Nothing's impossible when love is on the menu. In Peggy Jaeger's luscious series, the only thing more tempting than a delicious meal is a truly delectable romance . . .
Look for exclusive recipes in each book!

Photographer Gemma Laine is looking for arresting faces on the streets of Manhattan when her camera captures something shocking—a triple murder. In that moment, she becomes a target for the mob—and a top priority for a very determined, breathtakingly handsome FBI special agent. With deadlines to meet and photo shoots on her calendar, Gemma chafes at the idea of protection, but every moment she spends under his watchful eye is a temptation to lose herself in his muscular arms . . .

With two of his men and one crucial witness dead, Special Agent Kyros Pappandreos can't afford to be distracted. But Gemma is dazzling—and her connection to Kandy Laine's high-profile cooking empire makes her an especially easy mark for some very bad people. Keeping her safe is much more pleasure than business, but as the heat between them starts to sizzle, Ky is set to investigate whether they have a shot at love . . .

Also by Peggy Jaeger

Cooking with Kandy

A Shot at Love

Peggy Jaeger

LYRICAL SHINE
Kensington Publishing Corp.
www.kensingtonbooks.com

LYRICAL SHINE BOOKS are published by

Kensington Publishing Corp.
119 West 40th Street
New York, NY 10018

All Kensington titles, imprints, and distributed lines are available at special quantity discounts for bulk purchases for sales promotion, premiums, fund-raising, educational, or institutional use.

Special book excerpts or customized printings can also be created to fit specific needs. For details, write or phone the office of the Kensington Sales Manager: Kensington Publishing Corp., 119 West 40th Street, New York, NY 10018. Attn. Sales Department. Phone: 1-800-221-2647.

Lyrical Shine and Lyrical Shine logo Reg. U.S. Pat. & TM Off.

First Electronic Edition: October 2017
eISBN-13: 978-1-5161-0108-5
eISBN-10: 1-5161-0108-1

First Print Edition: October 2017
ISBN-13: 978-1-5161-0111-5
ISBN-10: 1-5161-0111-1

Printed in the United States of America

For Stephanie Krist…your talent with a camera and your love of photography shines through every picture you take. Hey—you even made me look good! No small feat, that.

Chapter One

Special Agent Kyros Pappandreos scanned the midtown Manhattan street in front of him and swore.

"I want to see the cops who were first on scene *right* now," he demanded of the uniformed NYPD officer next to him. Ky turned to his partner. "How did this happen?"

"It looks like a blitz attack." Jon Winters squinted an eye at the midday sun. "They'd finished lunch, were walking back to the car."

"We didn't have eyes or ears on them?" Ky asked, surveying the gory scene. Two of his best agents were dead and his witness lay with his face kissing the curb, pooling blood drenching his inert form, arms bent back in unnatural angles at his sides.

"Neither," Winters said. "They were out of touch for an hour, tops. Our guys had their cell phones, but no communication since they left the hotel."

"This is unbelievable." Ky squeezed the bridge of his nose between his thumb and index finger and let out a heavy breath. Three years of work shot to hell in a matter of seconds.

"Agent Pappandreos? You wanted to speak with me?"

Ky turned to the metro officer who approached him, noting the name badge over the left breast pocket of his blue uniform shirt. "Officer Johnson, you got here first?"

"Yes, sir. My partner and I responded to a *shots fired* at one fifteen."

"I want details. Where were you when the call came?"

"Outside the deli between Madison and Fifth, two blocks over. Dispatch alerted us, we raced down, saw the victims on the sidewalk. Whole thing was done by the time we got here."

"Any ID on the shooters? Witnesses? Did anyone see anything?"

"It was pretty chaotic when we arrived. The area's packed this time of day with lunch business. Lotta banks and professional offices are headquartered around here. People heard shots, ran for cover." He referred to his notepad. "I got a few statements about a black van, dark blue, maybe. No one got a license or has been able to give an accurate description of the vehicle. It pulled up, shots were fired, it sped off. Matter of seconds it was all over and your three vics were on the ground."

"Johnson, I've got a witness," another metro uniform called as he sprinted up to the trio. Ky turned in the direction of the voice.

"This is my partner," Johnson said.

"Where's this witness?" Ky asked.

"I've got her isolated by my squad car." He shot his thumb in the direction behind him. "Says she saw everything, and—get this—she's a professional photographer. Filmed it all as it went down."

"Take me to her," Ky said. "Jon?"

"Yeah, Papps, I know. Go interview this witness. I'll coordinate from here."

"Let's go," Ky commanded the officer.

"That's her." The officer pointed to a police vehicle in the middle of the barricaded street a moment later. "Name's Gemma Laine."

A woman stood next to the vehicle, a cell phone at her ear, her back to him. Tall, maybe as tall as him, and slender, her back tapered down to a miniscule waist, her legs clad in tight, faded jeans. When she turned Ky almost stopped midstride, the questions he intended to grill her with jumping out of his head. His breath caught as he simply stared at the loveliest woman he'd ever seen.

Hair the color of midnight, straight as a board, fell to just below her shoulders, blowing back from her face in the gentle afternoon breeze. Blunt, chopped bangs fringed a pair of large, bright-blue eyes. Plump, coral-colored lips moved as she spoke into the phone and for a brief, hot second, Ky wondered if they'd taste as delicious as they looked.

Her gaze stayed on him as she spoke.

"I've gotta go," she said into the phone. "Yeah. I'll call when I'm done. Love you, too."

"Miss Laine?"

She tucked the phone into her back pocket.

"I'm Special Agent Pappandreos. I need to speak with you about what you saw."

"Special Agent?" Those delicate brows furrowed under her bangs. "Like, FBI?"

Jesus, where does a woman get a voice like that? Whiskey laced with honey and rolled into one smooth pitch.

"Yes. I understand you witnessed the shooting? You photographed it?"

She nodded. "I was working when it all started. I took a series of shots while it was happening."

His gaze flicked to the camera she held in one hand.

"I need to see those pictures."

His first impression of her height had been correct. She was maybe three or four inches shorter than his six-foot-one frame. As she moved closer, the hairs on the back of his neck stood straight at attention. She smelled as good as she looked and his nostrils flared from the scent of sweet cherries blended with some hot exotic spice.

"It all went down so fast," she said. "But I got some good shots." Handing him the camera, she added, "Press this button to advance."

The first few pictures showed his witness ambling along the sidewalk, hands in his pockets. There was a smug, satisfied smile on his face as he was flanked by the two agents assigned to protect him. Ky pressed the button a few times. Another series of pictures showed the impact of the bullets as they pierced one of his agents, the next detailing the second man as a single shot impaled the center of his forehead. Shock, horror and stark fear replaced the smile on his witness's face as he bent forward and appeared to run from the bullets. The next few photos showed him struck and then felled by several shots, all clustered in his chest. Ky depressed the advance button again. The photographer had moved to view a black van with no windows on the sides nor any identifiable markings on the body. He wanted to curse when he saw it, thinking the van would be a dead end, when he flipped the advance button again to see she'd zoomed in on the license plate.

Elated, he glanced up and found her eyes trained on him.

"I need you to come with me." He grabbed her arm.

"Where?" She stretched across him and tried to take back her camera. Ky held it up and away from her reach.

"My office. I need a written statement from you about what you saw. It's better to do it now, right away, so you don't forget any details, anything of importance."

"I never forget details," she said, reaching across him again. "Can I please have my camera? I don't like anyone carrying it but me."

"This piece of equipment is the only link to finding out who killed my men. It's not leaving my hands."

She stopped and tried to pull her arm out of his grip. Ky tightened his grasp.

"Look, Agent PappaJohn—"

"Pappandreos," he corrected. It was a common mistake, one he'd heard a number of times in his career, but hearing her say it, wrapping the syllables around those pouty lips with that husky voice, for some reason charmed him.

"Whatever." She swiped her free hand in the air. "I want my camera."

"You'll get it back, I assure you." He started walking, giving her no choice but to follow.

Before she could protest again, he stopped. "Jon?" His partner turned from the interview he was conducting with a restaurant waiter. "Can you have someone escort Miss Laine back to the office? She needs to have her statement written up."

"Sure, Papps."

"Wait a second," Gemma said, wrenching her arm from his grip. The smooth, natural warmth in her voice had turned to frosted ice. "I'll be happy to give you a statement, but I want my camera. *Now.*"

"I won't break it, Miss Laine, if that's what you're worried about."

"Then stop holding it like it's a cheap piece of tin! Give it back to me. I'll hold it."

"This is digital, right?" Jon Winters stepped between them and asked.

"Yes, and it's very expensive," Gemma said, still trying to take it from Ky's hand.

"We really only need the SD card then, Papps, not the camera."

"True." Ky examined the device, found the button to expel the memory card and depressed it. He took the card and slipped it into his pocket. "Here." He handed the camera back to her.

"Wait a minute." She clutched it to her chest as if she were protecting a child from a threat. "You can't keep the card. All my work is on it."

"We won't erase anything you need," Ky told her. "Or let anything happen to it."

"This is ridiculous." Gemma blew at her bangs. "How do I know you won't keep it as some kind of evidence? I haven't uploaded the pictures I took today. I need those shots."

"I told you you'd get the card back," Ky said, his patience wavering. "Now we're wasting time. Jon?" Dismissing them, he walked away and over to the scene of the shooting.

* * *

Gemma paced the small room for the hundredth time, her arms folded across her chest, desperately wanting to hit something.

No, not something. *Someone.* Agent Pappa-pain, or whatever the heck his name was.

For over two hours she'd been confined to this cramped, windowless, and drab room. During the first hour she'd written, in full detail, everything she'd witnessed on the street corner. Agent Winters had guided her through the questions while she wrote the answers in her smooth, precise script. When they were finished, he'd left her, promising to return shortly.

Winters's definition of shortly was exceedingly different from hers.

With a heavy sigh, she plopped back down into a metal chair, arms still crossed, and thought about Winters' partner, Special Agent Moron. Reconsidering, she added, a hunky moron, but one nonetheless.

Gemma had been speaking on the phone when she'd turned and seen him approaching. Her first thought had been *serious eye candy.* Clad in a supremely well-fitted dark-blue suit, he simply tore up the pavement on his way to her, those long legs striding with purpose and determination in each step. His face was a contradiction in origins. Deep, milk-chocolate colored hair, cut just a bit too short for her liking, with soft, gold flecks framing his temples and the top of his head. His skin was a light golden brown, giving the impression he spent a great deal of time in the sun. Eyes the color of the sea at sunrise, so light green, they almost appeared crystal with the sun hitting them, were surrounded by jet-black eyelashes Gemma admitted she was jealous of. His face was angular, the jaw tapering into a rock solid *V* at its tip, a small crevice winking out right below his lower lip.

All-in-all it was a face she wanted to photograph, knowing just the way she'd capture it. The fact he'd yanked her along after him like an errant child got her dander up. Coupled with the way he'd carelessly held her camera, it made her want to kick some sense into him.

God, what a day.

All she'd planned on doing was spending a few hours walking along the city streets, shooting interesting faces. She was almost done when the dapper-looking gentleman alighted from the restaurant, a self-satisfied smile on his lips. Gemma recognized that smile. It was the same one she always had after treating herself to some well-deserved Cherry Garcia ice cream after a tough, demanding day. She knew without a doubt the man had just eaten a pleasant meal. Satisfaction like that came only from two things: good food or great sex. Since he was walking along with two testosterone hulks in conservative suits, she figured it was the food part of the equation dancing on his face.

In the blink of her camera shutter's eye, the scene had changed to one of horror. Professional instinct made her continue shooting the events as they unfolded, capturing the slaying of the three men. She turned her camera when she realized the direction the shots were coming from, and through her viewfinder found the van speeding off. Pointing her lens at its retreating back, she zoomed in on the license plate. Without even thinking about the composition of the shot, she snapped as fast as she could, trying to record as much information as possible.

After the van escaped, she ran to the victims to see if she could help in any way. It was too late for all three of them. The sound of sirens glued her to the spot. She'd located the first officers to arrive, told one of them she had footage of the incident, and then had been led away from the scene to wait. A quick call to her brother-in-law Josh was interrupted by the arrival of the arrogant FBI Agent.

* * *

Ky watched her pace the length of the room from the video camera mounted on the wall in the corner. "What do we know about her?"

"Aside from the obvious?" Jon's grin was quick. "She's awfully easy on the eyes."

"Aside from the obvious," Ky said, his own gaze never leaving the monitor.

"Twenty-eight, single, lives alone. Her professional rep is pretty impressive."

"How so?"

"Ever heard of chef Kandy Laine?"

His eyes widened. "My mom and YiaYia love her. They have all her books, used to watch her show every time it was on. Laine? Any relation?"

"Sister. One of seven. Owns her own photography business called GAL Photos. Pretty famous in her own right. Last month alone she shot three magazine covers. She's what's called in the entertainment biz 'the go-to' when you need a great headshot."

"So why was she in midtown today when our witness bought it?"

"Seems she's doing a coffee-table book of faces. Today she was walking around, looking for interesting ones, spotted Calafano and thought he'd make a good subject. She started snapping away and then the proverbial shit hit the fan."

Ky nodded.

"Here." Jon handed him a copy of her typed statement. "Read it for yourself."

Ky took it and within a few minutes had it committed to memory.

"You don't think there's anything more to this, do you?" Jon asked. "I mean, she was just in the wrong place at the wrong time, right?"

"Appears that way," Ky answered. "I have a few more questions before we let her go, though."

"She's still asking about the SD card. Wants it back, undamaged and unaltered. Now."

"She'll get it back when we're done with it," Ky said, buttoning his jacket.

When he entered the conference room a moment later, he thought he was prepared for the jolt seeing her in the flesh would cause again. He was wrong. The second he opened the door and saw her eyes tracking him like those of a caged animals, he realized just how wrong. A subtle, unmistakable, pang of unease sliced right into his midsection, cutting off all circulation except to his groin. With a mental and physical shake, he approached her.

Anger percolated through her from across the room.

"Miss Laine—"

"Why am I still here? I gave my statement. I want my memory card and I want to go home. I have a ton of work to do."

Ky reached down deep to curb his temper. "I need to clarify a few things first."

"What things?" She leaned back against the wall, leveling him with a hard stare. "I told your partner everything I remember. In vivid detail."

"Yes, I read your statement. Please." He motioned to a chair. "Have a seat."

"I'd rather stand."

He couldn't tell if she was being purposefully obnoxious when her chin tilted up defiantly at him or if it was a character trait. Regardless, he pulled the facing chair from the table and sat.

"You mentioned in your statement you were out walking when you noticed the shooting."

"No, that's not correct." She must have forgotten her reason for standing because she moved back to the chair and settled into it. "I said I was out working and noticed the trio of men coming out of the restaurant."

Ky knew that. He wanted to see if she'd change any of the details with time.

"The older man had an attention-grabbing face," she continued, resting her arms on the table. "I'm on the lookout for interesting faces."

"So you notice him, see his face and decide, what? To take his picture? Just like that?"

She nodded. "It's what I do. I'm working on a book called *Faces of New York*."

"What was so fascinating about his?"

"It wasn't so much his face as the expression on it," she said. "He'd just come out of Sam's. I figured he'd eaten lunch because he was patting his stomach and had a contented, gratified smile on his lips. So I took his picture. A series of them, in fact, as he continued walking."

"Why did you continue snapping away? You had your shot. Why take more?"

Gemma blew out a breath and leaned back in the chair, arms crossed over her chest again. "Do you know anything about photography?"

"No, not really."

She sliced a finger through the side of her hair and tucked the strands behind her ears. It refused to settle and fell back across her cheeks the moment she removed her hand.

"There's more to getting the shot you want than merely pressing a button. You have to consider the lighting, the motion, or absence of it. A million different things go into capturing the perfect image. A person's face changes in a millisecond. You can go from an expression of rapture, to the simple turning up of the lips in the time it takes for a heart to beat just once. I wanted to make sure I got the look I wanted to convey. Taking several shots in a continuum ensures I will."

Ky nodded. "So the only thing you knew about the older man was you liked the expression on his face?"

"Yes."

"You had no idea who he was?"

"No. I still don't. All I know is he and two other men were gunned down on a New York City street. And because of some quirk of nature, I was there when it happened."

Ky waited a beat. "What made you continue taking pictures after the shooting started? Most people ran for cover, got out of harm's way. You stayed where you were and continued to photograph what was happening. I have to ask myself why?"

Gemma's eyes narrowed. "What do you mean?"

"You're not a news reporter or photojournalist. You don't work for any national news publications. You own your own business, work for yourself. What were you hoping to gain from continuing to shoot?"

Gemma shot up, the chair falling to the floor behind her with a resounding thwack. "Your implication is insulting. You think I continued filming for some dark ulterior motive, don't you? Like I wanted to sell the pictures, or in some way benefit from them. That's not only insulting, it's disgusting."

"I don't think I said anything along those lines."

"Your veiled wording implies otherwise. For your bigoted information, my brother-in-law is in private security. I've assisted him a few times with surveillance photography, even helped his partner in various filming techniques when he's gone undercover. I'm not a paparazzo looking for my next big photographic score. Agent—," she flipped her hand in the air in lieu of addressing him by name, "I'm a professional photographer, and I reacted as one today. I kept filming because I could. I didn't think I was in any danger. The van was speeding away from me, not toward me."

Ky looked across the table at her, weighing her words. "For the record, again, it's Pappandreos, and I never assumed you were anything other than what you've stated, Miss Laine. I simply need to make sure you had no prior knowledge of the men who were gunned down today."

"I don't know them from Adam." Her voice dropped a notch as her gaze bore into his.

Ky wanted to believe her, but a cautious regard for human nature had always served him well.

"Do you recognize the name Mario Calafano?"

Her eyes narrowed again, her gaze never leaving his. "It sounds familiar, but I'm not sure. Why?"

Instead of answering he asked, "How about Jackson Hunter or Paul Ingersall?"

She shook her head. "No."

Ky nodded. Rising, he told her, "I think we're finished here, Miss Laine. We have your contact information. We'll call when we're done with the memory card."

"I can't have it now?"

The childlike whine in her husky voice reminded him of his nieces and nephews when they didn't get their way.

"We haven't finished with it yet. But I assure you, I'll get it back to you."

"When?"

"As I've said, when we're finished with it."

"This blows." She frowned and crossed her arms in front of her again, this time her hands were fisted.

It wouldn't have surprised him if she stomped her foot next. Reaching into his pocket, he pulled out his card. "These are my contact numbers. If you don't hear from me in a few days, feel free to call."

"A few days?" she cried. "That's a lifetime to someone on a publishing deadline. I have a lot of work on that card and it needs to be uploaded and edited."

"A few days are all we need."

She mumbled something he couldn't hear and didn't think he wanted to, figuring it was something derogatory about himself. Ky made arrangements for an agent to drive her home and then watched as she was escorted out of the office.

"Hell hath no fury." Jon chuckled.

"The quote pertains to a woman scorned."

"Scorned or not, she's one seriously pissed but fine-looking female."

Ky agreed, on both counts. "Come on. We've got work to do."

* * *

Gemma let herself into her condo, threw her keys down on the entrance table, toed off her shoes, and then plopped down onto her couch.

"Jerk." She rubbed her tired eyes with the heels of her palms and dropped her chin to her chest. "Special Agent Jerk."

Seething, she thought about all the shots she'd taken before the shooting. Pictures she now couldn't work on. An entire day's filming, shot. *Literally.* Shot to hell.

And there were some great images in the batch, too. The toddler twins running down the street with their parents laughingly chasing after them; the tiny, elderly woman carrying her equally frail Pomeranian; the Asian shopkeeper sweeping outside her grocery store, an e-cigarette dangling from the corner of her mouth.

All pictures she knew would be perfect for the book. Only now she had to wait for them to be returned. And if there was one thing Gemma Laine hated, it was waiting.

That, and arrogant special agents.

She blew out a breath, her bangs dancing up off her forehead. Since seven o'clock that morning, she'd been walking around Manhattan, looking for inspiration. She hadn't stopped to eat or drink before the shooting, and waiting at FBI headquarters had chewed up another few hours with nothing in her system. A loud growl snarled up from her empty stomach and echoed in the apartment.

A quick inventory of the refrigerator reminded her she'd wanted to stop at the local grocery today when she'd finished working. All that stared back at her from the cool interior was a pint of skim milk, a few bottles of beer from the last time her sister and brother-in-law had visited, and three eggs.

"Oh, well. An omelet it is."

She put the frying pan her sister had given her for Christmas on the stovetop and turned the coil to medium heat. She'd never be the chef

Kandy was, but she knew the basics for making a great breakfast. After whisking the eggs with some of the milk, she added a sprinkling of black pepper and nutmeg to the mix.

When the pan was the perfect temperature and she was about to pour in the eggs, the doorbell rang.

Since she lived in a doorman-controlled condo and all her family were well known to the man on duty, she assumed it was one of them. Without looking through the peephole, she opened the door. Her smile died in an instant.

"Scream and I'll shoot," a man holding a gun aimed at her face declared.

Gemma's first instinct was to run. She pulled back, using the door as armor and pushed. Her intruder pushed right back, knocking her to the floor when the force of the door smashed into her. Flat on her butt, she crab crawled backward and tried to stand while the man flew into the apartment, banged the door shut and was on her in a second.

He grabbed a fist full of her hair and pulled her up by it.

Tears of pain sprang into her eyes. She ignored them, slipping into full defense mode. She flattened one of her hands over the one he had on her hair, pushed down and twisted, turning to face him as she'd been taught to do. If she stood upright she knew she'd be taller than he was, so she stayed stooped. He was attempting to yank on her hair again, but Gemma pulled her other hand back and, opening the web between her thumb and index finger wide, shot her hand out like a snake, striking him with the "V" straight in the throat.

The hit had its intended effect. He let go of her hair and staggered backward, one of his hands flying to his gullet. Gemma took a split second to stand tall, stepped one foot behind her and then, raising her opposite leg, kicked him full force straight in the chest with the ball of her foot, knocking him back. The gun dropped from his hand and she ran to it, but he reached out and grabbed her leg, jerking her down hard to the floor. Gemma felt her knee splinter into the hardwood floor and she recoiled into a fetal position from the impact. With his advantage, the intruder jumped over her, grabbed the gun and pointed it straight at her face again.

"Bitch! I should kill you now." His neck was bright red from her strike, his voice raspy and raw like sandpaper gliding along fresh-cut wood.

"What do you want?" The gun bobbed up and down in his hand as she stared down its barrel.

"Where is it?"

"What?"

"The camera you were using today."

His eyes flicked around the living room and then back to her, the gun still pointed straight at her face. "Where is it?" he repeated.

"I don't have it. The police took it." She rubbed her knee, gauging if she'd be able to stand on it. It wasn't broken, but she'd landed hard.

"Try again. I watched you leave the FBI building. You had it in your hands. Now stop wasting my time and give it to me."

Gemma quickly ran through all her options. Her knee was pounding, she had a lethal weapon pointed at her face and she was on the floor flat on her butt: a very bad position to deal from. Her gaze swept from the gun to the man's face, memorizing it, detail by detail.

"It's in the kitchen," she told him, rolling over and trying to rise up on her uninjured leg.

"Get it. Now."

"My knee is blown," she told him, standing upright on her good foot. "I can't move fast."

To prove her point she tried to walk and hobbled, almost going down to the floor again.

Her intruder swore. "Forget it. I'll get it." He turned his head, the gun still directed at her. "In here?"

"It's on the table."

He never moved from her sight as he went into the kitchen. Gemma took the few moments to think what to do.

With the camera in his hand, he popped the back open and asked, "Where's the memory card?"

"The FBI took it."

He swore again and threw the camera against the wall, smashing it. The anger on his face was murderous as he came at her.

"You stupid bitch. You could have told me that instead of wasting my time."

He lifted the gun to her eye level and just as he pulled the hammer back, Gemma went into action. Sidestepping backward on her uninjured leg, she brought the other one up to her chest and in one fluid, swift move, knocked the gun from his hand with the front of her foot. Pain recoiled all the way up her leg, but she ignored it. While the gun bounced across the floor she spun and, using her injured leg again, struck three swift kicks to his temple, knocking him to the floor. The effect of the single-footed spin unbalanced her, and she fell flat on her backside again. Her recovery was swifter than his, though, and she shot up, jumped to the door on her good leg, and, throwing it open, screamed as loud as she could.

She fell into the hall and, due to the early evening hour, doors around her opened, quizzical heads popping out from the commotion of her shouting.

The intruder didn't waste a second. He sprang up and ran from the apartment, sprinting down the hallway toward the stairwell.

Breathing hard and in serious pain, Gemma collapsed against the wall as her neighbors gathered around her.

Chapter Two

"She gonna be okay?" Ky asked the emergency room resident when he came out of Gemma's cubicle.

"You family?"

Ky held up his badge.

"Oh. She should be. Knee is pretty tender. Not broken though, which is good. She needs to keep it elevated for a while, ice it down. Other than that, she should be good in a day or so."

Ky thanked him and turned to his partner. "Anything?"

Jon shook his head. "Not yet. She gave a dynamite description of the guy. Profetti's making copies of his sketch right now. She's got a good eye for catching details."

"Considering she was getting pummeled at the time." Ky sighed and pinched the bridge of his nose. "Okay, I'll get her statement. Why don't you try to find out what you can about the guy who attacked her."

"CSU should be done with her apartment. I'll see if he left any prints. The gun might be an avenue."

Ky nodded and turned his attention back to the emergency room cubicle.

When her call had come through to his cell he'd been packing it in for the day, just about to head back to his apartment. She sounded totally in control when she told him about the armed man who'd shoved his way into her apartment, demanding her camera. In less than ten minutes he and Jon were at her condo, which was already packed with people, including two paramedics and most of the neighbors on her floor. She was being tended to by one of the EMTs when she spotted him. He'd told himself he wasn't going to feel that right jab to his stomach when he saw her again, but the minute she lifted those china-blue eyes and caught his stare, it came: quick, hard, and undeniable.

With little emotion, she told them what happened. When Ky asked Gemma if she could describe the man, figuring the answer would be "no," he was shocked when she gave them a detailed rundown of the intruder's appearance. She told Jon to get a sketch artist and she could give even more details, and he'd arranged for one to meet them in the emergency room. While waiting to be x-rayed, she'd done just as she'd told them. The sketch was almost like a photograph, it was so comprehensive and thorough. Just as Agent Profetti had finished, Gemma's sister and brother-in-law arrived and were with Gemma now.

Ky entered the room and the conversation between the trio stopped.

"Agent Pappandreos?" Kandy Laine came toward him, her hand extended. "I'm Gemma's sister, Kandy."

"I recognize you, Miss Laine. The women in my family are huge fans." He gave her a small smile and took her hand.

"Actually," Kandy said, turning to her husband, "It's Keane. This is my husband, Josh."

The men shook hands, and Ky was quick to note he was being sized up by them both.

"Can I leave now?" Gemma asked from the bed.

He turned his attention to her. She was still clad in the hospital gown she'd been given when her leg had been x-rayed.

"I believe the doctor is signing the discharge papers right now."

"Hallelujah." She threw her arms up in the air.

"Have they found the man who did this?" Kandy asked Ky. "Do they know who he is?"

"No, ma'am. But your sister gave a very extensive description of him and my partner is running his likeness through our database. As for why he did it, well, that part's obvious."

He turned to Gemma.

"He thought I had the pictures of what happened today," she said, folding her hands into her lap. "He said he saw me leave your office and followed me home."

Ky nodded.

"Is my sister in danger because of this?" Kandy moved to Gemma's side and placed a hand on her shoulder. Gemma snaked her own hand up and covered it.

Ky shot a quick glance at Josh. "I'm afraid so. They know who she is and where she lives. And now she's seen one of them up close and can identify him. That makes her a liability."

"*Jesus,*" Kandy said, tightening her grip. "Josh—," she looked over at her husband, a plea on her face. He nodded.

"Agent Pappandreos, take a walk with me," Josh said.

The men left the room together and Ky heard Kandy say something in a soothing voice to her sister.

When they were about halfway down the corridor, Josh stopped. "So who'd she see get taken out?"

Without giving him too much information, Ky filled him in on the federal case he'd been working for the past three years.

Josh whistled through his teeth.

"She was in the wrong place at the wrong time," Ky said, "and now she's in danger because of it."

"She needs to be kept out of sight until you find out who's behind the killings," Josh said.

"Oh, I know who's responsible," Ky told him. "It's a question of being able to prove it before anything else happens."

His phone pinged, and Ky looked down at the number written across the screen. "Excuse me. I've got to take this."

Ky walked away from Josh. "Pappandreos."

"I want a full report right now," his boss, Special Agent in Charge Colin Tiege blared into the phone. Succinctly, Ky told him everything they knew of the attack, including the description Gemma had given. "Jon's working it through the system now, see if we get a hit. But I know it's connected to Ritandi. I feel it."

"I agree. This has his stamp all over it. Who else would take out a hit on Calafano?"

"No one. It makes sense it was him. Calafano was set to do serious damage to Ritandi's business with his testimony."

"And now you have no witness. No one who can detail the operation like Calafano could."

Ky remained silent. The anger and frustration filtering through the phone was identical to his own.

"To top off a lousy day, I just got my ass chewed out by that little pissant from the AG's office."

"Barly?"

"Yeah. Davison 'I'm-an-asshole' Barly. Jerk had the nerve to accuse us of sabotaging the case, of leaking Calafano's whereabouts to Ritandi. He's calling for yours and Winters's heads on a platter, so don't be surprised if you get a call. *Prick.*"

Department of Justice lawyer, Davison Barly, was, in Ky's opinion, one of the most unpleasant, rude people he'd ever had the misfortune to work with. Over the year since he'd been assigned to the Ritandi task force as the attorney general's assistant, the politically ambitious lawyer had tried to push the case forward at every turn, whether they had enough evidence or not. When Mario Calafano had been arrested, Barly was the only one who'd balked against making a deal with the bookkeeper, insisting instead on sending him to trial as a warning to Ritandi.

Ultimately it had been the attorney general's call to offer a deal and witness protection.

None of which mattered now, though, with the bookkeeper's execution.

"What are your plans for the witness you do have?"

Ky blew out a breath and swiped his free hand around his neck to massage the tightening muscles. "Her brother-in-law's in private security. He can keep her under wraps."

"Not a good idea, Papps. I don't want any more civilians involved in this."

"The guy owns his own business, boss. Protection is what he does."

"I don't care. You and Winters take care of it. Put her in a secure place and have her guarded. What happened today shouldn't have been possible. No one was supposed to know where Calafano was being kept. The fact someone did has me wondering if there's a leak somewhere down the chain."

Ky rubbed his eyes with the pads of his fingers. "Yeah, I was wondering that as well. Okay. We'll take care of it."

He ended the call and went back to a waiting Josh.

"From the look on your face," Josh said, "I can tell that wasn't pleasant."

Ky shook his head. "My superior." He slid the phone back into his pants pocket. "He wants your sister-in-law secured."

Josh nodded. "I can do that."

"No. He doesn't want any non-agency people involved in this. We'll be providing her with protection and some place safe to stay until this is resolved. She can't go back to her condo now, since they know where she lives."

Josh blew out a breath. "Good luck getting her to agree. Gemma's not known for taking orders well. You'll have a fight on your hands for sure."

"Can't be helped, Mr. Keane. I've got my orders."

"It's Josh, and I know. I just want you to be prepared for what she's going to do when you tell her."

* * *

"No frigging way!" Gemma jumped up from the bed with a lopsided jerk, causing the IV pole to tumble to the floor. "There's no way in hell I'm going into hiding."

Ky reached for the pole and righted it. "I'm afraid there really is no other alternative, Miss Laine. They'll come after you again, try to find out what you know, what you saw."

"But I don't know anything. All I did was take some pictures. That's it. I don't even know who the dead men are."

"Gemma, lower your voice," Kandy said. "We can all hear you."

"I'm sorry, Kan, but this is ridiculous." Gemma crossed her arms over her chest. "Why do I have to go into hiding? I didn't do anything."

"It's for your own safety," Ky told her.

"Can't I just go with them?" she asked, pointing to her sister and brother-in-law. "Josh can keep me safe."

"Think that one through, Miss Laine. You'd be putting them in potential danger as well as yourself. No, we need to put you in a safe house for a few days until this situation is resolved."

"A few days? I've got work to do, photographic commitments to honor. I'm booked for two shoots this week alone. I can't afford a few days away from all that."

"Gem, calm down," Josh said, his voice soft, but firm. "Agent Pappandreos is right. The FBI can do a better job of protecting you than I can. It's that simple. They have better resources, more manpower."

"But I don't trust *him*." Gemma pointed a finger at Ky, her voice rising again. "I trust you."

"I know, kid." Josh rubbed a hand down her arm. He looked over at his wife, raised his eyebrows.

Kandy nodded. "We'll take you back to your place and get everything you need," she told her.

"I'm afraid I can't let you go back to your apartment," Ky told Gemma, noting she was now squinting at him, her brow creased, her fury aimed directly at him. "It might still be staked out by whoever did this to you. It's not safe."

Before she could protest, Josh said, "Kandy and I will get what you need and bring it all back here. Okay?"

"Do I really have a choice?" Gemma said, dragging her hands through her hair. "This sucks. Big time."

Silently, Ky agreed.

* * *

An hour later Kandy kissed her goodbye after dropping off Gemma's overnight bag, the laptop she used for editing her photos, and two of the cameras she'd requested, nestled in their carrying cases.

When Josh leaned in to give her cheek a brotherly peck, he whispered, "Be good. This guy is just trying to keep you safe. Don't be a pain."

She narrowed her eyes at him when he pulled back, but didn't say anything.

Right after they left, Jon Winters came into the cubicle. "It's all set," he told Ky. Looking at Gemma he asked, "Are you ready, Miss Laine?"

Without a word, she nodded and grabbed for her bags. Ky reached for them at the same time. When his hand twisted over hers, they both stopped moving. Gemma lifted her gaze up to his and tightened her grip over the suitcase handle. His large palm engulfed her hand and all she could feel was heat flowing from it, warming her, searing her. A strange, unexpected spark fired right through her system, down to her stomach—and lower— causing a quick shudder to blast from deep within. For a moment Gemma forgot to breathe.

"Allow me," he said, looking down at her. With his lips curving slightly at the corners, he added, "I'll take this, since I figure you don't want either one of us to touch your cameras."

Gemma's mind stopped working and all she could do was stare at his mouth. The center of his top lip held a small bow that indented and outlined the upper half of his lips. The bottom one was full, and on a woman, it would have been called pouty. On him, though, it was sensual, erotic, and just begging to be kissed.

Gemma couldn't stop staring at it. For a few seconds her gaze stayed glued to his mouth, forgetting everything else.

"Miss Laine?" he said. "Is something wrong?"

Gemma tore her attention from his sexy lips up to his eyes, where a question filled them.

It was as if she was seeing his eyes, really seeing them, for the first time. As adept as she usually was at describing things, she couldn't find the words to do justice to the unusual flecks of colors and shades filtering through his irises. The green was so light it appeared crystalline, with a darker rim that mimicked deep moss circling the inner, lighter colors. The lids were heavy-hooded, so even when wide awake and staring straight at her, he gave the impression he was just pulling out of sleep.

Bedroom eyes, Grandma Sophie had called a look like his. Sensual, sexual, and carnal, as if they could look right into your soul and know your deepest, darkest, most erotic secrets.

Gemma realized in that instant she would love nothing more than to commit those eyes to film. But even thinking it, she knew no photograph could ever capture the beauty and the essence of the colors staring back at her.

"Is something wrong?" Ky repeated.

The quizzical expression on his lined brow snapped Gemma out of her thoughts. With a slight shake of her head she glanced down at her hand, his still over it, and said, "No. No. I'll take the cameras."

Ky relaxed his grip and let her move hers from the handle of the suitcase. When she let go, he grabbed the bag, lifting it. "Ready?"

Gemma nodded once and picked up the camera cases. "As I'll ever be, I guess."

* * *

"It's not the Ritz," Ky said, "but as safe houses go, it's not half bad."

The Ritz it wasn't. Not even close.

"Your room is at the top of the landing, second door on the right," Jon told her. "I'll drop your stuff up there." He moved up the staircase, her suitcase in his hand.

"Quick lay of the land," Ky said. "Two floors and the basement. Living room, den, eat-in kitchen, bathroom down here. Three bedrooms upstairs, two baths. You'll have your own room with an adjoining bathroom."

"You'll both be staying here?" Gemma asked.

Ky nodded. "In addition to some of my other men. We'll take shifts. I still need to coordinate with the rest of my team while we're here, but for the next day or so the three of us will be together constantly. Hopefully, we can end this whole thing before it drags on too much longer and we can get you back home as soon as possible."

"Hopefully is the operative word in that statement," Gemma said.

The frustration in her tone was obvious. She'd been quiet on the drive from Manhattan to Queens, sitting in the backseat, arms folded across her chest, staring out the window with a look of childlike petulance on her face. The few times he'd glanced in the rearview mirror, he could see the barely controlled anger filtering through her eyes. To say she wasn't happy about the current situation would be a total understatement. This was one pissed off woman. A fine looking one, but furious nonetheless, and Ky couldn't blame her. Through no fault of her own she'd been thrown into a situation where she'd tried to do the right thing, and it wound up coming back to bite her in the ass.

He knew he wouldn't be happy, either, if his world was suddenly turned upside down. His only hope was they could quickly find the assassins and her attacker and allow her to go back home, as he'd told her.

"A few house rules," he said. When she just stared at him, her mouth tight, eyes narrowed, he could feel the irritation sliding off her.

"You can't use your cell phone to call anyone or check data. It needs to be shut off at all times."

"No one? Not even the clients I'm being forced to bail on because of this, this—" her hand flailed out and swept the room, eyes blazing.

Ky shook his head. "Cell phones are traceable, as are computers. Since Ritandi knows who you are, I'm sure he's already had one of his people find out all your basic information. Cell phone number, e-mail address. All the accounts linked to your phone and computer. A digital fingerprint spans a wide berth these days, and it's easy for a hacker to find you. Too easy."

"This gets worse by the minute. What am I supposed to do? Just not show up at my client appointments? Do you know what that will do to my professional reputation? I'll never get another job offer if people think I'm unreliable and capricious about my work commitments."

"You can use my phone to call your clients and any staff members you have. It's blocked and untraceable. There's about fourteen layers of security attached to it. As long as you make the call quick and don't linger to gossip or chat it should be sufficient."

The anger barely contained beneath the surface bled out in full force.

"First of all, I work alone. I don't have any staff or anyone helping me. It's my name, my business."

Ky nodded.

"Secondly, and more importantly, I don't gossip with clients. I'm a professional. I'm there to do a job, a job they've hired me for. What am I supposed to tell them when I call to cancel? Sorry, but I can't photograph you today. I've got this little annoyance of a maniac looking for me?"

Ky forced his annoyance down. "You can tell them you're sick and will call to reschedule when you can."

"It doesn't work that way in my world," she said. Her breathing had quickened, her beautifully sculpted nose flaring with the effort. "If I can't make my obligations, my clients, my *powerful, rich, and unforgiving* clients, are going to hire someone else, someone who they can depend on to do the job. My world is one of deadlines. Quick, harsh, you'd-better-meet-them-or-else deadlines. Calling in sick to cancel, whether real or otherwise, is professional suicide."

Her arms were crossed over her chest again, the corners of her lips pointed down toward her chin.

"Would you prefer to honor those commitments knowing someone, someone who doesn't hesitate to kill those around him he considers inconvenient, is looking for you? And just say you do go to your scheduled appointments. Forget the danger you're putting yourself in by doing so. Have you thought about the danger you're putting your clients in?"

The space between her eyebrows pulled into a thin, tight line.

"What are you talking about?"

"The man who I think ordered these hits today has shown, many times before, that collateral damage means nothing to him."

"Collateral damage?"

"Yes. In order to get to you, he wouldn't think twice about having your clients killed as well. He doesn't leave witnesses behind. Ever."

Her color blanched and for a moment, Ky thought she'd faint.

"I'm sorry to be so blunt about it," he said, softening his tone, "but you need to understand the gravity of this situation. Two of my men died today, just for doing their job. I'm sure you wouldn't want the same fate for your clients."

"N-no," she said, her head shaking violently. "No. I wouldn't."

Ky nodded. "Then please, just do as I ask. I'm only trying to keep you and everyone else around you safe."

They stood, silent, each watching the other.

Gemma Laine was a woman used to being in control of her life, not relinquishing that control to anyone. He'd figured that out within five minutes of meeting her. Ky hated the fear and uncertainly he saw in her eyes now, knowing he'd forced her to confront the reality before her.

"How is your knee feeling?" he asked, wanting to divert her thoughts. She'd only been limping a little from the car to the inside of the house, but he knew the emergency room doctor had given her something for the pain before discharging her.

Her delicate shoulders rose once in a careless shrug and she took a deep breath. "It's tolerable."

Ky remembered how bruised it had looked when he'd seen her in the x-ray suite. It had already started turning deep purple and green, and he knew from experience the stiffness that accompanied the hurt would be worse in the morning.

"The ER doc gave you something to take with you for the pain, didn't he?"

"I'd rather just ice it down. I hate taking pills."

Because he did as well, Ky didn't push the point. "Do you want to go upstairs and lie down for a while? You've had a pretty exhausting day."

Gemma shook her head and when the fringe of her bangs swished across her smooth skin, Ky felt that sudden, increasingly familiar tightening in his midsection.

"I need to do some work," she said. "I'll rest later."

"Whatever you want," he said.

Gemma turned and, with care, walked to the stairs, her cameras slung across her shoulder. Ky watched her plod up the steps, her uninjured leg taking most of the weight. He knew her knee was sore, but instinct told him she would never admit it. Another thing he'd learnt about Gemma Laine since meeting her was she was a woman who would never show weakness. To do so was tantamount to an admission of frailty. And frailty was not a word in her vocabulary.

While she made her way up to her room, Ky slipped out of his jacket and laid it across the back of one of the kitchen chairs, then opened the refrigerator and took stock of their provisions. The house was kept well supplied with non-perishables in the event it needed to be used quickly. When he'd been ordered to move Gemma, he'd called one of his men to ensure there was enough to last them for a few days. He hoped they wouldn't be staying longer.

With his encrypted work laptop on the counter, he booted up the electronic files and pictures of the Calafano murder scene. Once again, he thought Gemma's photographs were perfect in their detail. When viewed one after the other, they almost looked like a video. The former mob accountant walking down the street, a smug expression on his face, his ample stomach pushing through in front of him one minute, his white shirt drenched with a streaming flow of blood the next. Ky could almost feel the impact the first bullet made when it hit its mark, just from the expression Gemma had captured on Calafano's face. Lips curled back in what had to be agony, eyes bulging wide with shock, and hands flailing backward to break his fall, his face was a portrait in stunned alarm and terror. The pictures of Ky's men as they, too, felt the impact of the bullet's stream were haunting, detailed, and exceptional.

Gemma Laine was a world-class photographer, there was no doubt of it. In the span of a few seconds she had captured an act so heinous and violent that if seen through a normal person's eyes would have been unbearable. Through her talented ones, though, she'd immortalized the scene.

"Is that my SD card, or did you upload the pictures to your laptop?" Gemma asked from behind him.

He'd been so engrossed with the photographs he hadn't heard her approach. "I uploaded them," he told her.

"Do you have my card?"

"No. It's still being examined."

She sighed. "I have some really great shots on that card," she said, leaning against the kitchen counter. "There isn't any way I can get just those back? Never mind the shooting stuff. I don't want to lose a whole day's work, especially since it was really productive."

It took him a moment to reply. "The FBI IT techs uploaded your pictures onto the main data frame and I did the same with my work laptop. I copied the ones we don't need to a flash drive. I was going to give it to you later on, after you'd rested for a while."

For the first time since he'd met her, Gemma smiled. The joy that filtered through it almost knocked him backward. Her entire face changed with just the parting and uplifting of her lips. Ky had thought she was a gorgeous woman without it, but when she looked into his eyes, her own glistening with happiness, he realized just how beautiful she truly was.

"Really?" she asked, wobbling closer to him. "Can I have it now? Please?"

He reached into his pants pocket, took out the flash drive and handed it to her. "Like I said, the kill shots aren't on this."

Her hand rolled over the drive, no bigger than a stick of gum, as she held it. Like a lover stroking a mate's naked flesh, her long fingers twined around and fondled the drive as she spoke to him.

"Do you know…anything?" Gemma asked.

Ky shook his head. "Not yet. The man who attacked you, I believe, is one of the soldiers in the Ritandi mob family."

"This Ritandi. He's the one who killed your men today?"

"He didn't do it personally, but he ordered it. I'm certain."

Gemma shuddered. She rubbed her hands up and down her arms and then crossed them in front of her, the flash drive tight in her grasp. "Curiosity compels me to ask why. But I really don't want to know."

Ky nodded. "Believe me, you're better off not. Just know that we're doing everything in our power to find the man who attacked you."

"In addition to this Ritandi guy?"

"Oh, I have a good idea where he is," Ky said.

"Then why haven't you arrested him?"

"Knowing where someone is, and proving they did something are two different things."

Gemma's lips formed a small *O*. "I get that. But if you know where he is and you know he's responsible for what he did today isn't there some way, some piece of information, that can help you link the two?"

Ky put his hands in his pants pocket. "That's exactly what my men are trying to do right now."

Gemma nodded.

"I'm betting you're a little pissed off you have to sit here and babysit me, because I can guess you'd like nothing more than to be out there on the chase yourself. I know I would be if I were you."

Ky stared across at her. He shouldn't have been surprised by her statement. She seemed an astute woman, attuned to what was going on around her.

"Don't get the wrong impression," he told her. "I'm not pissed off, to quote you, at being here to keep you safe. It's part of my job. But I will admit I'd like to be there when we locate the guy who attacked you. Once we know who it is, I'm positive there'll be a link to Ritandi. One I can use to take him down for good."

The corners of Gemma's lips turned up in the slightest of smiles. "Yeah, you're pissed off. And I can't say I blame you."

They stared at one another for a few moments. Neither spoke. Finally Gemma shrugged and said, "Thanks for the flash drive. If I have to be stuck here at least I can do some work."

At that moment her stomach rumbled loudly. When she laughed and placed her hand, open palmed, across it, Ky didn't know which was stronger: the jolt that leaped around his heart at the sound of her laughter—low, but so seductive—or the heat that palpated through his lower region as he watched her hand flex and contract against her abdomen. Even though she was fully clothed Ky knew the skin under the material would be soft, tight, and hot.

"Obviously, you're hungry," he said.

"*Obviously*. When all hell broke loose this afternoon at my apartment I was in the process of making something to eat. I'd been working since early this morning and when I got home after being at your offices for over three hours, I realized just how hungry I was."

Ky didn't miss the irritation in her words. "We keep this house filled. There's plenty to eat. What can I make you?"

Her eyes widened with surprise. Ky wasn't in the habit of cooking for people other than his family or friends. Not that he wouldn't. The women in his family had seen to his culinary education while he was growing up. Standing in the safe-house kitchen with this incredibly desirable woman,

Ky realized he not only wanted to cook for her but he wanted to make something that would be satisfying both nutritionally and emotionally.

"You don't have to cook for me," Gemma said. "I'm a big girl. I'm used to fending for myself." Her lips lifted in one of those smiles Ky was starting to want to see on her face all the time. "I couldn't be Kandy Laine's sister and not know how to cook, even a little."

"I just thought, with your knee and all, you wouldn't want to be hopping around the kitchen. I'm more than willing to whip us up something quick."

He couldn't read the look she tossed him.

"If Ky is offering to make dinner, let him," Jon said as he came into the kitchen. "At least we'll get something edible."

With a shrug, she said, "Okay. Mind if I sit here and upload these to my laptop so I can work on them?" She held up the flash drive. "The lighting is better in here than in my room."

"Not at all."

"I'll get your laptop," Jon said. "You rest that knee."

When Gemma smiled her thanks, Ky swore the feeling dropping in him wasn't jealousy. He wanted her to smile at him like that: naturally, and with warmth. So far, she'd scowled at him more than anything else, and although it was tantalizing to see the passion in her anger, he realized he'd like nothing more than to see that emotion revealed in a much more enjoyable way.

"Do you have any food restrictions?" he asked as she sat at the breakfast bar, her injured leg propped up on the stool next to her.

"None."

With a nod, he set about making a simple dinner for the three of them. But he never forgot she was in the room.

With a dishtowel tucked into the front of his trousers as a makeshift apron, he got to work. While the chicken breasts browned in olive oil in the pan, she typed away, every now and then exclaiming, or drawing in a breath while she fiddled on her laptop. As the orzo softened, he glanced over his shoulder and saw her unlined brows meeting in the center, those gorgeous blue eyes zeroed in on the screen. Whatever she was looking at had her total and complete concentration as her fingers flew across the keyboard.

"It smells great in here," Jon said at one point when he came back into the kitchen.

Gemma's head shot up, a look of puzzlement on her face. "Oh, my God, it does," she said. "I didn't even notice."

"You've been pretty engrossed in your work," Ky said while he dropped a handful of parsley and some lemon wedges into the pan.

"You making YiaYia's lemon chicken?" Jon asked, settling onto a bar stool next to Gemma.

"YiaYia?" she asked, her gaze ping-ponging between her two protectors.

"My grandmother," Ky explained.

"She can make shoe leather taste good," Jon said with a laugh.

Ky filled their plates. "Jon, get drinks."

"Water okay for you, Miss Laine?"

"Water's fine, and it's Gemma."

He handed her a bottled water from the refrigerator. She uncapped it and waited for Ky to sit with them before eating.

"Oh, good Lord!" she said after the first mouthful went in. "My sister is going to kidnap your grandmother and hold her hostage for this recipe."

Ky's fork stopped halfway to his mouth, the pleased grin dying on his lips from her praise when he looked over at her.

Her beautiful eyes were closed, her head thrown slightly back, giving him a full view of her long, smooth neck, as her tongue skimmed from one side of her bottom lip to the other.

"Right?" Jon said, grinning. "The first time Papps ever cooked for me I asked if he had any unmarried sisters at home who cooked as good as he did."

With an eyebrow tilting up to her hairline, she glanced over at Ky and then back to his partner. "Papps?"

Jon's grin split his face.

"You're not the only one," Ky told her, "who's had difficulty with my last name." He forked a helping of chicken into his mouth.

Gemma's cheeks turned a lovely shade of pink.

"It was our boss who started calling him that," Jon said. With a good-natured grin, he added, "It stuck."

"Well, whatever people call you," Gemma said, addressing Ky, "this is the best meal I've had since the last time I visited my sister."

Before he could thank her, his cell phone pinged.

"Excuse me." He stood from the bar and moved out of the kitchen when he saw the caller ID.

In the living room across the hallway, Ky punched the connect icon. "Pappandreos."

"We got an ID on the attacker," SAC Tiege barked into the cell.

"One of Ritandi's guys?"

"Yes. Charlie 'Little Chico' Faldo. Low level jackass, but definite ties to our boy."

"Any idea where he is?"

"Not yet. I've got people working on locating him. His rap sheet's a mile long, but I'm confident he'll be found. They located the van about an hour ago."

"Where?"

"Under the Brooklyn Bridge. Empty. Crime Scene Unit's all over it."

"How do they know it's the right van?"

"Descriptions and license plate number your witness gave us matches."

"I'm surprised it wasn't torched. CSU won't find anything." Ky shook his head, frustration boiling in his chest. "This hit was too well orchestrated and coordinated to leave something as helpful as a fingerprint or any kind of a DNA trail to one of the shooters behind."

"You never know. The van's VIN number was eradicated, but I'm guessing it was a chop-shop steal, probably from one of Ritandi's own. How's your witness?"

"Pissed," he said, "but cooperative."

"How certain are you, Papps, she's not connected to this, other than as an innocent bystander?"

The question had been rolling around in his head all afternoon. Her explanation for being on the street at just the time Calafano was executed seemed coincidental. But if there was one thing Ky had learned over his years at the bureau, it was to dissect and inspect everything, whether it seemed plausible or not.

"I wouldn't say *certain*, but I really can't see any other scenario that would put her on that street today other than the one she's given us."

There was a moment of silence and Ky wondered if his boss knew something he didn't about Gemma Laine.

"I agree," he said at last, one tired sounding breath wafting through the phone. "Listen, I've got a meeting to brief the director and the attorney general, so I've got to go. I'll call again if CSU finds anything or if Faldo turns up."

"Appreciate it, boss."

Ky shot his phone back into his pants pockets, pinched the bridge of his nose, and closed his eyes.

Calafano's execution shouldn't have happened. He'd had two of his best, most experienced agents assigned to the bookkeeper for two months, ever since the man had been convinced turning over evidence and being put in witness protection was a better option than spending the rest of his life behind bars where one of Ritandi's men would have easy access to him.

His men knew—*knew*—they weren't supposed to leave the hotel for any reason. Ky had ordered them repeatedly to stay put. All they needed to do was keep him safe for one more week until the attorney general could file charges against Ritandi.

One week. And now, because his agents had disobeyed a direct order, they and the bookkeeper were dead.

Why had they left the hotel?

Today's events had all but destroyed three years of work, gathering information that would lead to the arrest of mob boss Antonio Ritandi for money laundering, tax fraud, and extortion.

Three years of endless wiretaps, surveillance, and subpoenas that had yielded nothing substantial until Mario Calafano made one small slip up with a bank deposit transaction, and Ky and his partner had roped him in.

A sudden thought danced around his head but was quickly killed when the sound of Gemma's laughter pulled him like a magnet back into the kitchen.

The smile he'd seen for the first time just minutes before was now broad, free, and lit with mischief. The throaty laugh, lusty and filled with enough just-woken rasp to make his pulse bounce filled the small kitchen at something his partner was telling her.

"That can't be true," she said, grinning at Jon. She'd nestled her head against the palm of her hand, her elbow propped on the table.

They'd finished their dinners while his had sat, uneaten.

Jon, ever the fervent storyteller, swiped his index finger across his chest. "Swear to God, it is."

At that moment, Gemma's smiling gaze found his across the room.

It should be illegal to have eyes that blue. Ky had to willfully hold himself back from saying it out loud.

"What story are you spinning, partner?" Ky came into the room after he was able to check his thoughts.

With a sly wink to Gemma first, Jon said, "No spin, just facts, Ky. I was telling Miss Laine—"

"Gemma," she corrected.

"Gemma." Jon nodded. "About the first time I met your family."

With an inward groan, Ky shook his head and brought his plate to the microwave. "I'd rather forget that," he said, timing the appliance to reheat his food.

"It sounds like you would," Gemma said, a wry little line dancing across her lips.

As much as Ky loved his large, boisterous, and utterly lovable family, they could be trying on his soul, especially his six older brothers, who never missed a chance to embarrass their baby brother.

"I've got older sisters," Gemma said, lifting her water bottle. "I know what it's like."

"I have to think the torture a brother employs is different from a sister's," Ky said over his shoulder.

She considered it while she took a mouthful of her water and he brought his reheated dish back to the table.

"Maybe," she said. "Brothers will probably be more physically exacting while sisters are more like emotional hit men, getting inside your head, niggling, and torturing you to death."

In the next breath, she sat her water bottle down on the table with a plop, her face going gray.

"Are you okay?" Ky asked. He wanted to reach out and touch her, but knew it wouldn't be wise.

"Sorry." The vigorous shake she gave her head tossed her hair to and fro. "That was a poor choice of words after what happened today."

The trio was silent for a few moments.

"It's getting late," Gemma said. Ky was quick to notice the smile she'd had moments before was now just a memory.

"Don't worry about the dishes," Jon told her when she started to bring hers to the sink. "Ky and I have a system. Cleanup's my job."

She nodded and grabbed her laptop.

"Everything you'll need should be in the closet in your room," Ky said. "Towels, fresh linens. Just let me know if there's anything you might want that your sister didn't pack."

"It's fine," she told him. "I've got all I really need."

Before quitting to her room she turned to them. "I—well."

Both men allowed her a moment to collect her thoughts.

"I just wanted to thank you. Both. I know being stuck here with me is the last thing you want to be doing about now, and believe me, if I could undo what happened today, I would."

"Don't worry about any of that," Jon said.

"It shouldn't take long to find the men responsible," Ky added. "And we'll get the man who hurt you."

She looked from one of them to the other, her gaze coming to rest on Ky. "I have no doubt about that."

Chapter Three

She should have slept like the dead after everything she'd gone through, but sleep eluded Gemma most of the night.

It wasn't that she was in an unfamiliar, uncomfortable bed; Gemma could sleep anywhere easily, and the bed was sound.

It wasn't that her bruised knee was causing her discomfort; she'd propped it up on a pillow and hadn't needed to resort to any of the pain pills the doctor in the emergency room had prescribed.

It wasn't even because she was concerned about cancelling her shoots for the week; when she'd called her clients on Ky's secured cellphone, explaining that she was "sick," they'd been beyond accommodating, both telling her they would wait until she was better and could fit them into her schedule. They wanted her to do their photographs, no one else. Gemma got a mild ego boost knowing her work meant something special to them.

No, the unease that filtered through her mind all night had nothing to do with any of those things and everything to do with Special Agent Kyros Pappandreos.

He was annoyingly arrogant, professionally polished, too handsome for his own good, and made Gemma's stomach flutter every time he speared those ocean-blue-green eyes her way.

When was the last time a man had made her insides quiver?

In all truth, it had been a long, long while and it bothered her in more ways than she could count.

Gemma wasn't ignorant of the way she looked. She knew she was considered attractive and had only to glance at her sister Kandy for confirmation. The two of them could have been twins and Kandy was gorgeous by anyone's standards. But even though they looked alike, they were very different in their thoughts about certain things, men being the uppermost.

Kandy had given her heart freely and unconditionally to her husband, Josh. He'd come into her life to protect her from a stalker and wound up breaking down all the walls and barriers she'd erected to make sure her heart was never broken by a man. Gemma's walls and barriers were made of much stronger brick and mortar.

She'd been a shy and scared ten-year-old when her father had decided being married and having to support a wife and seven daughters was more than he'd ever bargained for.

Gemma, too young to understand the grown-up events which had led to her parents' split, felt the biting sting of abandonment hard. She grew introverted and distrustful of anyone but her family.

As a teenager she'd grown into her height and blossoming beauty but had still been crippled with the paralyzing shyness of her younger years. When Kandy had given her a camera for her fifteenth birthday, Gemma blossomed like a rose waiting for spring sunshine.

Overnight, she found her life's passion. Behind the camera lens she became a different person: cool, self-assured, and cocky. Her shyness flew the moment she winked an eye into her viewfinder.

With her new self-confidence, Gemma allowed herself to start acting like a teenager and did the one thing all her contemporaries did that simply terrified her: date.

There was no lack of boys who wanted to be with her. Hair the color of ink framed a face with eyes a vivid blue no one could look away from. Tall, lithe, and angular, she quickly became the *It* girl in her class. And just as quickly lost her heart.

Her first boyfriend, being a typical teenage male ruled by raging hormones, had wanted nothing more than to claim he'd had sex with her, which he did, to one and all. That it was a lie, no one cared, despite Gemma's protestations. Just as soon as the rumor started, he'd broken up with her.

The next boy to come into her life had expected her to do the same with him as he'd heard she'd done with the other. When Gemma refused, he'd become physical, smacking her and forcibly restraining her in the backseat of his car while he brutally shoved his fingers inside her. He laughed when she cried, telling her no one would believe her if she tried to get him in trouble. Her easy-girl reputation would negate any claims she made about being assaulted. He dropped her off at home without so much as a word or another look. Mortified, Gemma never told anyone what he'd done to her. Thoughts of her father's betrayal, coupled now with this boy's attack, consumed her and she spent the remainder of her high school career the whispered subject of rumors and painful innuendo by her peers.

College had fared little better. She'd hoped higher education and age would have instilled a sense of maturity into the male species. Disappointment met her at every corner when the reality of drunken and sex-starved frat boys spilled around her.

When Kandy hired Gemma as her primary photographer and launched her professional career with the very first cookbook she'd photographed, opportunities opened left and right, and with them an influx of new, available men.

The lessons of her early days stayed with her, though, and Gemma protected her heart like a lioness protecting its young. To truly love a man she knew she'd have to give away the two things she could not and would not: her trust and her control.

She'd been lucky so far. No man had made a lasting impression, and she'd easily kept up her guard. The number of people she trusted could be counted on one hand. Gemma took care of herself financially, physically, and emotionally. But now she was being forced to put her safety and trust in a man she didn't know, wasn't sure about, and who made her feel just the slightest bit uneasy in a way she didn't like.

Before rising from the bed, she straightened out her injured knee. It was a little stiff, but the pain had abated. When she stood she was able to put her full weight on it. An internal sigh of relief blew through her when she dropped to the floor and began her daily stretches.

Twenty pushups, forty crunches, and five minutes of meditation later, she thought to check her cell phone and e-mail when she remembered Ky had her phone, and he'd disabled the Internet connection to her laptop.

"This just sucks wind," she mumbled while moving to the adjoining bathroom.

When she emerged, dressed and ready for the day, she made a silent wish for her confinement to come to a swift end.

In the kitchen, Jon Waters was standing by the counter speaking with two men she'd never seen before.

"Good morning," Gemma said.

Jon's smile was bright and fast. "Morning."

When her gaze flicked to the two others in the room, Jon said, "These are Agents LaRoux and Coble, Miss Laine."

Both men nodded at her.

"They're part of our team and have been assigned to help with keeping you safe."

Gemma moved forward and shook hands with both men, committing their faces to their names. Both had the basic look of all the government men she'd met so far: six foot, square jawed, and somber.

"Any news?" Gemma asked Jon when the men left. "Have they found the man who attacked me?" She shook her head when he lifted the coffeepot.

"I haven't heard anything yet," Jon said. "Sure you don't want some of this?"

"I don't usually drink coffee or tea, but thanks."

His eyes widened. "No? I don't think I've ever met anyone who doesn't need a hit of caffeine in the morning."

She smiled at him, having heard that line many times in her life from scores of people. "Oh, I need a caffeine hit just like the rest of the world," she said. "But I prefer to get it from a cold soda. I don't like hot liquids as a rule and rarely drink them."

"Unfortunately we don't have any, but if you tell me what you like, I'll have LaRoux or Coble get it for you."

"That's okay, you don't have to."

"You don't have to what?" Ky asked as he came into the room.

Gemma mentally steeled herself before turning to face him.

Clad in a muscle hugging T-shirt and loose-fitting sweats with the FBI logo running down one leg, his body was bathed in shiny moisture. He reached into the refrigerator and pulled out a bottled water. When he tipped his head back and took a long chug of it, his Adam's apple shifting and bobbing with the effort, Gemma found herself swallowing as well.

"Our guest doesn't overdose on coffee like you and I do, Papps. She prefers soda to get her going in the morning."

Ky recapped the bottle and leveled his gaze at her.

His breathing was fast but even, his shoulders and chest rising with each inhalation, pulling against his drenched shirt.

Gemma's fingers itched for her camera. He was so profoundly male, so starkly masculine, bathed in sweat, testosterone gushing off his body in waves, she knew exactly how she'd photograph him.

"Soda?" His gaze zeroed in on hers, and her back instantly stiffened at the judgment she heard in his voice.

One word. It had taken just one word from him for her to get irritated again. Okay, maybe not the word itself, but definitely the mockery in his tone. She was all set to ask him if he had something against drinking soda, but before she could get the words out, he forced them back into her, unspoken.

"My sister Ariadne drinks soda for breakfast, too. Diet Mountain Dew by the case. Drives my mother nuts."

Gemma's grin came so fast she couldn't have prevented it if she'd tried. "A girl after my own heart. And taste buds. That's my morning wake-up drink, as well."

"I'll have LaRoux go pick some up," Jon said.

"Please don't go to any bother on my account," she told him. "I can do without it for a day."

The look that passed between Ky and his partner had Gemma's internal radar kicking up. "What?" she asked, her question aimed at Ky.

Before answering, Ky uncapped the water again and took another long draught. Gemma's nerves, frayed to begin with at the circumstances she'd been forced into, went into overdrive waiting for him to respond.

"You might need to stay here," he said after he swallowed, "a little longer than another day or so."

"Why? You said it wouldn't take long to find the men responsible."

Good Lord. Was that her voice whining like a three-year-old?

"If you'll remember, I said it *shouldn't* take long to find them."

Gemma sliced her hand in the air. "Whatever the wording you used, your implication was it would be soon. What's changed?"

His expression gave away nothing. He must be awfully good at his job, she thought. The average person would look at his face and see a blank wall. But Gemma wasn't an average person. She was a trained and keen observer of subtle body language, telltale motions, and minute physical changes the average person never noticed. So, even though his face remained a mask of calm emptiness, the slight constriction of his pupils, flare of his nostrils, and tension in his fisted hands told her quite the opposite.

Ky shot a quick look at his partner. "Why don't we all sit down?"

He pulled a chair at the table for her, waited until she grudgingly sat in it, and then took his own seat across from his partner.

"Well?" Gemma folded hands across her chest.

"I got notice just a few minutes ago that the man who attacked you, Charlie Faldo, was located this morning."

"Where?" Jon asked.

Ky glanced at him and then back to her. "The Hudson River."

She gasped, the noise bursting from inside her.

"He was fished out about five-thirty when a jogger on her morning run noticed something floating in the water along the waterway."

"How?" The word came out before she could stop it.

Ky's gaze hardened as he focused on her. "His throat was cut. Clear through to his spine. Then he was dumped."

"Ritandi's a big fan of slice and dice," Jon said, as if he were discussing the weather.

Ky nodded and finished his water. "We need to keep you hidden," he told Gemma. "Faldo was executed because he failed to kill you. Ritandi won't stop looking for you."

"But I don't know anything about any of this! I never even knew his name until you told me." Gemma bolted up from the table and backed into the counter. "Jesus!"

Ky was up and on her in an instant. "Easy," he said, reaching out to grab her arm.

The strength she felt seep from his touch, for some unknown reason, instantly calmed her.

And irritated the hell out of her.

With a quick jerk, she pulled out of his grasp and folded her arms in front of her chest again, flattening herself against the counter ledge. Ky's hands drifted slowly down to his sides as he took a step back. His gaze, though, never wavered from hers.

"We can keep you safe here. We just need to ride this out a little longer than anticipated."

"What about the men who killed your agents?" Gemma asked.

"The bureau has every available agent searching for them."

"Searching? That tells me you have no idea where they are, do you?"

He didn't answer her, but merely nodded.

"This just sucks," she said, repeating her thoughts of earlier.

Whatever appetite she'd woken with was gone now, killed by the knowledge that her life had been turned upside down and wasn't about to be righted any time soon.

She wanted to fly out the front door, grab a cab and run back to her condo. She'd shut and lock the doors and spend her solitary days working, pushing the horror of the past twenty-four hours from her mind.

She wanted to immerse herself in work until her eyes bled and her head begged for relief.

She wanted to punch something—anything—hard enough to free her mind of the fear and anger soaking through it.

She wanted to do all that and more, but what she wound up doing was storming from the kitchen, back up to her tiny, safe bedroom, and plopping down, face-up, on the bed that wasn't her own.

* * *

"She's been up there all day," Jon said hours later.

Ky looked up to the clock on the wall above the couch.

They were in the den, the room they'd fashioned as a command center, each at a desk, their laptops opened in front of them, files scattered atop the desks. For most of the day they'd been reviewing documents, arrest forms, witness statements, phone records, anything and everything that might give them a lead on how Ritandi had known where to find Calafano. So far nothing had popped for either of them, and Ky was getting more frustrated by the moment.

Live video feed of the outside of the house streamed on six different screens, each focused on a separate area of the perimeter, the back yard included.

"Didn't come down for lunch," Jon added, looking up at the ceiling. "And she didn't have any breakfast before you told her about Faldo. She's got to be hungry, don't you think, and lonely, up there all by herself."

Ky glanced over at him. "You sound like my mother, worried if someone skips a meal they're going to die from starvation."

Jon grinned.

"She's upset about the situation," Ky said, simply, leaning back in his chair. "Being stuck here, unable to do what she wants to do. Go where she wants to go. And I don't imagine she wants to be around either of us since we're part of the reason she's here."

"Don't you think one of us should check on her, though? Make sure she's okay? See if she needs anything?"

Ky regarded his partner through slitted eyes. "When did you become such a mother hen?"

"I'm not." Jon's grin turned wry. "I'm just saying one of us should make sure she's okay."

Ky shook his head. "Okay, *YiaYia*." He rose from the chair and stretched his arms over his head. "My eyes are starting to cross from looking at all this anyway. I'll go check on her."

"Ask if she wants something to eat," Jon instructed.

Ky turned from the doorway. "I'm getting the distinct impression you're not as worried about her stomach being filled as you are about your own."

His partner's face split into what Ky's oldest brother, Chrystos, mockingly called *a shit-eating grin*.

"Well, it is almost time for dinner. And we do have our deal, remember? You cook. I clean. It works."

Ky threw him a speaking glance and then started up the stairs.

The door to Gemma's room was closed over, but not shut. Ky tapped gently on the doorframe. When he got no response, he pushed it open just a bit so he could look in.

The bed was made but empty, the sheets rumpled as if she'd lain on top of them; the bedside light off. The sound of water running had him glancing at the accompanying closed bathroom door. A thin line of light beamed from under it.

His gaze was drawn to the desk and chair situated under the open window. Shaking his head he realized he needed to have a conversation with her about sitting in front of it since she didn't seem to realize she was making herself a target.

Atop the desk her laptop was open, a slideshow moving across it, littered with photographs. Like metal to a magnet, it pulled him closer, the images scrolling by calling to him.

He'd known she was an exceptional photographer just from viewing the untouched photos she'd captured of his crime scene. But what he hadn't realized was what a magnificent eye for detail and color she possessed.

Every single picture that slid by was better than the one before. Black-and-white images of city buildings, buildings he recognized and had even been in, never realizing how beautiful their architecture truly was; colored images of sunrise at South Ferry station, gazing out over the harbor; the Statue of Liberty at sunset, Lady Liberty looking as if she were going to jump down and walk away from her pedestal.

His breath caught in the back of his throat when the next series of photographs scrolled through. They had to be family portraits because each woman bore some resemblance to the one before. When a shot of a beaming Kandy Laine holding an infant popped up, her husband next to her, his arm thrown possessively across them, Ky knew the photos were of Gemma's own family. But not one picture in the collection was of her. Gemma Laine was the face behind the camera, never, apparently, in front of it.

"What are you doing?"

Surprise banged through him first. He'd been so engrossed with the slide show he hadn't heard the water shut off or the bathroom door open.

When he turned and found her standing next to the bed, her arms, as usual, crossed in front of her, primal awareness replaced the surprise in an instant.

Her mussed hair, wrinkled shirt, and the sheet mark indenting the left side of her cheek told him until quite recently she'd been on the bed, probably sound asleep. The mistrust in her eyes as she gazed across the room told him she was still wary of him. The fact she'd caught him in her room, uninvited and examining her computer screen, told him he deserved her watchful glare.

"I knocked," he said. "You didn't answer. I just wanted to make sure you were okay."

She uncrossed her arms and walked over to the desk. The scent of fresh-picked cherries floated with her and her hairline was damp as if she'd just washed her face.

"Did you think by going through my computer you'd discover if I was?" She slammed the laptop closed and leveled another piercing stare at him.

Ky dug deep for calm. He'd never had such trouble reining in his annoyance before. But ever since he'd met Gemma Laine, her attitude piqued his irritation to levels he was usually able to ignore. He waited a beat until he was sure he could at least speak in a civil tone, and then said, "I wasn't going through your computer. I'd never invade your privacy like that. I was simply watching the slide show, waiting for you to come out of the bathroom."

Before she could shoot a snarky comeback at him, he added, "Your photographs are amazing. I can see for myself why you're so successful."

His words shocked her into silence. Her shoulders relaxed under her sleep-wrinkled blouse and she dropped her hands to her sides, unfurling them from fists as she did.

"The pictures of the city buildings are so lifelike, I felt like I was standing right in front of them, looking up at them. You're extremely talented."

"Th—thank you."

Confusion replaced the wariness. Her brow, still crinkled, had his fingers tingling to reach up and rub it smooth. Why did she feel she had to constantly be on guard around him? She certainly hadn't reacted to his partner like she did to him. Why, with him, did she feel the need to shield herself?

"I'm sorry you thought I was snooping," he said, as he dropped his hands into his pants pockets. "I wasn't. Jon made me realize you've been up here, sequestered, all day, and we just wanted to make sure you were doing okay. Find out if you needed anything or if you were hungry."

Gemma ran her fingers through her unruly hair. "I'm starving, actually," she admitted. "At home I keep snacks around my workspace so I don't have to stop and make something to eat." Her sigh was deep and long. "I've got nothing up here."

"I can have the room stocked for you. All you need to do is tell me what you want."

"What I really want is to get out of here," she said, her plump lips pulling into a pout. She picked up one of the cameras sitting next to her computer and played with the buttons. "But since that's not happening anytime soon, I'll have to deal with it." She let out a sigh and shook her head. "I was just on my way downstairs to see if I could get something to eat." She slung the camera around her neck.

Ky nodded. "Come on, then. Jon's already thrown hints about dinner."

He descended the stairs first, checking over his shoulder to make sure she was able to navigate without any problems.

"You're not limping. Knee's feeling better?"

She nodded. "It's a little swollen, but no pain. By tomorrow I should be back up to speed."

He reached the foyer first and stopped to wait for her.

"I don't suppose I can go for a run, can I? I'm not usually inside all day long and I'm feeling pretty restless."

She looked so beaten down he wished he could tell her she could, but it just wasn't wise for her to be out where she'd be seen. It was much safer to keep her isolated and hidden.

"Don't," she said before he could speak. "The answer's written all over your face."

"Feeling better?" Jon called from the den. He closed his laptop and joined them.

"More like a lazy slob."

Why couldn't she smile at him the way she did at his partner? Where was the guarded expression she perpetually had for him, whenever she spoke to Jon? He'd give anything to know why she felt so mistrustful of him when he'd given her no reason to. At least none he could think of.

"I worked for a few hours and then I wasn't able to keep my eyes open, so I crashed for a bit. I never realized sitting around all day is so exhausting."

Jon laughed.

"Ky and I have been on enough stakeouts to know exactly how you feel," Jon said. They walked into the kitchen and he pulled a chair for her to sit at the breakfast table.

"At least I got a ton of work done," she said, accepting the bottled water Ky gave her from the refrigerator. "I was able to finalize some of the photos I'm using for the book."

While Ky set about putting together the simple stew he'd planned for dinner, he had Jon assemble a salad for them to eat first. While the stew simmered, they sat and ate their first course.

"You mentioned going for a run," Ky said while he watched Gemma attack the salad as if she hadn't eaten for days.

"I usually get one in three or four times a week," she said. "I missed yesterday's and now today is all but over. Why do you ask? Can I?" Her eyes lit up as she looked across the table at him with such childlike expectation, that Ky momentarily forgot what he'd been about to say.

He gave himself a mental shake.

"Not outside, no. It's not safe." And just as quickly, her excitement disappeared. "But we've got a treadmill and workout set up in the basement. Free weights, mats. You're welcome to use anything down there."

"Really? Is that where you worked out this morning?"

Her cheeks instantly colored and Ky couldn't for the life of him figure out why she'd be embarrassed at the question.

"I mean, I noticed when you came into the kitchen you were, you know… you looked like…maybe you'd been running. Or something. Working out. You were all…sweaty."

She stopped and took a large gulp of water. Across the table Jon's eyebrows rose as he turned his gaze from her blushing face to Ky's.

Not understanding the cause of her awkwardness, Ky replied, simply, "Yes, it was. Do you think your knee is up to a run?"

"Maybe not a full one. But walking on a treadmill is better than doing nothing."

"After dinner I'll show you the setup," he told her.

While he saw to their meal, Gemma asked them both, "Have you found out anything new? Who killed your agents? Or…anything else."

"No," Jon answered.

"Oh."

The disappointment in her voice echoed throughout the kitchen.

"I don't suppose you could tell me anything, anyway," she said, "since I'm not a cop or involved in any official way."

"It's not that," Ky said. "Believe me, you have a right to know what we find out. We both agree on that." He nodded at Jon. "But your life is in danger now and our priority isn't only finding the hit squad, but in keeping you safe as well."

She laid her salad fork down on the table.

He didn't know what to make of her silence. In truth, he liked it better when she was sparring with him, showing her strength and will.

Ky rose and served them the now ready stew.

"We'll get them," he told her. "I'm certain."

Gemma's gaze tracked his movements while he ladled their dinner into bowls. "I keep telling myself that, but…"

"No buts," Ky said and sat. "For now, just eat."

"Good Lord." Gemma closed her eyes when the first spoonful passed her lips. "Is this another of your grandmother's recipes?"

He shook his head. "This one belongs to Mom. Although, I'm sure my grandmother added something to it."

"You really need to write these down so I can give them to Kandy. She's always on the lookout for new recipe ideas for her shows. She'll probably want to do an entire hour on Greek cuisine after tasting this."

"I thought her show wasn't in production anymore?" Ky said.

Gemma squinted at him. "How do you know that? I didn't peg you for a cooking show groupie." Her lips pressed into a small line, her head cocked to one side. Something akin to a playful glare danced in her eyes as she regarded him.

In that second, Ky had such an overwhelming desire to kiss the grin off her face that he had to count to five before replying, fearful he'd give into the temptation.

"Not me, the women in my family," he said when he knew he'd be able to control himself. "They're all big fans. My sister-in-law Phaedra was the one, I think, who mentioned a while back the show wasn't live anymore."

Gemma didn't reply, and when the grin disappeared from her lips, he wondered at the cause.

"Everything okay?" Jon asked, noticing as well her quick mood change.

She laid down her spoon and took a swig of her water. "I just realized something. Something I hadn't even considered before right now."

"What?" both men asked.

She lifted her gaze to Ky and swallowed. The camera that had slung around her neck until she placed it next to her salad bowl before eating, she now pulled back into her hands and fiddled with again. It was almost as if holding it gave her some sort of comfort, of solace, like a child with a favorite blanket or toy.

Why is she nervous?

"I've been so wrapped up in thinking about how my life has been turned upside down with this whole situation. I never even considered what it might mean to the two of you, having to be stuck here with me. Being away from your families. Loved ones." She looked down at the camera and then back up at Ky. "Wives."

The air in the room suddenly flared with an unseen electrical charge Ky couldn't put a cause to. He swore her eyes changed colors: darkened from crystals to pale blueberries while she gazed across at him. Her sculpted brows pulled together above her eyes while she bit the inside of her cheek.

"No worries on that front," Jon told her. "Neither of us is hitched. Although," he slanted a look at Ky, "it's been rumored around the office Papps is married to his job."

The jest had its intended reaction. Gemma's quick, unfiltered laugh broke the sudden tension at the table.

She leveled her gaze at him. Ky couldn't read what she thought about Jon's statement in her eyes, if she believed it, or not, but the wall of wariness had fallen down.

She turned to Jon and, with a gentle, questioning lift of her brows said, "And you're not?"

His own grin was fast and boyish. Ky knew what a flirt his partner was, and usually wasn't bothered by it. Jon Winters was a top-notch agent, a crack shot, and there was no one else Ky wanted covering his back during a hairy situation.

But he wished his partner would tone down the charm a little with Gemma Laine. That quick, hot bead of jealousy he swore he hadn't felt yesterday had been a lie he'd told himself so he wouldn't get blindsided. They had a job to do; several, in fact. Aside from keeping Gemma safe, they needed to find out who had leaked Calafano's whereabouts to Ritandi and figure out another way they could put him away for good. Flirting with their present witness wasn't a good idea. On any level.

When he saw how easily and freely she interacted with his partner though, Ky knew the little stab in his midsection had a name.

"No, ma'am," Jon replied. "I'm too young and good looking to be tied down at this age. I'm single, bilingual, and ready to mingle."

Gemma's gaze narrowed.

"I've got a pretty good life outside the bureau. It's a great job, but it's just a job."

"Really?"

"Yup. Life's too short to make the job the be-all and end-all."

"Keep telling yourself that," she said, her lips quirking. "Maybe someday you'll actually convince yourself it's true."

She turned to Ky while Jon let out a whoop.

"Gorgeous, talented, and she can cut straight through the bullshit," Jon said. "Finally I've found the girl of my dreams. Gemma Laine, will you make me the happiest man alive and marry me?"

"No," she answered, immediately. "Not in a million years."

Jon's hands flew to his chest, a hurt pout on his face. With his eyes closed and clasped as if in pain, he declared, "You wound me, woman, to the quick."

"You'll survive." She rolled her eyes and shook her head, a ghost of a grin billowing on her lips. "You're too much of a *playa* not to."

For the first time Ky had an unfiltered view of her natural persona. Unguarded and quick, feisty, with just enough snark to be sassy but not derisive; this Gemma Laine was a delightful surprise.

She turned her attention back to Ky. "To answer your question," she said, ignoring Jon now, the mirth drained from her face, "you're right, Kandy's regular cooking show isn't in production anymore. But she signed a new deal to give the network three cooking specials a year. She wanted a complete out, but EBS knows what a golden goose she is. They gave her carte blanche and a ridiculous payday as long as she agreed. I can see her devoting an entire hour to food like this," she lifted her spoon, filled with stew, "so you'd better warn your mother and grandmother to be prepared for her call."

"They'd be honored," he said.

Honored? They'd be hysterical, but he didn't say that out loud.

He could picture them now, both women, plus his sister and his brothers' wives, all standing in his mother's kitchen, cackling away in Greek, each talking at the same time, offering their own special twist on a recipe.

While they ate the rest of their meal, Jon asked Gemma questions about her family and her business, while Ky sat and listened.

When they each rose and took their empty dinnerware to the sink, Jon reminded her it was his job to clean up.

"You guys really don't have to wait on me, you know," she told them. "I'm used to doing things all on my own. I'm not useless."

"No one thinks you are," Ky said. "Let Jon clean up, though. It keeps him humble."

"That's one word for it," his partner said while he filled the sink with water.

"Come on," Ky told Gemma. "I'll show you the layout in the basement."

Chapter Four

Gemma opened her eyes and for the second day in a row had a momentary flash of panic.

Not her bed; not her bedroom.

She sprang to a sitting position and as soon as her gaze landed on her laptop where it sat on the desk across from her, a desk Agent Pappandreos had insisted—*ordered*—her to move away from the window the night before, she remembered where she was.

And why.

She fell back on the pillow and scrubbed her hands down her face.

Another day in paradise.

Not.

Habit had her reaching for her cell phone. Immediately, she remembered she didn't have it.

Stretching her arms above her head, she did the same to her legs, noting her knee felt fine, a little stiff, but no pain, and flexed her toes, lengthening her body along the bed.

A quick glace out the open window told her the day was just beginning, and she decided to begin it the way she usually did. With a workout.

Up and dressed in the exercise gear Kandy had packed since she knew her sister so well, Gemma tied on her running shoes, twined her hair into a short ponytail and made her way to the basement.

When she opened the door to her bedroom, the hallway light was lit. She cocked her head and listened for any sounds of life in the house. Hearing none, she gingerly walked to the stairs, down to the first floor. The den was vacant, the security screens glowing in the dark room like an eerie montage, perpetually streaming. Gemma stopped to see the two other agents she'd met, LaRoux and Coble, each on a separate monitor, walking around the outside of the house.

They're on patrol, she told herself, making sure no one breached the house and got to her.

With a shudder, Gemma tore her eyes from the screens and exited the room.

The kitchen was empty, the coffee machine on and the carafe half-full. Guessing the caffeine was for the outside agents, she moved to the basement door and opened it.

Muffled sounds drifted up the stairs from the lit room that ran the length of the house.

When Ky had shown her the area the night before with the invitation to use whatever she wanted to and at any time, Gemma had been impressed by the quality of the equipment. A top-notch elite treadmill, stair climber, and a full array of weights were displayed for her choosing, along with two boxing bags suspended from the ceiling and a life-sized Slam Man punching stand. But Gemma's eyes had zeroed in on the nontraditional gear along one area of the concrete. Nunchakus, a series of different lengths of jo staffs, and several kamas of differing sizes were secured to the wall.

Gemma's eyes had gone wide when she'd viewed the fighting weapons. As much as she valued a good run, keeping up with her weapons training was equally as important. She hadn't been to class in several weeks due to her book deadline, and her fingers and arms had twitched with longing when she realized she had the weapons at her disposal.

With as little noise as possible, Gemma crept down the basement stairs, drawn to the sound of a fist connecting with something hard. It was an unmistakable sound, one she'd hoped to make herself this morning.

Dressed in similar sweats to what he'd worn the morning before, his body bathed in gleaming sweat, Ky pummeled one of the suspended bags. His hands were wrapped with white gauze, his arms toned and taunt as he executed each strike with perfect precision and technique.

Gemma stopped on the final riser and watched him batter the bag, fists moving with swift, defined actions, the jabs fast and hard, the recoils even faster.

Shoulders raised, elbows tight, hands balled and up blocking his cheeks and jaw line, he threw a right jab, left, then two rights, all aimed high, and a final forward thrust left, lower on the bag, his knees bending to give him balance.

Gemma wanted to race back to her room, grab her camera and capture the scene before her.

Kyros Pappandreos was the epitome, the very definition of a natural-born fighter. Distinctly male, uniquely the warrior, his body moved with the grace of a panther, the stealth of a tiger stalking its prey, and the accuracy of a cobra striking. There was something so sensual, so primal, so animalistic about him, she knew she had to photograph him just this way.

She'd capture him in slow motion first, his tight fist connecting with his target, the sweat of exertion flying from his forehead. Then, she'd move to rapid fire, the image blurring with the speed of his hits. A pugilist, enigmatic, tough, and hard bodied, the bulging muscles and corded sinew in his arms distended with his action, outlined and bathed in the shiny moisture pouring from him.

Ky repeated the moves in the same series of strikes three more times before dropping his hands to his thighs.

He swiped at his forehead with the back of his hand, his breathing hard, but not labored, and turned.

"I'm sorry," Gemma said as soon as his widened gaze trained on her. "I didn't know you were down here, and when I realized it, I didn't want to interrupt you. You looked so…intense. So focused. I'm sorry."

Good Lord, she never babbled like an idiot. Never. What the hell was it about a simple glance from this man that cranked up her nerves?

"No need to apologize," Ky said. He began unwrapping one of his hands, tugging at the gauze with his teeth. "This room is as much at your disposal as it is for any of us."

"I know, but…here, let me help."

She grabbed the edge of the gauze from him and began twirling it around his hand. Close to him now, she could feel the heat escaping him, the scent of his sweat distinctly male and surprisingly arousing. A hot jab of awareness punched her stomach, almost as if he'd actually been the one to throw it.

Gemma kept her gaze on the wrapping, but from the corner of her eye she watched his substantial chest rise and fall with each breath he took. The T-shirt was plastered to him, his pecs and abdominal muscles defined under the clinging, wet fabric. One lone droplet cascaded down along his jaw to settle in the deep notch at his throat, and in a moment of blinding lust, Gemma experienced such a profound need to run her tongue along the area, knowing she'd savor the taste of salt and man mixed together, she had to bite down on the inside of her bottom lip to avoid doing it and mortifying herself.

When the wrapping was finally off, Ky took his now freed hand and began working on the other one while Gemma held on to the gauze.

"Thanks," he told her. "It's always easier and goes quicker when someone else does the first one."

Gemma nodded and backed up, crossing her hands behind her back.

"You planning on using the treadmill this morning?" he asked.

It took her a moment to answer. She'd been staring at his now naked hands. Had she noticed how long and thin his fingers were before? How dexterous, how exact each movement was? A flash of his fingers moving over her naked flesh popped into her head and she had to will herself not to slam her eyes shut.

"No." She swallowed and took a breath. "I think I want to practice my weaponry skills today. It's been a while since I've been able to get to a class and I don't want to get rusty."

He nailed her with a hard glaze. "Weaponry skills? You study martial arts?"

She nodded. "Kempo. Jujitsu. Some escrima."

"Really?"

His bald disbelief sailed down her spine, stiffening it. Annoyance killed the sudden lust swimming within her.

"Yes, *really*." She fisted her hands on her hips. She'd had her fill of arrogant and superior sounding men over the years condescendingly question her abilities. It had only served to make her more of a devotee of the practices. She wasn't surprised when Special Agent *Pompous* sounded skeptical.

"How long?" Ky asked.

"How long what?"

"Have you been studying?"

Gemma shook her head, wondering why he asked. "Eleven years. I started in high school. Kept at it."

"Dedicated," he said. "That's admirable. Why'd you start?"

She couldn't tell him the real story behind her initial desire to learn how to defend herself. Gemma had never shared what had happened to her in the back seat of that car long ago and wasn't about to start with the man standing in front of her. So she opted for a half-truth.

"I took a basic karate class as a high school gym elective one year. The teacher told me I had"—she shrugged—"a natural ability for the art and the movements and that I should consider pursuing it. So I did."

"What's your rank?"

She never hesitated to tell him, proud of her achievements. "Third-degree black in kempo, second in jujitsu."

Ky whistled. "Nice." He glanced over at the weapon wall. "You like working with sticks?"

"They're my favorite weapons next to nunchakus."

"Okay. Let's see what you've got."

"*What?*"

He moved to the storage wall and selected two pair of three-foot fighting sticks, and handed her one set.

"Seriously?" Because it was second nature to her, she weighed the sticks in each hand and found her balance, legs spread hip distance apart and equalized on the balls of her feet, arms and shoulders lifted, the sticks pointed upward. "You know how to stick fight?"

His mouth lifted in a tiny arc on one side. "I've been known to hold my own," he told her, adopting an equal stance. "Drill first to get a feel for one another?"

Gemma nodded. "High, low, then triples?"

The tiny grin he'd tossed her spread into a full-fledged smile that had her mouth watering.

She counted them down.

From the first series of strikes she knew without a doubt he could more than just hold his own. Kyros Pappandreos had some serious skill.

They started slow, each gaging the other's reaction time, "getting the feel," as he'd said, for the other's ability. But in less than a minute the pace jumped. They parried and danced in a circle, each counterbalancing a move made by the other. For every lift of his stick to strike high, Gemma met his move and then changed the angle, first striking low, then lifting her arm. Back and forth, each maneuver challenging the other, the sounds of the sticks striking, wood to wood in a staccato rhythm, bounced off the walls.

At one point they were moving so fast, the sticks blurred in her vision and all she could do was let instinct and training take over her hands and arms, the weapons becoming an extension of her body.

How much time passed, she couldn't guess, but her arms began to scream with the effort and speed they mounted.

Gemma met him, hit for hit, strike for strike. It was exhilarating, mentally and technically, to work with someone so well-schooled in the art. For many of the past several years, her master had recruited her into helping the less experienced students. When she'd been able to spar and fight with him, his proficiency level had elevated hers, forcing her to defend against moves no novice or amateur could. She'd grown as a fighter, cherishing each time she was able to implement her abilities.

And every one of those skills was put to the test with Ky as her partner.

Eventually, he slowed them down to where they were simply just tapping their sticks together, high strikes then low. Gemma was breathing hard, but wasn't winded; she was elated. She wanted to push herself, push him, to see where they could take this.

"Enough," he said, taking a step back and lowering his sticks to a neutral position.

Gemma mimicked his movement.

"You know what you're doing," she told him, measuring his breathing by the pace of his chest rising and falling. It gave her a subtle ego boost to realize he was breathing a little rougher than she was.

"As do you," he answered. Respect and something deeper filled his gaze as he considered her. Gemma's toes curled inside her sneakers as those hooded eyes regarded her. "You've had top-notch training."

"My sensei believes if you're going to learn something, you should master it to understand every nuance, every aspect of it."

Ky nodded. "A sound practice." He reached out a hand for her sticks. Mild disappointment flowed through her. She'd wanted to play some more.

"What else can you do?" he asked while he replaced them.

"I'm good at staff technique and knife."

"How about hand-to-hand?"

Her brows pulled together. "Like sparring or grappling?"

"Either. Both. The disciplines you train in require you to be proficient in all aspects of combat, yes?"

"Yeah."

"What would you say you need to work on more?"

She lifted her shoulders. "Grappling, probably. I don't practice it enough. I haven't done any for a while."

Ky nodded. "Okay. Let's go."

"With you?"

Ky made a show of turning around the room. "I seem to be the only one here, so, yes."

His mocking tone stood the hair on the back of her neck upright.

"Don't worry," he said. "I won't hurt you."

Pride, anger, and just plain pissed-off-ness broke through her. She lifted her chin and glared at him, realizing a little splash of hurt had mixed in with the other emotions.

"That's a condescending thing to say."

"I didn't mean it to be." His brows kissed over his eyes. "I was thinking more along the lines of you getting injured by taxing yourself. You're still only a couple days out with that knee."

She stayed silent.

"Want protective gear?"

"Protective gear's for sissies," she said, automatically. Her pulse shot up when his hooded eyes widened. "I train without gear. Always. My teacher believes it's the best way to mimic the real world, and I agree."

Ky nodded.

Gemma couldn't help herself when she added, "But feel free to wear some if you think you might need it. I wouldn't want you to hurt...anything."

If her unconscious attempt had been to put him in his place, it backfired.

"Don't worry about me," he told her. "You're sure your knee is up for it?"

"My knee's fine. I wouldn't have decided to work out if it weren't. And having gear on wouldn't have prevented what happened to me in my apartment," she said. "I managed to hold my own even though I had a gun pointed at my face."

It was his turn for silence, his gaze, though, never wavering from hers. The intensity of the scrutiny had her insides squirming.

"Okay," he said at last. "No gear. But we use the mats. If one of us falls, at least the mats will cushion us."

"I have no intention of falling," she told him.

The slight lift of his full lips distracted her for a moment, just enough so that when he moved toward her she wasn't as quick as she should have been.

In no time at all, he'd grabbed both her forearms, the strength of his hold imprisoning her. His slight height advantage dazed her as he loomed above her, his hands clamped down together.

When the shock of his approach wore off, Gemma's trained brain kicked in. Most people would instinctively pull backward to try and yank their arms away from an attacker's hold.

Not Gemma.

She knew the futility of moving back, so she stepped into his space, their bodies so close she could distinguish the cacophony of colors in his eyes, and in one continuous motion rolled her arms inward so her palms were now facing the ceiling, snapped her forearms together—making his knuckles clunk against each other—and then spread them apart again.

The power and swiftness of the combined movements forced Ky's hands to fall open, freeing her arms.

Gemma wasted no time.

She stepped behind him and wound one hand around his waist, the other under his chin to try and grab the opposite side of his jaw. The purely male aroma of sweat and hot, sexy, man wafted to her. She bit down the longing to slide her nose along his neck and sniff.

Ky tucked his chin to his chest and turned into her hold, an elbow aimed at her stomach. Gemma felt the intent of his move with her body, so she loosened her hold and took two steps back, dragging him with her.

He snaked a hand under the arm secured at his waist, grabbed her thumb and yanked it back. Pain shot through her palm as she released her hold, a tiny grunt escaping through her lips.

Ky spun to face her. A momentary flash of something crossed his face before his hands went to her throat.

He'd barely tightened into the strangle hold on her neck before Gemma took a step back and to her right side, lifted her left arm high and close to her face and then smashed her elbow down on his inner arms, aiming for the inside notch on his own elbows. The moment his hold was broken, her right hand came up to punch him in the jaw.

Gemma was impressed with Ky's reflexes when he checked the move by slapping her wrist away and spinning her so her back was to him.

Before she could recover her balance he grabbed her around the midsection with his arms locked and lifted her up, her back plastered against his front as he swayed backward with them.

Gemma snapped her head back, clipping him on the jaw, registered the muffled groan he let out, lifted her knees to her chest and began rocking back and forth.

She'd misjudged his strength.

Instead of his hold slackening from her jerking motions, it tightened around her waist, her back now completely molded to his. Her breathing came in spurts from the effort it took to fight him and the tension of his grip on her body.

"Come on," he said, so close to her ear his breath warmed her neck, the sensation shooting straight down her spinal column. She was beginning to sweat and knew it wasn't just from all the physical exercise.

Ky's body was one long, solid, fortress of muscle and power. Imprisoned against him, his every cord and tendon flexing against her back as he held her securely in place, the heat firing off her body was as much from excitement as it was from the exertion of fighting.

"You should be able to get out of this, easily," he said. "It's a rookie maneuver. You learned it in self-defense 101."

Irritation flashed through her.

Damn him!

Gemma closed her eyes and tried to center her anger. He was right. She did know how to get out of a hold like this, and if one way didn't work, there were others that had been drilled into her. Her mistake had been in being distracted by the incredible feel of his body against hers.

She let her entire body go slack and limp, dropping her knees and legs back down, touching the floor with the tips of her toes. The moment the tension left her, Ky struggled to keep his balance and his hold as tight as he had on her. Gemma took the opportunity of his loosened grip to elbow him in the midsection first with one arm and then rapid-fire with the other, knocking him back.

She whirled around, pushed against his chest with the flats of her palms and hooked a foot around one of his ankles.

Ky lost his balance and dropped backward to the mat, just as she'd planned. Unfortunately for her, though, Ky'd grabbed her wrists when she pushed against him and hung on. When he landed flat on his back she fell on top of him. Face to face, both their breathing labored and harsh, they stared at one another.

Where did a man get off looking like walking sex, sprawled on his back, drenched in sweat? His golden skin glistened in the daylight shafting through the small windows near the ceiling. Her professional eye traced along his temples, down his jaw, across his neck, and the corded muscles there, wet and pronounced.

He'd photograph like a Greek god and she desperately wanted to film him just this way.

While they stared at one another, Ky's hands remained wound around her wrists. The second she realized she should snap out of his grip, he lifted his hips and in the time it took to register his intent, Gemma was flipped flat against the mat on her back now, two hundred pounds of hard, solid, able-bodied male on top of her.

He'd imprisoned her arms above her head causing the entire length of his body to cover hers from chest to toe.

Every quickened breath she took had her breasts bumping against his broad torso.

Her nipples tightened and pulled inside her sports bra. When her heaving chest skimmed against his, the scraping pain shooting across the swollen peaks of her breasts was equal parts excruciating and stimulating.

Her abdominal muscles contracted when his hips pressed down against her, his unmistakable arousal settling against her pelvis.

Hypnotized, she stared up at his face, unable to move her gaze away from the swirling colors in his eyes disappearing as his pupils dilated.

A muscle in his cheek quirked, tightened. His lips parted, a warm, soft puff of air pushed through them, and billowed across her face.

When he swallowed, Gemma had to mentally force herself not to lift up and slide her lips against the bulge at his neck.

Never in all the times she'd fought in class or practiced with any male partner had she been so turned on.

It was customary for the sexes to be paired, most physical attacks occurring to women by men. The need to understand how to protect oneself against an assault dictated this pairing. Gemma had sparred and grappled with all ages and types of men. As she'd risen in rank, she'd earned the respect of many of them and the admiration of all the female students.

But she'd never experienced any kind of sexual pull before now and wasn't quite sure she knew what to do about it.

The tension in her body was coiled so tight, her reflexes all standing at attention, it took her a solid few seconds to respond when he calmly asked, "Had enough?"

For an answer she closed her eyes, centered her mind as quickly as she could and unwound that coil.

The move caught him off guard just as she'd hoped it would.

As her shoulders and the rest of her body relaxed against the mat, Ky struggled to keep his hold secure on her. Using his instability against him, she clasped her fingers together, and with her imprisoned arms, lifted and wound them around his neck, making him lose the tenuous balance he had left.

In a heartbeat she flipped him to his back again with a single thrust of her hips and had his own arms plastered above his head while she straddled him.

Gemma's hands were strong. Lifting and carting cameras, tripods, and a plethora of heavy photographic equipment over the years had made them so, so when she pressed against his arms to keep them in place, she thought he'd push back.

He didn't.

He simply let her hold him.

Her shoulders lifted and dropped with each breath she took, her gaze glued to his. Ky's breathing was as deep as her own and with each shift in his chest, she pushed down a little further, a little harder, until she was balanced right above him, their faces close enough to feel the heat of the other's breath.

And still, he didn't fight back.

Her gaze glided to his mouth where a fine line of moisture outlined the notch above it. She stared at his full, solid lips, fantasizing about what they would feel like pressed again her own. Would they be hard and rough? Or soft and intoxicating?

Ky bent his knees, a move she instinctively interpreted meant he was going to try and gain the upper hand again, and, as a counter measure, Gemma dropped her knees to the mat, settling solidly and completely on top of his groin.

The feel of him, hard and long, against her was the most erotic sensation she'd experienced in some time. Even though they were both fully clothed, she felt naked and exposed where their bodies came in contact and touched. The moisture drenching through her thong wasn't from sweat. And if she knew it, he probably did as well.

A harsh moan grumbled from deep within him when she settled her weight down fully on his pelvis.

For a hot second her entire body stilled as she simply allowed herself to *feel* him.

Good God, he was huge. Gemma realized right then how long it had been since she'd felt such a strong burst of arousal fire within her. That it had to be for this man, a man she didn't even like, and one she didn't want to trust, was beyond vexing.

When he shifted and pulsed against her, growing even larger, her vision blurred, then cleared as she stared down at his mouth.

It would take nothing for her to close the minute amount of space separating their faces and claim it.

That she considered doing it proved just how long it had been since she'd felt the need for a man. He watched her as she watched him. When his tongue swiped against his bottom lip, Gemma's gasp echoed in the room.

His eyes turned to slits and his shoulders heaved with each deep breath as he stared up at her.

Sexual electricity crackled in the air between them and when Ky lifted his head slightly from the mat, his gaze never moving from her face, Gemma inched downward to meet him halfway.

His lips silently formed her name.

Gemma.

Just when their mouths were a whisper from kissing, Ky blinked, opened his eyes wide and dropped his head back to the mat, all the while keeping her prisoner with his gaze.

Confused, Gemma pulled back, lifted herself from him and forced her body upright. When she stood flatfooted, she moved back, taking a few literal and mental steps away from him.

"Enough for today?" he asked after a moment while he pushed up on an elbow and regarded her with eyes that gave away nothing.

But did his voice sound a little tighter than it had?

"Yes." She attempted to pull her gaze from him, but when he leaned forward and stood, every muscle and joint unfurling in a single line, she couldn't have forced her eyes away from his body if commanded to.

Once again he reminded her of a panther, sleek and lithe, his every motion calculated, stealth, and powerful.

Dangerous.

That was the word to describe Kyros Pappandreos. His calm and cool façade belied the danger seeping through him, hidden, and ready to unleash at a moment's call, and God help her, she longed to witness that side of him.

Gemma shook her head. She had enough danger in her life with a crazed mob boss hunting for her.

He stood before her and swiped the back of his hand across his wet brow. "How's your knee feel?"

"It's fine," she answered, automatically. Even if it did twinge a little, she wasn't going to admit it to him.

"You gonna do anything else down here, now?" he asked.

"No. No, I'm...done for today."

He nodded and moved to a table in the corner she'd hadn't noticed. He lifted his gun from it, slid it into the waistband of his sweats at his back, and then clipped his phone on.

When he turned back to her, his face could have been carved from granite, the expression blank and rigid. "I'm gonna take a quick shower and then make breakfast. Any requests?"

"No, I—. No." she shook her head, trying to force the image of him naked and wet in the shower from her mind. "Whatever you make is fine."

It was his turn to nod. "There's plenty of hot water. You can shower now, if you want, as well. No need to wait."

She wouldn't let words form in her mouth. She was afraid that if she spoke, she'd give voice to her thought that they share a shower, so she simply nodded once and followed him up the stairs.

Chapter Five

Ky let the icy water sluice down his neck and shoulders as he bit back an oath from the freezing shock of it against his bare skin. He'd told Gemma there was plenty of hot water, but he wasn't taking advantage of it.

He needed to cool down.

Christ, he needed to calm down. He was so hard, walking up the two flights of stairs to his bathroom had his hands shaking and sweat pouring off him.

If sanity hadn't taken over just when it had, he'd have flipped Gemma flat on her back again and given in to his roaring desire to possess her mouth.

And possibly more than just her mouth.

From the moment he'd turned and found her staring at him, her eyes wide and filled with nerves, he'd been fantasizing about what she would taste like, feel like. In truth, she hadn't been far from his thoughts from the moment he'd shut his eyes the night before until he opened them again.

Gemma was an enigma in every way imaginable.

She'd shown him a stubborn side, a determined side, and even a vulnerable side of her personality. She'd been flirty and quick-witted with his partner, something he imagined she was in her daily dealings with men, but reserved and self-contained with him. She was passionate about her profession but obstinate about her safety. She'd actually argued with him when he told her she needed to move the desk in her room from under the window for fear anyone on the street could look in and see her. Pouting like a three-year-old and insinuating he knew nothing about technique or lighting, she'd done as he'd asked.

So many conflicting facets written into one woman.

To discover her hidden talent and finesse with weaponry had almost been too much for him to take in.

Beauty, brains, talent, *and* she was skilled at martial arts. He'd had to fight to keep the smile from his face when she questioned his own abilities with the escrima sticks. What would she have done if he'd confessed the numerous trophies he'd won in the sport? Or that he'd been studying the discipline longer than she had?

He had no doubt she'd have still consented to fight with him, her own pride and sense of self-worth would have made it impossible to refuse.

Where the thought to spar with her, hand to hand, had come from, he could only guess, but the unshakeable need to touch her, to have his hands all over her, to have her willingly consent to it, had pushed the question from his lips.

He'd thought to hold back, go easy so she wouldn't reinjure her knee, but she'd proven her defensive skills were exemplary, outmaneuvering him twice. He could have argued it was because he was distracted by how perfect her lean, toned body felt against his, or how cottony-soft her skin was under his fingers, or even how she smelled like ripe cherries.

But they would have just been excuses.

Gemma Laine, he'd been thrilled to learn, was a worthy opponent on several levels.

When she'd reversed him to his back and settled over his growing-by-the-second erection, he stopped fighting and simply reveled in the exquisite, erotic feel of her body against his.

The raw need that surfaced as he'd lain there overwhelmed him to the point of the almost-kiss. He'd forgotten every rule, every regulation, every oath he'd ever taken. In that moment, all he knew, all he could see, feel, and want, was Gemma.

She'd been as caught up in the moment as he'd been, he was sure of it. While he watched her head bend down, bringing those amazing lips closer to his, Ky had sensed something floating in the air between their bodies: something frightening, something real.

He'd pulled back at the last moment when the realization of what it was came to him. Equal parts thankful and regretful the kiss hadn't happened, Ky knew down to his core he had to keep a close watch on his emotions from now on and think with his head and not other parts of his treasonous anatomy where Gemma was concerned. He couldn't give in to his desire for her, couldn't allow it to surface again no matter how strong or forceful it was.

He had to keep her safe, avenge his agents, find Ritandi, and put him away for the rest of his natural life.

That was the objective. He needed to remember it.

When his body finally turned numb from the cold water, his erection now a memory, he shut the shower off, towel dried and dressed. He glanced at himself in the bedroom mirror and resolved to clamp down on the unexpected tightening in his system whenever he was near her. He could do it. Like *YiaYia* was fond of telling him, he had the blood of his warrior ancestors flowing through him with a matching will of iron.

From the staircase he heard the sound of voices drifting up. Jon said something he couldn't make out, and then Gemma's laughter rang through the hallway.

In that instant, Ky knew no matter whose blood flowed through his veins, it couldn't stop the yearning coursing through them for this one, beautiful, stubborn woman.

Her laughter died the moment he walked into the room, but for a brief, small second, he'd seen her face before the internal shade came down over it. Eyes the color of cobalt crystals were moist with mirth, her cheeks plumped by the rise of her lips. Happy. She'd looked genuinely happy.

Ky wanted to see her that way again, and by something he'd done or said, not his partner.

"Did you leave me any hot water," Jon asked. He filled a coffee mug and held it out to his partner.

"Plenty." Ky crossed to the refrigerator. From its depths he removed a carton of eggs, milk, and bread, then reached up into a cabinet and found cinnamon and sugar.

"French toast?" Jon asked.

Ky nodded.

"I hope you're hungry," Jon addressed Gemma, "because Papps makes the best French toast this side of, well, *France*."

Her lips lifted. When she turned to him, he thought a challenge drifted in her gaze as she fiddled with the buttons on the ever-present camera slung around her neck.

"Mine has been known to bring grown men to their knees," she told him, her head cocked at a jaunty angle, her hair swishing across her cheeks, "so yours better be good."

While he whisked the ingredients together he tossed her a quick glance over his shoulder and said, "I've never had any complaints."

"Hey," Jon said, his attention bouncing between them, "why don't you two have a cook-off? See whose is better?"

"Why do I get the feeling you're suggesting that just so you can eat more?" Gemma asked him, then grinned when his hand flew to his chest.

"Woman, you wound me. Again."

"Deny she's wrong." Ky dipped a few slices of bread into the bowl, then placed them on the now-sizzling griddle.

He looked over at his partner when they were settled to his satisfaction and screamed, "Down!"

He grabbed Gemma and dragged her off the chair and under the table.

Just as she yelled, *What the*—, an explosion detonated the coffeemaker, hot liquid spurting and raining down all around them.

"Stay down!" Ky ordered, one hand restraining her, the other holding his gun, cocked and ready. He'd positioned his body as a shield over hers.

A spray of rapid and unending gunfire blasted through the kitchen, destroying everything it hit. Ky felt a scorching stab on his back as the skillet was struck, the oil spurting from the implosion.

"Shit!" Jon crouched next to them, his own gun drawn.

"Perimeter breach," Ky told him, keeping his body over Gemma.

A slight pause in the hail of bullets was enough for them to reach up and return fire. They discharged their weapons in a swift series of blasts.

The kitchen window was shattered, blown from its frame, but Ky was able to get a good view through it.

"How many?" Jon yelled.

"At least two," Ky told him, crouching back down. "Front lawn and moving."

Jon nodded. His eyes did a quick dance from Gemma back to his partner. "Cover me."

Ky nodded. Jon mouthed, "three...two...one," and then jumped up, sprinting.

At the same time, Ky sprang up and fired three shots in swift succession, giving his partner enough time to bolt from the room, his own weapon primed. Several shots and then a scream shattered the air.

Gemma squatted under the table, her hands covering her ears.

"Stay here," he commanded. "Don't move."

Raw and stark terror drenched her face when she looked up at him.

"Understand?"

She nodded a staccato assent.

Ky stood cautiously, every muscle in his body tensed, the sound of gunfire coming from his right.

He slithered to the doorway then plastered his body against the frame as more shots rang through the house. A flash of movement came from his left and he spied a figure drenched in black, a hood barring his face, an automatic weapon braced in his hands. He spotted Ky and took a stance.

Ky was quicker. He fired first, once toward the head, once, the body.

The gunman went down, his weapon banging from his hands.

Ky kept his gun trained on the man as he approached, kicked the gun across the floor, and checked him.

Dead.

The blast of more gunfire made him drop to a squat and position himself behind the staircase bannister. The commotion was centered to his right, the living room.

Suddenly, an eerie silence boomed in the house.

Ky, his weapon at the ready, mentally counted to five.

"Jon?"

When he got no response, he moved stealthily down the hallway.

The living room was in shambles, the front window blown, the walls littered with caverns from the bullets.

Another body, identically dressed as the first, lay across the entrance to the den.

Just as Ky checked the man's status, a faint, "Papps?" met his ears.

Jon was sprawled across the floor, his gun gripped in his hand, a deep crimson stain drenching the front of his shirt.

"I'm hit," he said when Ky reached him.

"Did you see anyone else?" he asked. He tucked his gun into his shoulder holster, then ripped Jon's ruined shirt apart. A single hole lodged squarely in Jon's upper arm spewed bright red blood from its center. Ky took the edge of the shirt and pressed down hard.

A hiss blew past his partner's lips. "No. I think there were only two." His color was pasty, sweat drenching his brow and upper lip.

The faint sound of sirens tinged the air. While putting pressure on his partner's wound, Ky pulled his cell phone from his belt and pressed a single number. A voice answered immediately.

"What?"

"We've been attacked," Ky said without a greeting.

"Status?"

"Two intruders down."

"Agents?"

"Winters is hit. I haven't found LaRoux and Coble."

"Get out of there, Papps. Take your witness. Contact me when you can."

"Winters—"

"Now!"

The call disconnected.

Jon looked up at him. "Gemma?" he asked. He swiped his tongue across his mouth.

"I'm here," she said from behind them.

Ky's head snapped up.

Gemma ran to them, her gaze flitting from Ky to Jon. Her eyes were wide and glazed, her skin alabaster white. She still had her camera slung around her neck. Relief surged through him when he realized she hadn't been shot during the firefight.

When she dropped to her knees next to them, his relief flew and anger got the better of him. "*I told you to stay out of sight!*"

She stopped short, glared at him, her brows tugging together, and for a moment he was afraid she'd lash out at him for yelling at her. But in the next second she pursed her lips, and, silently dismissing him, gave her attention to Jon. She yanked off her hoodie, then pushed Ky's hand and the drenched shirt out of the way and placed the garment over Jon's wound.

"We need to keep pressure on this." A shaking warble drowned her voice. "I hear sirens. That means help's on the way."

"You've got to get out of here." Jon laid a hand over the one she held across his wound. "They know where you are."

"I'm not leaving you."

Jon shook his head. His color paled even more and a swift gasp shot from him.

"Don't move," Gemma said. "Please."

"Papps?"

Ky looked down at his partner.

"Take her out of here."

"Jon—"

"I'll be fine. But if they found her once..."

He didn't need to finish. Ky nodded, hating to leave his partner, but it had to be done. They were sitting targets.

He grabbed Gemma's upper arm. "Let's go."

She snapped it out of his hand and screeched, "Get your hands off of me!"

The sound of sirens was louder now, almost on top of them. They didn't have much time.

"If we don't leave right now we won't be able to once the police get here. Now, come on." He tried to tug her again.

"Gemma, go with him, please," Jon said. His breathing sounded wet and harsh. "I'll be fine. Go."

"But—"

"Go."

Her indecisiveness was costing them valuable time. Ky gripped her arm again and lifted her up, giving her no recourse.

She didn't resist when he pulled her from the room, jogged them through the destroyed kitchen and out the back door.

He stopped, once, to listen. The sirens were blaring from the front of the property. Assessing their best route of escape, he tugged her hand and brought her through the backyard, around the garage and toward the parallel street.

Gemma stayed silent, one hand secured in his, the other wrapped around her camera strap.

"We have to get out of this neighborhood," he told her. "Can you keep up with my pace?"

"Yes."

He stole a quick glance at her, then nodded. It was apparent she was terrified. Her hand shaking beneath his proved it. But he could tell she was angry as well, and knew he was the cause.

Fine. He'd deal with her anger later. For now, he had to get her someplace she'd be safe.

Chapter Six

Gemma stood behind Ky, quiet and composed, while he paid for their room in cash. The motel manager, an e-cigarette dangling from one corner of his mouth, brought to mind every seedy film noir character she'd ever seen. Balding, the tufts of his sparse comb-over greasy and wispy, he wore a drab sweater an eclipse of moths had eaten holes into, his baggy pants were held in place with a belt almost wrapped around him twice, and she could tell what he'd had for breakfast from the egg-colored crumbles stuck to the stubble on his jaw.

What kind of person greets paying guests looking like this?

And didn't he think it unusual they had no luggage, no bags? He hadn't even asked Ky for identification when he'd requested a room.

When the man opened his mouth and said, "Twenty bucks an hour," the e-cigarette glowing as it bounced with his words, "a hundred for the night," she knew why he hadn't.

They weren't exactly checking into a five-star hotel. She had no idea how much Ky paid him.

The manager handed over a worn key card, his eyes never wavering from the cash now secured between his fingers. Gemma bit back a swell of bile at the clutter of dirt under his fingernails.

With a firm hand placed at her back, Ky ushered her from the lobby without a word.

He kept them close to the outside wall while he brought them to the room, his gaze darting all around, never stopping, watchful, on edge.

The moment he secured the lock behind them, Gemma took her first full breath since fleeing the house. She leaned back against the faded wallpapered wall and swiped one hand down her face, the other still clutching the straps of her camera. She hadn't let go of it once since running from the safe house.

Ky made a show of closing the blinds and the dingy curtains over them, then moving to the room's small bathroom, checking behind the door, the shower, then the tiny closet.

When he looked convinced they were truly alone, he turned to her.

"Are you all right?"

She didn't answer him, fearful the moment she opened her mouth she'd let loose all the pent-up anger, rage, and heart-stopping panic she'd been forced to curtail during their flight. She didn't want to lose control. Not here, not now, and certainly not with him.

He crossed the small expanse of the room to stand in front of her. She wouldn't look at his face, couldn't allow him to see the weakness or the total fear she knew was swimming in her eyes.

Ky tipped his head to try and establish eye contact. In a feeble attempt to divert his attention, she said, "You have blood on your shoes."

She should have realized he wouldn't be distracted.

Gently, so gently the move made her want to weep, he lifted her chin with one finger.

"Look at me," he told her, leaving his hand in place. It was as if he'd hypnotized her with the sound of his soft, warm voice. Gemma was unable to resist the command.

"Breathe."

Her shoulders lifted as she inhaled deeply, then let it out.

"Answer me," he said when she focused on his face. "Are you all right?"

Her lips trembled and she bit down on them to quell their quaking.

"No," she confessed, the word small and hollow to her ears. She swallowed, her gaze glued to his. She hated she'd admitted it. Experience had taught her to never show or admit any frailty. Never give a man the power to see you as weak. It was a rule she'd lived by all her adult life. Trapped in the searching heat of his gaze though, she found she couldn't hide the horror pounding through her. "This is all my fault."

The words caught in her throat, a sob mortifyingly breaking through.

"No, it isn't."

"*Yes.* It is. Can't you see that? Jon got shot because of me."

"Not because of you. Jon got shot doing his job. A job he agreed to. A job he loves."

How his voice stayed so calm and even she couldn't begin to fathom when every inch of her being wanted to scream and rail.

"What else can I think?" she yelled, her raw nerves finally snapping, the emotions she'd curtailed unable to be contained now. She knew she was in danger of becoming hysterical, but couldn't find a way to restrain herself. "If Jon hadn't been protecting me from a maniac, he never would have been shot. I'm the reason. Me. My God, if he dies—"

She choked on the word and pushed against him, forgetting what a solid wall of concrete he was made of. Ky's hands gripped her upper arms and gave her a shake.

"Lower your voice." His clipped command snapped through her, anger at him now clawing through the fear. His fingers squeezed through her skin, a single stab of pain shutting off her words. His eyes were flat and hard as he continued to look at her. "You're not responsible for any of this. Not for Jon getting shot, not for witnessing the execution, nothing. Do you understand? Ritandi is. This has his stench all over it. He's responsible for it all, not you."

She glared at him, tasting bile again as she tried to clamp down on her fury.

"I need you to calm down and focus," Ky said, freeing her arms. He stayed rooted, in front of her, his expression tight. "Jon will be taken care of. It's you I have to worry about."

He turned away from her, went over to the window, and pulled the curtain back a little. He dropped it back in place after a moment. "We can't stay here. I don't think we were followed, but I can't take the chance. It's impossible to keep you safe here."

"Then why did you drag me to this dump? Why didn't we just stay put?" Her voice rose again as her anger overtook her fear.

"I asked you to lower your voice. These walls are paper thin."

Gemma's mouth clamped shut.

He stared at her a moment, as if waiting to see if she'd comply. "We couldn't stay at the house. I had to get you out since I had no way of knowing if more of Ritandi's men were coming. Jon and I took out two of them. Would you have preferred to wait and find out if there were more?"

The words sliced through her like a hot serrated blade. Not trusting her voice, she shook her head.

"I didn't think so."

"Why didn't we take the car, then? Or call someone to pick us up? It would have been faster and we wouldn't have to be...here." She swiped her hand around the room.

"Think that through. If they knew where we were keeping you," he shook his head, "they probably knew what our vehicles looked like, or even the license plate numbers. I couldn't take the chance we'd be followed by using one of our cars."

It made sense. She hadn't considered there might have been more men in the background waiting for them.

A deadly chill iced down her spine.

"Now, please just give me a minute," Ky said. "I need to think."

He sat on the edge of the bed and ran a hand through his hair from temple to nape. He leaned forward, his elbows on his knees, hands crossed together, almost in prayer, lost in thought.

Gemma's adrenaline surge finally wore off. Her legs began to tremble and she was afraid she'd slither down to a puddle on the floor if she didn't sit. The sparsely furnished room was devoid of a table and chairs. The only place to sit was on the bed next to Ky.

Without saying a word, Gemma crossed to the bathroom.

"Are you okay?" he asked again.

Gemma folded her arms across her chest, cast a quick glance his way and nodded. She moved into the bathroom and closed the door behind her.

The room was no larger than a cabinet. A single shower stall covered with a plastic liner scattered with dots of mold took up most of it; a child-sized toilet and sink completing the windowless room. Two, threadbare, once white towels, were haphazardly folded on a wall rack. She shivered at the thought of who had touched them before her. Gemma turned the sink water on, then sat on the closed toilet lid. Her legs were shaking in a disjointed rhythm, her hands now following suit.

This made the second attempt on her life. A life that, up until three days ago, had been normal, happy, and safe. Happenstance had placed her on a city street while a heinous crime took place and turned her world on its axis.

It wasn't fair. She'd done nothing wrong, but fate didn't seem to care.

She dropped her head into her hands and let the tears finally come through. The running water would silence them from the man on the other side of the door—a man she refused to let see her as weak. More times than she could remember Gemma'd locked herself in a bathroom, running from her mother's angry shouts and her father's profanities, seeking refuge from the war raging through the house. The sound of her father's deep and menacing voice as it bellowed over her mother's shrill and emotionally raw one was a sound Gemma could still hear in her dreams to this day.

No longer a child, Gemma now faced her fears with fortitude and resilience. Locking herself away in a bathroom wasn't who she was any more. She wanted her life back. Her normal, happy, and safe life.

She ran a finger under the running water to gauge the temperature and then tugged one of the threadbare towels from the bar and wet the edges. When she pressed the cooled cloth to her closed eyes she sighed.

No, she wasn't a child any longer, and the need to hide from fearful and upsetting things had long since passed. Her life was her own, her choices, her desires, her every action, hers alone. Staring at herself in the faded glass mirror, she took a deep breath and raised her chin. She wasn't going to allow a madman to play with her life.

No. Fucking. Way.

She was taking back her life. Starting right now.

She heard Ky talking when she turned off the water. The walls truly must have been paper thin because she could hear every word distinctly.

"No, I don't think that's a good idea," Ky said in that same firm, intractable voice he'd used on her. "Because there's obviously a leak."

He was quiet, apparently listening.

"Let me take care of this. I have an idea."

Gemma opened the door to find him at the window, peeking out, his cell phone at his ear. He nailed her with his intense gaze the moment he saw her. A quiet gasp broke from her when she caught the heat in his eyes as they zeroed in on her face. She'd come to recognize the subtle changes in his expression over the past few days. The way he looked at her now she'd categorized as his *cop face*. Eyes flat and filled with icy calm, mouth set into a determined, take-no-prisoners line that brokered no arguments. Chin firm, jaw immovable.

A different look from when he'd shoved her under the kitchen table and thrown his body over hers to protect her from the hail of bullets. Then he'd looked like a warrior, eyes glazed with the heat of battle, focused and hard, intent on his attackers, his full mouth drawn into a tight and narrowed line, preparing to defend, to kill. One look at his steadfast expression, one feel of the furnace of scorching heat pouring off him as he covered her body with his, and Gemma had likened him to a god of his origin, preparing for a battle of epic size.

Her fingers itched to film him just this way.

"Yes. Soon."

He never stopped looking at her as he ended the call.

"Are you okay?"

"You don't have to keep asking me that." She moved into the room, her gaze locked with his. "Who were you speaking to?"

Ky's eyes tightened at the corners as he considered her. After a moment, he slipped the phone into his pocket.

"My boss."

"Does he know how Jon is? Is there any…news?"

Ky nodded. "The bullet tore through the fleshy part of his arm and stuck. He's heading to surgery, but it's expected to go well."

Gemma swallowed. "So he'll be okay?"

"Yeah. He should. But LaRoux and Coble are dead."

He was trying to control his anger and again, if Gemma hadn't been such a keen observer, she would have missed the slight hitch in his voice, the tightening around his mouth and jaw. He'd balled his hands into fists right before sliding them into his pants pockets.

"And Ritandi's men?" she asked.

"Dead."

"Good." It was her turn to nod now. "They deserve to be, working for such a monster."

Ky cocked his head at her. "The house has been secured already."

"What's next?" she asked. "As you've said, we can't stay here."

"No, we can't. We have no resources, and I only have a few dollars in cash with me. We can't use any credit cards, anything where we can be tracked. Ritandi shouldn't have been able to find us."

"And yet, he did."

Ky stayed silent, then repeated her words back to her. "And yet, he did."

She moved to the bed and sat. Since Ky was at the window, she wasn't as concerned about sitting on it now.

"What are you going to do?" she asked.

Ky didn't answer. Instead, he pulled back a corner of the curtain and took a quick peek outside. Gemma remembered seeing an empty parking lot as they'd made their way to the room and she wondered what he was looking for.

"Wait."

"For what? Another attack?"

He sliced her with an annoyed flick of his eyes, but didn't respond. Instead, he stayed vigil at the window, his gun drawn in his hand.

Suddenly, he dropped the curtain edge. "Come on. Our ride is here."

Without a word, Gemma rose from the bed, then halted when he motioned for her to stand behind him. She couldn't see what was waiting for them through the dirt encrusted curtains, but apparently she didn't need to.

"Ready?" Ky asked.

When she nodded, he slid a hand around her upper arm, his grip firm and, oddly, comforting. Easing the door open he slipped through it first, then tugged her with him.

A midnight-black Escalade was parked, the engine running, right outside their door. Two men in nondescript dark suits stood on either side, automatic weapons drawn, sunglasses covering their eyes. As soon as they spotted Ky, one of them pulled open the back passenger door.

Gemma took it all in as Ky hustled her into the back seat and climbed in after her.

In the blink of an eye, they were speeding from the parking lot.

"Flight leaves in twenty, Sir," the driver called back to Ky.

"Flight? Where are we going?" Gemma adjusted her seat belt and shot her gaze to Ky.

Cop face stared back at her: hard, focused, lethal.

"The safest place I can think to keep you right now." He turned and looked out the window. "The FBI."

Chapter Seven

Ky closed his eyes and squeezed the bridge of his nose. The dull thud of the headache that had started right before they'd taken off from the private New York air strip had metastasized into a roaring earthquake, pounding and pummeling behind his eyes once they'd landed in DC. Being screeched at by the assistant State's attorney for the past fifteen minutes hadn't helped ease the pain one bit.

"What kind of a shit-show are you running, Pappandreos?"

Ky met the ASA's disgusted glare and counted to five. It wouldn't do to give into the anger raging within him and flatten the man where he stood.

Davison Barly, all six feet, six inches of him, used his substantial height and width to intimidate and bully all those around him. He ruled his office with a fist encased in iron, brokered no excuses, and was rumored to have lofty political aspirations. All of the people assigned to him came to work daily in a state of nervous tension.

He stood in front of Ky, hands bunched into bowling-ball-sized fists, a look of abject fury on his face.

"I want you removed as lead investigator in this case. My primary witness has been assassinated under your watch, and now four agents are dead, another wounded because of your incompetency."

"Now hold on a minute, Barly," Colin Tiege said. "You can't pin those things on him. It's obvious there's a leak somewhere—"

"In *your* department," Barly insisted.

"—we need to plug," Tiege continued, as if the man hadn't spoken. "The leak can be from anywhere. There are multiple agencies involved in this investigation. Your office is just as much suspect as ours."

The red in Barly's face deepened. "My office had no knowledge of where Miss Laine was being kept. Therefore, it's your own house you should be combing through, your own men you need to look into." He turned back to Ky, his meaning clear.

"But," Tiege said, from his seat behind his massive desk, "You were the one who insisted Calafano be kept in a hotel so you'd have easy access to him, and not in a safe house of our choosing. Everyone in your office knew where he was being held."

Before Barly could respond, Ky jumped in. He'd had enough of the infighting, backbiting, and accusations. He needed to get Gemma somewhere safe and this pissing contest wasn't speeding up the process.

"Look," he said, his gaze going from one man to the other. "There's a crack in security, but right now that's not my priority. I've got four of my best men dead and my partner out of commission and I still need to secure Miss Laine." He turned to face Barly. "I realize Calafano's hit has set you back, but you have his testimony on disc. That should count for something in court."

The man actually snarled at him. "Your lack of knowledge of the judicial system is pathetic. Ritandi's lawyers have the right to interrogate the witness, which they can't do if he's dead, so the taped testimony will most likely never be allowed."

"What does that do to the indictment, then?" Tiege asked.

"It'll get tossed since Calafano is our only direct link to Ritandi."

Tiege picked up a pen from his desk and tapped it between his fingers onto the desktop. "The license plate on the photographs of the getaway van connects the vehicle back to one of Ritandi's chop shops. That's a direct link. And a mistake his crew made."

"But it can't be tied to Ritandi *personally*," Barly said. "His defense can argue just because the van came from a business allegedly owned by him, it doesn't mean he was the one who ordered the hit. The appearance of involvement is not the same as having actual proof he called for Calafano's execution."

Barly turned to Ky. "You need to get me more."

Ky wasn't about to remind the man he'd just said he wanted him off the case. Even if he made a formal request, caused a big stink about his participation and got him thrown out as lead, Ky wasn't about to drop his investigation. He had the funerals of four of his best men to attend because of Ritandi. There was no way that was going to go unpunished.

"What are you going to do about Miss Laine?" Tiege asked him.

"I'm in the process of moving her to another location. Once I know she's secure," he turned and addressed Barly directly, "I'm going to find Ritandi."

"How?"

Ky shook his head. "Let me worry about that. You just be available when I bring the bastard in."

"Don't you dare order me around." Barly stood up to his full height and peered down his substantial nose at Ky. "I'm a federal attorney—"

"Assistant," Tiege said dryly.

Barly whirled on him. "You son of a bitch!"

"Calm down, Barly. Your face looks like a tomato. I don't need you to have a stroke in my office."

Without another word to either man, the ASA stormed from the room, banging the office door against its hinges.

Ky moved and closed the door.

"If I knew it was that easy to get rid of him," Tiege said with a chuckle, "I'd have insulted him sooner."

Ky came to stand in front of the desk. "Sir, I need to get Miss Laine secured."

Tiege nodded. "What do you need from me?"

Fifteen minutes later Ky walked back to the room he'd sequestered Gemma in when they'd arrived at the federal building. With a nod to the agent he'd assigned to make sure no one entered or exited the room, Ky opened the door and walked in.

The room was a windowless cubicle used for interrogations. A single desk and a few metal chairs surrounding it were the only furniture. Gemma sat, an irritated scowl gracing her face, in one of the chairs. She had her camera in front of her and looked as if she were flipping through the photos.

The moment Ky walked in she vaulted up from her seat. "Where have you been? What's going on?"

"I'm sorry you had to wait so long," he said. "I had to brief my boss on what's happened, plus I had a meeting with the State's attorney in charge of the case."

"Any news on Jon?"

"He's still in surgery. That's all I know."

"Oh." She glanced down at the camera she held.

"I've been making arrangements for you to be moved, as well."

"What do you mean moved? I thought we came here because you said it was safe. We're not staying?"

"No. I need to get you out of here and someplace where you can't be reached until I locate Ritandi."

"Wait"—she put up a hand—"what do you mean until *you* locate him? You're not staying with me?"

Was that regret in her voice? Or was she happy she'd finally be rid of him. Ky couldn't tell from her tone.

"With Jon out of commission, no one else on my team knows Ritandi as well as I do. I need to coordinate the search for him and I can't do that and keep watch over you. I'm sorry, but I promise, I'll make sure you're safe and secure. I've handpicked the agents being assigned to you."

She didn't respond at once, but a moment later her shoulders dropped. "So I still can't go home?"

"Not until the threat against you is eliminated. I'm sorry. I wish there was some other way."

She nodded.

"I need another few minutes to get everything coordinated and then we'll leave. Okay?"

When she just nodded again, Ky was struck by how exhausted she looked. And more: worried. She bit down on the corner of her bottom lip and sat back down in her chair, an air of resignation about her that pulled at him.

It killed him to leave her safety up to another agent, but at this point he didn't think he had any other choice. Ritandi had to be located. It was obvious the security of their investigative team had been compromised. Someone had been able to discover the safe house and get word to the mobster. Ky needed to focus all his attention on apprehending the man. The quicker he did, the quicker he knew Gemma's nightmare would be over.

* * *

"Stay close to me," Ky said as he walked her out of the elevator and into the underground garage. He had that familiar grip on her upper arm again—strong, hard, and secure —as he propelled her to a waiting vehicle. The giant black SUV was surrounded on all sides by armed men.

Ky removed his hand once he'd helped her into the SUV, and for some strange reason, she missed the contact. Two agents slid into the front passenger and driver's seats. Once the doors were closed and locked, Ky handed her the black backpack he'd been holding.

"I thought you'd like to have these back."

Gemma zipped open one of the pockets and found her laptop and her spare camera .

For the first time in hours she smiled. "Thank you," she told him. It was a kind gesture, one she appreciated more than she could put into words.

Ky nodded. "They were cleared at the scene, so there was no reason we had to keep them in storage. Just FYI," he said as they started out from the garage, "the computer techs checked the wireless capability on your computer and the internal tracking system. Both are still disabled. When this is all over, the systems can easily be reactivated. But at least you'll be able to work where you're going and I'll know no one can track your location."

"Thank you, again." She tucked the camera she'd brought with her next to the spare and re-zipped the pack.

They moved into the metropolitan DC midafternoon traffic. Not familiar with the area Gemma couldn't tell in what direction they were heading.

"Where are we going?" Gemma asked.

"Alexandria. I want you out of the city. My men have already arrived and they're getting the safe house set up for you."

"How many?"

He cocked his head, regarding her. "Eight."

Twice as many as last time. Somehow, the knowledge of the increased number didn't make her feel as secure as it should, knowing that Ky wouldn't be counted among them.

"They're all excellent agents," he told her.

She sighed. "I'm sure they are."

The groove between his eyes deepened. "I promise, you'll be safe with them."

She nodded and turned her head to look out the window again.

They rode in silence for a while.

"Approaching the outbound, Sir," the driver said after several minutes. "Traffic's moving well for this time of day."

The SUV moved into the on-ramp lane and sped up to merge.

Ky turned to her and said, "We should be there in about a half ho—"

A loud blast exploded from the back of the vehicle and Gemma was thrown against Ky when it swerved. Another boom came from the back passenger side.

"We're under fire!" the agent in the front passenger seat yelled.

"Get down!" Ky shoved Gemma's head into the space between the seats. He'd drawn his weapon and was frantically turning left and right. "Speed up, Cassidy."

The van pitched forward with such force Gemma fell forward, banging her head on the seatback in front of her.

"I don't have a clear shot," she heard the front agent call to Ky.

She watched in horror as Ky undid his safety belt and knelt up on the seat, facing backward. "Two, maybe three vehicles," he shouted. "Get in the left lane."

The driver zipped the SUV toward the left, causing Gemma to flail again. She reached out for the safety strap as an anchor to keep from being pitched around.

"Stay down!" Ky commanded again. He'd slid to her seat and opened the window enough to lean his weapon out. Three rapid pops blared as the sound ricocheted around her.

She heard two return shots pierce the back end of the van. Ky fired again in quick succession. The unmistakable sound of tires squealing filled the air next and then a loud crashing noise.

From her vantage point, Gemma couldn't see what happened to the chasing car, but a red fire ball reflected off the windshield a moment later.

"Kilburn?"

"One still on us, Sir." He leaned out the window and sent a barrage of bullets behind them.

Ky pulled back in and reloaded. "Get us out of here, Cassidy."

"Trying, Sir."

The SUV pitched forward. For several seconds Gemma felt the force of the vehicle increasing its speed and swerving left then right.

"Get off at the next exit," Ky told the driver, "but don't slow down until we're almost there. I don't want them to know until it's too late."

A series of bullets hit the side panel on the driver side, imploding the window. The van veered sharply to the right then corrected.

"Cassidy?"

"I'm okay, Sir," the driver said. Gemma thought he sounded anything but. "Exit's another mile."

Cassidy kept up the speed as ordered, as another shower of bullets came from behind them.

Gemma felt the car jolt to the right, several horns blasting at them, as Ky and other agent continued firing from the windows.

"Don't stop for anything," Ky ordered.

"Copy that, Sir," Cassidy said.

"He's gaining," Ky announced. He slid back over to the passenger side of the vehicle, glanced quickly down at her, and then opened the window, firing behind him.

Bullets rebounded at them, shattering the windows, glass raining down on the seats and floor. Ky had a bloody gash on his hand, another on his jaw.

The fire play continued.

"Cassidy?"

"Almost there, Sir."

The van continued to move at speeds Gemma knew were beyond dangerous. Car horns blared loudly as she felt the car swerve in and out of lanes.

The van careened to the right suddenly and from her position on the floor, Gemma was bounced and tossed again. From behind she heard the sickening squeal of brakes slamming, then metal crashing against metal.

Horns continued to blast, as Cassidy navigated through what she assumed was now street traffic. He'd lowered their speed and from the movement of the van right and left, she knew he was weaving in and around other cars.

A quick swerve with the tires screeching and Gemma was pitched into semi-darkness as the SUV slammed to a stop.

She counted to ten, the silence in the van overpowering after the cacophony of the fire play.

A whirr of sirens echoed in the distance.

"Are you hurt?" Ky asked her. He helped her from the floor, swiping glass off her shoulders and lap.

"I—I don't think so." She sat up, her entire body shaking. White and yellow pops of light flashed in front of her eyes. Her lips felt tingly as did her fingertips. Before she could draw another breath, Ky shoved her head down between her knees.

"Breathe," he told her, keeping his hand secured to the back of her neck. "Slow, now. Don't force it."

Kilburn's voice was muffled and very far away, but she heard him say, "Cassidy's hit, Sir. We need to get out of here."

Gemma tried to sit back up, but Ky's hand hadn't moved from her neck.

"I'm okay," she told him.

He eased back. "Don't come up fast. Take it easy. Take a breath or two." His gaze flicked to the back of the driver's head. "How bad?"

"Left shoulder, Sir," Cassidy said. "I think it's a through and through."

Gemma opened here eyes to find Ky's gaze narrowed on her. "We need to get out of here," he said. "Now."

"You're bleeding. You've got a cut on your jaw as well as your hand."

Ky looked at his hand then reached into his pocket, extracting a handkerchief. A quick swipe across it and the blood was gone. "It's just a scratch."

"Here, let me have it." She took the handkerchief from him and, angling his chin with her free hand, she pressed the cloth against the gash with shaking hands. Gently, she dabbed at the jagged line, willing her hands to stop trembling.

"Probably from flying glass," she said, inspecting it. "I don't see anything in the wound, though, which is good."

"Okay, leave it." Ky yanked away from her hold. "We need to get out here."

He said something under his breath to Kilburn while he helped her from the car. Once out from behind the seat, she got her first view of the van's exterior.

A ball of bile swelled up from deep within her. She shot her hand over her mouth and turned away. The black SUV was peppered and pierced with bullet holes, the smell of heated metal harsh, filling the air with a rank, coppery odor.

"Let's go." Ky pulled her upper arm again. This time his grip was tighter. "Stay next to me, do you understand? Don't let go of me no matter what."

She nodded and tossed the backpack over her shoulders. She hadn't let go of it the entire time they were under attack.

"They're not coming with us?" she pointed her chin at his men.

"No," was all he'd tell her.

She finally let herself look around. They were in an alley, the van stopped between two buildings and secreted behind a large industrial garbage container. The acrid smell of urine and rotting food was overpowering, but Gemma didn't have a chance to notice anything else because Ky was moving so quickly she needed to concentrate on keeping up with his pace.

He was taking them in the opposite direction they'd come from, keeping them close to one building, his gun drawn in his right hand but pointed down, the other holding her arm. The sounds of traffic and voices from the street in front of them grew louder.

"We need to get as far away from this area as possible," he said.

When they reached the street, Ky shoved his gun into his pocket. She wanted to ask him why he didn't put it back in his shoulder holster, but she realized it was because it wouldn't be concealed if he did, but out in the open where anyone could see it. They walked for what seemed like miles, weaving in and out of the sidewalk traffic, keeping close to doorways.

Finally, Ky stopped and glanced up. "In here," he told her.

He hadn't removed his hand from her arm the entire time they were moving, so when he let go of it to pull out his cell phone, Gemma felt an unusual emptiness engulf her.

They were standing in a darkened entranceway, a worn and battered staircase just beyond them, behind a locked glass door.

"Where are we?" she asked.

Ky put up his index finger, a signal for her to wait.

"Yeah," he said into the phone. "Downstairs."

A buzzer pierced the air and he pushed open the door.

"Up."

She repeated her question.

"At a friend's."

From the top of the stairs a door opened and the dark hallway was bathed in shards of sunlight. A massive silhouette stepped in front of the light, blocking it.

The skin on the back of Gemma's bare arms chilled. Instinctively, she moved back a step and rammed into Ky. The feel on his hand winding around her waist calmed her immediately. She told herself she'd think about exactly why that was, later. For now, just knowing he literally had her back eased her fear.

The giant said something to Ky in a language she didn't recognize. She felt his own voice reverberate along the length of her spine when he responded in kind and she realized they were speaking Greek.

The giant stepped back, swiped a hand through the open door and said, "Please come in, Miss Laine. I assure you I don't bite."

She stumbled into the room when he added, "Unless I'm asked to, of course."

* * *

Gemma looked around the room and tried not to gasp. There wasn't an inch she could see that wasn't covered with some sort of computer device. Dozens of colored electrical wires dropped from the ceiling, cascading down the center and sides of the room, attached to at least ten computer hard drives that were visible. She counted an equal number of differing sized monitors all in a row, set across two massive tables, each one of them on and processing data across their screens. Two forty-inch flat-screen televisions took up one complete wall. They, too, were turned on, both tuned to opposing financial market stations.

A dull, persistent, mechanical hum permeated in the air.

The windows were covered with clear plastic from pane to pane with what looked like aluminum foil surrounding the borders.

Once the door closed behind them, the giant grabbed Ky into what Gemma truly could call a bear hug, and slapped him on the back several times.

"It's been too long, brother," the man said.

"Truth." Ky turned his attention to her. "This is one of my oldest friends, Theo Kanikaredes. Theo, Gemma Laine."

She took her first clear look at him. He really did look like a bear; a *teddy* bear. Yards of unruly, curly black hair covered his head, and an equally messy beard, his face. He was at least half a head taller than Ky and twice as wide, with shoulders as broad as the back of a truck. A faded, elbow-bare MIT sweatshirt covered his torso, the same logo gracing the side of his baggy sweatpants.

Eyes the color of fresh coffee beans crinkled at the corners when his face broke into an open smile.

"Theo and I went from kindergarten to high school, and all through Greek school, together."

"*Xaipete*. Welcome," Theo said, slapping Ky on the back again. "But I don't think you're here to talk about old times, *eh?*"

"We need your help." Ky quickly filled him in on the reason they'd appeared at his door.

Theo's gaze shifted several times from his friend's face to Gemma's and then back again.

"First things first." Theo moved to one of several desks in the room, opened a drawer and pulled out a bottle and two shot glasses.

"Theo, I can't," Ky said, watching his friend pour. "I'm on duty."

The giant said something in Greek that Gemma knew was an oath. She'd heard Ky grunt the same thing when they'd been in the hotel room. He downed a shot glass full of the liquid, re-poured, and downed another.

With a full body shake, he put the bottle and glass back into the drawer.

"Now," he addressed Ky. "Tell me what you need."

While the two men talked, Gemma sat on the only cushioned chair in the room. The computer monitors scrolled continuously around her, scores of numbered columns flashing against the blackened screens in a continual motion. It looked like a scene out of movie about an underground cyber world.

She scrubbed her hands down her face. Her nerves felt like flayed and exposed electrical wires. There was a fine tremble in her hands that wouldn't completely quell. She'd never been so scared in her life as when they'd been fired upon. That she might die in the van, never seeing her family again, never taking another picture, ran through her mind in a continual loop while they were under attack.

Anger pushed through the raw, stark fear, the churning bile. The urge to scream at the top of her voice, to hit something hard, to fight against this seemingly endless nightmare, was powerful. She was supposed to be safe now; he'd promised her she would be. No one knew where they were heading, but yet again, they'd been found and ambushed.

It was obvious he couldn't keep her safe, no matter how hard he tried. And Gemma did believe he had done everything he could. Even through her anger she recognized that. He'd never let go of her hand during their entire trek, never once. He was her protector, her defender, her guard, and he hadn't shirked his duty for one moment since she'd been placed in his care.

Despite all his efforts, though, she was still in danger.

Leaning back into the cushion, she allowed her eyes to close and tried to calm her mind while the men spoke in Greek.

An idea wormed its way through her exhaustion.

A gentle hand on her shoulder pulled her back to the land of the living. She startled instantly awake. "Wha—"

"You're okay." Ky squeezed her shoulder.

Gemma bolted upright in the cushioned chair to find him and his friend staring down at her.

"I fell asleep?"

"Only for a few minutes, I think," Theo said. "And totally understandable."

"We need to get moving," Ky told her. "I need to get you out of here, out of the city."

"Where?"

"That's what we've been trying to figure out," Theo said. "It seems as if no place is out of this wacko's reach so far."

Ky shot him a speaking glace, then looked back at Gemma.

Before he could say a word, she swallowed and said, "I have an idea."

Chapter Eight

Ky swerved around the narrow bend in the road, barely missed grazing a low-slung tree branch, and bit back the curse dancing on his lips. Next to him, Gemma consulted a map using a flashlight.

How Ky got talked into this crazy scheme, he couldn't begin to understand. But here he was, in the dead of night, driving a beat-up, ready-for-the-crusher two-door sedan that should have been junked ten years ago, up a mountain thoroughfare that barely qualified as a road and not a rut.

"It looks like we make the next right turn," Gemma said, pulling the map closer to her eyes. "Another quarter mile or so. There's a marking on the right side of the trail that'll read: Gossamer Way."

A thoroughly stupid name for a road in the middle of nowhere. "How far is the cabin from the turnoff?"

"About a mile," she said. "Give or take."

Ky shook his head. So far, as a human GPS, Gemma was doing a fair job—they hadn't gotten lost yet, but he would have preferred an actual navigational system. They couldn't take a chance on using anything that could be electronically tracked, though.

"The text says it's the only place for ten miles in any direction, so we should be safe enough for the moment."

For the moment was the operative phrase, he told himself.

After speaking with Theo for over an hour and still having no idea what he was going to do, Gemma had the idea to contact her brother-in-law and ask for help, since, as she put it, "he was the best at what he did and would know what to do." Ky's pride had been wounded, the not-so-veiled implication being that *he* didn't. At first he'd nixed the idea, but Gemma had argued her case astutely, telling him that Josh was used to subterfuge and even if Ritandi's men had him and his business under surveillance because of his connection to her, Josh was an expert and knew how to help them without being seen to do so. The pride and love she felt for the man rang through her voice, once again shooting his ego down.

Gemma trusted her brother-in-law implicitly with her life; that was a fact. It was obvious she didn't afford him the same assurance.

Ky had given in to her request and so far her confidence in Keane had proven sound.

Through an untraceable cell Theo had provided, Ky had contacted Keane on what Gemma called his bat phone—a cell no one but those closest to Josh had access to—and had been able to relay what had occurred during the past day.

Several back-and-forth calls later from various phones, and Keane had arranged for them to pick up the barely alive car they were currently in from a *friend* who, Josh told them, owed him a favor. Under the front seat they'd found an envelope with more than three thousand dollars in small bills with a note that read "For gas and sundries," and two bags of groceries in the trunk.

When Ky met up with the private investigator again, he was determined to find out what the favor had been.

They were on their way to a cabin in northern Pennsylvania that belonged to Josh's partner, Rick Bannerman. Josh had texted them the access codes to the cabin's security system, telling them not to worry, the name on the deed wasn't Rick's and couldn't be connected back to him.

That was the single reason Ky had consented to driving them out of state. No matter how deep the moles who worked for Ritandi dug, they shouldn't be able to locate the two of them. Theo had provided several disposable burner phones, in addition to a laptop he guaranteed Ky was "invisible." To Gemma, Theo explained it meant no one would be able to zero in on their location when they used it.

If this panned out and he was able to keep Gemma safe, and get back on track with trying to locate Ritandi, Ky knew he owed Gemma's brother-in-law big time.

"There's the marker." Gemma pointed through the windshield.

He turned the car down an unlit, unpaved road, riddled with potholes and channels. He was forced to keep their speed down to a little above a crawl just to ensure the chassis wouldn't fall off before they reached their destination.

"At least we'll know if anyone approaches the cabin."

"What do you mean?" she asked.

"They'll need ATVs or loud heavy machinery to get safely down this poor excuse for a road."

When she didn't reply, he took his gaze from the dead-of-dark view in front of them and snuck a glance at her. He wasn't sure, but he thought the ghost of a grin pulled at her mouth.

She had to be beyond exhausted. He knew he was. The punch of adrenaline had run through both of them once they'd made it safely from Theo's apartment to the arranged pick-up place for the car. They hadn't stopped to eat, wanting to put as much distance between themselves and any more of Ritandi's men as they could, opting to share a bag of potato chips and a liter of water they bought at a rest stop along the highway when they'd gassed up.

Tomorrow, he promised himself, he'd make her the French toast she'd missed—God, was it only this morning? It felt like days since they'd fled the safe house.

"I can see it up ahead," he told her. The bright headlights cut through the inky darkness to outline a small, rectangular structure.

He pulled the car right up to the front of the cabin and stopped. When he didn't shut the engine, Gemma turned to him. "What's wrong?"

"Nothing. I just want to get a look at it before we go in."

Gemma glanced out the front windshield and then turned to the passenger side window. "I can't see a thing in all this dark, *but* dark." She opened the door and slid her legs out.

Ky was in the process of reaching around to the back seat where she'd tossed the flashlight before he could stop her from exiting the car. A sudden, brilliant burst of light exploded from the front porch.

"Motion detector lights. Rick thinks of everything." Gemma jogged up the porch steps, punched in the alarm code they'd been left and opened the door.

Damn it. Did the woman not realize even after all that had happened, she was still in danger?

"Wait!" he called, bolting from the car, but she'd already gone into the cabin.

Ky sprinted up the porch steps after her, his gun poised.

"It's bigger than it looks like from the outside," he heard her say. "Why do you have your gun out?" she asked, her brows pulled up under her bangs when she turned toward him.

"Because you can't just sprint ahead of me into a place I haven't made sure is secure." He cursed and moved right up into her face, unable to leash his anger. "You have no idea if anyone is in here and you barge into the house without any regard for your safety or the consequences. That's just stupid and careless."

He realized he was yelling when her back went ramrod straight and her eyes darkened. "Don't you dare call me stupid—"

He cut her off with a swipe of his hand. "Then don't act without thinking. Running into a building without checking it out first *is* a stupid move. We've already been ambushed twice today. I'm not in the mood to be blindsided again."

If looks could kill, he'd be six feet under just from the deadly heat in her squinting gaze. In the next instant, her eyes went wide and the lips scowling at him turned pale.

He'd forced her to remember the details of their day. A small amount of guilt at bringing the fear back to her shot through him, but with it, resolve, because he was right to call her on her reckless behavior.

"Look." He pulled down deep for calm. "I know you thought this place was fine because it's your friend's house. I get that. But you need to let me do my job, which is keeping you safe. You had no idea if this place was empty, you just presumed it was because you were told it would be. I can't think that way. I have to assume and prepare for every potential threat, and running into an empty house without first making sure it is, in fact unoccupied, is one of those potential threats."

She swallowed, the movement of her long throat making the motion almost erotic.

"Do you understand?"

"Y-yes. I'm, I'm sorry. I didn't think. I…I'm just…sorry."

He gentled his voice even more, hating the fear now glazing over her face. "I understand this is all confusing and unfamiliar to you, and if there were any way I could turn back time to before you ever saw Calafano walking down that street, believe me, I would. But I can't. You're in danger and I need to ensure that nothing happens to you. I can't do that if you don't listen to me and let me lead you through all this. Okay?"

She nodded. "I'm sorry I didn't wait. I never even thought to."

It was Ky's turn to nod. "And I'm sorry I yelled at you."

He knew what the apology cost her, so he felt giving his own would even things between them. He was happy to see some of her color returning. "Let me take a quick look around and then we can bring in our gear. Okay?"

It was Gemma's turn to nod.

"Just stay here." The front door opened into a wide, wall-to-wall living area. Ky's eyes swept the room. A stone fireplace took up space to the left, an L-shaped sofa and chairs in front of it. A remodeled kitchen and breakfast bar was at the opposite side of the room, three closed doors along a hallway beside it, and an open staircase leading to a second floor. While Gemma stood in the center of the room, Ky took a quick tour of the upstairs.

"From the outside this place looks like just one story," he said when he came back to her.

When he was satisfied the house was truly empty except for the two of them, they brought in everything from the car without a word. He hoped Gemma's silence meant she was considering what he'd told her and accepting how serious the situation was for them.

They were in a secluded cabin in the middle of nowhere with no Agency backup, no one except her brother-in-law and his partner knew where they were, and he had no weapons except for his Glock to protect them.

He'd never felt so powerless and unprepared in his life.

Gemma placed the bags of food on the kitchen counter and then opened the closed doors off the hallway.

"Small bathroom, pantry," he said, following behind as she peeked inside each, "and bedroom."

She opened the door fully and stepped inside. "Lucy and Ricky beds."

"What?"

He came into the room with her.

Two dressers, two twin-size beds, and a small closet were the only furnishings. The beds were made; colorful Americana quilts atop them.

She turned around to him, a look of confusion sliding across her face. "Lucy and Ricky?" she said. When he didn't answer, she added, "The Ricardos? The television show? No?"

Ky dropped his hands in his pockets. "Sorry. We didn't watch a lot of TV in my house."

"But you have to know about *I Love Lucy.*" Her eyes actually widened. "The whole planet knows who she is."

Ky shook his head and again said, "Sorry."

Her mouth closed into a thin line of what he assumed was disgust.

"Who doesn't know Lucy Ricardo?" she muttered, as she shook her head, went past him, and out of the room.

He knew he'd gone down another notch in her esteem. Ky pressed the bridge of his nose between his thumb and index finger, squeezed once, and then followed her from the room.

"The two bedrooms up here have a connecting bathroom," she called from above him. When he looked up she was leaning against the stair rail.

"Do they have, what did you call them? Ricardo beds, too?"

For the first time in hours, she smiled. It was as if the sun had decided to come out in the dead of night. She came down the stairs, her smile still in place. "Lucy and Ricky beds, and no. These are kings, not twins."

Ky nodded, pushing the thought from his mind of what she would look like spread across a king-sized bed, naked and waiting for him.

"Okay." He prayed his voice didn't betray his thoughts. Thoughts he had no call letting slip into his conscious mind. "It's late. Why don't you get to bed? I'm sure you're tired."

"That doesn't even begin to describe it."

He could read the fatigue in the small purple smudges under her eyes. They'd both been awake for over eighteen hours.

"I'll bunk down here and we can unpack everything and get the lay of the land in the morning."

"You're gonna stay down here?"

"Yeah."

She cocked her head at him. "I don't mind if you want to be upstairs. The beds are bigger. They might be more comfortable than the twins."

"True, but from a defensive viewpoint, staying down here makes more sense."

For a moment he thought she might argue with him. There was a question in her eyes he couldn't fathom.

Instead, she grabbed one of the overnight bags Josh's friend had put together for them, since they'd fled the safe house with nothing, and with a shrug, said, "'K."

"I'll make sure everything is locked up and secure," he said to her retreating back.

"No surprise there," she muttered as she went up the stairs.

* * *

She'd tried to ignore the rumbling and churning noises coming from her empty stomach for the past hour, hoping they would quiet and let her get back to sleep, but they'd hung on like a feasting leech. In fact, she was hungrier now than she thought she'd ever been before. The chips she and Ky had shoveled in during the drive had quieted her hunger for a while, but now, like a caged beast roaring for escape, it blasted through the silence in the room, demanding relief. Other than those chips, she'd had nothing to eat all day, since she'd been robbed of her breakfast by the gunmen.

Good Lord! How much had happened in a single day. Never in her wildest imaginings would she have thought she'd be stuck on a mountain in the middle of nowhere, miles from civilization, rooming with an armed man sworn to protect her.

The bedside digital clock told her it was three a.m. Too early for breakfast, but she'd never get back to sleep if she didn't do something to squash the hunger blasting through her.

Gemma slipped from under the covers, thankful she'd donned socks before climbing into bed because she knew the wooden floor would be cold at this time of night. The cabin was deep into the woods, more than half way up a mountainside, and even though it was summer, the night air chilled without the sun's heat. Wearing only a thin T-shirt and boy-shorts she'd found in the suitcase, Gemma wrapped her arms around herself and went on a mission for something to ease her demanding stomach.

Thankfully, the floors didn't creak as she crept from the room, out to the landing, and down the stairs.

The light under the kitchen range was on so she was able to navigate around the living room and into the kitchen without knocking into any of the furniture.

She hadn't unpacked the nonperishables before she'd gone to bed, knowing nothing needed refrigeration, but the counter was free now of the bags they'd brought in from the car.

Ky must have put them away before heading to bed.

Gemma said a silent curse because now she had to hunt through the cabinets as quietly as she could so she wouldn't wake him. His bedroom door was cracked halfway open and any noise might disturb her sleeping special agent. Something she most definitely did not want to do.

With care she opened one cabinet, found it empty and moved on to the next. At the third she found success. She grabbed the first thing she could reach—a box of crackers. That would get her to breakfast, for sure. She opened the refrigerator, hoping he'd put the case of bottled water they'd brought in it to chill. The fridge looked as new as the rest of the appliances, and when she pulled the door handle to open it, a loud sucking noise barked into the air.

Gemma turned to stone, the door handle glued to her hand. She listened for a few moments, heard nothing but silence come back to her, then peeked into the fridge.

The water bottles were aligned in perfect precision on the top shelf, the rest of the unit empty.

She bent in and just as her hand clasped around a bottle, the silence was split by a loud, *"Freeze!"*

Gemma gasped, dropped the crackers and the full water bottle, which landed with a thud on her instep, and jumped back, banging her hip against the sink's ledge.

"Christ on the cross!" She grabbed her foot, tears springing into her eyes as she leaned back for support, and glared across the kitchen at Ky. "Give a girl a heart attack, why don't you?"

Poised in a shooting stance, his Glock pointed straight at her head, all sentient thought flew from her mind the moment her gaze cleared and connected with him. Clad in black boxers—and nothing else—he simply took her breath away.

Who knew that under the stiff, polite, and contained exterior was the body of a true Greek God? There was no other description for him.

A chest as finely chiseled and sculpted as any carved statue she'd ever seen, every muscle was covered with perfect, smooth, and sun-kissed golden skin. His nipples were two darkened discs perfectly aligned in the center of a pair of pumped and defined pecs. He gave a whole new definition to the term "eight pack" as each groove and trench of his abdominal muscles was pulled tight where he stood, his waist slim and sleek. Thick, powerful thighs jutted down from the snug-fitting boxers into calves that were both muscular and lithe.

There wasn't a visible inch or ounce of extra flesh on his entire body. Every bit of skin she could see—and it was a lot!—was simply perfect. A thin gold chain hung around his neck, a small pendant dangling from it.

He exuded strength and raw power from every pore, and in that moment, Gemma forgot about her injured foot. She felt her insides quiver while she grew, unexpectedly, wet with desire for this man.

"What are you doing? It's the middle of the night." He lowered his gun to his side and came toward her.

The harsh tone in his voice had the hairs at her neck springing to attention, despite the growing moisture between her thighs just watching him walk produced.

Dear Lord, the man really did move like a panther; sleek and silent, determined and focused.

"Getting something to eat," she snapped. "I'm starving. And I know what time it is, which is why I was trying to be quiet so I wouldn't wake you."

Ky bent and retrieved the water and cracker box from where she'd dropped them. Her eyes raked over the corded muscles in his back—his broad, hunky, naked back. The sinewy ripple of his shoulders and arms as he placed the items on the counter next to her had her biting down on her bottom lip so the moan breaking within her would be silenced.

He stood right in front of her; so close, in fact, she could reach out and run her tongue along his poured-from-concrete jawline. Gemma blinked hard when the notion hit her to do just that.

Ky reached out and touched her foot. She was still holding it up, one hand around the ankle, the other kneading the spot where the bottle had thudded. He rubbed his fingers over hers. "I'm sorry I scared you. I heard a noise. Thought you were an intruder."

"You must have hearing like a bat."

A tiny grin pulled at one corner of his mouth. "I'm a light sleeper. Consequence of the job."

He hadn't stopped rubbing her foot and the rhythm from his soft touch was hypnotic.

And wickedly arousing.

"Does it hurt?"

She shook her head. "Not so much anymore."

Ky removed his hand and took a step back. He glanced over at the cracker box and asked, "Want something more substantial than just those?"

Gemma cocked her head. "Like you just told me, it's the middle of the night. I wasn't planning on anything more substantial. Just something to tide me over until breakfast."

"Yeah, but you're hungry, so it really doesn't matter what time it is. Neither one of us ate anything of significance yesterday. Want me to fix something?" He set the safety on the gun, placed it down on the counter, then turned on the overhead light from the wall switch. The sudden harsh light had her squinting.

He opened the pantry door. "We've got some essentials. There's bread, a jar of peanut butter and some jam. Looks homemade. Want a sandwich?"

"Homemade? Let me see."

He handed her the jar and her stomach growled when she recognized the label.

Ky's low laugh was fast and sounded, God help her, panty-dropping sexy. "You really are hungry."

"I wouldn't be sneaking around at this hour if I wasn't."

Ky reached into a cabinet and pulled down two plates. The light from the overhead fixture silhouetted his body, shadowing all the contours and outlines of his muscle groups.

Gemma swallowed and moved her gaze back to the jar. "This is Kandy's jam, from Grandma's old canning recipe. She makes it every year and gives it out as presents to family and friends."

"So, I'm assuming that's a yes for the sandwich." He found the utensils drawer and grabbed a knife.

Gemma blinked, watching him.

How surreal was this? Standing in a strange kitchen in the middle of the night with a man clad in nothing but silk boxers, looking like a visiting God from Olympus, discussing a sandwich?

Gemma shook her head, wondering when she'd wake up from this dream. When she caught a glance at the way the muscles in Ky's arm undulated as he spread the strawberry jam on the bread, she hoped she'd get to sleep a little longer.

"Can you grab me a water?" he asked as he picked up their plates and walked over to the breakfast bar.

Seated across from him a moment later, Gemma stared at the chain dropping down almost to his pecs. "What's the pendant?" she asked, curiosity getting the better of her.

"St. Michael the Archangel. Patron saint of law enforcement officers. My baby sister, Ariadne, gave it to me for my birthday a few years ago."

"The Diet Mountain Dew girl?"

He nodded.

"I don't know why, but I didn't think you were Catholic." She dug into her sandwich and tried not to devour it in one breath.

"I'm not. My whole family is Greek Orthodox, but Dini's the most superstitious of us all so when saw the pendant online she thought it might help keep me safe."

"Dini?"

The corner of his mouth lifted again and his eyes softened. "Family nickname."

"Like Papps?"

His left eyebrow quirked. He took a bite of his sandwich and Gemma had an uncontrollable urge to press her thighs together when his neck bobbled as he swallowed.

"My family doesn't call me that, only my coworkers do. Pappandreos is a mouthful for some people." When he nailed her with a look that was equal parts mocking and hot, Gemma squirmed, remembering how difficult she'd found his name at first.

"She doesn't like that you're an FBI agent?"

"More that she worries. A lot. All the women in my family are worriers." He shook his head, his lips tugging into a half-grin. "She thinks if I wear the medal I'll be protected because it has a built in tracking device. I didn't tell her I've never turned it on, but,"—he lifted a shoulder—"if it helps calm her worries, it's no big deal to wear it."

"That's actually pretty sweet."

"Dini's a sweet girl."

She wanted to tell him she meant he was being sweet, not his sister, but before she could, he cut her off.

"I did a larger scale sweep before turning in," he told her. "Your friend Bannerman's got a top-notch security system in the back of the pantry. Took me a few minutes to figure it out."

"Rick's the most tech savvy guy I've ever met. Even Josh is surprised by some of the stuff he brings to the table. And Josh is no techy-slouch in his own right."

"It not only looks like the house is alarmed, but I think the surrounding property is as well. I'll get a better, more in depth look at it in the morning, but we should be okay here for a few days at least. In the morning I'll also try and make contact with my superior."

"Find out how Jon's doing, if you do. If he's okay."

Ky stared at her for a moment. She was a little aggravated she couldn't read the expression in his eyes.

"As soon as I know anything, I'll tell you."

It was amazing how swiftly he could go from being and sounding calm and nice, back to stern and hard.

"Your sister cans this jam?" he asked, changing the subject, and then took a pull from his water bottle.

Gemma nodded, confused at the topic switch. "Every year since she was nineteen and inherited grandma's recipes."

"I think this is the best strawberry jam I've ever had."

Gemma chuckled. "No lie. And you're not the only one. In the beginning she only gave it out to family. Once word spread, she increased it to friends and then friends of friends when they begged for it. Everyone keeps telling her she should market it commercially, but she won't."

"Why not?"

She shrugged. "Kandy's very faithful to our grandmother's memory. Some recipes she just doesn't want the whole world to have access to. Keeping them private makes it seem like Grandma's still with us, cooking only for us and no one else."

She polished off her sandwich, silently wished she had another and then licked the jam that had seeped out from the bread and onto her fingers.

Ky's swift inhale had her gaze whipping across the table. Nothing had changed in his outward demeanor. He sat, leaning back in his chair, his body relaxed, yet she felt he was anything but. It was his eyes. The green and blue flecks swirling in them had melded into one solid ball of deep and vibrant seafoam, mirroring the color at the bottom of the ocean. They were trained, unblinking, on her mouth. So intense was his stare, Gemma stopped, one of her fingers frozen in place between her lips.

The overwhelming sensation of being trapped and unable to move shot through her.

He lifted his gaze to her eyes and her heart quite simply stopped.

A well of sexual heat so deep it seemed bottomless, stared back at her. Want, desire, lust and—*God save her*—need, poured from him.

In the next instant he blinked, that blank wall of ice she was getting used to seeing, back in place as if she'd only imagined the scorching heat of a moment before.

But she hadn't.

That longing had been as real and as potent as the dangerous situation she currently found herself surrounded by. Where she was terrified of one, the other, she was surprised to admit, she'd welcome. If he so much as leaned in toward her, gave her any indication the hunger she'd seen in his eyes was real and needed to be slaked, Gemma would have crawled onto his lap and cleaved herself to his body without another word.

But she knew in the light of the morning she'd be filled with regrets.

Kyros Pappandreos, all six foot plus and dangerously handsome, was the type of man Gemma was drawn to because of his looks, but the kind of guy she'd made a lifetime habit of avoiding. He was a man she knew instinctively would claim her body and demand her heart and there was no way Gemma was going to ever give her heart away. She would never put herself in a position of actually caring enough for any man that her heart would get involved.

Ky struck her as the type of man who'd want a woman to be all in: mind, body, heart, and soul. Total intimacy, shared thoughts and feelings, a true couple in every sense of the word. He didn't strike her as player, like his partner Jon did, and she knew down to her toes he wasn't. A woman who found herself involved with him would have to be willing to forego part of herself for the sake of true intimacy.

Gemma had dated a fair share of men since she'd grown out of the naiveté of her teens but had never been truly emotionally vested in any of them. Sex was one thing. Affection was quite another.

It dawned on her as Ky's gaze zeroed in on her mouth that, sitting across the table from him in the dead of night, barely clothed, and eating a simple sandwich while they talked was the most *intimate* thing she'd ever done with a man that didn't involve sex.

Her initial impression of him as an arrogant and self-important jerk had subtly begun to shift over the course of the days they were forced to be together. Yes, he was single-minded and stiffly superior at times, but the realization he presented that face to the world in order to meet the demands of his job was starting to change her opinion of who he really was. A man who, if she let him in, had the ability to destroy her.

Gemma pushed back from the table and lifted her plate. She needed to stop thinking about him as if he were a potential bed-mate. He wasn't. He was her protector and nothing more. Lusting over his body would get her nowhere, fast.

"I'm making another one?" she asked. "You want?"

He nodded and took a sip from his bottle.

While she fixed the sandwiches, she gave into more of her curiosity. "Tell me about Theo."

"What do you want to know?"

She set his plate before him and shrugged. "He's been your friend forever?"

"Since we were little kids. His family lived next door to mine. His parents still do."

"He seems a little...eccentric."

Ky nodded. "As good a word as any, I guess." He took a bite of his sandwich, chewed, then swallowed.

Across from him Gemma pressed her thighs together and squirmed in her seat as she watched his throat work. The overwhelming desire to stretch across the table and lick his neck barreled through her again like a speeding bullet.

"Theo's a genius," Ky said. "A real one. His IQ's been tested as off the charts. He went to MIT at fifteen, had three doctorates—math, physics, and computer science—before he hit twenty-five."

Gemma's eyes widened and her mouth fell open. "Wow."

"I know. Genius doesn't even really do him justice. His mind works like a computer."

"He must have been fun at sleepovers."

Ky's lips quirked before he took a draught from his water bottle.

"So smart, yet he seemed a little, I don't know, *lost*?"

Ky held the bottle suspended in his hand while he gaped at her.

"What?" she asked.

"Why do you think he's...lost?"

She shrugged.

"He was wearing clothes that were clean about six days ago, his hair's a few months from a pair of scissors and he looked a little like a kid whose puppy died."

Ky lowered the bottle to the table with such exquisite precision and controlled timing, Gemma worried she'd said something wrong.

"I imagine being such an astute observer is what makes you such a fabulous photographer," he said after a moment.

She was too stunned to respond.

"You're not too far off the mark. Theo lost...someone. Someone very special to him. Violently. He's never recovered from it."

Gemma stayed silent.

"He's pretty much a recluse now," Ky continued. "Rarely leaves his place. Won't see people."

"He welcomed you in pretty fast."

Ky lifted a shoulder. "I've known him for most of his life. We're like brothers. I'm one of a very small number of people he trusts."

And she knew how important trust was to Ky.

"What's up with all the computers?"

With a sigh, he picked up the last bit of his sandwich. "He's trying to locate something. He's devoted his life to finding it, in fact."

"I'm no expert by any sense of the word, but it looked like he had financial stuff on those monitors. Like you see scrolling along at the stock exchange."

"Some of it probably was."

"What he's looking for involves stocks?"

Ky shook his head and then said, "Not the stocks themselves, but the person buying them."

"That tells me something and absolutely nothing."

Gemma realized what a good friend Ky truly was, by his silence.

With a deep breath, he sat back in his chair, his hands crossed over his chest.

His naked chest.

Her thighs vibrated again.

Bad thighs.

"Theo met a woman a few years ago when he'd been asked to speak at an international banking conference in London. She was a financial analyst, also speaking at the conference. They...hit it off right away." A small, sad smile tugged at the corners of his mouth. "She was everything Theo ever dreamed of in a woman, including the fact she was first-generation Greek, something his parents were thrilled about. He proposed within a month of meeting her."

"Yowza. That's fast, but not unheard of. Josh asked Kandy to marry him a week after they met."

"*That's* fast. But we all knew Theo and Calista were made for one another."

"I don't get the impression this ends well."

He nailed her with a gaze that was at once sad and angry. "It didn't. Calista was killed. Murdered."

"What? By who?"

"That's what Theo's been searching for: a name. Calista discovered a huge insider trading scheme within the European and American stock markets. She'd been doing research on certain branches of stock holdings and saw some kind of connection or imbalance, or something. I don't know the whole story. She told Theo about it and he encouraged her to go public. Before she could, she was gunned down."

"Oh, good Lord. And she didn't tell Theo the names of the people involved?"

"No. She died before she could. He's been searching for the people responsible ever since, because he believes her death is connected to what she'd discovered."

"Do you?"

"Yes. He's promised when he finds the link he'll let me know. I've vowed to help him bring those responsible to justice. Justice for Calista. And closure for Theo."

"When? Not if?"

"There is no *if* with Theo. If it takes him until the day he dies, he'll find out who did this."

Gemma stared across the table at him for a moment. "I think you're a very good friend and he's very lucky to call you one."

When he didn't say anything else, Gemma realized something else about Special Agent Pappandreos: he was a man who kept his word.

"Okay, well," she said, rising. "It's getting later by the second. Thanks for making me the sandwich and not shooting me." She rinsed the dishes in the sink.

"There was never any danger of that happening."

She jumped when he came up next to her.

Jesus, the guy moved fast. She hadn't even heard him rise from his chair.

"Well, okay, but you weren't the one with a gun pointed at your face. I could have been shot just because I was hungry. I'd like to see you explain that to my family."

Ky rinsed his own dish, turned sideways to her, laid one hand down on the counter edge, the other on his waist and leveled a serious glare at her.

"What?"

With a shake of his head, his lips pulled into that subtle grin that was beginning to drive her crazy—with need. "I'm too tired to tell if you're being serious or joking around, but either way, you're welcome."

"Thanks," was all her mind gave her to say.

"Think you'll be able to get back to sleep now?"

"Yes. I'm not hungry," her gaze flicked to his mouth, "anymore. The sandwiches helped."

He nodded. "Good."

"Well, then." She backed away from the sink and hugged her arms across her chest. "'Night."

"Good night."

She felt his eyes on her until she turned the corner and headed up the stairs. She wanted to look down from the landing to see if he'd moved to watch her, but chickened out at the last second.

Snuggled back under the covers, her rumbling stomach at last calmed, Gemma took a deep breath and closed her eyes, determined not to drift off to the image of a pair of eyes the color of a calm ocean, and a man whose name conjured up thoughts of Greek Islands and warm, white sandy beaches.

Chapter Nine

Ky lay in the comfortable single bed, thinking, for close to an hour after he'd bid Gemma good night. His thoughts ran the gamut from safety and security to desire and need.

When he'd heard movement in the kitchen, he'd assumed it was her, but he couldn't let his guard down even so. When she'd backed away from the refrigerator door, a quick, powerful and overwhelming bullet of lust shot right through him, ricocheting from his head to his toes. The fridge light silhouetted her body, framing it and giving him a pretty clear view of what lay underneath her miniscule T-shirt and shorts. He got hard in an instant, unable to prevent his body from reacting to the gorgeous, nearly naked, woman before him.

Yards of slim, smooth, and bare leg had his imagination shooting straight to what those legs would feel like wrapped around his waist. The shirt came to just above the shorts' waistband, affording him a glimpse at a very toned and flat abdomen. She was braless, a fact that was illustrated in full detail when his gaze zeroed in on her pointed nipples.

It took every ounce of willpower and thought he could muster to tamp his reaction down to prevent her from seeing what she did to him. He'd been able to suppress his raging desire until she'd unconsciously sent it roaring again when she licked her fingers where some jam had trailed. The sight of those perfect bow lips and that pink, wet tongue sucking at her fingers threw him into a tailspin of need. When she'd gotten up to take her dish to the sink, he'd started reciting the Pythagorean theorem in his mind in a feeble attempt to get his body under control before she realized what was happening and went screaming back to her bedroom.

It was a sincere testament to his sense of control that he was able to contain himself.

The woman pulled at him in a way no other ever had. He wanted to protect her, while at the same time knowing she was totally capable of defending herself if she had to. Her martial arts skills alone rivaled his, a fact his ego didn't even mind. It was time to find out if she could use a gun. He hadn't asked, never thinking she would need to with him around. But now that they had to rely on themselves for the foreseeable future, he wanted to ensure she had more in her weapons arsenal than just her bare hands.

Ky knew she was an independent, successful woman used to fending for, and taking care of, herself. But he found, much to his surprise, he wanted to be the one to take care of her, to satisfy her needs. All of them. He wanted her to lean on him, depend on him, turn to him when she wanted something.

It was simply ridiculous to feel this way for a woman who barely tolerated being in the same room with him.

When sleep finally came, he treasured the few hours of solid rest he got.

Used to rising early no matter how tired he was, Ky was up when the sun cracked its way into his room. He rose and quickly showered, forgoing his usual morning exercise routine. For a little cabin in the woods, the shower was refreshingly hot and soothing.

Dressed, he put on a pot of coffee and cocked an ear at the staircase listening for sounds of movement from above.

When he decided she'd opted to sleep in, he took the opportunity to, as he'd told her the night before, get the lay of the land.

In the bright, piercing light of day, their charming, tiny cabin in the woods proved to be more of a fortress built to survive Armageddon.

On his first walk through the night before, Ky found the sophisticated alarm system he'd mentioned to Gemma housed in the pantry off the kitchen. On further inspection he'd been able to discern that it not only alarmed the house, but did indeed, have a co-system meant to protect against an invasion from outside. Ky's opinion of Bannerman went up several notches.

Before exiting the pantry, a little niggle of a thought wormed its way into his head and, after inspecting the dimensions of the room, solidified into certainty. The room was smaller than it should have been. That told him one thing: the pantry was more than a pantry. Cautiously, Ky tapped the walls surrounding the shelves and within a minute's time, discovered where one part of the wall sounded hollow. He pulled back the shelving and a false partition was revealed. Thinking it might be spring activated to open, he pressed against it and was rewarded when the wall swung open into a closet.

Ky squeezed around the opening and found something that warmed his heart and spirit: a secret stash of weapons.

Dozens of handguns, automatic assault rifles, Berettas, and even a rocket launcher were affixed to the pegboard wall inside the room, with more ammunition than he'd seen at gun shows aligned in boxes on a metal-framed rack.

The perfect setup to teach Gemma about guns, assuming she wasn't already proficient with a firearm.

Ky's opinion of Bannerman climbed even higher when he found the garage behind the house. It hadn't been visible when they'd arrived. But now, standing in the full light of day, Ky saw a structure almost as tall as the cabin, and just as wide, nestled into the berm on the back slope of the hill.

The entrance door was locked, a numbered keypad affixed to the door. Ky took a chance it was the same numerical code for the front door and his gamble paid off when he heard the mechanical clicks shifting after he hit *enter*.

The garage was big enough to house two full-sized vehicles and Ky considered parking their clunker in it to keep it out of sight. That would take half the storage space, the other already housed with a four-wheel ATV. The gas tank was full, the keys in the ignition.

Ready for a fast exit.

One they'd, hopefully, be spared.

A one-hundred-pound heavy bag was suspended from the ceiling beams, something he'd be using later on for sure.

For the most part, this little mountain retreat would serve to keep them safe and isolated.

Ky checked his watch and realized it was time to call in.

"Who is this?" the assistant director said immediately when the call connected.

"It's me, boss."

A long, deep, and steady draught of air pushed through the phone.

"Are you alone, Sir?"

"Yes. Where are you?"

"I can't tell you. Just know Miss Laine is safe and we're secured."

"Dammit, Papps!"

"Sir, please. I don't have much time on this phone and I need to get some information from you."

An infinitesimal moment passed. "Go ahead."

Ky had been working out what he wanted to say ever since the long car ride the day before.

"First, how's Jon?"

"As good as can be expected after taking a bullet to his arm and having to undergo reparative surgery."

"What's his prognosis?"

"Full recovery says the surgeon. Guy's got a real shit bedside manner, but he's the best, so I'm confident Winters will recoup."

"Good." Ky waited a moment before saying what needed to be said. He rubbed a hand across the back of his neck and prepared for what was to follow once he'd said his piece.

"I'm convinced we have the mole, Sir. There's no other explanation. No one but my team knew where we were going."

He waited for the explosion, was staggered when it didn't come.

Tiege inhaled deeply again. "You need to include me in that group, Papps," he said into the phone. "I knew, too."

To cover his surprise, Ky said, "Sir, I'm fairly confident I can eliminate you as the source of the leak."

A dry chuckle floated to his ears. "Well, thanks for being fairly sure. No, I agree with you. I knew it the minute I heard about the second attack. I've tapped everyone connected to this case and can't eliminate or confirm anyone."

"How in depth have you gone?"

"Trust me when I say deep. LaRoux and Coble were clean. I made sure of it. I even had you and Winters looked at." He made a disgusted sound and clicked his tongue. "Barly insisted."

Ky wasn't surprised or upset at being targeted. It made sense from an investigative stance. That Davison Barly had pushed for it was the disturbing point.

"Man is the most annoying pissant I've ever had to work with. Why the AG assigned him to this case is one for the books."

Ky agreed.

"He screamed bloody murder when I told him I didn't know where you and your witness were and had no way to reach you." That dry chuckle sounded again. "It was almost worth having to deal with him to see how hot and bothered he got. Asshole."

"He's worried the case will fold now because of the Calafano hit. Has anyone been able to get a bead on Ritandi's whereabouts?"

"No. Guy went to ground right after Calafano bought it. No electronic communication, all his networks have been offline. That court order to freeze his accounts you pushed for finally panned out. Barly had some cockamamie answer for why it took so long, but as of yesterday Ritandi can't access the accounts we know about. That includes the ones in Italy and England."

"Good. With those funds cut off he'll have some serious cash flow issues."

"Unless he's got some stashed someplace you weren't able to locate from Calafano's info, I'd say he's sitting pretty pissed at you about now."

The phone beeped, signaling the prepaid minutes were almost complete.

"Sir, I don't have much time left. I can't do much from where I am because I don't have access to my files—"

"Don't worry about that, Papps. I've got it covered. I'm betting as soon as the doc will let him, Winters will be all over this. Maybe even before he's discharged. Just keep your witness safe."

They agreed on another set time for Ky to call to check in.

"And Papps?"

"Yes, Sir?"

"Watch your six."

"Always, Sir."

Once the call disconnected, Ky dropped the phone to the ground and smashed it with the heel of his shoe.

Looking up, he winked an eye against the sun's glare.

Time to make breakfast.

* * *

The smell of bread turning to toast pushed her eyes open. For a brief moment the unfamiliarity of her surroundings sent her heart pounding with fear. Memories of the past twenty-four hours flooded through with the next breath and the panic was replaced by irritation.

Irritation at being forced into hiding; irritation at not being able to see her family; irritation at missing work deadlines.

Standing under the scalding-hot shower spray, the one thing she admitted irritated her most was her utter loss of independence. Gemma simply wasn't used to taking orders from other people, nor was she someone who dealt well with being confined.

Living in Manhattan, she could leave her condo any time, day or night, and she did, often going out to take pictures of the city and its people under the cloak of darkness. Some of the photographs she'd chosen for the new book she'd snapped at a women's shelter on a cold, rainy midnight several weeks ago. Taken with the wide variety of ages and economic situations of the women who sought refuge from the potential threats of the night, Gemma had tossed an idea around in her head to do a book just cataloging the faces and stories of the indigent and forgotten. She was in the process of solidifying the proposal with her publisher when she'd decided to venture out the day of the shooting.

Gemma scrubbed her skin with a surprisingly soft face towel and sighed. So much work to do. Frustrated wasn't strong enough to describe the feeling surging within her.

After towel-drying her hair and dressing in the comfortable yoga pants and T-shirt she found in the suitcase, Gemma went in search of food.

The aroma of fresh coffee lured her down to the kitchen where she found Ky standing with his back to her, a mug in his hand.

The tiny jump in her pulse at the sight of him clad in trousers and a collared pullover was mildly annoying.

"Hey," she said as a way of greeting.

Ky turned and that little jump catapulted to a leap.

Why did he have to be so damn good looking? Why couldn't he look like a troll?

"Good morning."

And why couldn't he have a cringe-worthy voice, and not a deep, sultry, tummy-fluttering one?

The bad mood she'd woken with shot up ten degrees.

"Did you ever get back to sleep?" he asked as she came around to the coffeepot. She assumed the empty mug sitting next to it was for her so she grabbed it, poured it full of the hot liquid, and shrugged.

"Took a while, but yeah."

"I thought you didn't drink coffee."

"I do when I've got a headache from lack of caffeinated soda."

He pointed to the plate of toast. "There's that or oatmeal for breakfast. No eggs or milk. And no butter. We'll need to get provisions if we're gonna be here more than a few days."

"Toast is fine." She slid two slices onto a plate and took it and her coffee to the breakfast bar without another word.

Ky watched her movements.

When the first hit of hot, slightly spicy liquid washed over her taste buds, Gemma groaned, tipped back her head and closed her eyes, letting the steam from the coffee drift up over her face.

Ky's warm and throaty chuckle filled the space between them. "You may be the only person I've ever known who has as much of a deep visceral reaction to that first sip as I do."

Taking her time, Gemma opened her eyes. He'd moved to sit across from her as he had in the middle of the night, elbows resting on the table, his own cup suspended in his hand. The slight upward tug of his lips softened his features but did nothing to douse his blessed-from-God sexiness.

Gemma swallowed. "My sister makes her own brew from a recipe she got from our grandmother. She tweaked it by putting in some different herbs, spices. I never liked the taste of coffee until I had hers, and now when I have a rare cup, I don't drink any other kind. This," she lifted her mug, "tastes remarkably like Kandy's mixture."

"It probably is, since a jar of it was in the pantry next to the jam."

Gemma grinned, her mood lifting considerably. "When I see Rick again I'm going to give him a big kiss on the mouth for stocking it here."

Ky's eyes darkened. His gaze flicked to her mouth, her cup just touching her bottom lip, and then back up to her eyes. She caught that cauldron of flaming emotions she'd noted before in him blazing to the surface again, and as quick as she recognized it, he extinguished the fire.

Very carefully, Ky put his mug down on the table. "I need to go over a few things with you."

And there was the ice again.

"'K."

Ky told her the conversation he'd had with SAC Tiege about Jon Winters.

"So, he's okay physically?"

"From the sound of it, yes. Or he will be."

"Will he be able to shoot again? I mean, if the doctor says he'll make a full recovery, isn't that what it basically means? He'll be able to use his arm for everything?"

"I don't know the answer to that. I'm hopeful, as I imagine Jon is." His brows tightened together. "Why do you ask about shooting?"

Gemma took a sip of her coffee. "It's important for you all to be good shots, right? You've told me how much he loves his job. Being able to shoot is an important part of that. Where does it leave him, career wise, if he can't?"

Ky stared at her for a few beats, the intensity of his gaze boring down on her, making her want to squirm in her chair.

"What?" she asked when he didn't answer.

Ky shook his head, almost as if he was pulling himself out of a trance. "Nothing. I just keep forgetting how very astute and observant you are."

Surprise at his words warred with the little jolt of pleasure that shocked through her.

The pleasure won.

"I guess we'll have to wait and see how well he recuperates," Ky continued. "If his arm affects his shooting, he'll deal with it. Trust me, Jon is nothing if not resilient."

He finished his coffee, rose, and filled his mug again. When he held the pot up to her and cocked an eyebrow, she shook her head.

He brought his filled mug back to the table, sat, and said, "Speaking of guns, do you have any experience with them?"

"Yes. I've got a license to carry. Why?"

"Even though we're isolated here, and maybe more because we are, we need to be vigilant and prepared for anything." He went on to describe the weapons stash he'd found that morning. "What kind of firearms have you used?"

"Glocks, mostly. I like revolvers with six-inch barrels the best, but you have to load the bullets one by one after the chamber empties, so it's time consuming. But I love the feel of a revolver in my hand. It feels, I don't know," she shrugged, "comfortable and solid are the best words. Josh showed me how to use an automatic assault rifle once, but the kick was too much. Bruised my shoulder like a bitch, so he thought I should stick to handguns."

"He ever take you to the range to practice?"

She nodded. "Couple times. Rick was the one who gave me most of my info and instructions. He was a sniper in a previous career, one he never talks about, so I learned a lot. It's like with my martial arts training." She shrugged. "I'm good at it."

"I would bet it's because, as a photographer of your caliber, you have excellent hand-to-eye coordination."

She lifted her shoulders again. "I guess. I don't own a gun, personally, though."

"When you're finished I'll show you the room and you can choose the weapon you want. There's enough ammo that we can practice. It makes sense for the both of us to be armed while we're here."

"Okay. Do you think—" She stopped, hating she had to ask permission for something. For anything, really.

"Do I think what?"

She scrunched up her face, her lips pulling in at the corners. She began rubbing her palms on her thighs, much as she did as a child and had done something to incur a scolding from her grandmother.

"Well, I've got my cameras. I'd like to…explore a little. Just around the property. Maybe take some pictures? We're isolated here, like you said. No one knows where we are. I've been cooped up for days and I just need…to work."

It had all come out in a rush and when she stopped, she felt a wildfire of heat rush up from her neck to her face.

Ky stared down at his mug for a moment. When his gaze hit on her face again, compassion warmed his eyes. "I know you do," he said. "I know how hard this all must be on you, I really do. Witnessing a murder, getting attacked, then shot at. It's not what you're used to."

"No lie," she muttered.

His mouth quirked as he took a hit of the coffee. "Let's do this. You can choose a gun and we can get in some target practice just so I'll know you'll be able to use it, and then we can take a walk around the property."

"Together?"

Laughter danced at his lips. "That's what *we* usually means. Yes. Together."

"I wanted to go…you know…alone."

"Not gonna happen." And just like that, once again, frost formed in his eyes.

She wanted to fight him on it. A few days ago she would have. She would have argued relentlessly. But in the end, she knew it wouldn't do any good. She'd come to understand his intractable stubbornness where her safety was concerned. He wasn't going to leave her side, no matter what.

So Gemma did something she never did if she could help it: she acquiesced.

Chapter Ten

"How many do I have to hit for you to be satisfied?"

Ky looked over to where she stood at the side of the garage, the Glock in her hand, its barrel aimed at the ground. Her eyes had gone wide at the hidden supply of weapons Bannerman had in the pantry access room, but her only comment had been a muttered, "Why am I not surprised?" before she'd made her choice.

He'd watched her load the clip, then weigh and balance the gun in her hand like she did it every day of her life.

"This'll do," she told him.

He found a box of empty beer and wine bottles in the garage and set them up at varying distances from where he'd told her to stand. He wanted to ensure she was comfortable shooting up close and far.

"All of them." He came and stood next to her.

"Are you kidding? All of them?"

"You might never get a second chance if a first bullet misses an attacker, so yes. All of them."

She moved to the line in the grass he'd drawn for her to shoot from, mumbling something he couldn't hear, but guessing it wasn't something complimentary.

"Ready?" he asked.

"Yup. Any particular order you want me to hit them in?"

He had to bite back the grin threatening to fly free at her snooty, disgruntled tone.

"Your call."

Gemma nodded and planted her feet. He wasn't surprised when she angled her body with one foot slightly behind the other in a Weaver stance—a more aggressive, weight-forward position—and not the triangular, or Isosceles stance. Gemma held her gun up to her face, lining up her shot, both elbows bent and close to her torso. Her brother-in-law, Josh, had been a New York City cop, and if he'd taught her to shoot, it made sense he'd taught her this way. Although the Isosceles stance was the more popular, Ky knew the Weaver was a power stance, and Gemma was a woman for whom power could have been a middle name.

She flexed her shoulders and neck, the motion so subtly erotic, it made his pulse quicken, and shifted her weight. From his viewing position behind her, he appreciated just how tall and lean she was. Narrow shoulders were relaxed and tapered down into a waist no bigger than a hand span. How many times in the past few days had he thought what it would be like to slip his own hands around that tiny area and pull her in close? Too many for prudence, that was for sure.

The first bottle, the one he'd placed the farthest from them, shattered into a thousand fragments. Before he could take a full breath, she'd hit the next two.

The final three closer ones she dispatched with equal ease.

When she turned to him and asked, "Satisfied?" in a tone filled with condescension, Ky had to physically restrain himself from running to her, lifting her up in his arms, and kissing the gorgeous smirk off her mouth.

Because he'd discovered how much he liked sparring with her—go figure that out—he pursed his lips and nodded. "Not bad."

Gemma's smirk grew into a self-satisfied grin.

"But they were all stationary targets. Really adept shooters practice with moving targets, so I really can't gauge how well you'll do with that. But for now, you'll do."

The squinty-eyed glare she aimed at him would have made a lesser man run for the hills.

"Trust me." She dropped the empty cartridge case from the weapon into her free hand. "I can shoot those as well."

He handed her another clip and watched as she loaded it.

"Let's hope you never have to prove it to me."

Gemma slapped the cartridge in place. Ky handed her a holster and waited until she fastened it around her waist.

After tightening it, she secured the gun in place, dropped her hands on her hips and asked, "Can we go now?"

She looked like a warrior armed for battle. Strong, self-possessed, and so bad-assed sexy standing in front of him, her bangs blowing back from the slight breeze surrounding them, her perfect chin tilted up defiantly.

He could imagine her leading an army into a crusade against evil, each soldier following her blindly, minions pledged to fight for her, perhaps die for her without hesitation.

And he'd be one of them.

"Sure. Get your camera. I'll secure the house."

* * *

"I think we should head back," Ky said.

They'd been walking for hours. The woods surrounding the cabin had, just as she'd hoped, provided her with an overabundance of perfect beauty to film.

They'd started out as soon as she'd secured her camera around her neck and checked the availability of the memory card for space. With the Glock on her hip, and Ky's own gun in his hand, they'd ventured out from the back of the cabin, into the thick, lush woods surrounding it.

After a few moments the house was no longer visible. A mild sweep of alarm brushed through her, but when Ky looked down at a compass he'd pulled from his pants pocket, it dissipated.

"Were you a boy scout or something?" she asked, pointing to the compass in his hand.

His response had been a tiny lifting of his lips and an, "or something," in reply.

He'd led her in every direction she'd asked to go, following the sunlight from above them.

She took hundreds of photos. The break in the canopy when the midday sun had peeked through, slitting light through the trees, giving the illusion the leaves were wet and shimmering like glass mirrors; the raging brook they'd happened upon, the water barreling over lichen-covered rocks, tiny white bubbles bursting around them as they came in contact.

A trio of foraging deer munching on several bushes had frozen in place when Gemma aimed her camera at them. Just as she'd captured three shots in succession, they'd bolted, their white tails bouncing away from the noise. A monarch butterfly had decided to follow them at one point. When it settled on a leaf, Gemma played with all the stops on her camera, photographing the insect on zoom, in black and white, even out of focus. She couldn't wait to transfer them to a computer and play with the composition.

In all, it was just the break she needed. She'd let her mind clear of the events of the past few days and simply enjoyed the beauty, the quiet, and the natural splendor surrounding them.

But she'd never for a moment forgotten the man walking with her, ever vigilant, his eyes darting and surveying every inch of ground they covered. Positioned a few steps in front of her at all times, guiding her way, alert to any noise and movement before she saw or heard it, Gemma knew even in this secluded, apparently safe environment, Ky was still protecting her from any and all potential threats.

He'd been patient and agreeable the numerous times she'd asked to stop to capture something with her camera. He hadn't been chatty, peppering her with questions or making comments on her shots. Instead, he'd allowed her the pleasure to walk quietly, lost in her own thoughts, and simply *be.*

When was the last time she'd felt so comfortable with a man—with anyone other than her family, really—and didn't need to keep up a conversation? Didn't need to engage in small, inane talk to quell the nervous anxiety seeping through her? Didn't need to explain why she was taking this shot, not another?

"How far do you think we've come from the cabin?" she asked.

"Hard to tell." He consulted the compass. "We've circled around a few times. We're facing the front of it now. We should get back."

Gemma nodded and followed him.

A few minutes later they saw the cabin come into view. They were, as Ky had said, approaching it from the front road they'd traveled on the night before.

He disengaged the alarm and preceded her into the house, motioning for her to stay behind on the porch. He entered the cabin, did a quick, thorough sweep of the great room, and when he gave her the signal that it was safe to enter, she realized, with utter astonishment, that she'd obeyed him without hesitation.

The realization she'd blindly and compliantly consented to his command floored her. Never before with any other man had she followed what amounted to an order.

Why now?

Despite his primitive male sexiness and the fact that he made her quake at times with the sheer power of it, Gemma still wasn't even sure she liked him, much less trusted him. She'd all but proven to him that morning she could defend herself if need be against an assault and he was aware she was as proficient in hand to hand combat as he was. She could take care of herself, and had been for most of her adult life.

"Are you hungry?" He re-holstered his gun. "There's some canned soup I can heat. Some bread." He'd moved to the kitchen and opened one of the cabinets. "It's not much, but it'll do."

She didn't answer him, still lost in thought.

"What's wrong?"

He moved so quickly, before she could blink and lift her head he was standing in front of her, his hands locked on her upper arms.

She stared at his hands, securely, yet gently wrapped around her. Each finger was long and lean and she could feel his natural heat passing through them and burning into her skin. She lifted her head. His brows were pulled in tight to the center of his forehead, concern swimming in his eyes.

"Nothing," she said, astounded her voice sounded as steady as it did, despite the cyclone of emotions spinning within her. "I'm just not hungry. I think I'll go upstairs and lay down for a little while."

"Are you okay?" His splayed fingers squeezed around her arms and she wondered if he realized he was doing it.

"I'm fine. I'm tired. The walk…" She shrugged. "It tired me out some."

He kept staring at her, an unasked question burning in his gaze. Finally, he released his hold.

For the life of her, Gemma couldn't explain why she suddenly felt lonely.

With a nod Ky said, "Okay. I can imagine you're exhausted after not sleeping so well last night."

He took a step back, dropped his hands into his trouser pockets. "If you get hungry, let me know."

Gemma snuck one last look at him, then turned and walked up to the second floor. She could feel his gaze, following her, burning on her back the whole way and had to clamp down on the need to turn and look back down at him.

After she shut the bedroom door, she clasped her hands together and realized they were shaking. She laid her camera carefully down on the dresser top, every movement precise and slow, un-holstered the gun and put it alongside the camera. Mindlessly, mechanically, she crawled into bed, not bothering to pull the covers up over her body. On her side, with her knees drawn up to her chest, she closed her eyes, and on a ragged breath, fell almost instantly to sleep.

And dreamed of a God-like man with eyes the color of a calm sea.

* * *

Shadows from the afternoon sun played along her face, forcing her eyes open. Gemma rolled to her back, stretched, and listened as her stomach told her it was time she gave it something to eat.

The great room was empty, the bedroom he'd used as well when she peeked in. The entire downstairs area was quiet. Too quiet.

Knowing Ky would never purposely leave her alone, she nonetheless gave in to a few seconds of panic when she couldn't find him. A slow, dim, thudding sound came from what she thought might be the garage, so she moved through the kitchen's back door after disarming the alarm, and out to the building.

The sound was loud, accompanied now by grunting noises. Fear pounded through her. Gemma pulled her gun from its holster and crept along the side of the house. She stopped at a small window facing into the garage, held her breath, and peeked in.

The noises she'd heard were coming from Ky. Her fear flew when she realized he was pummeling the punching bag suspended from the ceiling.

The moment she wished she had her camera in her hand, she bolted back to the house, ran up to her room and was back at her viewing spot within a few seconds, the lens pointed at the powerful image in front of her.

Ky was slathered in sweat, his hair stuck flat to his head. His hands were wrapped in gauze as they'd been in the safe house basement. Shirtless, the muscles in his neck and chest flexed with each roll and thrust of his arms as they connected with the bag. The St. Michael's medallion bounced against his neck with each move he executed. Moisture poured down his torso, dipping and pooling in the curves and indentations of his abdominal muscles.

Gemma snapped dozens of pictures, alternating the settings on her camera with every shot. She wanted to capture each and every movement he made without worry of blurring or distorting the image.

He was simply magnificent to watch, even more so because he hadn't a clue he was being observed. Free and unfiltered, every motion he made was pure and raw, true to form, and unadulterated. His breathing was coarse but controlled, heavy sounding but not labored. A few times she heard him suck in air then let it out in a natural, easy rhythm as his fist connected with its target.

The bag swung and shifted with every hit as if it weighed nothing more than a fistful of cotton balls. Gemma appreciated just how powerful and focused Ky's punches were when he jabbed two fists in rapid succession and the bag swung away from his body with such a force, he had to sidestep it on the recoil.

It was at that moment he became aware of her.

Standing square with him now, Gemma saw his face fully for the first time and not in profile. Her heart actually missed a few beats, then made up for the deficit by rebounding to a skipping cadence.

Primal, savage fury encompassed his features. His eyes were so filled with heat she was astounded she didn't burst into flames when they lit on her. His luscious full mouth was open, dragging in huge gasps of air; his massive shoulders rising almost to his ears with each inhalation. Visible steam floated from the heated sweat evaporating off him.

Ky dropped his hands to his sides as he watched her, silent.

"I'm sorry," Gemma blurted, clutching her camera to her chest. "I didn't want to interrupt. I woke up...I couldn't find you and I got worried... I'm, I'm sorry."

She clamped her mouth shut.

Ky shook his head and, like a dog shaking wet fur, his sweat fanned and danced around him. He pulled one of his wrapped hands to his mouth, saying first, "You don't have to be sorry."

Like she had once before, Gemma said, "Here, let me help." She swung her camera from its strap to rest on her back. She crossed to him and felt the temperature in the air surrounding him shoot up a good twenty degrees. Taking his hand from his mouth, she pulled it down and began to unfurl the wrapping.

With her eyes trained on her task, she could feel his penetrating stare covering her. She wanted to look up at him but was fearful once she did, she wouldn't be able to look away. Ever.

She was eye level with his chin and watched, mesmerized, as moisture pooled in the deep indented notch at his throat. She swiped her tongue across parched lips and, in one insane moment of mind-numbing lust, wished beyond everything she could lap the area dry.

And then proceed to lick the rest of him.

When she felt her own cheeks flame with heat, she cursed her fair skin.

Standing toe to toe with this man who defined the word *male*, Gemma felt every part of her body that made her a woman scream out with desire and want.

And she did want him—in the purest, most sensual, mating sense.

When the drenched gauze fell freely, unwound from his hand, Gemma rolled it into a ball and finally ventured a look up at his face.

If she wasn't mistaken, that dark, graphic, just barely constrained force she saw mirrored back at her told her he felt the same way she did. Her detailed and creative imagination went into overdrive, giving her a full and erotic sense of what the two of them would be like if they ever fell together.

Oh my! Bad imagination.

Her nipples pulled into two tight, painful pebbles beneath her bra. Stomach muscles she didn't even know she possessed cramped and clenched as her lower body tensed. When she pressed her thighs together in a purely involuntary move, she felt the area at the top of them throb and moisten with need.

"Want me to do the other one?" she asked before she gave into the urge to jump up and wrap those throbbing thighs around his waist.

It took him a moment before he replied, "I'm good, thanks."

Gemma took a mental step, and a few physical ones, back as he removed the second gauze.

"You got some sleep, then?" he asked.

She nodded.

"Feel better?" He reached out for the gauze she still held. She dropped it into his hand, careful not to touch him because she didn't know how she'd react if she actually did, and then he tossed both over his shoulder and into a trash pail.

"Yes."

It was his turn to nod. "Let me grab a shower and then I'll see about dinner."

"Let me help," she said. When his eyebrows shot up his forehead, she realized how he might have misinterpreted her meaning. "With dinner, I mean. Cooking. You've…you've been doing everything. All the cooking, and such. I want to help. And I *can* cook. You know who my sister is, after all. I know my way around a kitchen. Even an unfamiliar one."

She came slamming to halt. She never babbled, so why did just having this man look at her with a question in his eyes cause her to turn into a nonstop chatterbox?

Taking a deep breath, she counted to three, then said slowly, enunciating each word clearly, "You go have a shower. I'll make dinner. Deal?"

He bent over, grabbed his gun from its resting spot on the floor, said "Deal," and then moved by her and into the house.

Once she was alone, Gemma flattened a hand over her shaking abdomen and took in a deep, slow breath. There was no sane reason the thought of Ky naked and standing in the shower, lathered in soap and essence of, well, *man*, should make her knees goes soft and her thighs tremble.

But when she passed the closed bathroom door on her way to the kitchen and heard the shower kick in, they did just that.

Bad knees.

* * *

Ky was starting to realize the benefits of a brutally cold shower. Not only did it cool off the total body swelter his workout had heated him with, but it helped tamp down the lust raging through him.

Walking around in almost a full state of arousal for hours on end was starting to take a toll on his body and his nerves.

From the moment Ky'd watched Gemma hit all her targets like a sharpshooter, to the hours he'd spent with her in the woods, watching her work, his body had been on hyper alert.

Taking an hour to try and sweat off his ravenous desires, he'd almost gotten his body back to normal when he saw her watching him, her camera poised. The workout may have calmed him for the moment, but the sight of her in the garage had him hard and pulsing in an instant again.

This is insane.

He was charged with keeping her safe from a madman. He couldn't do that if every time he looked at her all he could envision was what color those beautiful eyes would turn to when she came; what her skin would taste like as he ran his tongue over every inch of it; the noises she'd make when she fell apart in his hands.

Insanity. Lusting after a woman who didn't even like him and only tolerated his company because she had no other choice.

With her brother-in-law, the other agents, even with Jon, Gemma had smiled and spoken to them as if they were old friends. With him, she continued to be reserved and quiet, nervous and unsure, all traits he didn't think she usually possessed.

He wasn't naive by any sense of the word—he knew when a woman liked him, desired him, wanted to be in his company.

Gemma Laine gave no indication she felt any of those things. In fact, she'd been peeved he hadn't let her go off on her own to wander through the woods. She may have yielded to his demand to go with her, but he knew she hadn't been happy about it. They'd walked for hours with barely a few sentences said between them.

It was obvious his desire was one sided, which was probably a good thing since he had a job to do. If his ego was a little bruised because of it, well, he'd just need to live with it.

Ky toweled off, dressed, and checked his gun before inserting it back into his shoulder holster. He needed to remember why they were hiding out here. He had to keep his mind alert and focused, his guard up, to make sure nothing happened to either of them. He had to do his job, no matter what was going on in his mind.

He took a quick glance at himself in the bedroom mirror and nodded, determined to keep himself in check now. He knew he could do it—he had to.

The smell of tomatoes simmering hit him the moment he opened the bedroom door.

"It smells great out here," he said.

Gemma turned from the stove, continuing to stir a steaming pot of something, and in that moment he knew he'd just lied to himself yet again. There was no way he could keep his body, mind, or imagination from reacting to her.

She'd pulled her bangs off her face with a headband and for the first time he realized she had a well-defined heart-shaped peak on her forehead, the base separating her face into two perfect sections. Her features were so symmetrically balanced, if she weren't the one taking photographs, he could see her in front of the lens, gracing the covers of beauty magazines.

"I found a box of pasta and what I'm pretty certain is a quart of Kandy's homemade sauce."

Ky moved to stand next to her and dipped his head to get a whiff of the sweet-and-spicy smelling brew. Gemma gave a little jump when his shoulder bumped her arm, but Ky just closed his eyes, ignoring it, and took in the heady aroma.

"If this tastes as good as it smells, I'll need the recipe for my mother." When he turned his head and opened his eyes she was staring at him. She was eye level since he'd ducked his head, and all it would take was a subtle shift on either of their parts to bring their lips together.

Her gaze flicked to his mouth and it took every ounce of will Ky possessed not to move in and discover exactly how she tasted.

He pulled upright and sidestepped away from her.

The little shudder he caught her make solidified in his mind how she felt about him.

He watched as she took a breath and flexed her neck from side to side in a move that had his mouth watering. She'd done the same thing that morning before proving what a good marksman she was, and it elicited the same reason from him now as it had then: he went concrete hard.

"You're out of luck with that request." She went back to stirring the sauce. "This is one of those recipes of Grandma's that Kandy will never share. It's strictly for family."

Something he wasn't and never would be.

She'd set the table and put bottled waters at each place setting.

"There's no wine," she said as she poured the sauce into a serving bowl. "I really wish there was wine."

He grinned at the wistfulness in her voice. "Water is fine."

He waited until she had everything ready, then sat with her.

"This is beyond delicious," he said after his first forkful of the sauce-laden linguini.

"No lie."

They ate in silence for a few moments, the only sounds the movements of their forks across the plates.

Raised in a family with six brothers and a sister, Ky was used to mealtimes being loud and lively. At the safe house, Jon had always been able to keep the conversation flowing, eliciting responses from Gemma without any effort. Sitting here quietly, just enjoying the meal was a rare treat. He wondered if she felt awkward with the silence, but when he stole a glance at her, she seemed content enough.

After a while she cleared her throat. "Can I ask you something?"

"Yes."

"And you'll be honest with me in your answer?"

Taken aback by the question and the hidden implication behind it, he said, "Of course I will. I'll always be honest with you."

Gemma considered his words, then nodded. "How much longer do you think we'll need to stay here?"

The question wasn't what he expected, but she'd asked for the truth, so he gave it. "I wish I could tell you, give you an exact date and time, but I just don't know. My division is doing everything it can to find Ritandi, but until he's in custody, he's a threat to you, so we have to keep you out of sight. I'm sorry I don't have a better answer."

Her shoulders fell as she stared down at her plate. "I figured as much."

His heart broke at how resigned she sounded. They ate the rest of the meal in silence.

"Since you cooked, I'll clean up," he told her once they were done.

"No, I'll help." She shrugged and picked up her plate and utensils. "There's nothing else to do."

She washed while he dried, both remaining silent.

When the kitchen was cleaned and everything put away, Gemma leaned against the sink and sighed.

"What's wrong?" Ky asked, standing across from her, his hands dipped into his pockets.

Her full mouth pulled down into a frown and her arms crossed over her chest. "What if he isn't caught?"

"Ritandi?"

She nodded. "What if your men can't locate him?"

"They will, believe me. The access to his money has been cut off. His passport has been rescinded and he's been tagged by the FTA both here and abroad. We know his closest contacts and they're being watched. Believe me, he'll be found."

"But when?" She yanked the headband from her head and scrubbed her fingers into her temples. Her bangs swished back across her forehead, perfectly aligned once again, the peak hidden from view. "It could take years. Am I supposed to spend the rest of my life running from him? Hiding out? Not able to work? Never seeing my family?"

He told himself it was because her voice broke on the last word that he moved toward her and pulled her into his arms. She looked so forlorn, all he wanted to do was comfort her, keep her from falling apart. The moment she slipped her hands around his waist and laid her head down on his chest he knew he'd told himself yet another lie.

He shouldn't touch her. He knew it. But the need raging within him to offer whatever he could to this woman was beyond something he could fight.

"I can't live like this," she mumbled against his shirt. "This isn't my life. I'm not the criminal, but I'm the one caged and cut off from the world. It's not fair."

Because he agreed, he whispered against her temple, "No, it isn't."

The delicate aroma of cherries drifted up from her hair. Ky closed his eyes and rubbed his hands down her back. She felt like a piece of porcelain against his fingers, delicate and fragile, her skin smooth and soft wherever he rubbed. But he knew the strength under that velvet covering, the backbone forged in steel. In all the time they'd been forced together, from the initial attack in her apartment, to the gun spree at the safe house, she'd never cracked. Even now, when he'd expect any other woman to dissolve in tears or rant and rave at the situation, Gemma was angry more than anything else.

Well, he could deal with anger. He didn't know what he'd do if she ever fell apart.

"I promise, we'll get him."

Gemma pulled her hands from around him and shifted back. Her gaze scrutinized his face, darting back and forth between his eyes, looking for what, he didn't know. She seemed fascinated with his mouth all of a sudden, her attention focused on the lower part of his face.

Her tongue slipped out and fanned her bottom lip while she regarded him. Why hadn't he noticed before how it was so much plumper than the top one? It glistened with the moisture her tongue had drawn across it. Ky tensed, every nerve in the lower part of his body firing with longing.

He knew he shouldn't, but the need to know what she tasted like was too powerful a temptation to defy. Ky bent, just a fraction, as Gemma pushed upward toward him, their gazes locked.

With eyes wide open, his lips pressed against hers, gently, just a slow, thoughtful graze. He thought she'd push him away, verbally castigate him—or worse. But she didn't. She leaned into the kiss. Soft and smooth and warm, the feel of her lips pulled him closer. He wanted more than just a simple taste he realized in that moment. He wanted to devour her.

A tiny sigh pushed from somewhere deep within her. Gemma slid her hands around his waist again, her lips exploring his—sampling, wanting.

He could feel her heart jackhammering against his chest, or was that his own pounding against her?

A quick swipe with his tongue and she opened for him, inviting him in, the warmth of her accepting response urging him on. He tasted spice and sugar, arousal and need all mixed together in a heady blend that had him reeling.

The hands at her back slipped down to cup her perfect ass, molding her to his body, showing her everything that was happening to him. He nipped at her mouth, skimmed his lips down her chin, across her jaw. He swallowed a chuckle when she palmed his head between her hands and dragged his lips back to hers, telling him what she wanted without words.

And he was happy to give it to her.

He felt her tug his shirt from his pants, the feel of her soft, strong hands on his bare flesh sending him into orbit. He hissed when she raked her nails across the small of his back and then slipped them under his waistband to hold on, grinding her body against him.

Her hot and impatient mouth never left his, her tongue caught around his own as she sucked it into her mouth. He pushed her back until she hit the counter and then snaked his knee between her legs. A whimper whistled from her lips when he ground his thigh against her heat and felt her pulsing response.

Ky snaked his hands up under her shirt, up her torso, sliding his thumbs across hard and pebbled nipples through her bra. Her breasts were heavy in his hands, filling them with each breath she took. While his tongue wound around hers pulling her deep into his mouth, he squeezed those perfect mounds of flesh and felt Gemma's response when she double fisted his hair and tugged.

Every warning bell he possessed sounded and pinged in alarm, but he ignored them all. This is what he wanted. *She* was what he wanted.

It would be so easy to simply haul her up in his arms and to his room where he could help them both disappear into one another for a few hours. Just as the thought to do so bloomed, they were wrenched apart by the piercing shriek of the house alarm blasting through the air.

"Wha—?" Confusion drenched her face when Ky pushed her out of his arms and immediately grabbed his gun from its holster.

He yanked on her hand and tugged her behind him. "Where's your weapon?"

"Up-upstairs, I—"

"Get up there. Now. Lock the door." He pushed her toward the staircase. She wouldn't let his arm go. "What—?"

"Don't argue Go. Now." He shoved her up the first riser, then ran to the front window. He hit the light switch next to the door and the room was thrown into late afternoon darkness. The sound of Gemma's feet as she ran up the staircase was muffled under the continued boom of the alarm.

The bedroom door slammed shut.

He spied the incandescent glow of a vehicle's lights as it came slowly up the gravel drive. Whoever their visitor was, he wasn't trying to hide his arrival.

A bold tactic, or a stupid one?

The engine cut and the driver door opened. Ky's Glock was ready as he stood behind the front door, waiting, his muscles tensed, his breathing sparse.

The automatic lock shifted on the door.

Their visitor knew the entrance code.

Ky had only a moment to consider that before he flattened himself against the wall. The door pushed open and a large figure crossed the threshold.

Without waiting, Ky struck.

Jumping from behind the door he slammed into the figure's back, shoving him to his knees.

"Don't move!" he barked, the Glock aimed at the man's head.

His command went unheeded.

An arm as thick as a tree trunk shot out and swiped at Ky, clipping him behind the knees. He fell back, flat on his ass, knocking a table lamp to the floor, his gun bouncing out of his hand. Before he could right himself, the behemoth straddled him, his ham-sized hands pressing Ky's shoulders into the floor. Unable to move his arms or use his hands, he arched his back, lifted his pelvis and scissored his legs. The hulk barely moved, but Ky was able to shift him so the grip on his shoulders slackened and the man fell forward. Without waiting or taking a breath, Ky shoved, shot up and spun around him, twisting his arms around his neck in a chokehold.

The man flailed, trying to grab and smack at Ky's face. Ky locked his knees together and tightened the hold.

"Who sent you?" he snarled into the man's ear.

An elbow with as much force behind it as a speeding train, slammed into his midsection. A loud "oof" blurted from him, and he strained to keep his stronghold. Another jab, this time a little lower had Ky shifting back to avoid any damage, and his attacker took that split second of movement to toss Ky over his shoulder.

Flat on his back again, Ky reached out and grabbed one of the man's forearms, rolled with it and repositioned himself on the man's back, shunting his arms around the massive chest, imprisoning his attacker's arms to his sides.

The room was thrown into stark light, stunning him. Just as Gemma pounded down the stairs, screaming something he couldn't make out clearly due to the alarm's unceasing squawk, the giant pried Ky's arms apart and shot both his elbows back, knocking Ky back again.

Instinct and training waved through him like a tsunami. Ky jumped up and back onto the intruder, who was still on his knees, his hands flattened on the floor, his breathing harsh and labored.

A right hit to the man's temple knocked him over onto his back. As he'd had done to him, Ky straddled his legs and dropped two quick hits to a massive jaw.

All the while Gemma continued screaming behind him. A gunshot exploded in the room, paralyzing Ky from landing his next hit.

With one hand gripping the intruder's collar, the other poised to deliver another punch, Ky looked over at the fireplace where a large, round and jagged hole pierced the brick overlay, dust and mortar blowing from it.

He was dumbfounded when he spied Gemma, glaring down at them, the Glock in her hands.

"I'm charging your sweet ass for that," he heard the man tell her. "Can you please disable the alarm," he added. "I've got enough of a headache now from being pummeled."

"Oh, my God, you're bleeding!" Gemma ran to the kitchen, the gun still in her hand.

It was then he realized what Gemma had been screaming since she flew down the stairs.

Their invader wasn't a threat.

She came back into the room, a dish towel in her hand, shoved her Glock at Ky and then pushed him out of her way, taking his place.

"Here." Gently, she pressed the towel against the man's bleeding cheek.

He reached up and laid his hand over hers while she held it in place. Ky's eyes narrowed at the tender gesture and his immediate, irrational jealous response to it.

"Thanks, but you're still paying to fix my fireplace, Cleo," he said.

Gemma sat back on her haunches and shook her head.

"What are you doing here, Rick?"

Chapter Eleven

"I think this needs stitches," Gemma said once she'd secured the bandage over the deep cut on Rick Bannerman's cheek. "Otherwise, you're gonna have a scar."

He smiled and grabbed her hand, kissing the knuckles. "A scar is always a great conversation starter," he said. "I'll get a lot of pick-up mileage out of it."

She smacked his arm and pursed her lips. "God help the members of my sex."

When she looked up from her brother-in-law's business partner, she found Ky leaning against the kitchen counter, watching them.

Unlike Rick, Ky's face was unmarked from the fight, but she'd noticed him rubbing a hand across his abdomen a few times while she tended to her friend.

Lord, she'd never been so scared in her life as when she'd cracked open the bedroom door, the gun secured in her hand, to see the looming hulk of a man come through the front door. Ky had him on his knees in a heartbeat and it was then she saw the dim light from the late afternoon sun cross his face and realized it was Rick Bannerman who was getting the crap beat out of him.

"Are you okay?" she asked Ky.

"Fine. Mind explaining why you're here?" he asked Rick in a tone that told her he wasn't hurt as much as pissed off.

Bannerman fingered the bandage at his face and flicked his gaze from Gemma to him and then back to Gemma.

"Josh wanted to make sure you two got here okay, encouraged by Kandy, I'm sure. She's worried about you, Cleo." He dragged the finger down Gemma's cheek.

She wasn't sure, but the sound that came from over her shoulder sounded a little like a growl.

"You need to stop calling me that," Gemma told Bannerman.

He winced when his smile burst fast and easy. "Ow. I think you might be right about the stitches. Anyway, after you two got in touch and Josh set you up here, he realized he had no way to make sure you'd arrived safe and sound, or to check on you. Since I'm between jobs at the moment, and this is my place, he asked me to come. Sent me with supplies, too. They're out in the car."

He turned his attention to Ky. "I was surprised you'd found and programmed the boundary line alarm. I didn't set it the last time I was here."

"Good thing I did, then," Ky said. "We knew you were coming."

Bannerman considered him. "I've never had it go off when I've been here. How much warning did you have?"

"Thirty seconds, give or take."

"You got the drop on me pretty quickly, then. Good job."

Gemma couldn't tell if Ky was pleased by the compliment or not. The unreadable expression on his face never wavered.

Cop face, again.

"He found your weapons stash, too," she said, a little pride singing through the words.

"Okay, so now I'm impressed. And a little ticked off. I thought that room was well hidden."

"I'm going to assume all those weapons are licensed and registered."

Gemma's head whipped around to glare at him. Why was he acting like such an asshole?

Rick's response was to shrug good naturedly and smirk. "Free country. You can assume anything you want. How'd you find it?"

"The dimensions in the pantry seemed off."

Bannerman nodded. "Good eye. I added it when I got the place a few years ago. Seemed like a good space to hide a room." His eyes went to half-mast. "I may have to reconsider that, now."

When Ky didn't respond, Gemma jumped in, uneasy with all the testosterone floating around the room. "You said you brought supplies?"

The men glared at one another for a moment, then Bannerman nodded and turned back to her.

"In the trunk of the car. I told Kandy I only stocked emergency rations here, so she sent some stuff. Josh did, too. I'll go get it all."

"I'll help," Gemma said.

"Hang on a sec." Ky reached out and grabbed her arm.

Bannerman looked between them.

"Go ahead. I'll be right there," she told him.

Just a simple touch from Ky had her breath catching. The memory of what they'd been doing when the alarm sounded jumped back to her.

"You didn't stay out of sight like I told you to," Ky said, his mouth flat, nostrils flaring, when they were alone.

Gemma glanced down at his hand and then back up at him.

"It's a good thing I didn't," she said, tugging her arm away. She might as well have been trying to pull it through hardened concrete. He didn't let go. "You could have killed Rick if I'd stayed up there and then where we would be?"

Ky shook his head, took a deep breath, and Gemma could see for the first time he wasn't as much pissed off as he was furious.

"You didn't know that it was Bannerman—"

"Yes I did."

His eyes narrowed. "How?"

Gemma bit her bottom lip. "I-I opened the bedroom door when I heard the fighting. I could make out Rick's face from the light coming through the front door."

"You opened the door and looked out?"

"Y-Yes."

"After I specifically ordered you to lock it and stay out of sight?"

Her back shot up straight at his tone and word choice.

"Yes, I did. Why are you so angry at me?"

Instead of answering her question, he asked one of his own.

"Why?"

"Why what?"

"Why did you disobey me? Why, after all we've gone through the past few days, would you disregard what I said, knowing we were potentially under attack again?"

"But we weren't. I—"

"*Why*, Gemma?"

She stared at him with her mouth wide open, the response dead on her lips. It was the first time he'd ever spoken her name aloud and the sound of it across his lips made her knees shake.

He took a step closer and wound his free hand around her other arm, pulling her square to him. "Answer me," he whispered.

His eyes had turned to twin daggers, piercing straight through her.

"B-because I thought you were in trouble. I heard...the fighting...I was...worried."

"About?"

Gemma's lips slammed together.

He gave her a tiny shake. "About what?"

"You, damn it! I was worried about you!"

Ky stared down at her. From the way his brows lifted and his eyes widened, she knew hearing her statement had surprised him as much as it had her to declare it.

Gemma licked her suddenly parched lips. "We're all alone here. You have no backup. No one to cover you. No one to fight with you. *Damn it!* I wanted to make sure you were okay. I wanted to help." She squirmed against his grip, realizing her voice had a slightly hysterical pitch to it. "Now let me go."

He didn't. In fact, his hands tightened around her arms as he stepped so close she had to tilt her chin up to see him clearly. Those gorgeous hooded eyes softened under his glare. He cocked his head to one side and took a breath so deep, she felt the air around her pull into him. When he let it out, it fanned, hot and moist, against her face. She felt her nipples tighten, her stomach muscles go slack, as he continued to stare at her.

Good Lord, the man made her *want*.

He opened his mouth to say something just as Bannerman called into the house, "You coming to help me or not?"

* * *

She'd done it because she was worried about him.

Ky couldn't get that statement out of his mind.

Or, how she'd felt in his arms.

And let's not forget the way she tasted.

She'd disobeyed him, risked her life, because she had his back.

Ky didn't know whether to be mad, glad, or worried.

It was his job to protect her, not the other way around. He was responsible for her safety and well-being.

But Jesus, she'd purposefully put herself in potential danger by opening that bedroom door without any consideration for her own safety. She'd admitted she hadn't known their intruder was Bannerman until she'd seen his face. Until that moment she'd been prepared to fight the threat with him.

Funny thing was, he knew she could. Gemma was more than capable with a firearm, as she'd proven to him, and equally as able with hand-to-hand maneuvers.

The second her words penetrated through him, all his anger flew, replaced by something overwhelming. He wouldn't put a label on what he felt, it was crazy to, but something had changed between them. Something he was powerless to fight against and, truthfully, didn't want to.

Her response when he'd taken her in his arms had been surprising. Not to mention mind blowing. She'd never given him one single indication she found him desirable, in fact, until she'd kissed him back, he thought she considered him barely tolerable. But that kiss hadn't been one of tolerance. No, she was fully invested in it and if he wasn't mistaken, she'd been as turned on as he had.

If the alarm hadn't sounded he'd have tossed her over his shoulder and run into his bedroom, dropped her onto the narrow bed and climbed on top of her.

Then again, they might not have made it that far. The kitchen counter certainly looked sturdy enough for what he'd had in mind.

Her giggle pulled him out of his musings. She was standing in the kitchen, her arms leaning on that same counter he'd been thinking about, watching her friend eat the remaining pasta she'd cooked for dinner. Her eyes crinkled at the corners as she laughed.

"So when are you gonna marry me, Cleo?"

Ky's senses went on hyper alert, his insides clenching.

"You are so easy." Gemma rolled her eyes. "Give you a hot, home-cooked meal and you pledge your eternal devotion. That's so lame."

"I'm not easy, I'm smart. I know a good thing when I see it."

"Easy." She nodded and pointed her finger at him. "You don't want someone you might have to—God forbid—share emotions and feelings with. You don't want a wife, you just want someone around who'll feed you and clean up after you. Get a maid."

Bannerman laughed and shoved another forkful of pasta into his mouth. "You know me too well, Cleo."

"And remember what they say about how familiarity breeds contempt," she shot back, with a smirk.

Her eyes flicked to Ky and the smirk died.

"Why do you keep calling her Cleo?"

Ky regarded their visitor through assessing eyes. Roughly the same height as he, Bannerman's shoulders were doorway-wide, his arms and torso looking like they were a frequent occupant of a gym. Ky could still feel the force of the man's elbows against his ribs. It was surprising none were cracked.

Military-cut dark hair framed a wide forehead. His eyes were equally as dark, their expression guarded and closed as he looked across the room at Ky.

"It's because of the way I wear my hair," Gemma said for him.

It took him a moment. When the meaning burst through, he nodded. "Cleopatra."

"He started calling me that one day at the shooting range. It stuck."

"It fits," Bannerman said.

"It sucks."

He grinned at Ky. "She hates it."

"Which," Gemma threw up her hands, "is why he refuses to stop. Typical teenage-boy behavior."

"Yeah, but you love me, admit it, Cleo."

For an answer she blew a raspberry through her lips.

The good natured banter between them struck a quick spark of envy in Ky.

"As much as I love sparring with you, babe," Bannerman said, "I've got some stuff to go over with Agent Pappandreos."

"Oh. What stuff?" Gemma asked. "Can I hear it?"

Bannerman shot a quick glance at Ky, a question in his gaze. "Up to you."

Ky looked at Gemma.

"You know what?" she said. "On second thought, forget it. I'd rather go have a shower."

He tracked her the entire way up to the second floor.

"She's easy on the eyes, isn't she?"

Ky turned to Bannerman. "You're the second person who's said those same words to me in the past week."

Bannerman grinned again. "She's a good kid. And one of the most loyal people I've ever met, especially if you can get past those inch-thick defensive walls she wears like armor."

"Keane mentioned she has trust issues. I've seen it for myself."

"Yeah, she doesn't let a lot of people in, and even when she does, she tends to be guarded. I'm glad, though, she decided not to stay. Josh sent me with some intel for you and I'd rather she not hear it." He pulled out a laptop from a duffel bag he'd brought in from the car, along with groceries and food from Kandy. He'd given Gemma an overnight bag from her sister as well.

"This system is encrypted," Bannerman said as he booted up the laptop. "Josh figured you needed something secure to work with."

"I've actually got my own."

He went into the bedroom and brought back the device Theo had given him. "A friend gave me this before we left DC."

He'd been planning on doing research all day, but the walk in the woods and then the need to burn off his sexual steam with the punching bag had shoved the idea to the back of his mind.

"Let me see that."

Ky handed him the laptop. A few quick keystrokes later, and a low, appreciative whistle sailed passed his pursed lips.

"You got this from a friend?"

Ky nodded.

Bannerman's eyes went to half-mast again as he regarded Ky. "I'd like to meet this friend. This system makes mine," he chinned his laptop, "look like a second-generation throwback."

Ky's lips twitched. "You said you had some intel for me?"

He shifted to his device and typed. "After you got in contact, Josh asked me to do a little digging into Ritandi and his organization."

"I know everything I need to know about Ritandi."

Bannerman shot him speaking glance. "I'm sure that's true. To a point."

"What does that mean?"

Bannerman shrugged and flicked a hand at him. "Look, you're a federal agent. You go by the book because everything you find has to be above board and beyond reproach to get an indictment that sticks."

Ky nodded. "We can't leave any room for his lawyers to wiggle through."

"Right. So you go about obtaining info through legal and judicial avenues."

"Of course."

"I don't."

Ky just stared at him.

"I've got…access is the best word," Bannerman said, "to a whole other level of information. The kind you can't even imagine exists. The kind, if you wormed your way into, even accidentally, could get you killed."

"Who are you? Or should I say, what are you?"

"Nothing but a lowly private eye. But once upon a time, well..."

Ky remembered Gemma telling him Rick Bannerman had been a sniper in, "a previous life."

More than a sniper, he thought. *Much more.*

"So, assuming you found out something I can't use legally," he said, "what is it and how can I use it?"

"I'm going on the assumption the witness Gemma saw eliminated was under wraps and only a very few knew where he was, yes?"

Ky nodded. "Very good, wraps, actually. I haven't been able to figure out why my agents left the hotel with him that day. They were under strict orders to never leave the floor we'd had him sequestered on."

"Orders they disobeyed?"

"Apparently."

"No."

When he didn't respond, Bannerman turned this laptop around so Ky could see the screen. "This is the cell phone call log of your dead agent Jackson Hunter from the day of the killings."

Ky stared down at the screen, speechless. And furious.

"How can you possibly have access to this?"

"Don't get your panties in a twist. Just accept it as a gift, no questions asked."

"A gift?"

"Yeah. Your witness bought it at what time?"

Ky told him.

"Look at the log. An hour and half before they were killed, Hunter received a text from this number." He pointed to the screen. "Do you recognize it?"

"No. Whose is it?"

"That, I can't answer. It's an untraceable number and believe me, I tried. The only thing I can tell you is when I pinged the towers connecting the call, I got bounced through a shitload of routers. The closest I can come to figuring out the origination point is somewhere in DC, New York, or Philadelphia."

"That doesn't tell me anything. It could be anyone who called him, from his wife to another agent at the bureau."

"True, but it's a mighty big coincidence your agents were barred from leaving the hotel for what? Six weeks or so? And then ninety minutes after one of them gets this text, they're out the door and dead. Makes you wonder."

Ky had to agree.

"Any thoughts, then, on why they left?"

Through pursed lips, Ky said, "None."

"My guess, if you want to hear it, is someone told them it was okay to take Calafano from the hotel."

Ky shook his head. "No one had the authority to do that. No one but me. And I certainly didn't give permission for it. Every meal had been ordered in and eaten in the suite we had him secured in."

"Interesting. Who knew where you were keeping Gemma after she was attacked?"

"The remaining agents on my team, my superior, and the agency director."

"No one in justice?"

"No. Since we obviously had a leak, I figured the less people who knew her whereabouts, the better. Why?"

Bannerman typed again for a few seconds. When he was done he turned the screen back to Ky. "This number," he said, indicating the one on the screen he was referring to, "comes up four times on the ASA assigned to the case."

"Barly?"

"Yup. All the calls were made after you had Gemma in seclusion."

"Do you know whose phone the calls were made from?"

Bannerman sat back and lowered his chin, his gaze targeting straight to Ky's. He got the impression he wasn't going to like the answer.

"Yours."

Ky's mouth fell open.

"It's a number personally registered to you."

"That's impossible."

Bannerman nodded. "Josh felt the same way when I told him. That's the only reason you're still sitting here—alive." He said it as if they were discussing what to have for lunch: calmly, without any inflection in his voice.

"If he thought for one minute you were a danger to his sister-in-law," Bannerman continued, "we wouldn't be having this conversation and Gemma would be with me on a flight back to New York while your body rotted in the woods."

Ky believed him.

"So, it looks like someone's setting you up for a fall, son."

Chapter Twelve

Gemma stepped from the shower, wrapped a towel around her body, and swiped the steam off the wall mirror.

The image reflected back at her looked exactly the same as it had that morning. On the outside, she hadn't changed one bit.

On the inside was a whole different story.

How in the name of all that's holy could one kiss affect her so powerfully, change her so completely, and leave her so bamboozled that all she could think of was when could she kiss him again?

Because she really did want to kiss him again. *Really.* Kyros Pappandreos's kiss had been like no other she'd ever received.

His lips had been soft, like a newborn's skin, when they'd trailed along the edge of her jaw, and at the same time hard, solid, and demanding as they took total possession of her mouth.

She could have stood in the kitchen, just kissing him, for the rest of her natural life.

She trailed a finger across her mouth as she stared at herself.

Well, that was a bold-faced lie.

She didn't *just* want to kiss him. She wanted to do a lot more. A whole lot more. Like strip him naked and eat him alive.

Gemma shook her head. The image of Ky pummeling the punching bag in the garage, shirtless, his perfect body bathed in sweat, muscles flexing and extending, shot to the front of her mind. She'd wanted to lick every drop of that sweat off every place it touched his sun-kissed skin.

And then start all over again at the top.

Without even seeming to, he'd stripped all her self-imposed defenses raw as if he'd stripped her naked before him. Gemma never let a man make the first move, sexually. She was always the instigator, taking control of the situation, guiding it, and deciding what she'd allow to happen. She had to be the one in control. If the events that took place during her high school days had taught her anything, it was this.

But Ky had made the first move today without ever asking, and she'd allowed it, which was mindboggling to begin with. What made it even more so was that she hadn't resisted or pulled away. She'd let him assume control and had been a willing participant in the most sensual, fiery, and intoxicating embrace of her life. When his hands cupped her butt and pulled her straight up against what she knew was a major league erection, all she could think about doing was jumping up and wrapping her legs around his waist to get all that length and heat against her own roaring inferno. If Rick Bannerman hadn't made such a dramatic entrance, she could imagine she'd be doing a lot more than kissing Ky at this moment.

A whole lot more.

A quick glance at the bedside digital clock and she saw it was only nine o'clock. Still early, but she was tired, both in mind and body. She pulled on a clean T-shirt and some yoga pants from the suitcase Kandy had sent with Rick, and made her way down the stairs, guided by heated voices.

"I don't know how this is possible," Ky was saying.

"It's not easy, but it certainly can be done. Any hacker worth knowing has the access and capability to—"

"What's not easy?" Gemma asked.

Two sets of eyes trained on her. One pair was flat and as unreadable as always. The pair that resembled a calm ocean had turned stormy, filled with fire and rage.

"What are you guys talking about?"

Gemma noticed Rick slant a look at Ky, who hadn't taken his eyes from her since she entered the room. The same possessive glare she'd seen in them when he'd kissed her was there again. The one that told her she should run for the hills, only her feet weren't listening.

Oh my.

"Your brother-in-law and Bannerman have been looking into how Ritandi discovered where we were keeping you."

Gemma looked at Rick. "And?"

"Before I answer that, I want to ask you another question," he said to Ky.

"Go ahead."

"You called Josh from DC after you'd been attacked while moving Gemma to another location, right?"

"Yes." Ky's lips were pressed together so tight, Gemma barely heard him.

"So, again, who knew where you were relocating her? The same people as before?"

"No. I notified the agents I wanted assigned to the house, my boss, and the two agents who were in the van with us. That's it."

"No one else?"

"No, why?"

Rick didn't answer him. "You need to give me all their names so I can run a comparison. Then we can get a bead on who's setting you up."

"Setting him up? What are you talking about?" Gemma asked.

Succinctly, Rick told her what he and Josh had discovered; all the while Ky was focused on her face, watching her.

"Well that makes no sense," she said when he was done. She turned to address Ky. "If you were involved in this, you had more than enough chances to get me out of the way. Why run with me if you were planning on killing me anyway? It's dumb."

"Maybe not," Rick said.

When they both looked to him, he shrugged. "In a twisted sense, it might be brilliant." He turned his gaze to Ky and narrowed his eyes. "If you are involved, what better place to keep an eye on Gemma than while she's in your care. A few feigned attempts on her life, a few location switches, and then suddenly, bam! She dies and you can't be suspected because you've done everything in your power to keep her alive. It's a tragedy she's dead, but nothing points to you."

Gemma crossed her arms over her chest and cocked her head to one side, her lips pulling down at the corners. "That's just stupid. You just said these phone calls point to him."

Rick nodded.

"So if they do, then he'd be suspected. That blows your theory to crap."

"Only if the calls were discovered," Ky said.

Rick shot a finger at him. "Right. It's safe to say whoever orchestrated this is going to pin Gemma's death on you. Especially—" he stopped and cast a quick glance at her.

Gemma knew immediately what he'd been about to say. She turned to Ky. "Especially if you die, too. Because then you couldn't defend yourself against any allegations or charges. You'd be guilty after the fact."

The air in the room chilled and Gemma squeezed herself tighter.

"So," Rick said again, "who hates you enough to want to kill you and destroy your reputation in the bargain?"

* * *

It was a good question.

Ky stood and walked to the kitchen, head spinning. He grabbed some bottled waters from the kitchen and handed one to Gemma when he returned. A little shock sparked through him when his fingers skimmed hers and by the way she sucked in a fast breath, he knew she'd felt it, too.

"Ritandi is, of course, the name that heads the list," he said, sitting. "I've been a bug up his ass for three years. When I arrested Calafano I could practically hear him screaming."

"So it makes sense, then, he got to somebody in the bureau, maybe even on your team."

Ky sighed. "Unfortunately, it does."

He was still having a great deal of difficulty thinking any of the men he'd handpicked for his investigative team could be involved. He'd worked side by side with these men for over three years. He knew their families, their kids' names. He'd worked diligently to establish their trust and confidence in him as their team leader. To suspect one of them may be something they weren't, well, it was hard to imagine.

His gaze lifted to Gemma. She stood opposite from where he sat, the water bottle in her hand, a look of quiet introspection on her beautiful face. He'd give his right nut to know what she was thinking.

And his left one to take her in his arms again and disappear into her.

"Listen kids, I'm beat." Bannerman rose and stretched. "I've been on the road since late last night without any sleep, so I'm heading up. Get me those names and we'll start fresh in the morning, 'kay?"

Ky nodded.

Rick stopped, kissed Gemma on the forehead and swiped a finger down her cheek as he'd done earlier. "Get some sleep, Cleo. You're looking haggard."

It took every bit of control Ky could muster not to drag her away from him.

Gemma stuck her tongue out at Bannerman, and said, "I love you, too, *old man*."

With a chuckle, he jogged up the stairs. It was in that moment Ky realized the man would be sleeping in the room next to Gemma's. The room with one of the king-sized beds.

When Gemma turned her gaze back to him, her eyes narrowed. "What?"

Ky waited a beat. "You and Bannerman?" He cocked his head.

"Yeah?"

Ky just lifted his brow, his question clear.

"Me and Rick? Good Lord, *no!*"

"You two seem pretty…in sync."

"Is that what the kids are calling it these days?"

Ky bit the inside of his cheek.

Gemma sighed and rubbed her hands along her thighs. "He's like an older, totally annoying brother. The kind you love and who'll stick up for you in a fight, but who you really can only take in small doses because he's such a pain in the ass most of the time." She shrugged and added, "We've worked together on a few surveillance cases. I told you that the day we met."

He nodded.

"I've helped him with photography, and he's helped me with improving my shooting skills. That's it."

"He likes to touch you," Ky said before he could stop himself.

He sounded like a jealous idiot.

She rolled her eyes, shook her head, "Rick likes to touch *all* women. But it doesn't mean anything. Not to me, anyway."

Ky wanted to tell her how happy that made him, but he kept it to himself.

"Look, I originally came down here to say good night. I got a little sidetracked with all this talk of agency moles and potential deaths."

She crossed her arms over her chest again. "I wanted to tell you I'll do breakfast duty in the morning. You don't have to cook every meal. I can pitch in."

"I like cooking," he said, simply. "It…I don't know," he swiped a hand in the air, "calms me. Helps me to think. To focus."

Gemma nodded. "I get that. Kandy's the same way, but you don't have to do all and be all. I can manage. Dinner tasted okay, right?"

His mind immediately flew to how she'd tasted, not the pasta. The food had been nourishment for his body, but sampling her, savoring her, had been nourishment for his soul. His thoughts must have shown in his eyes because her face went bright pink and she bit down on her bottom lip again, a sign he'd noticed of nerves building in her.

"Dinner was delicious," he said.

He stood and crossed to her. He shouldn't do this. Not here. Not now. But he had to know the truth. Had to know what was in her mind.

When he was within the distance of a breath from her, he stopped and circled his hands around her upper arms. She jumped, ever so slightly, at his touch, but her shoulders immediately relaxed and he felt her lean into him, not retract.

"You believe me when I tell you I'm not involved in any of this, right?"

He captured her gaze with his own, wanting—*needing*—to see the truth in her answer.

Without a moment's hesitation she said, "Of course I do."

"Why?"

"Why do I believe you?"

He nodded.

Her eyes never left his. "Because you're one of the good guys, through and through. I knew it the moment I met you." Her eyes darted between his. "You were obnoxious, overbearing, and so arrogantly alpha, you practically oozed *cop* from every pore."

His lips twitched at the description. He knew it wasn't far off the mark.

"You'd never sell out your men. Or anyone close to you."

"You seem awfully sure."

She rolled her eyes again. "*Please.* In the brief time I was with you and Jon, I saw for myself the respect and loyalty you two had for one another. You can't fake that."

Ky's insides calmed and settled.

"Don't forget," she added, "I'm a trained observer. I see things most people miss. My internal bullshit-ometer is the best there is. I never doubt it."

He squeezed her arms. What he really wanted to do was yank her to his chest, put his mouth on hers again and slake the waterfall of desire cascading wildly within him.

Her belief in him was monumental. She may never admit it, her pride might not let her, but he knew she trusted him. And to Ky, trust was everything.

When he lowered his hands to his thighs he swore he heard a tiny whine blow through her lips.

He took a step back, never breaking eye contact with her.

Confusion creased her flawless brow and her luscious lips pulled into the hottest pout he'd ever seen. He was as hard as steel and the pressure of his erection pushing against his zipper was growing more uncomfortable by the second.

Gemma crossed her hands to the spot he'd just held and said, "Well, I guess I'll say good night then. Finally."

Ky nodded and dropped his hands into his pockets. "I'll make sure everything is safe and secure before I call it a night."

Gemma stared at him and then shook her head. As she walked away from him she muttered, "No surprise, there."

Once she closed the bedroom door and was out of sight, Ky fell back into his chair and dropped his head into his hands. With a deep inhale, he settled back, legs splayed, and his gaze flicked to Theo's laptop.

Work. He needed to work.

He had to get his mind off what he really wanted, which was to have Gemma underneath him, screaming his name while he made her come as many times as he could manage.

He groaned and readjusted himself, the pressure in his crotch growing at the image dancing across his imagination.

The scene in the kitchen jerked back to his mind and he remembered every sensation that had gone through him at the whisper-soft feel of her naked skin under his hands, the erotic sound of her tiny gasps as he sucked on her tongue, even the way he knew without a doubt her panties were wet when he'd snaked his knee between her legs.

The pressure in his pants grew almost unbearable.

He took several deep breaths and started reciting the names of the Greek gods in his head to clear his mind.

After a few minutes, he rose, took the laptop with him and went to his room.

* * *

Gemma rolled over and sighed.

Again.

She'd been trying to fall asleep for the past two hours to no avail. Every time she closed her eyes, all she could see was Ky's face as he'd kissed her in the kitchen.

Wild and wanting. Hot and steamy. So ridiculously sexy all she could remembering thinking was *kiss me, please, kiss me.* And when he did, holy mother!

Gemma flipped to her back and blew out an exasperated breath.

How had she gone from loathing the man to wanting his lips on hers—and on all her other body parts, too? She hadn't been fibbing when she told him she believed he had nothing to do with anything that had happened. The man was as rock solid and steady as they came, and he'd treated her with nothing but professionalism and actual concern.

She hated to admit it but she trusted him. To her core. After just a few days of being together she knew he'd do whatever it took to keep her safe. He'd proven it time and again.

Trust was the one thing Gemma never gave freely. But Ky had earned it—multiple times over.

Wiggling to her side, she drew her knees to her chest, unable to get comfortable no matter what position she got into, and she knew the reason why.

She didn't want to be in this bed, alone, and wanting.

She wanted to be in Ky's bed, with him, and satisfied.

It took one second to make her decision.

When she opened her bedroom door, the living room lights were off, but the small glow from the range hood illuminated all she needed to see as she made her way down the stairs.

From the kitchen, a small beam of light slipped through the partially opened door to his room.

Gemma licked her lips, gave a tiny knock, and opened the door at the same time.

Ky's eyes tracked on her immediately. Shirtless, he was sitting up in bed, the laptop across his thighs.

"Gemma?" His voice was soft, due to the hour, raspy and filled with just enough late night promise to make her fingertips tingle.

"You moved the Lucy and Ricky beds together." She closed the door and leaned back against it.

Ky glanced down at the beds and shrugged. "It's more comfortable because I'm so tall. I can stretch out better."

"Oh."

He stared at her for a few beats. "What's wrong?"

"Nothing. Why do you always think there's something wrong when I want to talk to you?"

His left eyebrow cocked. "Because there usually is."

Gemma pouted. "I just want to…talk."

And there went the right eyebrow in the same direction. "Talk?"

Gemma licked her lips and inched into the room.

He stayed silent as she approached the bed. Since he was reclined in the middle of it, she slid down on the edge and sat, drawing one leg up on the bed, bent, facing him.

Now that she was here, the realization that this might not be the best idea she'd had in a while shot through her. With any other guy she knew what do, how to convey what she wanted.

But Ky wasn't any other guy, as he'd proved all too many times.

"Yes. I want, well—" She stopped, bit down on the side of her cheek.

The air in the room suddenly changed and Gemma swore she heard his breath catch.

"What?" The low, soft, seductive timbre in his voice sent her thighs to shaking.

"Were you working?" She chinned the laptop.

"If you could call it that." He took a breath and scrubbed his hands down his face. "I'm trying to find any link I can between those phone calls Bannerman found and my men."

"Any luck?"

"None. I don't know whether to be happy or mad that I can't. It makes no sense. I know all these men. I vetted them." His gaze lit on her face. "But you didn't come in here to ask me about this."

Because it wasn't a question, she didn't respond.

"Gemma, come on. Tell me what's wrong, what's bothering you."

The Gemma Laine she showed the world, the confident, snarky, assertive one never at a loss for words and always able to state what she wanted in no uncertain terms, wanted to tell him, "What's bothering me is that you're not inside me right now."

The real Gemma, the shy, uncertain, untrusting one, couldn't bring herself to be the aggressor this time. The kiss they'd shared should have been proof enough he wanted her, but she just wasn't totally sure, a fact that unnerved her.

"I want to know why you kissed me," she blurted. "Before. You know? In the kitchen."

His face could have been a virgin slab of stone. He held her stare a few seconds, then his shoulders relaxed and he closed the laptop. He stretched across the bed to place it on the night table.

Gemma's pulse kicked up at the length of long, toned, and wickedly hard muscles rippling across his back. Her fingers actually itched to reach out and run across them.

"I want to apologize for that." He sat back again. "I shouldn't have. It wasn't very...professional."

Deflated, she said, "Oh. I thought..."

"What?"

"That, you know." She waved a hand in the air. "You, well, wanted to..." She blew out a breath and closed her eyes. "This was so much easier when I was talking about it in my head."

A movement on the bed had her opening her eyes. Ky had shifted toward her, enough that she could see he wore black silk boxers, the sound of the material as it whispered across the sheets intoxicatingly soft and supple. And if she wasn't mistaken, a very large, very solid, very *pulsing* erection was barely hidden under them.

"The simple truth is I did it because I wanted to," he told her.

"Really?"

Jesus, Gemma, do you have to sound so hopeful and needy?

"Yes, really. You were upset and emotional—"

"I was not emotional!"

"—and I felt bad for you."

The hope sailed away in a heartbeat. "You kissed me because you felt bad for me?"

"Yes-NO!" He scrubbed his hands down his face again and took another breath. "That's not what I meant."

"That's what you said."

"Gemma, please." His eyes lasered on hers. "I kissed you for several reasons, but mostly because I wanted to and couldn't convince myself right then why I shouldn't."

Okay, that shot some hope back into her. "Why would you need to convince yourself you shouldn't? It's not like I was fighting you. Or not kissing you back."

"Do you really need me to lay all the reasons out for you?"

She shrugged.

"First," he ticked one index finger with other, "you're under my care. It's my job to keep you safe and secure, and I take my responsibilities very seriously. Two, it's frowned on for agents to get involved with civilians in cases like this no matter how attracted to them they are. Emotions and physical desires have a way of shifting focus off the main objective. And three, you can barely tolerate being in the same room with me. I was staggered when you didn't drop-kick me in the balls afterward."

She cocked her head at him and wrinkled her nose. Okay, this might not be as hard as she thought it would.

"One," she ticked her own fingers together now, mimicking him, "It may be your job to keep me safe and secure, but I'm no slouch. I can take care of myself if I have to. I've proven that."

"But—"

"*Two*, no one in the FBI is here right now, watching and evaluating what you're doing or how you're acting toward me—"

"—I know how I'm acting."

"And number three is just too stupid to even really comment on. We've been constantly together for almost a week. Living, eating, running from maniacs together, so forget that excuse. It doesn't hold water. Let's remember, I *did* kiss you back."

He didn't say anything for a moment. Then, he shifted his legs, dropping them to the side of the bed, glared at her, and said, "Stupid?"

"Yeah. Major league stupid."

Her gaze bore right through his, challenging, not giving an inch.

His St. Michael medallion dangled in the cavern of his pecs, swaying as he moved closer to her, so close she could smell the clean, fresh scent of the soap he'd used in the shower. So close, she could see his eyes darken as he looked at her, those gorgeous seafoam colors roaming over her face and turning stormy. So close, she did what she'd been dreaming of doing since she first saw him without a shirt, drenched in sweat and looking like a warrior: she leaned in and trailed her tongue along the angle of his jaw. He didn't move, but did hiss in a breath, his abdominal muscles contracting inward.

A fine line of spikey stubble tickled her tongue and made her want to explore more.

Ky choked. "Did you just…lick me?"

When she pulled back there was surprised mirth crinkling in the corners of his narrowed eyes, his lips twisting up at the corners.

"Yeah," she sighed. "I've been wanting to do that for days."

Ky's mouth straightened. "You've been wanting to…lick me… for days?"

She nodded, feeling her cheeks burn like wildfire. Oh well, here goes nothing…

She kept her gaze steady, and said, "Well, yeah. Ever since that morning in the basement when we worked out together."

Something in his eyes shifted; eased.

"You were all sweaty and…hot."

And then they darkened again, but this time not in anger. No. This time the heat in his eyes wasn't to be laid at fury's door, but at something deeper, more primal. Sensual.

"And to be honest," she added, "I want to do more than just lick you. But, yeah. Days."

She didn't even have time to process what he was doing. Before she could blink Ky hauled her up to her feet by her arms and flattened her body against his. One hand snaked around her waist holding in her place, while the other cupped the back of her neck. His mouth hovered a breath from hers when he said, "You realize what you've just said, right?"

"That I've wanted you…like this, for days?" She nodded.

She watched the hard line of his jaw contract as he swallowed, his gaze intense and filled with raw hunger and she was his meal.

Oh my.

"Be sure, Gemma. Be very sure this is what you want to happen between us. I've been walking around as hard as nails, so before this goes anywhere, goes any further, be sure, because I don't think I'll be able to stop once we start."

Encouraged by those words more than she could possibly imagine, Gemma coiled one hand around Ky's neck and tugged. Against his lips she challenged, "Prove it."

His mouth crushed hers, possessed it, claimed it. His tongue plundered, took hers prisoner and stroked it with his own. He kissed her as if he were starved for a lifetime, drawing every bit of nourishment and sustenance he could from her.

And then he went back for more.

Her heart was pounding so wildly in her chest she swore she could hear it thumping in the air around them.

The man had a perfect mouth for kissing: hard, insistent, and punishingly gentle. If she was never kissed by another man, she'd die knowing what it was to be kissed by a man with no equal.

The hand at her waist crept below the band of her pajama shorts, roved along the curve of one butt cheek and squeezed. Gemma's body reacted unconsciously by contracting her muscles. Ky's lips danced into a smile as he pulled back from the kiss, a tiny sucking sound filling the air. His bedroom eyes twinkled down at her as he nuzzled her nose. "You've got the sweetest ass." His other hand followed the first. "Watching you and not being able to touch it has been driving me nuts."

While he squeezed them both, Gemma grabbed his head and dragged him back to kiss her. "Squats. Thousands of them," she said as she nipped at his bottom lip and kissed her way along his jaw. At the little notch between his neck and shoulder, she opened her lips, wet the spot with her tongue and sucked.

His entire body went rigid. A feeling of feminine supremacy eclipsed through her at eliciting such a reaction. The man oozed control from every pore. She was dying to see what would happen when he lost it and know she was the cause.

"You taste so damn good." She pulled his earlobe into her mouth and bit down.

In the next second she was flat on her back, the mattress springs bouncing against her.

Ky stared down at her, his eyes raking her body in one smooth, possessive glide. When his gaze settled on the top of her thighs, she squirmed, trying to draw her legs up. His hands caught her knees.

"No."

That one, small word was filled with such authority, such command, she was powerless against it.

He spread her legs apart with the flick of his hand. Even through the thin material of the shorts covering her, Gemma felt completely exposed.

And more turned on than she could ever remember.

He bunched the hem of her short T-shirt and pushed it up over her belly, his mouth following the shirt's trek, up, until he got to the underside of her breasts, where he stopped. The warm, moist sensation of his breath on her skin was glorious.

"Still sure?" he asked, looking her square in the eyes.

"Yup."

He lifted the shirt, exposing her breasts, then tugged it over her head and tossed it behind him. He weighed each breast in his hands, holding them as if they were precious jewels. With a quick glance at her, he bent his head, his mouth sucking one nipple to a hardened point, then the other.

Gemma squirmed against the sheets. Each time his tongue tugged, an invisible beat of desire pulsed to the lower part of her body. It was almost painful. Almost. But among the pain was exquisite pleasure.

"You're so beautiful," he whispered against her rib cage. "So soft."

He plumped her breasts in his hands. "So perfect."

Sitting back on his knees, his wove his fingers under the waistband of her shorts, and slunk his gaze up to hers again. Fiery didn't begin to do justice to the amount of heat staring at her.

"Still sure?" he asked again in that wicked bedroom voice that he had to know no sane woman could resist.

Gemma took a breath, loving that he thought enough of her to give her the chance of an out.

But she didn't want an out. She wanted an in—as in *him*. *In* her.

"Abso-friggin-lutely."

And let's not forget that sexy leer. He had to know what that little lift of the corners of his mouth did to the pulses of women in the room. Any room.

Slowly, so slow she grew impatient with the urgent need to feel him inside her, Ky drew her shorts down, exposing her skin inch by inch, while his mouth and tongue trailed after. She felt singed by fire every place he crossed.

Gemma lifted her hips so he could draw the shorts over her butt, her movement nudging her mound straight into his lips. When she gasped, he simply chuckled, dragged his nose and mouth from one side of her to the other, licking his way across. She closed her eyes and thanked the gods of beauty and timing she'd gone for a waxing the week before. Her shorts hit the floor with a dull thud.

Her eyes flew open when she realized Ky had stopped his travels.

He was sitting back on his haunches, his hands fisted on his thighs, just staring down at her. The bottom half of her.

"What?" she said, growing nervous and unsure. Did he not like a woman to be groomed? What is too much? Not enough?

She swore he growled, then murmured something low and quick, in Greek.

"That sounded hot. Tell me what it means." She pushed up on her elbows.

He cocked his head and lifted his gaze from her naked crotch to her eyes.

Good lord, the man invented the smoldering stare. She actually felt the moisture begin to drip between her legs from the look alone.

"It loses a little something in the translation," he told her, his voice dark and low as he gripped her thighs between his fingers and squeezed. "It doesn't sound as…romantic…in English."

"I don't need romantic words. What did you say?"

He uttered the oath she'd heard come from him before. "Roughly," he told her, "I said I want to fuck you six ways from Sunday."

Chapter Thirteen

Her eyes widened to the size of saucers, her mouth falling open into the sexiest, most perfect *O* he'd ever seen.

She swallowed. Then did it again.

"Still sure?"

He watched the question penetrate. A tiny head bob, and then "go for it," told him everything he needed to know.

In one swift move, he slid his hands under her butt, lifted her and settled his mouth between her legs, his tongue sliding into all her heat.

"Oh, sweet Jesus!" she gasped.

"Baby, you're drenched." He dropped a kiss on each thigh, then dragged his mouth to the top of them.

Little whimpers broke from the back of her throat when he dipped his tongue inside and tasted her, lapping every inch he could reach.

He found the little button of flesh, hidden at the top, licked it once, then sucked it into his mouth, his tongue swirling around it, while he pumped two fingers inside her.

Her body vibrated against him as his fingers curled and gently scraped at her walls, his tongue dedicated to pleasuring her.

Gemma's hips bucked off the bed, her insides clenching and squeezing around his fingers. From his vantage point he watched her shove her fist into her mouth to drown the scream of the climax whipping through her. Her breaths came in short, hard spurts, her breasts jumping with each swift intake of air. With his free hand he reached up and rolled one of her nipples between his fingers.

The muscles in her thighs clenched like a vise around him. One hand braced at the back of his head, holding him in place as he stayed with her until she rode the wave home.

God, she was beautiful, even more than he'd fantasized she could be. She might not think she needed romantic words, but watching her come, knowing he was the cause of such pleasure, made him want to say them to her.

When she opened her eyes, polished sapphires shined back at him.

He slid his fingers from inside her and sucked them into his mouth, smiling as he watched her face react.

She sat up in a flash and before he could draw breath she had him flat on his own back, her hands pushing his shoulders down against the bed, forcing him there as she straddled him.

He felt all her wet heat tantalizingly close, just nuzzling the erection poking through his boxers. He let out a ragged breath so deep his abdomen went concave with the effort.

Sitting on top of him, her weight balanced on her knees, he throbbed against her, wanting, needing, release.

Like a hunter finding prey, Gemma smiled down at him as she ground herself against him, then quickly pulled back.

"Are you sure you want to do this?" Her smile turned wicked and playful as she gave his words back to him. "Be sure you want this to happen between us. I've been walking around wet and wanting for days"—she bent to lick his nipple—"so be sure, because"—she licked the other one—"I *know* I won't be able to stop if we keep going."

He lifted his shoulders and pushed against her hold to grab the back of her neck and yank her in close.

"Still sure?" she asked and then swiped her tongue across his chin.

"Abso-frigging-lutely."

He reversed their positions before she could blink and nestled himself between her thighs, nudging them apart with his knees.

If it was physically possible he went harder when she giggled.

Gemma slid her hands along his back until they were inside his boxers. "Take these off," she commanded, pushing them off his waist and down over his butt. "Now."

"Bossy, much?" He shifted back on his knees and yanked them down and off, tossing them carelessly to the floor.

He kept a watchful look on her eyes. His heart stopped for a few beats when they drifted down to see him, naked and pulsing, and turned the color of ripe blueberries after a rainfall: shiny, moist, rich.

Gemma reached out and fisted her hand around his shaft.

"Talk about someone being perfect," she whispered. She ran her thumb along the top edge of him and massaged the silky drop of fluid she found around its head.

Ky threw back his head, stretching his neck and digging deep for control. The precise, smooth friction of her hand as it moved up and down the length of him was tortuous ecstasy. When her hand dipped down to cup his balls, he covered it with his own.

"Baby, you need to stop that or this will be over way too soon."

Smiling, she slid her hands around his back and pulled him down on top of her. "We wouldn't want that," she said against his lips.

Kissing her was an experience all in itself. From the back of his mind the notion bloomed that he could be happy for the rest of his life just kissing Gemma Laine.

Soon, too soon, he needed to do more than just kiss her.

Tucked between her legs, his erection pressed against her stomach and throbbing for release, her legs wrapped around his waist, he broke from her lips, touched his forehead to hers and inhaled deeply.

Gemma opened her eyes. While her nails raked gently up and down his back and across his shoulders, she said, "Okay. My turn to ask. What's wrong?"

He dropped a soft kiss to her nose. "I want to be inside you." His lips dragged to her neck, kissed the sweet spot behind her ear. When her entire body shuddered against him, he had to count to ten so he wouldn't embarrass himself and spill all over her. "I want to pound into you hard and fast, over and over, until I make you scream when you come."

Gemma moaned and tightened her legs around him.

"And then I want to do it all again."

An oath whispered through her lips. "Okay." She swallowed. "Are you asking permission? Because if you are then, *hell yeah*. Go for it."

How could a woman make him so hard he could drill through concrete and laugh at the same time?

He kissed her lips again and smiled. "I was pretty confident you were already on board," he told her, moving to kiss her cheek, then up to her brows.

"Okay, so? What are you waiting for?" She wiggled her hips again, making him blind for a second.

He lifted his head and looked down at her face, pinched now in confusion.

"I don't have anything to protect you with."

"Oh." Her expression cleared. "*Oh!*"

"I didn't plan on this...happening between us. I'm not prepared the way I should be. I don't want to take a chance on you getting pregnant." Her eyes shifted, softened. She lifted a hand to his cheek. He kissed her palm and swore he heard her sigh.

"Move back." She lifted herself and shoved against him. He sat back on his knees.

"Lay down," she commanded.

His lips twisted. "You like giving orders."

"Trust me, this time you'll be glad you obeyed," she said, while settling next to him.

"Now," she molded her hand against his erection and tugged. "While I'd simply love to have you inside me," she licked him from bottom to top on the underside of his shaft, "pounding hard and fast until I came screaming," she trailed her tongue down the other side, "it'll be more fun for me to watch while I make you come, screaming." She took him, all of him, in her mouth.

Ky almost shot off the bed. *Christ,* she was gonna kill him. He was just about to tell her that when all logical, sentient, conscious, thought flew from his head. Her hand followed her mouth as she pumped him up and down, her tongue doing wild and imaginative things to his tip.

No amount of counting, conjugating Greek verbs, or reciting geometry theorems could calm him. He felt a sharp twist in his lower back coil deeper and speed to his groin as Gemma's pace quickened.

When he came, just quick enough to clamp his lips together before he really did scream her name, she stayed with him until the end, as he had her, her lips cuddled around him with every thrust and explosion until he was empty.

The bed shifted, then the sound of the water running in the adjoining bathroom met his ears. Next time, he'd make sure to have a condom. No, several.

His eyes flew open to stare at the ceiling.

Next time.

Christ, his pulse hadn't even calmed yet and he was already thinking of next time. He closed his eyes again.

Yeah, there was gonna be a next time with Gemma. Many next times. They'd started something he wanted, needed to explore further. She was such a dichotomy of independence and need; physically tough, yet he sensed she was emotionally fragile. The hard exterior she showed the world, he knew hid the heart of a softie. She was an awful lot like the women in his own family. More times than he could remember his father had claimed the true head of the family was the woman because she had the strength of a lion and the heart of a dove.

Yeah, there were going to be many, many more *next times* with Gemma Laine.

His breathing hadn't calmed, his heart still hammering against his ribs when she came back into the room.

Flat on his back, his arms splayed at his sides, he didn't want to move; couldn't if he had to.

He opened his eyes again and found her standing next to the bed twisting her T-shirt and shorts in her hands, looking down at him. The corner of her bottom lip was tucked between her teeth.

He reached out a hand to her, and, when she slipped hers into it, he tugged her back down on the bed. "You okay?"

She nodded.

Her gaze dropped to the clothes in her hands and he realized she was nervous. Gone was the bravado and cockiness of just a few minutes before. He squeezed the hand he held. "Gemma, look at me."

When she did, he worried his thumb across her knuckles. "Stay?"

Surprise rose to her eyes first then traveled down to her mouth. He thought she was going to refuse, so before she could he added, "please?"

This time, when the surprise grew, she grinned. "I don't usually do sleepovers."

He understood since he didn't make a habit of them either.

But.

"Well," he shifted his head on the pillow and kept her hand in his, "it's not like a real sleepover. You room is just a few yards away, not in another location. It's really you're just sleeping in a different bed in the same house. Trying a new one on for size."

That glorious giggle was back and Ky swore he could live off just the sound of it and the expression on her face when she made it.

Her pajamas were tossed unceremoniously back onto the floor. Ky shifted, dragged the sheets down and then pulled her under with him.

Spooning, he wrapped an arm around her waist to hold her in place and smiled when she grabbed his wrist.

"Get some sleep," he said into her hair, inhaling the fragrance of cherries lingering there. For the rest of his life he knew he'd associate the scent with Gemma.

"I'm really glad we…talked," she whispered sleepily a few minutes later.

Ky fell asleep with a smile.

* * *

With extreme care so she wouldn't disturb him, Gemma unwrapped Ky's hand from around her waist. One finger, then the next, and then the next until, finally, he stirred, shifted, and fell to his back, still sound asleep. The medallion at his neck slipped to the side of the pillow. Gemma smoothed its raised edges and regarded the man lying next to her, the first and only man she'd ever spent an entire night with.

His hair looked like he'd just combed it, even though she'd almost pulled it bald the times he'd had his head between her legs during the night. After their first...talk...he'd woken her twice more, taking his time to wring any number of orgasms from her—she'd stopped counting at four—to the two more she brought from him.

In sleep his features were comfortable and relaxed. Gone was the coiled tension he'd been filled with since she'd first met him. She'd been able to give him a few hours of escape, as he'd done for her.

But now it was morning.

Watching him, she slid to the side of the bed, dropped one foot, then the other, onto the floor and eased up to stand. She crept to where she'd thrown her clothes, grabbed them and then went into the adjoining bathroom. When she was dressed, she exited through the hallway door.

The house was silent as she made her way back to her own room to ready for the day.

The connecting bathroom door was open and when she peeked in, Rick's room was empty, the bed made.

She hadn't known he was an early riser.

After washing and dressing in fresh yoga pants and a T-shirt, the majority of the clothing style Kandy had packed for her, she went downstairs to see what she could make them all for breakfast.

From the kitchen, she heard the water from the downstairs' shower go on.

So. He was awake.

Would he act any different toward her this morning? Would she? Gemma didn't do mornings after for a reason. All the speculation, the overthinking, the analyzing of what had been shared the night before; what did it mean, if anything other than a slaking of a physical need. What it could mean if continued.

Ky was such a professional Gemma worried he'd be filled with regrets at sleeping with the person he was responsible for protecting. Knowing how seriously he took his job and having seen it for herself, she didn't want him to feel sorry for what they'd shared during the night. She certainly didn't.

And they had shared something, some…connection. She could admit she'd never been so free and uninhibited with a man as she had been with Ky. Forget that he had the kind of body a woman, any woman, would want to run her hands and tongue over. Forget that just hearing the raspy, seductive bedroom timbre in his voice made her want to get naked and busy in a heartbeat. And forget the way he'd been considerate enough to give her multiple outs before they got too hot and heavy. Forgetting all those things, she actually *liked* him.

She'd been more intimate with him than with any other man she'd ever been with, and, in reality, they hadn't even slept together. They'd done everything but, and she'd felt more fulfilled, more satisfied, more just plain wanted than she could remember ever feeling.

Before he'd asked her to spend the night in his bed, she'd been wondering how she could broach the subject and ask him if she could stay without sounding needy or clingy. She'd been telling him the truth when she said she never stayed over at a lover's house. Gemma didn't feel the need to cuddle and share a bed for the night. Sex was one thing; tenderness and affection were something entirely else. She didn't do intimacy, didn't share emotions.

Until last night.

Last night, she'd wanted to fall asleep with Ky's arms around her; wanted to lie next to him all night, luxuriating in his warmth, listening to him breathe; she wanted to wake up with him.

He'd stripped her of all the protective maneuvers to safeguard her heart and pride.

Never let a guy get close enough to see your heart, your true self. It was a creed she'd lived by all her adult life, in every dealing with men she'd had.

Gemma dated. Often. Dinner, drinks, a few Broadway shows and a nightclub now and then. She didn't sleep with most of the men she dated, though. The guy usually got the message he wasn't wanted *in that way* and the offers to go out stopped. But they would remain cordial to one another, and no hearts were ever fractured or broken. It was a system she'd cultivated, and had some measure of success with, since none of her dates ever had a bad word to say about her.

But she hadn't dated Ky, and yet, somehow, he'd gotten her to break all her rules and personal commandments.

How? How had he done it?

Gemma shook her head. She wouldn't think about that now, afraid the answers might not be the ones she really wanted to hear.

In the past, Gemma had been gone before breakfast had ever been a thought. Not possible now since they were basically imprisoned in the house. She had to face Ky, face what they'd done. Face what they'd shared. For some strange reason she couldn't name, she wasn't as unnerved by the prospect as she would have thought she'd be.

Her one hope was he'd felt the same connection she had. Until she knew, though, she'd play it cool. It wouldn't do to have him know how much she'd treasured the night.

She opened the fresh bread Rick had brought with him, took the eggs and milk from the refrigerator, and snooped around in the cabinets until she found some nutmeg, cinnamon sugar, and apple pie spice.

The pan had just come to temperature, the butter sizzling, when Ky came out of his bedroom adjusting the collar on his shirt.

She'd told herself she wouldn't react to him until she was able to gauge his mood. The moment their gazes connected across the counter, she knew that was impossible. The fingers holding the spatula gripped the utensil harder. The quickened sound of her breathing filled the small cooking space, making it sound as if she stood in an echo chamber.

He looked, well…like a man who'd spent the night having sex: content, relaxed, sated. And as drop-dead gorgeous as usual. His sun-kissed hair was damp from the shower and finger-combed in place, his skin faintly flushed. His eyes were alert and when they zeroed in on her, she watched them rake across her face, a silent question in them.

"Good morning," she said, hating the tiny tremble in her voice.

Ky nodded. "Morning."

"I-I'm making French toast. For breakfast. We never got to eat yours the other day, and I, well, I've been craving it ever since then and now that we have the ingredients, I figured, why not? We haven't exactly been eating too well for the past few days."

Jesus, Gemma, shut up!

She clamped her mouth closed, mortified by her nerves. Turning back to the stove, she tossed in a few slices of the bread she'd already soaked. She hadn't even known Ky'd moved until she felt the air surrounding her shift and heat. When his lips brushed her ear—not a kiss, but almost—she startled.

His hand settled on her lower back. In that quiet, low and pelvis clenching voice he said, "First a sleepover and now breakfast. I'm feeling pretty grateful on both counts. And French toast, to boot."

When he chuckled and squeezed her waist she almost dropped the spatula.

She turned to him, an acerbic retort on her lips and simply forgot what she wanted to say when he pulled her into his arms and kissed her. The spatula hit the counter, freeing both her hands, which flew immediately around his neck and clutched.

He deepened the kiss, parting her lips with his tongue and then pillaging. When her knees started to shake he simply pushed her back until she hit the counter, never once breaking the kiss. His leg insinuated itself between her thighs, rubbing along her mound and her body shook all the way to her unshod toes.

Her worried thoughts of a few moments ago dissipated with each insistent lap and nip of his mouth. How could she have ever thought she could play it cool with him after last night? One look, one kiss, one swipe of his body against hers and she was lost.

Good Lord, the man had a mouth created for kissing.

His lips left hers to slide along her cheek, behind her ear, along her neck.

"Gemma?" He sucked her ear lobe between his teeth and gently bit down.

Her entire body hummed with arousal. "Hmmmm?"

"You smell like cinnamon and sugar." He licked her chin and crossed to her other side. "And you taste like…heaven."

Gemma tilted her head back and closed her eyes, giving herself up to the feel of his mouth caressing her body. She was starting to rethink her whole morning after avoidance. If this was what waited for her after a *sleepover*, well, why would she ever evade it?

"Baby, something's burning." Ky's mouth found the sweet spot at her collar and licked.

"Hmmm. It's me."

Oh, Christ! Did she really say that out loud?

A warm, deep chuckle blew into her ear as he squeezed her butt between his hands. "In addition to you," he said.

Gemma's eyes flew open. "*My toast.*" She pushed against the solid concrete wall of his chest and turned. The bread she'd placed in the pan was sizzling.

"Shit! Shit! Shit!" She grabbed the fallen spatula and turned each blackened piece over, the smoky smell of burning bread filling the air.

"These are toast. Literally." She threw them into the sink and ran cool water over them.

When he laughed behind her, she turned and glared at him. "You shouldn't distract a girl like that when she's cooking." The smoke detector shrilled on a second later, exploding into the room. Gemma dropped the pan into the sink and yelped. "Oh, great!"

Rick bolted into the kitchen from the door leading out to the garage a heartbeat later. He was sopping wet, sweat cascading down his entire body. A Glock poised in his hand, his gaze bounced from Gemma to Ky and then to the smoke wafting up from the sink.

Without a word, he slid his gun into the back waistband of his sweatpants and disappeared into the pantry. The smoke alarm quieted.

When he came back into the kitchen, his eyes found Gemma. With his hands fisted at his waist, a half twist to his lips, he said, "I am so busting you to Kandy."

"Traitor," Gemma mumbled. "It wasn't my fault." She slid her gaze to Ky. "I got…sidetracked."

She felt her face heat when he glanced from her to Ky, his eyebrows lifting, and then his jaw tightening. The fisted hands at his waist dropped to his sides, clenching and unclenching. A vein pulsed at his temple as he took a step forward. The look he threw Ky was part anger, part warning, and all seriously pissed alpha-male.

Knowing how his mind worked, how he considered her more sister than friend, and having seen for herself what he was capable of when mad, Gemma crossed the small expanse of the kitchen and stood between the two men, using her body as a barrier.

Ky hadn't moved. He'd dropped his hands in his pants pockets as soon as Rick sprinted into the kitchen, and maintained a nonthreatening stance. But Gemma could see the checked tension in his shoulders, the way his breathing accelerated, and knew if provoked, he'd fight back.

She faced Rick, placed a restraining hand on his chest. "Don't," she said. "Please."

His heated glare shot to her, swiped across her face, searching. The subtle lines on his forehead deepened. "Cleo?"

"It's okay. Really," she told him. "Everything is okay." Only when she stretched up and kissed his cheek did he relent.

"You smell like a locker room," she told him, punching him in the abdomen. He didn't even flinch. "Go have a shower. Go. Breakfast will be ready when you're done."

His eyes softened, the lids falling to half-open. "Promise you won't burn it?"

Gemma dropped her chin and glared at him. "Beggars and being choosey. Ever heard of it?"

He threw his hands up in surrender. "Just asking."

"Just saying," she shot back.

He grinned at her. When he shifted to stare at Ky, he dropped it.

Without another word, Rick went up the stairs.

When he was out of earshot, Gemma sighed.

"He's very protective of you," Ky said. "And he loves you very much."

Gemma turned around to face him, embarrassed and unsure, two things she never was. She shrugged and stared down at the floor.

Ky stepped toward her and wrapped his hands around her upper arms. "Look at me."

She did. The expression on his face was guarded, his eyes narrowed, his brow pulled low as he peered at her. On a deep breath, he said, "I can't believe I'm asking you this, but," he squeezed her arms, "I need to know. Are you having any regrets about last night?"

Gemma bit the corner of her bottom lip as she stared up at him. "Are you?"

She held her breath until he answered. Which was immediately and accompanied by his head shaking left to right.

"None." He smiled at her then. "Abso-friggin-lutely none."

His grin was infectious. She could live off it if she had to. "Ditto," she told him.

"Good to know." His lips softened as he drew her closer. When they covered her mouth in a sweet, gentle reminder of what they'd shared a tiny crack split along Gemma's protected heart, allowing the notion of possibilities and future happiness to weave its way in.

Why she wasn't scared out of her shoes at the thought was a mystery, but a mystery best left to figure out at another time.

"Now let me restart breakfast." She pulled away from him. "And no distractions this time," she added, shaking her finger at him.

His response was to grab her finger, then her whole hand and place a kiss to her palm.

That little crack widened.

* * *

Rick came back down, showered and dressed just as Gemma pulled the last piece of toast from the griddle pan.

"Well, it smells better in here than it did a few minutes ago," he said, pouring himself a mug of coffee from the pot Ky had made.

Gemma glared at him.

"Oh, hey, I forgot." He shot from the room and out the front door after disarming the security alarm. Ky filled his plate with toast.

"Here," Gemma said. She sprinkled a dash of cinnamon and then powdered sugar over them, a dusty white cloud gusting up from the plate. "Secret ingredients."

Ky grabbed her free hand and brought it to his mouth. He was rewarded when her eyes turned dewy and her lips lifted at the corners. He swore she sighed, but the sound was drowned out by Rick's intentional throat clearing.

"Excuse me." The sarcasm in his tone sounded terse and rude.

Gemma laughed. "Why? What did you do?" she asked, and then, on a squeal of delight ran to him and grabbed something from his arms.

"I left that in the car last night by mistake," he said.

When she threw her arms around him and kissed him soundly and loudly on the mouth, saying, "Thank you, Jesus!" Ky's stomach clenched. *Jealous.* Damn it, he was jealous.

He had no reason to be because he knew the kiss was innocent and bestowed in appreciation, but never the less, a quick, hot and resounding shot of possession bulleted through his gut, shooting his blood pressure up into the red zone.

He wasn't stupid. He knew the look Gemma had given him when he'd come in to the kitchen a while ago had been at best wary, at worst, remorseful for what they'd shared during the night. The thought she might be uncertain about how he felt in the light of day never entered his head until she'd bitten down on her lips and asked, "Are you?"

In that moment he added another descriptor to his growing dictionary of terms to associate with her: insecure. Not a word he'd ever think belonged to her.

Gemma Laine was a woman with impenetrable walls and enough trust issues to fill a psychiatrist's couch for years. Her own brother-in-law had affirmed her problems with trust at the hospital. Until she'd shown up in his bedroom, he'd thought she didn't like him and only tolerated him because she was forced to. The kiss aside, and it had been one hell of an unexpected response from her, Ky truly felt she'd rather be anywhere but in his company.

By some amazing twist of good fortune, though, she'd admitted to actually wanting him. He didn't think it was simply because she was feeling a sexual itch and he was available, either. Gemma didn't seem like the type of woman who'd easily give herself to a man to satisfy a basic need.

It had taken every ounce of self-respect, will, and internal fortitude he could muster to not toss her on the bed after she'd licked him—*licked him!*—and have at her without any further preamble. No, he'd called on all the gods he could name to slow him down, try to calm the raging lust driving through him, and bring her as much release and pleasure as he could.

It had been so worth it, too.

But he shouldn't feel jealousy. In truth, she wasn't his to be jealous over, but he had a hard time convincing himself of that.

"I'm surprised you've been able to go this many days without any," Rick said as both men watched her fill a glass with ice from the freezer and then pour the diet soda she loved all the way to the top. When it threatened to spill over, Gemma grabbed up the glass and slurped at the overflowing liquid.

"Very classy, Cleo." Rick smirked.

"Bite me." She gave him a sweet smile that didn't touch her eyes and then chugged a good, long draught.

Rick laughed out loud and shook his head. "Not an option."

She drank almost the entire thing in one, long pull. When she dropped the glass from her lips, the look on her face reminded him of how she'd looked after coming apart in his hands the night before. Those self-same hands started to tremble with need when she threw back her head, closed her eyes and smacked at her lips.

"You look like you've just had the best sex of your life," Rick said, giving a voice to Ky's exact thoughts.

Gemma's eyes sprang open, her expression wide and startled. Ky was dumbfounded when her cheeks turned candy-apple red, her pupils tuning to pinpoints.

Her eyes darted to him, her cheeks growing more heated.

Rick's eyebrows slinked upward as he turned from Gemma to him, a question pounding in his glare.

Ky met his query, measure for measure, not backing down, not offering anything verbal. With as much nonchalance as he could call up, he lifted his coffee mug, sipped, and then placed the cup back down on the table, all the while holding the other man's stare.

It was Rick who broke first. He lifted his plate to Gemma and asked, "Can I have some toast? Please?"

Gemma pulled out of her paralysis and dropped three pieces onto the plate.

Unlike with Ky, though, she didn't offer the sugar. He should feel small for being so pleased by that gesture, but just couldn't summon up any self-recrimination.

Gemma refilled her glass. She stole a glance at Ky, then said, "I'm going upstairs to work for a little while."

"Stay off the Internet," Rick said a heartbeat before Ky's mouth formed the words. He was glad Rick beat him to it, because Gemma threw him a contemptuous glare and, with a hand on her hip, pursed her lips together and said to Rick, "I'm not a moron, you know," before running up the stairs.

"I didn't say you were," Rick called after her just as the bedroom door slammed.

Alone now, the men regarded one another like young lions slinking around a new pride.

"So." Rick shoved a forkful of toast into his mouth. "What's going on with you and Gemma?"

Chapter Fourteen

"Dope." Gemma crossed her arms and pouted. She wasn't sure whether she was angry at Rick for saying what he had, or herself for reacting so viscerally to it. Her shocked response had all but verified what Rick suspected she and Ky had done. It wasn't that she was shy or ashamed of it. It was more she wanted to keep it private, between them, just for them.

She'd likened Rick to an annoying older brother and he certainly acted like one. She could imagine him right now, downstairs, giving Ky the evil, stink, interrogation eye and embarrassing him.

Ky was a big boy, though. He could take care of himself, so she wasn't worried.

The best sex of your life.

Yeah, that about summed it up in a nutshell.

Gemma opened the laptop and then connected a cable from it to her camera. After uploading all the new pictures she'd snapped in the past few days, she climbed up on the bed and got to work, knowing it was the one thing that would take her mind off the sexy FBI agent downstairs.

Scrolling through the hundreds of pictures she'd taken in the woods, and surreptitiously of Ky while he'd been hitting the punching bag, her attention was drawn to one particular photo of him she'd taken in slow motion. It was close-up shot of his torso and face as he hit the bag. She'd adjusted the camera settings perfectly to capture the beads of sweat that burst from his brow and face as he moved. She zoomed in on his hand, manipulated the filter and turned off the color to have the photo switch to black and white. The simple contrast of Ky's fingers wrapped in stark white gauze against the black background and bag was striking. Gemma sat back against the headboard and smiled. This was the kind of artsy picture she usually avoided taking, knowing her talent for capturing faces was where her true talent lay.

But this simple picture of a hand against a punching bag was beautiful, if she did say so herself.

The fingers, long and clenched, gave the observer a sense of their subtle power as they hit the bag, leaving a sizable dent in the process. The bag swayed from the hit, obvious in the blurriness surrounding it.

A sense of supreme satisfaction shot through Gemma. This, *this*, was why she'd become a photographer and worked so hard at her craft. To be able to preserve the perfect image, to know she'd captured something few ever saw or could even imagine, meant more to her than any awards, high priced commissions, or professional accolades ever could.

The fact that it was Ky's hand she'd immortalized increased that sense of accomplishment.

When her stomach started to rumble, Gemma glanced over at the digital bed clock and blinked.

She'd been working for five solid hours without a break. The glass of diet soda had long since been drained. After hitting the save icon on the photos and creating a special file on the laptop for them, she shut down the device, stretched, and thought about lunch.

And about the men downstairs.

The sound of voices drifted up the staircase when she opened her bedroom door. They sounded…civilized.

Gemma let out a breath and bounded down to them.

They were seated where she'd left them hours before, at the kitchen table, each with a laptop in front of them. Opened bags of chips and a few empty water bottles littered the table between them.

Ky was facing in her direction and when he lifted his gaze from the computer screen to her, her insides did a quick tumble and roll at the heat and intensity staring at her.

She felt naked, exposed, and so completely turned on that her knees actually knocked together, making her stumble off the last step.

Stupid knees.

"You okay?" Ky was instantly on his feet.

"Just stiff from sitting so long."

Lord, when had she turned into such a world-class liar? To cover her mortification, she plastered a smile on her face and asked, "Who, besides me, is hungry?"

* * *

He wanted to tell her he was starved for her, but kept his thoughts to himself. If Bannerman hadn't been sitting across from him, poking fun at Gemma's clumsiness, Ky would have crossed the room, taken her in his arms and feasted on her mouth.

"Kandy sent some of the soup she's featuring in the new restaurant, along with stuff to make her grilled cheese sandwiches to go with it," Rick told her when she opened the refrigerator. "There's a container of it on the second shelf."

Gemma opened the tub and took a whiff. "Hmmm. Grandma's tomato cream. Yummy."

"Your sister is opening a restaurant?" Ky asked. He'd moved behind her, helping to take down dishes and utensils from the cabinets. Just being physically close to her again brightened the foul mood darkening his soul from everything he and Bannerman had discovered.

"Several, actually," Gemma said. She filled a pot with the zesty smelling soup and placed it on the stove. "The first one opens in a month in Tribeca. Another in Orlando in the fall and then LA in January."

"Impressive."

"No. Kandy." Gemma lifted her shoulders. "This has been her dream since she was a kid, although she never told it to anyone until recently. A restaurant featuring only comfort foods, the kind we all had and loved as kids."

"An interesting premise."

She nodded and began slathering bread slices with butter. "No lie. This soup," she pointed to the pot, "is without a doubt the best tomato soup you will ever have. Hands down."

"Truth," Bannerman said.

"What makes it so special?"

Gemma's quick grin had him hard as stone and wanting in a heartbeat. "The showman in Kandy will tell you it's made with love added into every cup, but it's really the mix Grandma perfected of spices and herbs, plus the fact she used almond milk as the cream, and not cow's milk. Grandma was a pioneer when it came to using plant products for baking sauces instead of dairy ones."

The soup started to warm, its enticing aroma filling the kitchen.

"I wasn't hungry until just this moment," Ky said, sniffing the air.

Gemma laughed and said, "Wait until you taste the grilled cheese." She laid two sandwiches onto the griddle. "You'll think you've died and gone to comfort-food heaven."

A few minutes later the three of them sat at the table.

The only sounds for a while were them sipping the soup and chewing.

"You didn't exaggerate," Ky said, wiping his lips with a napkin. "This truly is the best soup I've ever had. Think your sister will give me the recipe for my mother?"

"Not a chance in a gazillion, but she can come into the restaurant anytime and order it." Her lips lifted at the corners.

Ky nodded. "I figured you'd say that."

"So, tell me." Gemma laid her sandwich down on her plate and looked from one man to the other. "What have you guys been doing all morning?"

Through silent agreement, Ky was elected to speak. Rick was still typing as they ate.

"The leak to Ritandi is directly from my department."

He still had trouble believing it, but the proof Bannerman and he had unearthed was irrefutable.

"Rick found an e-mail account in my name and several wire transfers from one of Ritandi's offshore accounts to an account in DC. Which is stupid when you think about it. The money can be traced to an American account so easily."

"Instead of like the Caymans or someplace like that?" Gemma asked.

"Yeah."

"Is your name on the account?"

"No."

"So whose account is it?"

Ky shook his head. "That's what he's trying to find out. There are several layers of encryption and password protected steps to sift through first. Whoever set up the account knew what he was doing."

Gemma's gaze flicked to Rick's side of the table. "That's Theo's device."

Ky nodded. "I called him and he told Bannerman all he needed to know about how to navigate through the layers."

"Guy's a fuckin' genius," Rick said, his eyes never lifting from the screen, his fingers drumming across the keyboard. "I'm gonna try and get Josh to hire him. We could use his skills on some of the tougher info probe cases."

"I can tell you right now Theo will say no. He's working on something that takes all his time and concentration and until he finds what he's looking for, he won't be diverted."

"We'll see," Bannerman said.

Before Ky could say another word, Rick's hands fisted and he pumped them over his head. "Yes! I'm in."

Both Ky and Gemma rose from their seats and came around to his side of the table.

"The name on the account is…Delaney Peterson. Who the hell is that? You don't have anyone on your team with that name."

Something tugged at the back of his memory. Ky sat back down at his computer and typed. After a minute a name scrolled across the screen. He cursed in Greek and then in English. "Son of a bitch!"

"Who is it?" Gemma asked.

Ky lifted his gaze. "My boss, SAC Tiege's wife. It's her maiden name."

Gemma gasped and Bannerman's eyes turned to blocks of stone.

"I can't believe this." Ky rose and shoved his hands in pockets to keep from hitting something—anything. He crossed to the living room, stopped in front of the fireplace.

"Well, now," the private investigator said, leaning back in his chair, arms crossed over his chest, "it makes sense, doesn't it? Who better to set you up for a fall than someone who knows you so well?"

Gemma followed Ky and placed a hand across his shoulders. "I'm so sorry."

"He was the last person I'd ever think would be involved in something like this." Ky stared at the empty fireplace. "I've always thought he had my back. He always has."

The betrayal stung, but not as much as knowing Gemma's life had been put in danger too many times by a person he'd put his complete trust in. Misplaced trust, it was apparent now.

"What do you want to do?" she asked.

He turned to face her. In reality, all he could think of doing was pulling her into his arms and letting her touch dissolve all the pain shooting through him.

"We need a plan to end this." He looked over at Bannerman.

"And we need to bring him and Ritandi down."

Rick nodded. "Let's get to it."

* * *

Something was holding her in place. Gemma opened her eyes to see that night had come. The open window curtain allowed the moon's glow to slink through the room giving her enough light to see the face of the man lying next to her, his arm wound possessively around her waist.

She had no memory of coming to bed. Gemma had joined Rick and Ky as they put together their plan, remaining silent for the most part, butting in with questions and concerns when she felt the need. Lunch had given way to a long afternoon of the men arguing back and forth about the best tactics to use. Before she reheated the lasagna and garlic bread her sister had sent for dinner, Gemma took an hour for herself and worked out in the garage.

What time she fell asleep she hadn't a clue.

Ky shifted to his back, his hand trailing across her stomach, but never leaving. Gemma cuddled closer, delighting in his natural warmth, and nuzzled her nose along his jaw. His eyes opened, instantly awake and aware as he turned his head to face her.

"Did you carry me up to bed?" she whispered.

He nodded, moved to his side, and ran his index finger along her cheek. "You didn't look comfortable on the couch."

"Thank you."

"You wouldn't let me leave." He smiled and kissed her nose. "I was worried Bannerman was gonna put up a stink about my staying in here."

His mouth slid down to hers. When he kissed her nothing had ever felt more natural, more comfortable, than to be lying beside him. Gemma ran a hand down his arm, then up again and over his shoulder.

"He's not the boss of me," she said, gliding her finger across his jaw. "He just thinks he is."

Ky's smile hit her squarely in the chest right before he took her lips again.

In no time at all the kiss went from sweet and tranquil to burning hot and insistent, each of them fully awake now, wanting, demanding. His tongue danced around hers, tugging, nipping, making a firestorm of need tornado up from within her. She grew restless, her feet and legs sliding along the sheets, along his legs, seeking relief. Seeking…him. An impatient moan pushed out of her when her hands met the fabric of his shirt, denying her access to his skin.

Gemma pulled away from his lips. "Take this off," she commanded, breathlessly. "I need to touch you."

Ky pulled back and touched his forehead to hers. "Baby, we can't do this. We can't let this go any further. Not here. Not now."

"Why not?" Frustration pushed the whine into her voice.

"Bannerman's right next door for one, and I'm still not convinced he won't try to beat the crap out of me. And I still don't have any condoms for another."

"We were okay without them last night." She really needed to have a conversation with herself sometime about the needy tone that kept escaping through her lips.

He kissed the corner of her mouth. "I know. And as amazing as that was, I need to be inside you the next time we make love. I want all of you, Gemma. All of you."

For the first time in a long time—maybe forever—Gemma couldn't speak. Ky's words stopped her cold. His eyes, even in the darkness, shone like winking stars as they gazed across at her.

No one had ever said those words to her before. No one. Gemma had had sex many times in her life. Some encounters had been better than others, and last night she counted among the best of the best. But in truth, she'd never *made love* to anyone. She'd never even considered it, because in doing so she'd have to give a piece of herself away, forgo some of her control. Allow the man making love to her to see her, really see her, all of her, and she'd never been willing to share herself that completely with anyone.

Until now.

"I want to see your face when I'm inside you and make you lose control." He kissed the other corner of her mouth. "I want you to look up at my face and know it's me making you come undone." He swiped his tongue across her bottom lip. "And then I want to lose myself inside you without worrying about anything but how good it feels to be there, for both of us."

His mouth ravished hers, there was no other word for it, she realized. He took complete control, claiming her, marking her as his. Why fear and uncertainty didn't follow she couldn't answer, so she just delighted in the knowledge that even though he desired her, he was willing to wait to make it perfect between them.

The widening crack protecting her heart opened to the size of a chasm.

Ky changed the kiss, softening it once again, turning it playful.

"I need to get back to my room." He dragged his finger along the lips he'd just caressed with his tongue. "Rick is leaving tomorrow to start setting everything up and you and I need to prepare for when we get out of here."

"So, stay with me now," she said. "We don't have to...do... anything. Just sleep."

Ky's grin was winsome, even in the dim light surrounding the bed. "Baby, if you believe I can get back to sleep with you cuddled next to me, and both of us on fire, you're crazy. I'm strong but not that strong." He pulled out of her arms. "I'm going to sleep in the bed downstairs. Alone. And I'm gonna dream about you."

With one last kiss, he left her.

* * *

They'd been over the plan four—no, five—times. Gemma's brain was starting to shut down. She wanted this to be over, but why did it have to be so complex? Why couldn't they just point the feds in the right place, to the right person?

With a shake of her head, she silently answered her own question. Tiege was a professional. He'd already made it look like Ky was responsible for everything that had happened. He'd be able to wiggle his way out of any accusations hailed at him, and the so-called proof would be the faked e-mail account and phone messages.

She let the men talk it out all over again while she kept them fed and hydrated. Without either of them uttering a word of complaint, she'd brought her camera down to the first floor and took dozens of pictures of the two of them, the house, and the view through the windows. By the time lunch was finished, they'd finally gotten everything set.

Rick lifted his plate and brought it to the sink. While he rinsed it, he told Ky, "I'm all packed and ready to leave. As soon as I get back to my office I'll start arranging things. It'll take a day, two tops. Then I'll call you and you can set everything into motion from here."

Ky nodded. "I think this will work." He glanced over at Gemma.

Cop face.

"Are you okay with everything we've laid out? Any questions or concerns?"

"None that I can think of."

"I really don't like the idea of using you in this," Ky said.

She cocked her head at him. "Because you don't think I'm capable?"

"No. You're more than capable. I know that." He took a deep breath and then blew it out slowly. "It's because you're a civilian and involving you in this just goes against everything in my training. You won't be armed; you'll be on your own. But I just don't see any other way out of this."

"Relax," Bannerman told him. He nodded his chin at her. "Gemma may be a civilian but she can handle herself. She'll be fine."

She turned her gaze to him. "You think Josh will go along with this plan?"

Rick's grin was fast and confident. "No worries. They want you home, Cleo. This is gonna guarantee it."

"I hate that name," she mumbled, bringing her own dish to the sink. "Remember how she ended up."

Rick reached out and hugged her to his side. That growling sound she'd heard escape from Ky before slipped out again.

"You're not gonna get bitten by a snake—"

"Asp."

"—hiding in a basket, so forget about how she bought it, and concentrate on your part of the plan."

"I know what to do," she told him, taking Ky's plate from his hand and joining it with the others.

Fifteen minutes later Rick pulled her into a full body hug and kissed her forehead. "Behave," he told her.

"Back at ya."

He moved to Ky and shook his hand. Right before he got into his car he leaned down and said something for Ky's ears alone, then pulled back and grinned, tossing a wave her way.

"Stay safe," she called out from the front door.

"Always."

Ky walked up the porch steps and watched the car until it crossed out of sight.

"What did he say to you?" Gemma asked when they walked back into the house.

While he set the alarm code, Ky answered. "I'll tell you later."

Even after being around him constantly for almost an entire week, Gemma couldn't read what was in his eyes as he looked across at her.

"I'm feeling like I need a workout," he said. "We've been cooped up here too many days and I'm starting to feel antsy. What about you? You up for a good sweat?"

"What did you have in mind?" she asked.

Chapter Fifteen

"You're overthinking it again," Ky told her.

He had her pinned from behind, his arms bracketing her own, forcing them to lay flat against the side of her torso, unable to break free.

Gemma squirmed and shifted her weight several times to no avail. Ky's grip was tighter than the Spanx she'd squeezed herself into last year when she'd attended the Daytime Emmy awards with Kandy. She was hot, thirsty, and pissed. A terrible combination on a routine day. Add in the stress, isolation, and worry about the next few days, and she was like a lit fuse, just waiting to burn down before igniting something.

"I can feel you vibrating with anger against me," he said into her ear, his hot breath washing over her skin like an erotic caress. For a millisecond she forgot what she was supposed to do and just melted into how good it felt to have his body holding hers. Granted, it wasn't a loving embrace, but all that hard muscle and coiled tension flat against her back was a blatant mix of sexual need and carnal arousal that had her toes curling in delight.

In the next second, Ky's arms tightened and plastered hers even more securely down to her sides. "Come on, Gemma. Focus."

Oh, I'll focus, all right.

She turned her cheek and rubbed it against the scruff on his jaw. He'd forgone shaving that morning in the last minute prep work he'd wanted to get done with Rick. When she purred at the delicious feel of his prickly stubble and her butt ground against his pelvis, her movements had the desired effect: distracted, his grip loosened just a tad, but enough for her to do what she did next.

A single, deep inhalation with a rapid fire exhale was all it took to disengage his hold.

Pivoting on one unshod toe, she grabbed his wrists, swirled them upwards and moved behind him, his arms now slung from her hands above his head, and yanked backward.

She bent her knee behind one of his and pushed. When he lost his balance and went down on the assaulted knee, she forced his arms to bend backward at the elbows, allowing her to restrain his hands together.

"Ouch!"

Gemma grinned at the back of his head. "You said to focus."

With his head shaking, she could feel his shoulders following suit. "You're nothing if not resourceful."

"I prefer the terms *skilled* and *expert*."

Ky dipped his head back to look at her. Upside down he was still gorgeous, so Gemma gave in to temptation and bent to kiss him on the lips. In the next breath she was flipped over his head to lay flat and sprawled on the mat.

Ky shifted and climbed on top of her, covering her body with his, pinning her arms above her head. That little smirk on his mouth was equal parts maddening and lust-inducing.

Gemma decided to go with the arousing part. Before Ky could say a word, she lifted her legs and crossed them at the ankles around his waist, effectively putting the part of her that was on fire in direct contact with the part of him that was growing by the moment.

Ky bucked up, flattening his weight on his bent forearms. "Oh, no. I'm wise to your tricks now, woman. You're not going to break my concentration again with your sexual charms."

"I'm not trying to break your concentration." She arched her back to bring them even closer in contact below the waist.

Ky hissed through barely open lips. "No?"

Her pulse tripled at the strain in his voice.

"Then what are you trying to do?"

"If you have to ask, I'm not doing it right." She laughed up at him.

She pushed up even higher on the mat, her butt and half her back now suspended, held in place by just her shoulders. He still had her arms restrained over her head.

Suddenly, his brow cleared and twin commas appeared at the corners of his mouth. Slowly, he lowered his head. So damn slowly she thought she'd expire from old age before his mouth ever came in contact with hers.

Body on fire for this man, she met him halfway and sealed her lips to his in a kiss that went from zero to ninety in less than a full heartbeat. Ky freed her hands and immediately moved them down her length. He hooked one under her butt, allowing his groin full body contact with hers now, the other circled around her shoulder to lift her head to his.

Gemma's hands went on a wild rampage, coursing over his body, scraping her nails under his sweaty, T-shirt clad chest, slipping below the waistband of his sweatpants to squeeze his butt. Their mouths never moved from one another, licking, nipping; exploring all their favorite hidden places.

Ky swore in Greek as his tongue danced down her jaw to stop and suck the notch at her shoulder.

"What does that mean?" she asked, licking her way to his ear, biting down on his lobe.

Ky groaned, tipped his head toward her mouth and panted. "Fuck!"

"Yes, please," she said against his jaw.

The choking sound of his strangled laugh filled the garage.

He nuzzled her nose and said, "You're gonna kill me."

"But what a way to go." She found his lips again, pushed them open and roamed free. "Are we done?" she asked against his mouth.

"Baby, we haven't even started."

Her thighs quivered at his savage growl. "No. No." She laughed. "With the workout. Are we done fighting? 'Cause I really want to be done fighting."

Ky's eyes dragged a molten hot trail across her face. A dark, seductive grin pulled at the corners of his mouth as he pushed back to his knees and then stood, pulling her up with him.

"Yeah. We're done with this." One hand crooked under her knees, the other under her shoulders, lifting her in his arms.

"Oh! What are you doing? I can walk."

"I know."

He carried her—*Jesus, carried her!*—through the breezeway into the kitchen and then up the stairs to the bigger bathroom. Gemma forgot all about protesting. She simply gave herself up to the amazing sensation of being carried effortlessly in Ky's strong arms.

He sat her down on the big bathroom counter, and, after a quick, hard kiss, turned the shower on.

"How do you like it?" he asked, yanking his sweaty tee off with one hand and dropping it to the floor.

"Um, fast and hard?"

Fingers hooked under the waistband of his sweats, he stopped cold and stared at her with such darkening embers glowing in his eyes, Gemma's nipples hardened.

Ky reached out and bracketed his hands on the counter at her hips. The heat from his body engulfed her. With his mouth a whisper from hers, his gaze holding her captive, he pressed his mouth to hers and said, "We can debate fast and hard over slow and bone melting later," he licked her bottom lip, "but I meant how do you like your shower temp?"

Gemma's nervous giggle echoed in the tiled room. "As hot as you can get it." She reached out and dragged her finger from the notch at his throat, down over his sweat-drenched pecs, to stop at his waist.

"Good. I've been taking enough ice-cold showers lately to last me a lifetime."

Why her pulse tripled in rate at those words she'd think about later… much later. For now, she continued her finger wandering until it came to rest on the pronounced bulge under his sweats.

"Take these off," she said, swiping her fingers up and down the length of him.

His lips twisted at the corners. He bent close to her, his mouth hovering over hers. "You sure do love to give orders."

She stretched up and took his lips in a quick, hard, promising kiss. "I love when they're followed even better."

Ky striped out of his pants, toeing them behind him and, before she cold blink, had her shirt over her head and on the floor joining his. The heat from the shower began to steam the room.

One flick of his fingers and her sports bra joined her shirt. Ky captured each of her nipples between his fingers and rolled them to hard, pointy peaks.

"God, that feels so good." Gemma's head fell back and connected with the clouding mirror.

"Ouch! It's a good thing I have a hard head." She rubbed a hand across the back of it and grinned.

Ky lifted her from the counter to stand her flatfooted, then slipped a hand inside her pants. "Come on, klutz. Let's get you out of these and into the shower."

"Now who's being bossy?" She let him tug her yoga pants down to the floor, her breath hitching when, on his way back up, he took his time to lick her from calf to the top V of her thighs. With a groan she could only term *wanting*, she shifted her legs, opening for him, and said a silent prayer he'd get the hint.

Bless the man for being smart.

He nuzzled into her for access, his breath sailing over her swollen, throbbing skin, making her skin tingle all the way to the roots of her hair, before he dragged his tongue along the length of her heat.

"You're wetter than any shower," he said, standing. He took her hand and helped her into the tub.

"Oh, sweet Jesus, that feels good," Gemma said when the pulsating water sluiced down her shoulders. She dipped her head back, wetting her hair, scooping her bangs off her face. "There's nothing better than a hot, steamy shower after a workout."

"I can think of one thing better." Ky wound his hands around her waist and covered her body with his. The temperature of the heated water at her back was nothing compared to the furnace of the man wrapped around her front. When his lips took hers she couldn't decide which was hotter: the water, him, or his kiss.

When his tongue pushed against her lips demanding entrance, she decided it was his kiss. Definitely. The man kissed her with a dedication and determination she could only equal to what she gave to her photography. He owned her lips, pure and simple. They were his to do with as he wanted, and Gemma wasn't the least bit unnerved about giving up her control of them.

"You taste like sunshine," he said, skimming her jaw. He pushed the wet hair back against her scalp, palmed her chin in his hands and changed the angle of the kiss, giving him deeper, fuller access.

Gemma felt the kiss all the way to her toes.

His hands roamed down her torso, lightly tickled her ribs and settled on her butt. He pulled her closer, his erection flattened against her belly, vibrating with need, engorged with desire. Gemma snaked a hand between their bodies and fisted him, squeezing with just enough pressure to make him shudder.

"And you feel like steel wrapped in velvet." She moved her hand up and down, slowly, knowing full well what she was doing to him. She could feel his thighs shaking against her own. He hooked a leg around her calf, pressing his knee against her quaking mound, the coarse hairs on his thighs rubbing against her skin and shooting erotic prickles down her spine.

"I want you inside me," she said.

Ky's smile was wicked. "First things first." He reached around her and grabbed the bottle of shampoo from the shower ledge. After squirting some into his hands he said, "Turn around."

Without even the thought of a retort, Gemma did.

Ky massaged the liquid through her hair, his fingers circling and swirling along her scalp as he brought it into a full lather.

Gemma groaned and reached out to plant her hands on the tiled wall in front of her for balance. Her knees were so weak, and Ky's hands felt so good, she wasn't sure she could keep standing for any length of time. "You can't imagine how good that feels," she whispered.

The low, deep rumble of his chuckle almost made her come where she stood.

"Face me," he said, with a subtle yank on her arm. When she turned around, he added, "You're getting better at following orders."

She opened one eye and regarded him through it. "I never have trouble following orders I want to obey. It's the ones I don't that get me into trouble."

With a smile, Ky pushed her head back and helped rinse her hair. That done, he took the bar of soap into his hand and worked up a lather between his fingers. "Open your eyes, Gemma."

She did.

"I want to watch your eyes when I do this."

"Do what? Oh, sweet baby Jesus!" Her eyes slammed shut again the moment his soapy fingers circled on her puckered nipples.

"Open your eyes."

That growl almost did her in. When she opened them to see him watching her face, his own so focused, intent, and—damn!—wild, her heart stopped beating for a second and then giddy-apped.

He rubbed and brushed the tips of his fingers around the mounds of her breasts, down along her ribcage and hips, swirling circles along each inch of skin he touched, lathering the soap to a luxurious mix of bubbles and cream. When he reached the dusting of downy hair on her mons, palmed it, and then slid a finger between her thighs, Gemma's spine shook from her neck to her tailbone.

Afraid she truly would slip and, god forbid break something in the shower, she reached out and braced against his chest for support. "Ky!"

"Love the way my name sounds on your mouth." He slid two soapy fingers fully inside her, pushing against her pelvis with his free hand.

Her eyes had a will of their own, because despite his growled commands, she couldn't keep them open. Wave after wave broke within her from his touch. Gemma came so hard and so quick, she wasn't prepared for the overwhelming sensations that shot through her. Ky held on fast, riding the climax with her, whispering words she didn't understand in her ear.

When her brain started to function again, she opened her eyes.

Ky's wet hair was plastered to his scalp, water droplets sliding down his cheeks to his jaw.

"Feel all clean now?" he asked with a self-satisfied smirk that had her wanting to punch him and kiss him at the same time.

"I feel something," she said, letting her hands roam down to cup him, "but I wouldn't exactly call it *clean*."

A breath whistled through his teeth when she scraped her nails along the thick line of hardened skin connecting his balls with his penis.

"I think the word I'm looking for is," she swirled her tongue around one of his wet nipples, rewarded when it hardened into a pebble, "dirty."

His eyes went from a hazy, drowsy ocean green to the color of smoke, burning and feral. For the thousandth time since they'd met she wished she had her camera handy. To capture him like this, wild and raw and completely untamed, unguarded and free, would have been a once in a lifetime photograph.

The artist in Gemma was captivated by his undeniable masculinity. The woman in her was simply captivated. By him. Only by him.

Ky reached around her and shut the shower off.

"Hey! I didn't wash you."

"No need. I'm just going to get all sweaty again. And so are you."

He picked her up allowing her legs to circle around his waist and stepped from the tub.

With a flick of his hand, he dragged a towel from the rack and threw it over her neck, sopping some of the water from her hair.

In two strides he crossed the room to the bed, tossed her down on it, and covered her body with his.

"Caveman, much?" Gemma laughed and slid her legs along the length of his, her toes scraping the muscles of his calves.

The corners of his eyes crinkled. "There's something to be said for that." He kissed her. "Stay put. Do not move. Under any circumstances but imminent death. Understand?"

Gemma wrinkled her nose. "Why? Where are you going?"

He took a deep breath in, his steady gaze never wavering from her. "Gemma?"

"Okay. Okay. This is me: staying put."

After another fast kiss, he went back into the bathroom.

"What are you doing in there?" she called when the sound of a cabinet door slamming reverberated out to her.

He came back to the room with a look of total satisfaction on his face. Her gaze immediately flew to her camera, lying on the bedside table.

"Nothing." He dropped something on the floor next to the bed and crawled over her again, pushing her knees apart with his own and settling between her legs.

"What did you throw on the floor?" Gemma squirmed to look down the side of the bed. Ky wasn't having any part of her moving, though.

With possession oozing from every pore, he kept her flat on her back. "A little present from your buddy Rick."

She squinted up at him. "A present? What?"

Right before he claimed her mouth he said, "Condoms."

Gemma raised a hand to his mouth. "How did you know they were in there?"

He kissed her palm. Gemma's heart went topsy-turvy. When he licked it, she felt the bed grow wet under her—and not from shower water.

"You asked me what he said right before he drove away. It was that he had a whole box of them in his bathroom and to feel free."

Gemma's body stiffened. "He said that? Feel free?"

"Yup." He kissed his way across her jaw, to just where her neck met up with her ear. "And I intend to take him up on the offer. Now." He pulled back and stared down at her, his mouth wet, his eyes moist with desire, and his lower body doing all kinds of lovely things against hers. "Are you done with the questions? Because I really want you to be done with the questions."

She laughed out loud, charmed that he could turn her body to sensual mush with her words repeated back to her.

Her arms wound around his neck and she pulled his head down to hers. "Done."

Kissing him and being kissed by him was an experience she couldn't liken to anything else she'd ever done or dreamed about. The thought that he truly did possess her lips, her mind, her body, was true. With any other man, Gemma would have resisted giving up the most important part of her: her control. But with Ky, it wasn't a consideration at all. She willingly, willfully, and gladly let him have every bit of her and had no regrets about it.

As his tongue and fingers did a wicked dance over her face, down her torso and belly to weave and claim the hottest and most wanting part of her, all Gemma could think was how happy she felt.

It wasn't lost on her how ridiculous that sounded. Pursued by a crazy mobster hell-bent on finding and killing her; her normal, perfectly sculpted life in shambles; missing her sisters so much she ached. All those things should have given her pause. And they did. But wrapped in Ky's arms, with him whispering words to her she longed to know the meaning of, all she could do was admit this man who'd come into her life for all the wrong reasons, had somehow managed to make her feel alive and vital for the first time she could remember.

So she did something she never thought she would: she simply enjoyed the moment and gave herself up to him.

His mouth, persistent and hard, continued its fevered pace on her.

"You need to start speaking in English. I want to know what you're saying while you do that," she chastised when he whispered against her thigh.

She could feel his smile against her skin right before he sucked at her inner folds.

"Oh, dear Lord!" Gemma arched, pushing herself closer into his mouth. "Forget it! Forget the words. Just keep...doing...that!"

* * *

How, how could a woman make him bleed with need, make him question every pledge he'd ever made to his job and country, make him want with such a powerful ache that he was defenseless against it, and still make him laugh?

Thank all that's holy Bannerman had told him about the condoms. He and Gemma still would have wound up in this exact spot, but now that he could be assured of protecting her in every sense of the word, he could explore this *thing* between them without worry.

And there was something between them. It wasn't just attraction, although that was powerful enough. No. In the span of time they'd been forced together and learned about one another, he knew it was much more than a sexual itch for either of them. Daily, hourly, Gemma came to trust him more and more, something everyone kept telling him she rarely did. If she could trust him with her life, she could trust him with her heart.

But right now he was happy she was trusting him with her body, because he really liked that.

He dipped his tongue inside her, deep, deeper, his breath catching when she almost arched off the bed to pull him even deeper. The words he murmured in the language of his ancestors told her what he was feeling. She might not understand them, but she certainly understood their intent.

"I think it's better if I show you what they mean," he told her, sitting back on his knees and reaching down to the floor.

She yanked the condom from his hand, tore the wrapper with her teeth and took it into her mouth. Ky almost embarrassed himself by letting go right then and there.

She shoved up on her elbows again, then pulled to her knees. With one cheeky slant of her eyes, she reached for him and then lowered her mouth. When she pulled up, the condom covered him.

When Ky let fly with his favorite oath, she sat back, grinned and said, "I know what *that* word means."

The grin died on her lips in the next moment when he shoved her back down and laid over her body. Knowing he wouldn't last long if he barreled through this, Ky recited an old geometry theorem in his head while he slowly, slowly slipped into her.

Her eyes went wide then slammed closed when she let out a groan that sailed right through him.

"Open your eyes," he commanded. When she did, he ground out, "We'll do it your way first." He shoved into her, pulled out, than dove home again. The sound of their flesh slapping bounced around the room. "Hard and fast, because I can't wait." He drove faster. "But next time, Gemma," his breath came in spurts and gasps now, his words distinct through each thrust, "next time we do it my way…slow and…mind-blowingly." With one final thrust he emptied into her, calling her name as he did.

Chapter Sixteen

She must be immortal.

However else to explain how she could have died from ecstasy and still be breathing?

Two hundred pounds of hardened muscle and satisfied male was on top of her, covering her from neck to toe in one warm and sated line. His lips a whisper from her neck, his rapid breaths fanning over her, his hips nestled against her own, all felt like heaven.

Gemma mindlessly scraped her nails up and down his back. Being immortal was going to be a blast if this was how she got to spend the rest of eternity.

Her sleepy contentment was disturbed when he propped up on his elbows, placed a swift kiss to her cheek and then slid out of her and went into the bathroom.

Gemma missed him immediately. She reached down for the sheets to cover herself, then became vaguely aware they were damp from their shower-slicked bodies.

A ridiculous joke about a wet spot sailed through her head and a laugh burst from inside her before she could stop it.

Ky materialized at the bathroom door, a filled water glass in his hand, and a frown on his forehead.

"You find something funny?" He bent a knee to the bed and handed her the glass.

Not even realizing how thirsty she was, she gulped it down, the chilly, clean taste refreshing her.

"I just thought of a really bad joke." She handed the glass back to him.

His left eyebrow arched. After placing the glass on the bedside table, he slipped in beside her. His hand fanned the bed around her. "These sheets are wet."

"I know. That's what the joke was about."

He stared at her for a moment, then shook his head. He rose and said, "Let's strip these so we won't be uncomfortable. We can wash them later."

They quickly remade the bed with the spare, dry set they found in the bedroom's closet. That done, Gemma's gaze slipped to her camera. She flexed her fingers a few times, the need to use it intense. Ky got into bed and reached out his hand for her.

"Gemma?"

She bit down on the inside of her cheek and couldn't for the life of her understand why she was nervous about asking him something she asked people every day of her life.

"Baby, what's wrong?"

She stared across the bed at him. "C-Can I ask you something?"

"Anything."

She sat on the edge and twisted her hands in front of her. When Ky separated them and brought one to his lips, she practically melted from the inside out. He didn't push, just waited, patiently.

"Would you consider, I mean…would you let me…Oh, hell."

With a gentle yank, he pulled her closer and cupped her cheek with his hand. "Baby, what's wrong?"

"Nothing. I just, well, I want to photograph you. Like this." She waved her other hand in the direction of his body.

His eyes went wide. He looked down at his naked form and Gemma realized he was already more than half aroused again.

"Like this? As in naked?" His mouth tripped down a little at the corners, the expression in his eyes, wary.

She nodded. "You have such a perfect body. It's made for being photographed."

He shook his head and glanced down at himself. "My ego is saying thanks, but my common sense is telling me this isn't a good idea."

"I was afraid you'd say that."

"Gemma, I'm a federal agent. I can't have naked pictures of me," he swiped his hand in the air, "lying around. Or worse, published."

Gemma pulled up her knees and crawled closer to him. "No, they wouldn't be. I promise that. I just want to capture you on film. Just for me."

His eyes went half closed at the same time Gemma noticed his erection grow. She licked her lips, swallowed, and edged nearer to him.

"You've seen my photographs."

He nodded, his body staying still.

"You've even said they're good."

"What I said was they're amazing. Good doesn't do your talent any kind of justice."

She couldn't have prevented the pleased smile from forming if she tried. Gemma knew she was talented, but hearing the praise come from Ky's lips sent a battalion of excited butterflies roaring through her stomach.

"I won't show the pictures to anyone, only you, so you don't have to worry about them being seen."

"Pictures? *Plural*? I thought you only wanted one."

She cocked her head and winked an eye closed. With her bottom lip between her teeth, she regarded him. "I think I told you when we first met that to get the shot you truly want, a photographer needs to take many along a continuum."

He nodded. "Facial expressions change by the moment. I remember."

"So, that's why I say pictures instead of picture."

What she didn't add was the thought that even just one photograph of him in this state of undress and—*gulp*—arousal, would be perfect.

She waited for his answer, hoping it was the one she wanted to hear.

With a confused shake of his head, he finally said, "Okay. But I want your word no one sees what you do except for me."

"You have it."

She grabbed her camera and adjusted the settings.

"What do you want me to do?" he asked. "Pose? Or just lie here?"

"Just lay back. Perfect. Look at me and think about something that makes you happy."

Through the viewfinder she saw his eyes go half closed, the same uber-sexy and hot twist of his lips that sent her pulse bounding, form across his mouth. She could feel the desire coursing from within him through the lens.

In rapid succession she fired off a dozen shots of his face and torso. From this angle, he looked like a statue, carved to perfection from polished marble, the muscles in his chest and abs cut and perfectly aligned. She reached out once to rearrange his St. Michael's medallion. Before she could pull her hand back, Ky grabbed it and kissed her knuckles.

The gesture, sweet and unexpected, shot a bullet of emotions through her.

"You almost done?" he asked, letting her hand go.

"One more."

She pressed down on the shutter button.

"That was six more," he said when she placed the camera back on the bedside table. She'd look at the photographs all in sequence later. But she already knew each and every one of them was perfect.

Her quick grin died when he yanked her flat on the bed and crawled over her. He was at full arousal now, throbbing against her as he nudged her legs open.

"I didn't think you could get any sexier." He skimmed her jaw and collarbone with wet lips. "But watching you work just now? That was hotter than anything I've ever seen."

"You're saying that because I did it naked." She chuckled and fanned her fingers across his shoulders. "I'm usually clothed when I work. Nothing sexy about that."

"I disagree." He kissed her once, twice; fast. "Naked or not, there's something stimulating about watching you work." This time he took his time with the kiss. "Your mind goes someplace else. You're incredibly focused and in control. Totally in control. That's beyond arousing in ways I can't even put words to."

"Speaking of arousing." She pushed up against him.

His breath caught. "I'm trying to pay you a compliment here, woman."

"I don't need compliments."

Ky's gaze bore into hers in a way that, if she thought about it, would have made her uncomfortable with its scrutiny. Too many times in the past few days he'd looked at her the same way, as if trying to get to her core, see into her soul; determine what made her tick.

"What do you need?" he asked in that growl that turned her insides to quivering mush.

"This." She ground her pelvis into his. "You. Now."

Right before his lips covered hers he told her, "You've got me."

* * *

After a quick nap that they both needed, they rose and, without showering again, dressed. Then, it was Ky's turn to make dinner. Kandy had sent several proteins with Rick, so he opted to make a chicken dish of his mother's he thought Gemma would like.

With a dish towel tucked into his pants, he set about cooking while Gemma uploaded her pictures to the secure computer Bannerman had brought for her.

"Again," she set her fork down next to her plate, sat back in the chair and closed her eyes, "you're gonna need to give this recipe to my sister. This chicken tastes insane."

"I'm sure my mother won't mind giving it to someone not in the family, since it'll be to her favorite chef-lebrity."

Gemma took a large sip from her soda glass. "Do all the people in your family cook?"

Ky nodded. "Two of my older brothers run a restaurant together, their wives included. My uncle is the head chef. My father grew up in the food industry so he's as good a cook as my mom and *YiaYia.*"

"I love that word," Gemma said with a smile.

His stomach muscles tightened at the expression on her face. Forget the dinner in front of him. He could live off that smile and never know hunger. "What? *YiaYia?*"

"Yeah. It sounds so, I don't know...like someone who's cherished and adored."

Ky considered that, then nodded again. "She is. Both. Her ninety-fourth birthday is in a few weeks. My parents have a huge celebration planned."

"Did you grow up with her in the house?"

"Yes. She's been living with my parents since before I was born. She came over from Greece when my grandfather died. My dad's the oldest, so naturally, she came to him."

"Why naturally?"

"In our culture, the oldest child assumes the adult responsibilities of a widowed parent." He shrugged. "She's been with us for almost forty years."

"She never remarried, or found someone else to be with?"

Ky laughed out loud at the notion of his grandmother hooking up with any other man. "No. Like swans, Greeks tend to mate for life."

Gemma sighed and glanced down at her plate.

"That doesn't sound like a very happy sigh," he said, lifting his water glass to his lips.

"No. It's okay. I'm okay. Just...I don't know." She took a swig of her soda then laid her elbows down on the table, hands clasped in front of her.

Ky stretched across the table and wrapped his hands around hers. "What? Tell me."

She lifted her eyes to meet his and he saw the sadness flitting in them. Worrying her knuckles with the pads of his fingers, he squeezed her hands and said again, "Tell me."

Her lips dipped at the edges as her gaze shifted to their joined hands. "That mating for life thing. I've only seen it happen once in my family, with my grandma Sophie and my grandpa."

"Your parents?"

She shook her head. "Dad bolted. After seven kids, all girls, he left."

"That's hard. Really hard. Did he keep in contact at all?"

"No. He cut off all ties."

"And he never came back? You never tried to locate him?"

"No. Kandy and I talked about it a few times when she was getting married and then again when she got pregnant. I'm sure Josh could find him in a heartbeat, but—" She shrugged. "I just don't think it's worth it at this point."

He squeezed her hands.

"I wonder, sometimes, if my life would have been different, if all my sister's lives would be different, if my father hadn't left us like he did."

"What do you mean? How did he leave?"

Gemma pulled back her hands and reached for her soda. After taking a long chug, she answered.

"They always fought, my parents. Loud, vicious arguments. Lots of name calling. Lots of tears from Mom. It wasn't until I was a teenager that I found out what the fights were about."

She stopped, glanced up at him, and then back down. Ky didn't push, realizing she needed to trust him enough to share. He couldn't force it out of her, no matter how much he wanted to.

With a shrug he knew wasn't as carefree as she intended it be, she said, "My father was a cheater. A serial cheater, according to Kandy. There were a lot of women over the years. Every time he'd cheat and Mom found out, he swore it was the last time, they'd...make up."

Ky's breath caught when a red flush spread up her neck and cheeks.

"Nine months later I'd have another sister. It went on for years until finally Mom'd had enough."

"What happened?"

"It was right after my tenth birthday, a party he missed because he was out with another new woman. When he came home two days later, drunk and mean, Mom told him to make a choice. His family or his girlfriends. He couldn't have both anymore."

She stood with her plate and brought it to the kitchen, Ky following. He pulled the dishtowel he'd tucked into his pants out and laid it across the sink counter.

Gemma ran hot water into the sink, added dish soap. While it bubbled, she continued. "He packed a single bag and left. He never said goodbye to any of us. Kandy, my sister Abby, and I were huddled together at the door to our bedroom, listening. The front door slammed and then we heard Mom go into her bedroom and close the door quietly." She took his dish from him and put it into the water with hers. "A millisecond later we heard her crying. Kandy went to her, since she was the oldest. Abby and I went to the others and told them Daddy left."

Ky didn't even think she realized she was washing the dishes while she spoke. She ran a soap sponge over the plates and utensils, rinsed them under a running water stream, and then laid them down on the towel he'd spread out. Ky leaned back against the counter, arms crossed in front of his chest, just listening.

"I always wondered, if he'd stayed, if we'd been raised with two parents who loved and supported one another, and us, would I or any of my sisters, have turned out differently."

"How so? I mean, I don't know your other sisters, but you and Kandy are highly successful women. You both have enviable and thriving, high-powered, lucrative careers."

She nodded, wiped her hands dry on a paper towel and turned to him. "We do. But until a few years ago when Kandy met Josh, she was basically a workaholic with no other real life. Much like me."

"I'm not getting your point, Gemma. How do you think your life would have been different if your father had stayed?"

* * *

How would it have been? It was question she'd tossed around in her head thousands of times.

Kandy had told her when Gemma had been introduced to Josh Keane, he'd pegged her as having trust issues with men immediately. He told Kandy he figured it had something to do with feeling abandoned by their father.

He wasn't wrong. The mistakes with boys in her teenage years and then college, proved she drifted toward men who would hurt her, much as her father had.

The impenetrable wall she'd built around her heart over the past few years, coupled with always needing to be the dominant one in any relationship, the one in control, had turned Gemma into the workaholic, relationship-avoiding woman she'd once accused her sister of being.

Now, at a time in her life when her career was where she wanted it to be, Gemma was beginning to realize how much she wanted to share her successes with someone who would revel in them with her. Someone who would support her, her decisions, her desires. Someone she should be able to trust.

"If he had stayed," she said, "and the fighting and the cheating ended, I'd like to think I would still be successful work-wise, but..."

"But?" Ky remained where was.

"Maybe...maybe I wouldn't be so hard and tough on people. So demanding of perfection of myself and everyone around me. Maybe I'd be able to trust people a little more and not always feel like I needed to be in charge and in control."

He continued to lean against the counter, but Gemma sensed something shift in his posture.

"I went to a lecture in college once," she continued, while she poured more soda into a glass, "about how your parents influence the kind of person you turn into when you age. If they love you unconditionally, or if they're cold and distant, you turn out one way. If they're supportive and accepting of your decisions, or disdainful and ridiculing, you turn out another. A lot of the talk was about how feelings of being abandoned as a child can lead to problems with trust and acceptance in adulthood."

Ky nodded. "I've read studies as part of my profiling training at the bureau like that. They all state the same thing. How a parent reacts and responds to a child when they're young influences the person they'll become in adulthood."

"So you know, then. You understand what I mean."

He pushed off the counter and crossed the small expanse of the kitchen. His fingers wound around her upper arms, drifted downward, and took her hands in his. The warmth spreading from them into her was soothing, calming, and arousing all at the same time.

"I do. What you're trying to say is you have trouble trusting people, men particularly, because the one man you should have been able to trust with everything, including your love, betrayed that trust by leaving you."

Gemma's shoulders relaxed when she let out the breath she'd been holding in. "Exactly."

"I can understand that, Gemma, I really can."

"That's the beginning of a *but* sentence if I've ever heard one."

His grin set of an explosion of firecrackers in her stomach. "*But*, despite that betrayal and how it should, theoretically, have affected you, you're a brilliant photographer, a savvy business woman, you can kick ass like no body's business"—she grinned at that—"and you're the sexiest woman I've ever known."

The blush she felt spring up her face at his words was unpreventable.

He tugged her into his arms, wound his hands around her waist, settling his body comfortably against hers.

"You're all those things and more, Gemma. And I think you would have wound up the same way, in the exact same place you are now, with your father's presence in your life or not. This is who you are, what you are, the person you were meant to be. And from where I'm standing," he wedged one knee between her legs and leaned in closer, "you're a pretty remarkable woman."

She cupped his cheek and rubbed her thumb along his lips.

Words failed her. In that moment, without a doubt, she knew she was starting to have real feelings for Ky; feelings she'd blocked herself from having for so long.

And feelings she didn't know how to deal with. Or more accurately, she told herself, couldn't deal with.

"Trust is hard for most people," he told her. "But getting hurt sucks, whether it's emotionally or physically, and whether you're betrayed or abandoned, or your heart is stomped on, it makes it harder to trust the next time."

She nodded.

"But you need to cut yourself some slack here. You were an innocent kid, as were your sisters. It's not your fault your father couldn't live up to his responsibilities, or grow out of his selfishness. And that's what he was: selfish. When you have kids, nothing else matters but them. Not what you want, what you need, even what you think you deserve. Just those kids, who are now dependent on you for everything. He walked away and truly, he doesn't deserve a minute's thought from you ever again."

"It's funny. I know that in my head, but just can't accept it in my heart."

He kissed her temple and sighed against her cheek. "You've made yourself into something any father would be proud of. The fact he doesn't know it, know you, is his loss, not the other way around. Know that."

"I do, but it's really nice to hear it," she said. "Thank you. For understanding and for saying that."

He pulled back and stared down at her. "You know you can trust me, right? I'm not like your father, like the other men you've known. I won't hurt you. I won't leave you. Do you trust that? Trust me?"

When she didn't respond, his brow pulled inward. "Gemma?"

Her mouth grew dry. She was unable to find the words to tell him, so instead, she decided to show him.

One hand snaked up and around his neck while she placed her mouth close to his. With a quick glance up at his still frowning face, she pressed into him and kissed him.

"Gemma." His eyes darkened, heated, bringing to mind the ocean churning just before a storm. He whispered something in Greek while he slid his lips along her jaw again.

"I may not speak the language, but I can guess the meaning of those words." She giggled and hugged him, tickled when his shoulders shook against her.

He pulled back and kissed the tip of her nose. "No translation will do it justice, anyway."

He ran a finger tenderly along her cheek, down to her neck, where he put his lips.

Gemma's head fell back, giving him all the access he wanted. In no time, he had her panting and primed.

"I want you so much," she said against his lips. "So much."

He held her head between his hands and shifted, deepening the kiss, reaching down into her soul.

Her hands were everywhere, all over his body, squeezing, scraping, pressing. She couldn't get close enough to him.

Ky broke away from her suddenly and spun her around so her back was against the front of him.

"Put your hands, flat, on the counter."

His beautiful voice had turned to flame-forged steel.

Without a word of protest, she did.

In the next heartbeat he tugged her yoga pants down to her ankles, her panties following.

"Wha—"

"No. Don't turn around. Keep your hands on the counter."

She felt him unbuckling his pants with one hand while the other slid down her butt, spread her cheeks, and cupped her.

Gamma's gasp echoed in the room.

"Spread your legs for me," he commanded, his breath hot near her ear, his voice tight.

More turned on by the sound of the just-barely controlled emotion in his voice than she ever thought she could be, she did as he commanded. When he slid his first two fingers inside her, she bucked and arched, falling forward on the counter.

"You're so damn wet and ready for me."

Only you, she wanted to say. Only you.

He pulled his fingers from her and the sound of a wrapper being torn filled her ears.

"Stay in this position," he said. "Don't move."

It never even entered her mind to.

He slid himself along her dampness, then, in one powerful thrust, he was completely inside her.

Gemma screamed, the sound muffled by the blood drumming through her head. She gripped the counter edge, felt Ky's hands spread over her hips, squeezing, anchoring, and met him, measure for measure as he moved in and out of her.

She came on another scream moments later, momentarily blinded when all the blood in her body rushed to where Ky had her completely under his control.

He followed her over the ledge, then collapsed across her back.

When he moved his hands to lie next to hers on the counter, she couldn't help the tingle of egotistical pride that tumbled through her when she noticed they were shaking.

I did that. I made him tremble.

His breathing was fast and uneven at her ear. She reached around and patted him on the hip, his muscles still quivering against her.

"See?" she said, unable to keep the laughter from her voice. "Like I told you before. Fast and hard. It's the best."

A laugh barked across her back as he wound his hands around her waist and hugged her tight.

Chapter Seventeen

Another day flew by while they waited for word from Bannerman. Gemma started to worry it would never come.

In the next breath, she almost wished it wouldn't.

Never in her life had she felt so free, which was completely ridiculous. She was as far from free as a person could get, since she and Ky were prisoners in the cabin, awaiting the okay to leave. For the first time in her adult life, though, she had no assignments, deadlines, or contracts she needed to honor; no clients she needed to appease and make look good; no worries other than what to make for dinner.

Well, except for the fact that a madman wanted her dead.

Funny thing was, she'd gone from hating every minute of her confinement while at the safe house, to treasuring the solitude and the company of the man with her.

In New York, she was on the go from morning to night, moving from one photo shoot to another, meeting with clients, visiting with her family. She had her beautiful condo that many days she simply used as a place to drop her equipment before falling into bed, exhausted.

Go, go, go, day after day, week after week, shoot after shoot.

The week before she'd witnessed the shooting she'd been in London for two days photographing one of the country's hero footballers for *GQ*, then Venice for a night to shoot a film star at her villa.

Here, the farthest place she could go was the surrounding woods, a far cry from the usual, bustling places she frequented.

Until a week ago she hadn't minded being alone for most of her down time, knowing she could always visit with a sister or two, or call Kandy for a quick meal. Now, she'd gotten used to having someone around her twenty-four-seven, and couldn't imagine what it would feel like to be left alone again.

Gemma scrolled through the photographs she'd uploaded of Ky after they'd made love, the pictures she'd cajoled him into agreeing to by telling him no one would ever see them. As she moved from one photo to the next in a slide show, she knew her original thought that every picture would be perfect was true. Ky's was, without doubt, the most perfect body she'd ever shot. And that was saying something since she'd photographed everyone from top sports athletes to Olympic medal–winners at the peak of their success and while in the best shape of their lives.

None of them could compete with the flawlessness of Ky's perfectly etched muscles, natural golden skin, or ocean colored eyes. She'd agreed to never show the photos to anyone but him and now regretted making the promise. Understanding his need for anonymity because of his job was a valid concern. Gemma knew how important the respect and trust of his coworkers and fellow agents was to him. But these pictures screamed to be seen by the public; admired; worshiped.

How to do that and still keep her promise was the problem.

Ky's fingers danced along his keyboard when she looked across the great room to where he was seated. He'd been trying to tie up some lose ends concerning the Ritandi investigation for as long as she'd been sitting and working on her photos.

After waking in each other's arms after another night of intimacy, they'd worked out in the garage, showered together, ran out of hot water because they'd lingered for so long under the spray, made a light breakfast, and then had each decided to work.

Gemma hadn't been alone with another person for such a substantial amount of time since before she'd left for college. If she'd have been asked a week ago, she would have said she loved living alone, being alone, and not encumbered with anyone else. No distractions, no awkward conversation lags to hurdle over; no need to make small, pleasant talk or worry that the other person wasn't feeling enough attention was being paid.

If asked today, she would have negated everything she'd said before. She felt…comfortable and at ease, was the best way to describe it, sitting across the room from Ky. He demanded nothing of her time, respecting her need and desire to work on her coffee-table book, and had silently asked for the same kind of consideration while he delved as deep as he could into the Ritandi-Tiege connection.

Comfort and ease. Two words she would never had thought to use to describe a relationship.

Gemma blinked. Hard.

A relationship? Is that what she and Ky had?

No, it wasn't. They were two people who'd been forced together by circumstances neither could have prevented or predicted, who'd found each other sexually attractive and acted on it. That was all.

Or, was it?

Just as she started to delve deeper into the question, the disposable burner phone Rick had given them beeped.

Gemma's gaze skated to Ky, and his to her. He reached for the phone and hit the *answer* icon.

"Yeah?"

Gemma's attention zeroed in on him. A second later he ended the call.

"It's a go," he told her, rising and crossing to where she sat at the kitchen table.

He pulled her up and into his arms.

"When?" She rubbed her hands down his back to rest on his waist.

"Tomorrow."

She nodded and leaned into him.

"Then this nightmare will all be over by tomorrow night?"

Ky pulled back and traced a thumb across her jaw. "Hopefully, yes."

"Are you okay with all this? It won't be easy."

His caustic laugh sent a shiver down her spine.

"I'm fine."

"Ky—"

He squeezed her arms. "I'm fine, Gemma. Really. This has to be done."

And he was the man to do it, she knew. The only man.

"Everything will be fine. We just need to stick to the plan."

She nodded and laid her head down on his shoulder.

In twenty-four hours this nightmare would be over. She could go back to her life, her work, her family.

And Ky would go back to his world.

Would she ever see him again? Would he even want to? They hadn't discussed what came after tomorrow. He'd told her she could trust him; that he wouldn't leave her. It was the truth. Ky was a man of his word. She trusted him to stand by her side and protect her. Stay with her. Ride out the problem to its end.

But when this was all done and behind them, what then?

"I have to make the call."

She nodded and slipped out of his arms.

Using one of the cell phones Theo had provided, Ky punched in a number from memory.

With his gaze glued to hers, he said into the phone, "Jon? Yeah, it's me. We need to meet."

* * *

"You're clear about what you need to do tomorrow?" Ky asked.

Gemma snuggled under his arm and kissed his neck, the bed still warm from their recent lovemaking.

"No worries," she said on a yawn.

No worries. If only it were that simple.

Tomorrow could go either way. The best made plans had a way of unraveling, but he was confident what he and Bannerman had devised would work. His FBI training had preached that people's underlying behavior didn't change, even when they were placed in dangerous situations. He was counting on that to be true. Tomorrow Tiege would hopefully be in custody, and if the planets all aligned, he'd have a solid bead on Ritandi. The FBI would suffer through a few raised eyebrows, an internal investigation-maybe even an external one-from the corruption he'd discovered, but it would survive in the end.

Gemma would be safe once again and they could both go back to their lives.

The problem with that scenario was Ky didn't want go back to his life. He wanted to start a new one. With Gemma by side.

He hadn't even known there was something missing in his life until he'd met her. Life at the bureau—a life he'd forged for himself—had, until recently, been enough. He enjoyed the work, celebrated in the successes, felt fulfilled when he brought someone to justice. He gave it his all, and as Jon Winters had jokingly told Gemma: "everyone thought he was married to it."

And right there was the problem. Much like Gemma, he had nothing else in his life but his family and work. No one to come home to at night, to share with, to talk over a bad day, or relive a good one. No one to make new memories with.

No one to love or be loved by. He wanted that. Badly. The realization hit home the first time he touched Gemma Laine. The first time he felt her body melt against his, match him desire for desire. Maybe even before that.

Ky closed his eyes and remembered that morning in the basement gym when she'd impressed and awed him with her weaponry and martial arts skills. She was a complete surprise, a happy one, in so many ways.

He'd finally met a woman who liked the same things he did, valued family as highly as him, was independent, successful, smart, witty, drop-dead gorgeous, and trouser-tightening sexy.

And she had a wall around her heart and issues with control and trust.

He stared up at the ceiling, considering. Well, he just needed to tear down that wall and wrestle some of that control away. He'd made a good start. The hot little scene in the kitchen had been about control and trust, and she'd willingly given him both without questioning or jockeying for the upper hand. Gemma had let him take the lead, something he guessed she seldom allowed a man to do.

"Why are you grinning like a fool?" she asked, lifting up on an elbow, the corners of her eyes narrowed.

The sheet pulled away from her torso, allowing him to look his fill at her lovely, perfect breasts. Apparently his hands had a mind of their own and weren't satisfied with him just looking, because before he could stop them, they reached out and cupped each one, his thumbs swiping across the flattened tips. In an instant they hardened and peaked.

Gemma's head reeled back as the blue in her eyes turned the color of cobalt. Through her parted, plump lips, a simple sigh escaped, her breath fanning over him.

He'd been semi-hard just thinking about her. Seeing her like this turned him to granite. In one move he had her beneath him, his body covering hers, his hips pressing against hers.

"Again?" She laughed and threw her arms around his neck.

"Again," he answered, his lips moving across hers.

And a thousand times more, he promised himself.

* * *

"You okay?"

Gemma turned to him and rolled her eyes. "You've asked me that four times in the past two hours. Yes. I'm okay."

They'd been driving for over six hours, after packing up and leaving the cabin before dawn broke.

Gemma's sleep had been fitful, even wrapped securely in Ky's arms. They'd made love one final time before finally succumbing to exhaustion.

Something had been different the last time. He'd seemed... anxious, almost as if he had to please her, had to wring out as much pleasure as he could from her.

Almost as if he were afraid it was the last time they were going to be together, and he wanted to make is as memorable as he could.

He'd been frantic for her, and she for him. If they'd been clothed, the garments would have been in tatters, so desperate were they to touch the other's skin, caress one another's bodies.

The sheets came undone from the mattress, the pillows flew in the air. They'd rolled, risen, and repositioned more times than she could remember. At one point, Ky sank to his knees to the floor, grabbed her legs and threw them over his shoulders so he could have better access to all of her.

Once, he'd been buried so deeply inside her, Gemma could feel him straight to her soul. He'd pulled back, his gaze skirting over her entire face, as if memorizing it. Every angle and plane, every dip and hollow.

Right before he climaxed the last time, he'd growled a command that she keep her eyes open. She wondered now if it was because he wanted to watch her lose control or if he wanted her to see him as he did.

Either way, she'd been overcome with a range of conflicting emotions.

"We have about another half hour," he told her, sliding into the fast lane.

Gemma nodded and fingered the medallion at her neck. After taking a quick shower before leaving, he'd taken it from his neck, slipped it over her head, and had given her a swift, thorough kiss, before dressing.

Now, as she dragged the medallion along the chain, she could almost feel the strength and warmth of its owner flowing through it, from it, and into her fingers. Knowing they'd activated the tracking sensor gave her a little reassurance that nothing untoward would happen to her.

"You don't seem nervous about any of this," he said, his gaze flicking from the highway in front of him, to her, and then back again, as if reading her thoughts.

"Oh, I'm nervous," she said, nodding. "In all honesty, my stomach is doing handsprings and tumbles like an Olympic gymnast in the gold medal competition."

She turned to face him. "But it's a little late now to be worried about what will happen. You've got a plan. A good one. Let's hope nothing deviates from it."

It was Ky's turn to nod. He reached across the seat and folded her hand into his own. When he brought it to his lips, Gemma's insides vaulted even more. Such a gentle gesture. So filled with…everything.

They drove without speaking for the remainder of the ride.

The arranged meeting place had been Ky's idea. Just north of Manhattan, the safe house was well known to the bureau, surrounded by woods and far enough removed from civilization that no one would unexpectedly come upon them.

Perfect, he'd told her, for what they needed to do.

"I think we're the first ones," Gemma said, when Ky turned up the winding drive.

A log cabin was situated at the end of a dirt driveway, buried deep behind a copse of trees. It hadn't been visible until they'd driven for a few minutes after coming off the county road. If the situation weren't so dire, Gemma knew she'd like to photograph the house and surroundings. Stark, bare, and barren, it would make for a surreal shot.

"Let's hope so," Ky said, parking and shutting the engine. He pulled her hands into his and squeezed. "You ready for this?"

"As I'll ever be."

He peered at her, his eyes that stormy mix of dark blues and greens she knew meant his emotions were high. "When this is over," he said, "when everything is settled and clear, I want—"

She could only guess what he'd been about to say.

"Papps?"

Jon Winters stood in front of the car. He was wearing a shoulder sling, securing his hand and arm to his torso. He looked pale and a few pounds thinner than the last time Gemma had seen him.

Ky squeezed her hands once more and then freed them. "Let's go," he said softly while alighting from the car.

"Jon. Thanks, buddy, for meeting us."

"Where have you been, Papps? The team's been going nuts for days with worry."

Ky slanted a glance at Gemma. "I know, but it couldn't be helped. I couldn't trust anyone close to the investigation. Like I told you last night, someone knew from the beginning where to find Miss Laine and I had to figure out who it could be. I needed time to find the mole in the department."

Winters' gaze shuttled from Ky to Gemma and then back to his partner. "Yeah. You mentioned that on the phone. How could you find something like that out when you were off the grid? No computer access or phone?"

"Let's just say I had some help."

Winters started at him, his face blank, his body seemingly relaxed. "Help? Who?"

"I can't tell you, Jon. I don't want to put my source in danger before this is all resolved."

"Smart. But you always have been. And resourceful. I've admired those traits in you."

Ky stood, silently.

"So, did you find out who the mole is?" Jon asked.

Ky nodded, his eyes trained on Winters. "Yeah. I did."

Before she could blink, Winters drew his gun.

"Jon? What are you doing?"

"Don't act like you don't know Ky. The minute you called me you knew where this was going."

"What are you talking about?"

"Stop. Just stop. I know you're the leak in the department. I know it. I have proof. And I'm taking you in."

Gemma didn't have a chance to breathe before Ky's gun was pointed at his partner.

"Jon," he said, his voice deathly still and calm, "you know that's not true. You know me."

"What I know is that I trusted you," Winters spat, his face hard, his eyes focused on Ky. "You betrayed that trust, Papps."

"What are you talking about?" Ky took a solid stance, his gun poised at his partner.

"You got four of our men killed. Four. And for what?"

"Jon—"

"Why did you do it? Did Ritandi pay you? Did he have something on you? What?"

"Jon, you know I'm not responsible for anything that's happened," Ky said. "You—"

"Drop your weapon, Pappandreos!"

Gemma spun around to see SAC Tiege and five men dressed in tactical gear move from the bushes surrounding them, guns drawn and pointed at Ky.

"No!" She ran toward Ky. "Stop! Don't shoot him!"

"Gemma, stay back," Ky yelled.

The force of the command stopped her cold. "Ky—"

"Don't get any closer to him, Miss Laine," Tiege said. "Drop your weapon, Papps. Now."

Ky's face turned to a slab of stone. Even his eyes went dead. Gemma couldn't see his chest rise and fall from breathing, and for a moment worried he wasn't.

"Don't make me shoot you, Papps," Winters said. "I will if you give me a reason to. Believe me. You deserve it for the traitor you are."

The words sliced through the air.

Slowly, so slowly Gemma wasn't sure he was moving at first, Ky raised his hands and then bent to lower his gun to the ground.

"Kick it over to me," Winter's ordered.

"Why are you doing this, Jon?"

"Why?" Jon said. "You have the nerve to ask that?"

"We know it was you, Papps," Tiege said, moving toward Gemma, his gun still aimed at Ky.

"Know it was me?" Ky asked, his hands bent and raised above his head, his eyes trained on Winters. "Know *what* was me?"

"You're the one who's been feeding Ritandi intel all these months," Winters said, his mouth pulling back in disgust. "It was you, all along, damn it! You played us. All of us."

"No!" Gemma shouted. "It's not him."

"I'm sorry, Miss Laine," Tiege said, "but it is." He grabbed her upper arm with his free hand. "Winters discovered phone messages between Papps and Ritandi going back several months now."

"It's a lie!" she shouted. "He's lying." She pointed at Winters.

"Miss Laine, please. Calm down. This isn't helping. We have the proof we need that it's been Pappandreos all along."

"No, you're wrong. Let me go!" She pulled as hard as she could, tugging the arm he held securely, then slapping at it with her free hand.

Tiege ignored her plea. "Winters? Do it."

"Yes, Sir." He holstered his gun and pulled a set of handcuffs from behind his back. He moved toward Ky and said in a voice that shot a dagger into her spine, "Down on your knees, Papps. Now."

Ky stood his ground, his gaze never moving from his partner's.

"Don't give me any trouble with this. You've got five weapons pointed at you. They won't hesitate to shoot a traitor. Understand?"

Ky knelt, his mouth twisting into a crooked like.

"Stop!" Gemma shouted at Winters. "Stop. You don't know what you're doing." Gemma again tried to squirm out of Tiege's hold, to run to Ky. He held on fast, crushing her arm in his big, beefy hand.

"Take him in, Winters. I need to get Miss Laine out of here."

Tears sprang from Gemma's eyes as she watched Ky being handcuffed by Winters then yanked to his feet by two of the men with him.

Again, she struggled against Tiege's grip, trying to pull away.

"Ky!"

He turned his head to look straight in her eyes. She had never seen such a cold, dead expression on someone so alive. Her blood chilled to ice.

His mouth barely moved, but she understood what he silently told her.

Trust me.

The tears started to cascade down her cheeks as she continued to struggle against Tiege. Gemma was strong, but he proved stronger as he all but dragged her along with him, down the drive, to an awaiting vehicle.

"Come on. I need to get you out of here."

"No. I don't want to go. I want to stay with him. Please!"

He ignored her protests. "You can't. He's in custody now and will be charged as soon as Winters brings him in."

"You're wrong," she told him several times as he pulled her along as if she weighed nothing more than a feather. "Ky isn't responsible for any of this."

"I'm afraid you've been tricked by him just as we all have." He helped her into the front seat of a black Escalade, not letting go of her arm until she was situated and had her safety belt in place.

He closed the door and sprinted around to the driver's side as if afraid she'd bolt the minute she got the chance.

A moment later he threw the car into gear and peeled away.

As the cabin and woods became a distant dot behind her, Gemma let go of the sobs she'd been holding inside her.

"I'm sorry you had to go through all this, Miss Laine. I thought Pappandreos was one of my best men."

"He is! You can't believe what Winters is saying. You can't. He's being set up—"

"No." Tiege shook his head. "Don't you think I've checked this out? I wouldn't willingly believe one of the best agents I've ever known is corrupt without making sure first."

"How could you make sure?"

"As soon as Winters brought me irrefutable proof, I had it checked out by our computer forensics team. They confirmed what Winters found. We set this whole thing up as soon as Papps called in."

"But Ky only called last night. How could you have proven it was him so fast? There was no time."

Tiege shook his head again, a habit Gemma was starting to hate. "Winters came to me two days ago with his suspicions."

"Two days ago? Wasn't he still in the hospital?"

"Yes, but he was working on the case even from his hospital bed. He discovered the agents killed in the ambush were texted from Papps' phone the day they were killed. Don't you understand? Pappandreos sent them to their deaths. Calafano was the target and my agents were collateral."

"But why would he do that? Hadn't you had that man in custody for weeks? I'm sure Ky had more than enough chances to kill him, the same way he had with me, and he didn't take advantage of them. Doesn't that prove he's innocent of all this?"

"No," he shook his head again, "it doesn't prove anything."

"Then why didn't he just kill me? Why did he escape with me? There were so many times he could have gotten rid of me and didn't. It doesn't make sense, which is why I know you're wrong about him."

She wiped her hands across her tear-drenched cheeks and then swiped her wrist under her dripping nose.

Tiege just shook his head again and kept driving.

Chapter Eighteen

Gemma opened her eyes. The sun glaring straight through the front windshield on its way to the horizon blinded her.

"Where are we?"

A piercing pain stabbed through her from a crick in her neck when she sat upright. She cupped her neck and massaged her shoulder. "We've been driving for hours."

"We're almost there."

"Where? You still haven't told me where you're taking me. I have no clothes, no equipment. Everything is in the car back there at the cabin."

"Don't worry about any of that." He turned and skirted a glance at her. "You'll be taken care of once we get there."

"Why won't you tell me where we're going?"

The SAC let out a deep, annoyed breath. "If it's so important for to you to know, I'm bringing you to another safe house upstate."

"Are we still in New York?" She glanced out at the road they were on and didn't see any identifying road markers. They could have been anywhere along the eastern seaboard. Or further in, for all she knew.

"Yes. And you can relax, we're almost there."

Gemma sat back and crossed her arms.

Tiege turned the car down a narrow dirt road. She spotted a blindingly bright body of water in the immediate distance.

So, they were by a lake. Interesting.

"What is it with the FBI and log cabins?" she asked, taking in the surroundings. The small, single-floor structure stood atop a small rise, wooden stairs leading down to a dock at the lakeshore from behind it, visible from the drive. A cabin cruiser was moored alongside the dock.

Peggy Jaeger

"They're easy and cheap," Tiege told her. He removed his seat belt and said, "Come on."

Gemma alighted from the car and took a look around. "Where are the other agents? I don't see any cars."

He didn't answer, just took her arm and led her up the two steps to the porch.

The front door opened and three men stepped out. Two were holding assault rifles, the third was unarmed.

Hair the color of a storm cloud, a little less than six feet, and clad in a well-cut suit with a bright, blood-red tie, Gemma's discerning eye put him between fifty and sixty years of age. Entirely too old to be an agent.

"About time you got here," the man said to Tiege, but his eyes were trained on her. "You've kept me waiting far too long."

"Couldn't be helped." Tiege shoved Gemma in front of him. "Here. She's all yours now."

He continued to hold her in his behemoth grip as he pushed her up close to the man.

Hands fisted on his hips, the man raked his gaze over her face, down her chest to her toes and then back up again. "You've proven to be a real pain in my ass, young lady." For the first time, a thin line of fear shivered down her spine. His spoken voice was low, but tinged with such hate and menace, Gemma knew instantly this was a powerful man used to giving orders and having them followed to the letter.

His mouth dipped at the corners, a snarl pulling back to reveal cigarette-stained teeth, decades in the making.

Gemma shoved her fear down as far as she could. "I'm sorry? What have I ever done to you? I don't even know you."

Beside her, Tiege's breath audibly caught.

The heat in the man's snarl turned volcanic. He moved toward her, the edges of his eyes narrowing, his bushy brows pulling down, almost closing off his eyes to her view.

"You don't know who I am?"

Gemma shook her head. "Why should I?"

His hand came up so fast she didn't have a second to pull back from the slap that lashed across her cheek. The force behind it knocked her to the side and she would have fallen to her knees if sheer will and determination hadn't kicked in, helping her to stay upright.

She whipped her head around, the painful sting from the slap throbbing immediately. The man grabbed a fistful of her hair and jerked her head so that his face was a kiss distance from hers.

"You should know the name of the last man you're ever going to see, little girl." His breath was hot, fetid, and foul as his words wafted over her face.

He yanked her hair, causing tears of pain to well up in her eyes.

"I'm Antonio Ritandi and I'm gonna kill you."

Gemma stopped breathing. It was the only way she knew she could keep control. Slow her breathing and it would slow her heart rate as well, allowing her to stay calm and focused.

"Let go of me. Now."

The snarl pulled back into a semblance of a smirk. "You're a ballsy thing, I'll give you that."

He jerked his hand from her hair.

Gemma refused to let him see how much pain he'd caused. Her scalp stung, and she could feel her cheek already starting to swell.

"So, you're the one responsible for making my life a living hell?" she asked, pleased her voice sounded steady and strong. As he'd done to her, she raked her gaze down the length of him, hoping the expression on her face was one of disdain. She'd flattened her lips, narrowed her eyes and fisted her hands on her hips.

It must have seemed so to Ritandi, because his face turned boiled-tomato red, the color spreading like wildfire up to his ears and then down his neck.

"*You little bitch.* I was gonna do you quick and easy, but that mouth of yours just made me think slow and painful is better."

He reached out a hand to her, but Gemma sidestepped him.

Ritandi stumbled, quickly recovered and snarled at her. Gemma took the moment's distraction to bolt. She sprinted around the house toward the dock.

"Get her!" Ritandi screamed. Just as she started down the steps she was grabbed from behind by Tiege. He yanked her to a halt and pulled both her hands behind her back, clasping her in handcuffs before she could fight him off.

"You're more trouble than you're worth," he spat into her ear as he spun her and dragged her back to the front of the cabin. "I'd have killed you first thing."

"Why didn't you, then? Why bring me here?"

"Not my call."

He shoved her so hard in front of Ritandi, she dropped to one knee. "Here. She's all yours now. I've gotta get back."

"Not so fast," Ritandi said.

It was then Gemma noticed the gun in his hand pointing at Tiege. Ritandi's finger hovered right over the trigger, cocked and ready. "You're not going anywhere."

"What is this?" The SAC yelled. "I brought this bitch to you, I got Pappandreos arrested. Calafano's dead. I've done everything you asked. Everything."

"Yeah, you have," Ritandi said with a smile that never made it to his eyes.

"So? What more do you want?"

Ritandi shook his head and seemed to ponder the question. When he gazed at Tiege, Gemma felt her insides turn liquid. His brown eyes were the deadest she'd ever seen on a live person; cold, hard, and scary as all hell.

His lips pulled back revealing stained teeth as he grinned at Tiege. There was a sharp edge of madness cut into his expression.

"Nothing." Ritandi pulled the trigger and shot Tiege straight between the eyes.

Tiege's body flung back, falling in one, single flat line. An eerie silence followed the echo of the shot as it moved through the tree line.

"Get rid of him," Ritandi told the two silent thugs. "I don't care how."

He trained his cold eyes on her while they dragged Tiege's body into the woods.

"And now you." He lifted the gun and pointed it at her face.

"I thought you wanted to kill me slowly," Gemma taunted. "Make me suffer."

Something shifted in his eyes at her words. He looked...gleeful.

She tampered down the bile pushing toward release. This man was truly the definition of evil.

A shot boomed from the direction the men had taken Tiege's body. Ritandi raised his head to the sound, then cursed. He pulled Gemma up from her knees and yanked her against his body.

"Walk!" he commanded as he pulled her along with him toward the dock.

"What's going on? Where are you taking me?"

She struggled against his hold. With her hands secured behind her back in the cuffs, she could do little more than wiggle and pull against him.

"Shut up and get moving."

She stumbled and would have dropped to her knees again, but his grip was as secure and tight as Tiege's had been.

"Stop! Federal agents!"

A bullet hit the ground close to them.

"Hold your fire! Hold your fire!" Winter's voice called.

Two agents in tactical gear appeared at the bottom of the dock stairs, weapons aimed up at them.

"Shit!"

Ritandi pivoted, keeping Gemma up against him as a shield, her back plastered against his front, his arm secure around her neck.

Ky and Jon came around the side of the house, several agents, all armed, their weapons primed, with them.

"Let her go, Ritandi," Ky commanded.

"Not a chance. She's my ticket out of here."

Ky shook his head. "It's over. You can't get out of here alive. I've got agents everywhere, surrounding you. Your men are in custody. It's just you and all of us. Let her go."

"I said not a chance."

Gemma could feel the man's heart jack-hammering against her back. His grip tightened around her, almost cutting off her air.

"I don't want to shoot you, but I will if you don't release her," Ky said.

"No you won't."

Ky's eyes shifted for a second to Gemma, then back to the mobster. "Yes, I will."

The man laughed, actually, laughed, at Ky.

He was enjoying this.

Gemma changed her description of him from evil to insane.

She needed to get Ky's attention on her again. She said his name. As soon as the word left her lips, two things happened.

Ky's gaze shot over her face and Ritandi's arm around her neck constricted even more. She couldn't move her hands, couldn't wind them under his to gain any slack in his increasingly tight hold.

With Ky looking straight at her, Gemma blinked and mouthed "Trust me" before closing her eyes and letting her body go slack.

The effect of her knees dropping, purposefully allowing them to relax, pitched her forward. Ritandi lost his hold as she slid down. When he tried to reposition her, he fired off a shot.

Gemma hit the ground, the sound of the gun's explosion above her deafening, as Ritandi's body fell backward. A hail of bullets from every direction sailed above her and the sickening thud of Ritandi's now lifeless body hitting the ground next to her made her slam her eyes shut again.

Gemma was hauled to her feet when she opened her eyes. Ky was saying something but her ears had gone silent, except for the high-pitched whistle screaming inside her brain. She shook her head at him. "I can't hear you."

He dragged her into his arms, his hold so safe, so familiar, she leaned into it. She could feel the reverberations of him saying something with her head against his chest and in the next instant her hands were freed from the cuffs. Immediately, she wound them around his waist and held on, while he smoothed her hair and kissed her temple.

The feel of his arms securely woven around her and the pounding of his heart against her cheek was nirvana.

Little by little the whistling eased and she was able to distinguish the sounds of the agents talking around her.

Ky's voice was the only one she wanted to hear.

He pulled back and stared down at her.

"Can you hear me yet?" He cupped her cheeks in his hands, settled his worried gaze on hers.

She nodded.

"Gemma." There was so much emotion infused in her name her knees almost went out on her again. He shook his head and placed his forehead against hers.

Around them the agents were inspecting Ritandi's lifeless body, removing his weapon, walking around the perimeter of the cabin. Jon Winters said something to one of the men and then came up to Gemma and Ky.

"That went well," he said with a grin. "Almost according to plan."

Gemma pulled from Ky's arms to give the agent a hug, mindful of the supportive sling that encased his arm to his chest. She dropped a kiss on his cheek.

"Except for Tiege and Ritandi getting killed," Ky said behind her.

"Hey, we got the son-of-a-bitch and rescued the girl," Jon told his partner. "That's what counts."

"Pappandreos! Winters!"

All three of them turned to the man barreling down from the drive toward them.

"Who is that?" Gemma asked, moving close to Ky again. When his hand spread across the small of her back, her shoulders relaxed. Just a touch calmed and comforted her more than any words ever could.

"ASA Barly," Ky told her.

"You were given explicit orders not to use deadly force," Barly shrieked at Ky.

"Couldn't be helped," Winters said. "We were forced to defend ourselves. And Miss Laine."

Barly's gaze flashed over Gemma. The photographer in her decided there was no conceivable way she could ever make him look appealing in a portrait. His reptilian eyes pulled almost closed while her stared at her. She felt as if she knew what an unsuspecting insect experienced just before a predator claimed it as a meal.

"I'll need a statement from you immediately," he told her, without even introducing himself. "Detailing everything you can remember about what Tiege said to you before and after you arrived here." He switched his attention to Ky. "Have one of your men bring her to my office now."

"It'll get done, Barly," Ky told him, "but Miss Laine's been through enough. Her statement can wait."

From over the man's shoulder's Gemma spied a familiar face in the sea of agents and personnel who'd descended upon the cabin, standing off at the tree line, hands in his pockets, just observing the scene.

"Excuse me," Ky said to the attorney, cutting the man off midsentence while he'd been castigating him about shooting Ritandi.

With Gemma's hand in his, he led her to Rick Bannerman. "I'm gonna be tied up for a while," Ky said while they walked. "Here and back at the bureau. I made arrangements for Bannerman to take you back to the city so you don't have to wait around. I know how much you want to get home."

"I don't mind waiting for you," she said. "I can give that statement Barly's so hot for."

He shook his head. "Like I told him, it'll get done. It's better if you go, Gemma. I need to finish this. I've got a lot of bureaucrats to deal with and reports to file, and I can't do all that with you around."

"Oh." Why did she feel like she'd been stabbed in the heart?

"Bannerman can take you home. Either Jon or I will be in touch as soon as we can about taking your statement. It's not necessary we have it immediately, despite what Barly says. It's not going to change anything that happened here today."

"Looks like everything went as planned," Rick said when they got to him.

"We didn't plan on Tiege getting himself killed," Ky said, letting go of Gemma's hand.

"Collateral damage," Bannerman said with a shrug. "You okay?" he asked Gemma, pulling her in for a hug.

She nodded. "My ears are still ringing a little but it'll pass."

"Yeah, it will. You did good, Cleo. Your boy here," he chinned Ky, "says you were very convincing when Winters was pretending to arrest him."

Gemma snuck a glance at Ky. "That was the plan," she said.

"You did well," Ky said. "It was obvious Tiege had no clue we knew he was the mole."

"If you don't need us for anything," Bannerman said to Ky, "I'd like to get out of here."

Ky turned to Gemma, took her hand and brought it to his lips. "I'll find you as soon as I can."

Swallowing, she nodded.

"Thanks for taking her," he said to Bannerman. "And for...everything else. Without your help we would never have been able to arrange all this."

Rick nodded and held out his hand. Ky took it.

"Never thought I'd hear myself say this about a bunch of feds, but working with you and your team has been a pleasure. Your partner couldn't stop singing your praises when I met with him at the hospital. Says a lot about a man when his men respect him like that."

Ky nodded. With a final look at Gemma, he turned and made his way back to his agents.

Her gaze followed him as he walked away.

"Come on, Cleo." Bannerman grabbed the hand Ky had just kissed. "Let's get you home."

Like an obedient child, she let him lead her away.

Chapter Nineteen

Bannerman drove her straight, without stopping, back to her condo to a waiting Kandy.

The sisters hugged, then Rick kissed her cheek and told her he'd check on her during the week. Once alone with just her older sister, Gemma collapsed in tears.

Over several hours, and fortified with an entire bottle of much needed wine, Gemma relayed everything that had happened to her for the past week, including how her relationship with Ky had gone from professional to personal. As she had for their entire lives, Kandy listened quietly, asking simple questions when she needed clarification, and held her younger sister's hand. She hadn't judged, offered advice, or asked Gemma what she was going to do next.

When Gemma's eyes started to drift closed, Kandy put her to bed and called Josh to come pick her up.

It was the next afternoon by the time Gemma opened her eyes again.

For the first time in what seemed like a lifetime, she reached for her phone. Kandy had plugged it into the bedside charger before leaving and when Gemma typed in her password the phone began chirping incessantly, announcing all the messages and e-mails she'd received while she'd been out of touch.

Gemma silenced the sound and took a quick glance at the screen.

She couldn't possibly have a thousand e-mails and text messages.

A quick scan through the scores of texts showed nothing from Ky. Gemma sighed and tried not to think about what that meant. Next to the charger was a glass of water with two aspirin.

"God bless you, big sister."

A long, hot, and steamy shower later, filled with memories of the last time she'd showered with Ky, Gemma dressed and then hit the kitchen.

The stocked refrigerator was a present from Kandy, but Gemma wasn't hungry for all the delicious food her sister had stuffed it with. She grabbed a bottle of her favorite diet soda and chugged it down.

Within seconds the caffeine hit her bloodstream.

Showered and caffeinated, she took a look around her, happy to see that her living space had been put to rights and cleaned up from the previous attack. With another bottle of soda in her hand, she went into her home office and started answering her e-mails.

Eight hours later she looked from the computer screen to see nighttime descending through the window. She'd answered a good deal of her e-mails, most of it scheduling requests, called her editor at the publishing house and explained about the delay with the *Faces* book, had spoken with her mother, Kandy, and the rest of her sisters who'd all been worried sick about her. Promises of lunch and shopping dates satisfied their questions that she was, indeed, home now, the threat eliminated.

She paid the bills that had come in while she was gone, checked her bank balance for any Internet transactions and payments deposited in her absence and then realized she was hungry.

Dinner was a bowl of Kandy's fish chowder and a couple slices of sour dough bread, after which exhaustion once again dragged her to bed.

One day home and no word from Ky. Before she fell asleep Gemma told herself he was busy righting all the wrongs Ritandi and Tiege had created. He'd call when he could.

Day two she awoke with more energy. When her phone was still empty of any word from Ky, she pouted, got ready for the day and decided to work.

Now that she'd joined the land of the living and employed again, she needed to pay attention to all her projects. She dug out her cameras and hooked them up to her home computer.

The images she'd taken of Ky in bed popped up immediately, filling her screen and kicking her pulse into high gear.

He truly was a magnificent man. Every curve and dip in his chest and abdomen, where the muscles grouped and flexed, was perfection. Memories of all that power and strength above her, surrounding her, inside her, shot to the front of her mind. Gemma closed her eyes and sat back, just letting them play through.

She missed him. Pure and simple. Alone in the privacy of her home, safe and secure from any threats, and free to let her mind explore, she could finally admit what she truly felt for him.

And it was more than the simple longing she'd tried to convince herself it was.

Much more.

Was she was in love with him? She'd never been in love with any man before, so her reference for what she was feeling was nil. But there could be no other explanation for what she was going through. Her mind drifted to his image no matter what she was doing. His was the last face she saw before falling asleep, the first thing that popped into her head upon awakening, and her dreams were filled with him. His voice, his expressions, the way his eyes stared at her when he was inside her, as if he could read her thoughts.

He'd snuck past her all her defenses, sidestepped her protective nature, and grabbed hold of her heart with his hands.

It wasn't just the physical part of him that she craved, either. Oh, that was great enough. Gemma was a woman who knew the benefits of physical pleasure and she enjoyed sex. Sex with Ky was amazing. He'd approached it the way he seemed to everything else in his life: calmly, thoroughly, and with full commitment. The way she'd felt when he kissed her, as if he owned her body and soul, had been a heady experience, and she'd remembered thinking what unbelievable and complete power there was in surrender. It sounded crazy, but to give all her control over to him, to trust him with everything she was and had, was stupefying.

Physically, they were a near-perfect match. In so many other ways, though, they were as well. He was a competent straight man to her many snarky remarks, able to toss out a dead-aimed zinger of his own now and again. They both enjoyed martial arts, and what she might lack in body strength, she more than made up for in skill. Ky had even admitted she was masterful with weapons. They both liked to cook, although she easily conceded he was the better chef.

Family had come first, last, and always to her, and it did to Ky as well. The way his eyes had gone soft and loving when he'd spoken of his siblings, or quoted his mother or grandmother, showed her he was the type of man who valued those he loved.

Every way she looked at him, inside, out, physically, mentally, and spiritually, Kyros Pappandreos was a man—the only man—she could picture giving her heart to and entrusting him with.

She hit the scroll button on her laptop and stopped at every photo she'd taken of him. In the garage while he'd been pummeling the punching bag, drenched in sweat and looking like a powerful machine; seated on the couch while he'd been hatching his plan with Rick, thoughtful and pensive; the pictures of him naked and spread across the bed, a sheet covering him from the waist down, a look of drowsy sexual satisfaction in his eyes. Satisfaction from what they'd just shared.

A single tear slipped down her cheek. Gemma laughed out loud, not missing the irony of crying over a man when she'd spent a lifetime protecting herself from ever doing just that.

Work was the one thing she knew would take her mind off missing Ky, so she squared her shoulders and got to it. The coffee-table book wasn't going to produce itself.

She had her memory discs, minus the Calafano pictures, and all the other photos she'd already taken around New York City.

Time to make some magic.

Hours later she stumbled back to bed, and, fully clothed, settled under the covers.

* * *

The number displayed across her screen was unfamiliar. Thinking, hoping, it was a certain special agent sent her pulse into race mode.

"Hello?"

Good Lord, was that breathless anticipation really her?

"Gemma? It's Jon Winters."

"Hi." She tried to infuse some warmth into her voice. It wasn't his fault he was the wrong agent calling her.

"We need to bring you in so we can get your statement about everything that went down."

She'd been expecting the summons. "When?"

"Is today good?"

She told him it was. "But you don't have to pick me up. I can get myself down there."

"No can do. I've been ordered to make sure you get here safe and sound."

Gemma wondered who'd ordered that.

An hour later he met her downstairs at her condo and helped her into another black Escalade.

"I'm beginning to think this vehicle is made exclusively for the FBI."

Jon chuckled. Seated next to her in the second row of seats, he peered at her for a moment, then asked, "So, how are you doing? Really?"

Gemma shrugged and gave him a smile. "It's good to be home. I've been working nonstop, after sleeping for about fourteen hours that first night back."

"The adrenaline drop," he said, nodding. "Happens to us all the time when a case is finally done. Exhaustion sets in and then after a day or so back to reality, you're looking for the next shot of it to hit your bloodstream."

She didn't think she'd ever heard the experience described so well before.

"We should be there in a few more minutes. Let me tell you what's gonna happen."

He took her through the steps of her testimony. Barly insisted she be videotaped and he would be present to conduct the questioning.

"Don't worry about him," Jon assured her. "He's a bit of a blowhard, and he might come across as an asshole, but you'll be fine. He already knows all about the plan with Tiege. I told him before it ever went down what we were going to do. When your friend Bannerman contacted me that was the first thing Ky had wanted."

At the mention of his name Gemma's body went on alert. She desperately wanted to ask how he was, *where* he was, why he wasn't the one bringing her in, but somehow, she couldn't get the words out.

"Ky's stuck in DC, by the way," Jon offered. "The director needed to go over some things concerning Tiege and our division with him, otherwise he'd be the one with you today."

"Oh," was all she could manage to say.

He cocked his head as his gaze traveled across her face. In the next moment he said, "We're here."

Five hours later, tired and drained, he dropped her back at the condo with a kiss to her cheek and a promise to call if anything else came up she was needed for.

* * *

Two more days passed, and she still hadn't heard from Ky.

Her mind was cluttered with thoughts of why, but the one that she gave the most space to was the simple fact that he didn't want to see her.

She was no longer in danger and his duty toward her was done. Done with the case, and with her.

The physical closeness they'd shared had been nothing more than a reaction to two adults experiencing simple desire in enclosed quarters, during a stressful time.

That had to be it, because if it had been more, if Ky had felt one tenth for her what she had for him, he would have contacted her. Would have been here with her. Would have made the time.

All her thoughts that what they'd shared was different from anything else she'd ever experienced with a man were true. Unfortunately, she now realized those feelings were one-sided. Hers.

She dragged herself from bed, forced herself to take a shower and eat. She wouldn't cry over him again or let his unexplained absence rule her life. She had clients lining up for appointments; she had the book to finish, and another to start. Tasks to keep her busy. Work to keep her from thinking about him.

She worked on her computer, editing photographs and e-mailing clients without stopping until late afternoon.

Just as she was finishing up and about to make something to fill her growling and insistent stomach, the doorbell chimed.

Without first looking through the peep hole or asking who it was, she pulled the door open and gasped.

"Ky!"

He looked…wonderful. Exhausted, but wonderful. About three days' worth of amber, honey-blond stubble lined his jaw, dark, half-moon shaped blotches circled under his eyes, and it looked as if he'd been wearing the same clothes for a while. He leaned against the doorframe, as if he needed it to keep him upright. Gemma wanted to wrap her arms around him and cuddle away all the pain and weariness she saw in his eyes and on his face. Then, in the next breath she remembered she was mad and wanted to punch him for not getting in touch with her.

"What are you doing here?"

"Can I come in?" he asked. Even his voice sounded close to the edge of collapse.

Gemma pulled the door open wide. He let out a breath, placed his jacket over his forearm, and entered.

"Thanks," he said when she shut it behind her. "I wasn't sure you'd be home. I took a chance without calling or texting first. I hoped," he shook his head, "I hoped you'd be here."

She led him into the living room.

"This is nice," he said absently, glancing around, his eyes tired but alert. "I wasn't paying attention the last time I was here."

The day she'd been attacked. The day they'd met.

Lord! Was it really just two weeks ago?

"Would you like something to drink? Or eat?" she asked. "I was just going to fix myself something."

"I wouldn't say no to a beer if you have one."

"I do. Sit." She pointed to the sofa. "You look about ready to drop."

He nodded. While she went into the kitchen to get them drinks she heard him settle down and sigh.

Her heart stuttered at the bone-weary fatigue in the sound.

She laid a hand across the quivering muscles in her stomach and set about making him a sandwich.

"Here." She handed him the beer she'd poured into a glass and set down the small plate with the ham and cheese she made on the cocktail table, and then sat down on the opposite side of the sofa.

"Thanks."

He took a long draught, tipping his head back as he drank.

Such a profound craving to reach out and run her mouth along his exposed jaw and neck pounded through her, she squirmed in her seat and settled her butt firmly into the cushion so she'd stay put.

When he leaned forward again, his gaze shot to her.

"How are you doing since you've been home?"

She shrugged. "Fine. Busy. Getting my life back in order again."

"No nightmares, trouble sleeping? No anxiety about what happened?"

"None." She mentally crossed her fingers against the fib.

Ky nodded. "Jon told me you gave your taped deposition. I'm sorry I wasn't here for it. For you."

Her heart gave a little shudder at his words. She bit down on the inside of her cheek before she asked, "How about you? Is the investigation closed now? Officially?"

"Almost. I've been tied up with the director and attorney general. I just got off the plane about an hour ago. I haven't even been back to my apartment yet."

So he'd come directly to her. Interesting.

"Was it bad?"

"It wasn't good." He blew out a breath. "The attorney general went on a rampage when he was told Ritandi was dead. He blames me."

"That's ridiculous. I'd think he'd be happy the man was brought to justice, no matter how it was accomplished."

Ky shook his head absently and took another drink of his beer. "He wants answers to questions and now he can't get them. With Ritandi dead we can't find out much more about his organization. There's still stuff we haven't been able to tie to him to, and now it looks like we won't be able to. And then there are the millions of questions about Tiege. How did Ritandi get to him? What was the leverage? Is anyone else involved? It's been a nightmare. My tech guys have been combing through Tiege's home and office computers since we got back."

"Have they found anything?"

"Nothing of use other than confirmation about the account Bannerman found with Tiege's wife's name attached to it. If there is anything it's buried so deep we may never find it. Tiege was assigned to the cybercrimes division for ten years before he was made SAC. He knew how to cover his virtual tracks well."

"Can't you ask Theo for help?"

He stared across the length of the sofa at her, his eyes half closed, his brows almost kissing. She'd give anything to know what he was thinking with a look like that.

"Unfortunately, I can't. Not officially. And if I did it unofficially and he found something, I wouldn't be able to use it since it wasn't legally discovered. Lawyers love that phrase: fruit from the poisoned tree."

"I thought privilege like that didn't follow you once you were dead?"

"Typically, it doesn't. But discovery from a non-agency source is grounds for survivors to contest. Possibly sue. The bureau doesn't need that kind of headache."

"Rock, meet hard place," Gemma said.

One corner of Ky's mouth kicked up. "My life for the past three years."

He finished his beer, placed the glass back on the table, then scrubbed his hands down his face and yawned.

"Anyway. It'll work itself out in time." He turned to look directly at her again. "I didn't come here to discuss all that with you."

"Oh?" She tried to ignore the little stab to her heart. She'd hoped he was here because he missed her, realized he couldn't live without her...loved her.

Wishful thinking.

"Do you want another beer?"

She rose, but Ky's hand shot out to grab her arm.

"No."

The touch sent an electrical frisson through her body. His long, strong fingers wound around her forearm, holding her in place. Gemma didn't know whether to sit back down or stay rooted to her spot.

Ky solved the problem when he gently tugged on her arm and brought her down next to him.

He slid his hand down her arm to lace their fingers together. Utter warmth spread through her from head to toes.

"Gemma."

Had her name ever sounded so sweet on any other man's lips?

"We need to talk."

Oh, God! Here it comes: the letdown, the brush off.

Historically, Gemma had been the one who always told the man she was with it was time to move on, that things were over between them. It was one of the ways she'd always been able to keep control of the relationship. She'd start it. And she'd end it. Her heart would remain unscathed.

But she couldn't bear to hear the words come through Ky's lips. It would break her in two.

"No, we don't, Ky. It's okay. I know what you're going to say, and it's okay. Really."

The corrugated lines in his forehead deepened as he regarded her. "What do you think I'm going to say?"

Pride, ego, and self-preservation bounded through her. She wouldn't let him see her come apart. Couldn't let him know her real feelings. She needed to dig deep for that lifelong cord of control that she'd never needed more than she did right now.

"Gemma?"

She sighed and placed her free hand over his, patted it, like she would a child who needed reassurance. "Like I said, it's okay. You don't have to say it. We're both grownups."

"Just what is it you don't think I need to say?"

"Ky." She shrugged.

"No. Really, Gemma. I need you to tell me, because I sure as heck don't know what you mean."

"Oh, all right." She tugged her hand from his, intending to stand and move away from him, but he wouldn't let it go. In fact, when she pulled, he squeezed harder.

She took a deep breath and looked over his shoulder at the lamp next to the couch. She couldn't look directly at him without coming undone.

"Look at me, Gemma."

From any other man's lips, that command would have sent her back shooting up straight as a pin. That she did exactly what he told her to in an instant was an indication of how much power he had over her.

"Baby, look at me." His voice softened with the endearment and, God help her, tears threatened to drop.

She swallowed them back, looked up at him and said, "You're going to tell me that since this case is done, and I'm no longer in any kind of danger, that, well…"

Gemma sighed, all the fight going out of her. "I'm trying to tell you I understand. We were in a dangerous situation, adrenaline gets flowing, emotions and urges get acted upon…"

He continued to stare at her with confusion on his face.

Did he really not understand what she was saying?

"We slept together, Ky. We used each other to get through a bad time. To give us each a little comfort, a little diversion. But it's over now and we can get back to our lives. Back to the way things were...before."

"You think I used you for comfort? For sex? Because you were, what? Available?"

She nodded, as one single tear broke loose and slipped down her cheek. Gemma cursed her weakness.

"I'm saying we both used each other. And then it all got to be too much, between us," she said. "I realize that. You were just doing your job, trying to keep me safe. Everything you did, everything you said, was because you were doing your job. I was the one who, well, made it go further than it should have."

Saying it out loud made it sound so real, so final.

"Gemma, look at me."

She did.

"In all the time we've spent together, through everything, the shootings, the running, *everything*, do you really think that I would have made love to you if I didn't want to? That you basically forced me into it?"

"N-no. That's not what I'm saying."

"It's what you implied when you said you let the situation between us get out of hand."

"I did. If you remember, I was the one who came to your room, not the other way around. I started this...this...*thing*, between us. I made the first move, not you."

"Only because I thought you couldn't stand to be in the same room as me."

"What?"

"From the moment we met, you were pissed off at me and didn't hide it. At the safe house it was worse. You were all sweetness and light to Jon but when you looked at me I felt like you wanted to squash me under your shoe like an annoying bug."

Gemma had the grace to blush, knowing how true his words were.

"Believe me," he said, his mouth quirking up in one corner, "if I'd known what you were thinking, what you wanted, I would have been in your bed after the first time we grappled together in the basement."

She blinked. Several times. "You would have?"

He laughed. "Baby, I was so hard when you were on top of me, even an ice cold shower couldn't calm me down."

"Really?"

With one tug on her hand she was in his lap. "Yes, really." He cupped her cheeks and leaned in to kiss her.

How had she lasted five days without this? Without his touch? Without his kiss?

Ky pulled away and stared hard at her face. "The minute you turned around on that street corner and I saw you the first time, I wanted you. That's never happened before."

She traced his bottom lip with her fingertip.

He sucked it into his mouth. Then he circled her wrist and pulled it out, biting gently down on the pad.

Gemma was glad she was sitting because she lost all feeling in her legs from her thighs down.

"The night you came to my room I'd been trying to work, but all I kept thinking about was that kiss in the kitchen."

"It was all I could think about, too. That's why I went to you. I wanted more."

He laid his forehead against hers. "Thank God you did."

Gemma nuzzled his jaw and set her head down on his shoulder. "I thought you didn't want to see me any more now that everything was resolved. You didn't call, or text. Nothing. Not one word since I got home."

A breath pushed passed his lips, slow and deep. "I apologize for that. The truth is, aside from being tied up twenty hours a day for the past five days with every government alphabet agency imaginable, I knew if I called you I'd never be able to finish what needed to be done. All I'd want to do was come to you and forget everything else. So I kept going, sat through every tedious, long, maddening meeting and interview I had to. I slept on the couch in my office at the FBI for the past four nights."

He pulled her head up and stared into her eyes. "The minute I was cleared of the investigation into Ritandi's shooting I hopped on a plane. I came straight from the airport hoping you'd be here."

When she cupped his cheek he turned his head into her palm and kissed it. "All I knew was I had to get here. To you, Gemma. And I'm not leaving for any reason, so you're still stuck with me whether you like it or not."

This time his kiss was urgent, wanting, needing. It was everything Gemma had remembered, and promised so much more.

When she came up for air, she wound her fingers into his hair and said, "I like it. Very much."

"Good."

* * *

Later, much later, she rolled to her side on the bed and curled into the crook of his arm. His fingers absently stroked her side, both their breaths still fast from their recent lovemaking, but slowly calming.

"I missed you." She kissed his chest, dragged a lazy finger across his nipple, and giggled when it came to a peak.

"Baby, you're gonna kill me," he moaned, then chuckled. He pulled her closer. "I missed you, too." A gentle kiss to her temple had her sighing.

"Oh, speaking of getting killed, take this back. I don't need it anymore." She pulled out of his arms, sat up, and lifted his St. Michael's medallion from around her neck.

Ky took it and rubbed the raised impression between his fingers. "I have to thank Dini for giving me this again the next time I see her. It allowed us to track you without Tiege knowing it."

Instead of putting it back around his own neck, he tossed it over onto her bedside table.

"Even though I knew you were able to monitor where he was taking me, I was still a little scared," she admitted.

"Come here." He tightened his arms around her when she melted into his embrace. He kissed her cheek.

"We were never more than a minute behind you the whole time. I still can't believe he didn't spot us following. You did a good job, by the way. Tiege really bought your act."

"He kept saying how Jon had given him irrefutable proof that it was you. That I'd been tricked into believing you were a good guy. That the whole bureau had. I was so mad I wanted to hit him more than once during the car ride."

Gemma felt his jaw tighten against her.

"I'm still pissed at myself that I never considered he was the one responsible for any of what happened. If I'd had even an inkling, maybe my men would still be alive."

It was Gemma's turn to tighten her hold on him. "Don't do that. Don't blame yourself."

His sigh was deep and troubled. "I do, though. There's no way around it. They were my men, my team. I'd handpicked every one of them the day we started the investigation."

Gemma sat up again and stared down at him. The exhaustion she'd seen earlier was joined by sorrow and anger now. "They were all seasoned agents, like you, right? Had been on the job for a while?"

He nodded. "I have the most time in, Jon next, but yeah. I had no newbies. I needed guys with history and experience in the bureau. Why?"

"Then they knew what to expect from the job? What might happen? What could go wrong?"

"Sure." He shrugged and then folded his arm around his head, cradling it on the pillow.

"So, knowing that something could go wrong, planning for it even, they still wanted to work with you, right?"

He nodded. "What's your point?"

Gemma considered what she wanted to say. While she did, she slid her legs over his abdomen, straddling him, her hands resting on her thighs.

Ky's hands moved immediately to settle on her hips. He was already half aroused and she could feel him swelling more now against her.

"My point is that these men were professionals who knew what they did was dangerous and did it anyway of their own choice. You didn't get them killed. You're not responsible for what happened. And despite the AG being mad that Ritandi is in a box and not a cell, I think you killing him was totally and completely justified."

She trailed her hands up over his pecs and rested them there. The steady, solid beat of his heart against her hand picked up when she wiggled and settled down against him.

For a moment he looked as if he was going to argue with her. Then, his lids went half closed and he nailed her with that hot, drowsy, sexy gaze of his that made her toes curl.

He slid his hands from her hips, lightly across her outer thighs to the inner skin sitting on top of his body. Gemma's breath caught when he pushed his thumbs along the tops of her legs and pressed into her flesh, spreading and exposing her most intimate, private part for him.

His full lips pulled up in a wicked grin. "Gorgeous, talented, successful, and," he swiped the pad of his thumb straight across her clitoris, circling it, "smart."

Gemma felt the pressure from his finger shoot a bullet of pleasure straight up her spinal cord.

"Everything I've always wanted in a woman," he added, slipping two fingers inside her.

Gemma threw back her head and arched her spine, giving him more than ample space to continue with this task, unheeded.

While he pumped his fingers in and out of her in a slow, thorough rhythm, she felt him grow larger and harder against her butt. Reaching back a hand, she fisted him and watched his eyes close, his mouth open on a moan when she tugged up his length and then slid down again.

Her laugh filled the room when he murmured in Greek.

"I don't need you to translate that. The meaning is universal."

In a heartbeat he reversed their positions. He made a nest for his hips in the cradle of her thighs, while she wound her long legs around his waist to cross at his back.

With his weight on his elbows, his shoulders pressed back, he looked down at her. His beautiful ocean colored eyes were sparkling, his long lashes glistening with moisture, as he whispered, "Gemma. *Se agapo.*"

She went as still as stone.

This phrase was new, different, *more.*

She was terrified to ask what it meant and terrified not to know. Instinct told her it was something profound. Something that would change her and...them.

"Gemma." He swiped her bangs back from her forehead and kissed her eyes closed. She opened them when he shifted his mouth to her cheek, then ran it along her jaw.

"Not going to ask me what that meant?" He sucked at the notch behind her ear.

"I—I think, I think it probably has something to do with what we're doing. Right?"

She felt him smile along her collarbone. "Kind of."

"So. Okay. No need to know the full translation, then. I'm getting the gist."

When he lifted his head and looked down at her, amusement filled his smile.

"What?" she asked.

"I never took you for a coward."

"*What?*" She dropped her legs back onto the bed with a thud and tried to push him off her, forgetting what a solid, unmovable tank of a man he was.

"I'm not a coward. And you know it."

Her inner voice mocked her as the liar she was.

"No?" He cocked his head as he continued grinning down at her. "Then why don't you want to know what I've just said? Every other time I've lapsed into Greek you've always demanded I translate. Why not this time? Do you know what the words mean?"

"N-no."

"Then why don't you want me to tell you?"

She didn't answer him. Couldn't. Instead, she bit down on the inside of her cheek.

Ky's gaze softened. He slid his knuckles across one cheek and kissed the other. "It won't hurt if I say it in English, I promise. This translation leaves no room for doubt." He looked into her eyes, and she swore he could see her soul. "Trust me?"

Without hesitating she answered, "With everything I am," and knew the words could never be truer. "You know that."

Right before he took her lips with his, he smiled and whispered, "I love you."

Oh. My. God.

She'd been correct. That phrase, those three words, changed everything. Everything.

"I can hear the fear flying around in your head," he said, as his lips moved down her neck to her breasts. He wet his mouth with his tongue, and then sucked the tip of one in, his tongue laving across the hardened peak.

"Oh!" Her hands fisted in his hair.

"There's no need to panic." He moved to her other breast, his free hand skating down and over her flat belly to burrow in the sparse hair at the apex of her thighs. "You trust me, right?"

"*Yes.*"

Did she say the word or scream it? She wasn't sure because the pressure of Ky's tongue and hands doing wicked things to her body made logical thought impossible.

"Then don't worry about anything." He ran a purposeful finger down the length of her wet heat, then back up again. "Just let me love you, Gemma."

He shifted, slipped on the condom he had ready, and in one, full, and elegant slide, was completely inside her.

"Ky!"

"Love when you call out my name, baby," he growled into her ear.

Gemma's mind shut off with each thrust and dive of Ky's body. Every nerve fiber in her body, every pulsation of blood coursing through her, was centered where they were joined together.

When he reached a hand between their bodies and pressed his thumb, hard and firm, against her, Gemma wasn't prepared for the magnitude of the orgasm that shook through her. Lightning flashed behind her closed eyes as she repeated the words he'd given her minutes before.

When he followed her over the cliff seconds later, she was still quaking around him, milking him with the aftershocks raging through her.

Buried deep within her, Ky nuzzled her neck. "I heard you, you know." He pulled up and grinned down at her. "It was kind of hard not to since you screamed."

She pinched one taut, firm butt cheek between her fingers.

Laughing felt so good, Gemma couldn't contain hers when he yelped.

"I want to hear it again," Ky said once she stopped. "Scream it if you want. But I want to hear it, Gemma. I want to watch you say the words."

"What?" She opened her eyes wide, batted her lashes at him, a move she'd always considered cheesy before, and asked, "That I trust you? I think I've told you that before, haven't I?"

One milk chocolate colored eyebrow crawled upward.

She giggled and threw her arms around his neck. With her lips hovering just a whisper from his she said, "Oh. You mean tell you I love you, again. Okay." She moved closer still, close enough to breathe in the air he expelled over her. "I love you, Kyros Pappa-whatever."

The corners of his eyes crinkled.

"It's crazy, but I love you."

"There, now," he said. "That wasn't so hard, was it?"

She shook her head. "But speaking of things being hard…" she lifted her hips.

Still nestled inside her, she felt him being to pulse and grow again.

"Again?" she asked on a laugh.

"Again," he answered with kiss.

Later, when their hearts and breathing settled, he rolled off her, and, with a quick kiss to her cheek, slid from the bed and to the bathroom. Gemma heard the toilet flush, and then water running. He came back seconds later with a filled glass of water.

He leaned a hip down on the bed and handed her the glass.

"Drink this," he told her, with a yawn. "Then we need some sleep."

Gemma drained the glass and after he put it on the bedside table next to his medallion, he slid under the covers and settled on his side, her back molded against his front.

With his arm draped across her waist, Gemma linked her fingers with his and closed her eyes.

"I love you," she whispered.

* * *

In the dark, Ky smiled.

Chapter Twenty

They'd been together nonstop since the moment he'd walked into her condo. After not taking any personal or vacation time in the three years of the Ritandi investigation, Ky had requested, and been granted, a month's leave. Every second he could, he'd spent it with Gemma.

The days she needed to work with clients were the only times they'd been separated. He'd moved most of his necessary things into her place without a formal invitation or discussion about it and she'd never questioned it. They were living together in every way. When she came home, exhausted and cranky from dealing with contrary and annoying celebrity clients, Ky had a glass of wine, a meal, and a willing ear ready that immediately elevated her mood.

They made love every night in her king-sized bed then fell asleep wrapped in one another's arms.

Many mornings she was out the door, late and laughing, because he'd *detained* her in bed, not wanting to let her go.

He was secure enough in his thoughts to know Gemma was the woman he wanted a forever with. Getting her on board with the idea was the problem, but if working at the FBI had taught him one thing these past twelve years, he was a first-class problem solver.

* * *

"Your grandmother is adopting Kandy," she told him, as she kicked off her shoes and went into the kitchen after arriving home from his grandmother's ninety-fourth birthday party.

Ky nodded and took the beer she offered him from the refrigerator, while she took a bottled water for herself.

"Before we left my mother pulled me aside and told me Kandy offered her and *YiaYia* jobs as special culinary consultants for one of her upcoming food specials. She's gonna do a whole hour on Greek cuisine." He heaved a theatrical sigh. "There'll be no living with her now. My poor father."

"He'll survive."

Gemma moved to the living room and collapsed onto the sofa.

"I liked your family," she told him when he sat with her. She lifted his arm and snuck under it, laying her head on his shoulder while he squeezed her upper arm and then kissed the top of her head.

"They liked you, too. Especially my uncle Stavros." He groaned then took a swig of beer. "I've got a feeling you created a monster when you suggested he get a job as an older male model."

"I wasn't kidding. He's extremely photogenic. His features practically leaped from the camera, just like—"

She stopped and busied herself with taking a long draught of water.

"Just like what?"

"I should have known you wouldn't let that go."

"Like what, Gemma?" He pushed against her arm.

She slipped from his under his arm, sat back on the cushions and folded her arms across her chest. "Okay, I'll tell you, but you have to promise to have an open mind."

He shrugged and looked at her with confusion. "Okay. Although I don't know why it would be closed."

"Stay here," she commanded, rising. "It's easier if I show you."

He heard her rummaging in her home office and then she came back with her work laptop in her hands. She sat back down facing him this time.

"I haven't shown these to anyone, just like I promised, which is a crying shame because they're some of the best work I've ever done."

"Gemma?"

She shook her head and booted up the laptop. After signing in with her password she turned the device to him.

An oath spewed from him before he could rein it in.

"That's the word you curse in Greek when you're either surprised or upset. I'm really hoping this time it's because you're surprised."

"Is that...me?"

He pulled the device onto his lap and continued to stare at the photo she'd cropped for her screen saver.

She'd blown up the image in black and white so that it started at his neck and went all the way down to where one thigh was peeking out from under the sheet tossed over his groin. His medallion glittered from a spark of errant light, giving the depression where it sat between his pecs an even more defined and toned appearance. Half lying, half sitting against the pillows, one arm was flung carelessly next to him on the bed, as if beckoning a lover to come back to him, the other braced on top of the sheet, casually covering his arousal. The curved, deeply corrugated rows of his abdominal muscles were contracted and taut, each muscular duo perfectly positioned atop, and next to, the other.

The sheet barely concealed him, and it didn't take any imagination at all to visualize the bulge under the strategically placed piece of material. One thigh was bent outward, a simple fold and pull of the same sheet allowing a small, almost imperceptible glimpse under it.

"It's the most erotic picture I've ever taken," Gemma said. "I've filmed hundreds of people who were totally nude and they didn't look this sexy. This is tasteful, doesn't show a thing that could be considered pornographic, and if I wasn't the one who took it, I'd say it looks like a high-class art piece."

Ky's gaze bounced from the screen to her face, then back to the screen a few times. His mouth opened, closed, opened, and then slammed shut as he gave his attention to the picture before him.

"This is really me?"

"Have you glanced at a mirror lately?" she asked. "Don't you know what you look like?"

"Not like this, that's for sure. What did you do to the picture? Photoshop it?"

He knew he'd hit a chord when her back went straight up against the couch. He expected a tongue-lashing but was floored when she took a breath and said, "I didn't do a thing to the photo except copy it in black and white and blow it up so your head wasn't shown." She pushed the keyboard to scroll through the others in the series to show him the originals.

"Here, this proves it's you."

The pictures showed up in a grid of four on the screen, each one untouched, in color, and with his face on display.

"I've said this before, you're an amazing photographer." He reached out for her hand and, bringing it to his lips, kissed it. "But I never realized what a true artist you are, Gemma."

She shrugged off the compliment, but her eyes softened when she looked across at him.

"You really don't know this is how you look? What I see every time I look at you?"

Peggy Jaeger

He shook his head.

He turned his attention to the photos with his face not cropped out. As he'd known her to do before, she'd snapped a half dozen within a few seconds to, as she'd told him, capture the perfect expression. He may not be an expert on technique, but in every shot he saw the same thing: a man looking at the woman he loved.

Truth in art.

"I want to use the one without your head for my portfolio on my website," she said.

"No."

"No one will know it's you, Ky. Ever."

"No."

"I promise. Without a face, it's just a gorgeous torso. It could be any guy."

"The medallion is a dead giveaway."

"I'll edit it out," she said quickly.

"It's not gonna show up in one of your books somewhere in the future?"

She grinned and slid over to him. Taking the laptop, she put it down on the coffee table and took its place on his lap, straddling him. With her hands twined around his neck she told him, "I promise I'll only do books of faces, famous people, or buildings for any future publications."

"Why don't I believe you?" He tugged her shirt from the waistband of her skirt, slipped his hands under the silk.

"Because you're a federal officer, trained to be highly skeptical and disbelieving. Oh!"

He smiled at her reaction to his hands teasing and pinching her nipples through her thin lace bra.

"Speaking of jobs," he said, slipping his hands under the band and unhooking the clasp, "your brother-in-law cornered me at the party." He cupped each of her now freed breasts and squeezed.

Gemma threw back her head, effectively pushing her breasts closer to him. "O-Oh? What did he want?"

The tiny panting breaths she pushed through her lips as he circled her now pebbled nipples with his thumbs had the zipper on his pants straining against him.

Ky lifted her shirt up and tossed it over his shoulder, her bra following. Naked to the waist now before him, he feasted on her beautiful breasts. He pulled one of the tight peaks into his mouth, bit down with just the right amount of pressure and grinned when her body vibrated against him.

"Somehow he found out that I've been thinking about not going back to work," he said against her warm soft flesh.

Gemma fisted her now shaking hands in his hair. "I might have mentioned...something when I met Kandy for lunch the other day. About you being disillusioned by...everything that happened. Oh, sweet Jesus! Don't stop that. Please don't stop that."

God, he loved how he could seduce her. The way she responded to his touch each and every time was a marvel. She'd begun gliding slowly, rhythmically, back and forth across his erection, and even through their clothes he could feel how wet she was.

He ran his tongue across her nipple, blew on it and then drew the other one into his mouth to suckle.

"Hmmm." While slowly making love to her breast, Ky dragged down the zipper on her skirt, shoved through the waistband of her panties and filled his hands with her firm butt cheeks.

"He offered me a job."

Gemma kept moving across him, when suddenly his words penetrated. She stopped, pulled back, her hands still in his hair and peered down at him, her perfectly sculpted brows disappearing under her bangs.

"He what?!"

"He told me if I was looking to leave the FBI he could use someone with my skills. Apparently, he's been more busy than ever lately, and with just Bannerman and him to cover it all, he's been considering taking someone new on."

She stared down at him, her expression watchful. A minute ago her body had been humming with arousal against him. Now, she was as tight as a well-tuned piano string.

"Baby, breathe." He pulled his hands from her skirt and rubbed them along her thighs. He wasn't quite sure how she felt about this news. In truth, he'd been hoping she'd be overjoyed. But she didn't look joyful at the moment, she looked...anxious and apprehensive.

Of what, though?

Once she did as he commanded and took a deep breath, her shoulders were still tense as she asked, "What did you tell him?"

"That I had to talk to you about it first."

"Me? Why? It's your decision to make."

Ah. There was the reason for the nerves.

Ky gripped her hips and shifted their positions until she was flat on the couch with him hovering over her. He pushed her knees open with his own and made a nice resting place for himself between her thighs, their bodies touching from waist to toes.

With her cheeks palmed in his hands, he smiled down at her. How to tell her without causing her to bolt up and run from him? He measured his response as he would when dealing with an interrogation: calmly, laying out the facts, and guiding her to the logical conclusion.

"Because every decision I make from now on concerns you."

"It does?"

"Yes, Gemma, it does."

When she bit down on the inside of her cheek he knew she was beginning to understand.

"I can hear your brain running around like a wild, mad dervish," he said with a smile.

"Ky, I—"

"No, baby. Let me say this before you blurt out what I know you're thinking."

She squinted, a perfect pout forming on her lips. "What are you now, a mind reader?"

He dropped one soft kiss on the corner of her mouth. Instantly, the pout disappeared.

"No. A Gemma Laine reader."

Her response to that was a quick snort.

Ky waited a beat. "The reason I told Josh I needed to talk to you first was because I wanted you to know the real reason I'm considering it."

"You are? Considering it, I mean?"

"Yes. Seriously. And it's not just because of my changing feelings about the FBI," he said quickly when she opened her mouth. When she shut it again, he continued.

"Gemma, until recently I thought my job was all I needed. Jon Winters wasn't kidding when he joked I was married to it. I've always thought I'd have a real family one day, but *one day* kept getting pushed back because there was another investigation or another case that needed to be completed first. I knew I could wait a while before I found the woman I wanted to share my life with."

He kissed the tip of her nose.

"Then, about a little over a month ago, all that changed."

The sound of her throat bobbing up and down filled the space between them. "It did?"

He nodded. "The day I met you. The circumstances couldn't have been worse, I'll give you that." He chuckled. "But however we met, whatever we went through, one good thing to come of it is that I fell in love with you. And every day we've been together, everything we've gone through, has shown me that *one day* is now. And I can see the terror jumping on your face when I say that."

"Ky, please—" Her eyes grew moist.

"I know you're scared Gemma. I know all about your feelings concerning your father's abandonment, and how it's hard for you trust. To commit. Hard to trust that love will last, that it's real. But this is real, baby. What we have, well, it's what I've always wished for."

She cupped his cheek with her palm. "Ky."

"I know you need time to get used to this. I'm not asking for you to marry me tomorrow—"

"Marry?"

Ky's eyes narrowed, then relaxed. "I really should be pissed off that you sound so horrified about the possibility, but I'm not." He pressed his lips against her palm in the softest, gentlest of caresses. "We're practically living together as it is, you know, and you haven't said boo about it."

"No, I—"

He wasn't going to give her any room for an argument. "You've let me in, Gemma, to your home and your heart, something I don't think you've ever done before. I just want you to know, to realize and believe, I won't be walking out of either. Ever. I love you. I want to make a life with you. I want you to believe when we go out the door in the morning we'll be walking back through it that night and every night after, together."

Emotions gamboled across her face. He knew she was conflicted. Who wouldn't be with her scarred childhood history? But he hoped—*wished*—she could get over the doubt and see what he was saying was the truth.

"Can I speak now?"

He grinned at her piqued tone. He'd never known until he'd met her what a turn-on annoyance could be.

With a nod, he said, "The floor is yours. Or, more accurately, the couch."

She did her darndest to fight the grin, but he saw it peek through.

With her hands still on his cheeks, she lifted and kissed him on the lips.

"I like the way you talk," he told her.

She pinched his cheek and laughed when he cried out, "Ow!"

Then her mouth turned serious, the glaze in her eyes intense.

"It's no lie I have trust issues with men."

"Given your past, it's understandable."

"I thought it was my turn to speak?"

"Sorry." He pressed his lips together.

She waited a second before saying, "I've always protected myself from falling in love. I never let any man get close enough that he could hurt me. Until you."

He wanted to tell her he'd never hurt her, but kept quiet, as she'd asked.

"Maybe it was because we were forced to be together, to depend on one another, to trust one another completely, to just…be with one another. I don't know. But what I do know is that despite all my efforts not to, I wound up falling in love with you, too. Totally."

She pulled his head down until it lay on her chest.

"I started to think maybe I was the kind of girl who *could* have her own happily ever after. A family. A life with a partner. I'd never pretended those things were possible for me before."

She stroked his back with the tips of her fingers, as he stayed silent.

"Those five days I didn't hear from you after I got back were worse than when I was confined to the safe house and not allowed to work. Everything you'd said to me ran through my head in an unending loop, assuring me you cared for me. But your actions, or inactions, were starting to prove you didn't. And that hurt, Ky. More than any hurt could have, because all I could think was I'd given you my heart and you'd left it. Abandoned it. Just like my father."

Ky hugged his arms around her waist and kissed her neck.

"When you came back, I thought, okay, he does care. I'll just enjoy the time we have together, knowing it won't last, but happy he's here for the time being. I won't let myself think about the future again. I won't let myself hope."

When she choked on the last word, Ky lifted up to see tears falling down her cheeks.

He swiped at them with the pads of his thumbs as he held her gaze in his.

"But when you told me you loved me—*me*—and then practically moved in—"

"No practically about it," he said.

"—I allowed that hope to worm its way back in. It's taken root and buried itself deep, deep down."

"Gemma? Baby, what are you saying? I need to hear the words."

She pulled him back until their lips were touching lightly. Against them, she said, "I want the same things you do. A future together, children, shared memories. Marriage, tomorrow, next week, or next year, if you want it—"

"I do."

They both laughed.

"I want it all and I want it with you, Ky."

She pulled him down so their lips were firmly pressed against one another now.

When they came up for air, he squinted down at her and asked, "You're sure?"

Her lips pulled into the wicked, heart-stopping grin he loved beyond all else. "I'm sure." She kissed him, hard and fast. "Trust me."

Recipes

Grandma Sophie's Creamy Tomato Soup

Grandma knew the benefit of using plant-based products way before they became the current rage. Adding unsweetened almond milk to this delicious soup instead of a heavy cream not only makes the soup more nutritious, it eliminates a ton of excess calories as well! Grandma used her own tomato sauce, canned from her garden tomatoes, but you can use commercially canned tomato sauce if you don't garden.

Ingredients: Serves 8
½ stick (¼ cup) unsalted butter at room temperature
1 small onion, peeled and chopped
2 cloves of garlic, peeled and chopped fine
¼ cup tomato paste—any commercial brand will do
2 quarts home-canned tomato sauce OR 2-28 ounce cans commercial sauce, plain and unflavored
2 tablespoons sugar, divided
8 cups warm water
¾ cup unsweetened almond milk at room temperature
½ teaspoon Kosher salt
Parsley flakes to garnish—to taste, if so desired.

Preparation:
Melt the butter in a heavy, large stockpot over medium heat. Do not let it burn. Once melted, add the onion and the garlic and cook until the onion is soft and translucent—about 10–11 minutes. Add the tomato paste and cook, stirring often, until the paste begins to caramelize—about 5–7 minutes. Do not let it burn.

Add the tomato sauce, 1 tablespoon of the sugar, and 8 cups of warm water to the pot. Increase the heat level to high and bring the liquids to a simmer. Once it simmers, reduce the heat and continue simmering, uncovered, until the soup reduces to about 2 quarts, total (8 cups). This will take one hour, to one hour and ten minutes.

After that time, remove the soup from the heat and let it cool for approximately 15 minutes. Then, in batches of two cups at a time, add the liquids to a blender or processer, and *puree* until smooth. Return the pureed soup to the stockpot. Add the remaining sugar, stir in the cream, and simmer for 15–20 minutes again, uncovered.

Once the flavors are all melded together, add the salt, stir, and serve. Garnish with parsley flakes, if you so desire.

YiaYia's Lemon Chicken

You can serve this with roasted potatoes or couscous.

Ingredients: Serves 4
2 teaspoons lemon zest
¼ cup lemon juice
2 tablespoons olive oil
4–5 minced garlic cloves
1 tablespoon oregano
¾ teaspoon Kosher salt
¼ teaspoon black pepper
1 green pepper, cubed
1 small onion, peeled and cubed
4 skinless, boneless chicken breasts

Preparation:
In a small bowl, combine the lemon zest, lemon juice, olive oil, garlic, oregano, and salt and pepper. Set aside.

In a large frying pan, drizzle some olive oil to coat the bottom and place over a low-medium flame (heat) on top of the stove. Once the oil is heated, place the chicken breasts in it, cover, and cook over low-medium heat for 4–5 minutes per side, until the chicken is somewhat brown and doesn't stick to the pan when pulled away. Remove when done and set aside.

Drizzle a large casserole pan with a little olive oil to coat the bottom and the sides. Spread the cubed vegetables along the bottom of the pan and then drizzle half the lemon mixture over them. Lay the 4, browned, chicken breasts over the vegetables and drizzle with the remaining lemon mixture to coat the breasts. Cover and cook on low-low/medium heat until chicken is cooked and vegetables are soft (approximately 15–20 minutes, depending on the type of stove and thickness of casserole pan.)

Uncover, check chicken for doneness, and serve with roasted potatoes or couscous as a side dish.

**Keep reading for a sneak peek at
Stacy's Story**

CAN'T STAND THE HEAT

Coming soon from

**Peggy Jaeger
And
Lyrical Shine**

Chapter One

"I can't believe I let Teddy Davis talk me into this," Stacy Peters mumbled as she rifled through her underwear drawer. "I could be on a tropical beach right now, sipping some exotic, fruity drink, instead of packing for a trip to Hell." She tossed two bras into the open suitcase on her bed.

"I wouldn't classify where you're going as Hell," her cousin Kandy said from her perch on the bed. While Stacy threw a few panties haphazardly into the suitcase, Kandy removed and neatly folded them.

"What do you call being stuck on a sweltering, smelly, cattle ranch in July with a director who has the temper of an erupting volcano?" Stacy flung open the doors to her closet.

"A strategic career move?"

Stacy's hands stopped in the middle of hauling out a blouse, turned, and frowned at her cousin. "This isn't funny, Kan."

"I know, sweetie, but just think how much Teddy will owe you if you do this for him."

"Oh, he owes me, all right. Big time. Before I left his office he green-lighted *Family Dinners.*"

One of Kandy's perfectly sculpted eyebrows rose a fraction. "I hope you got that in writing."

Stacy moved from her closet back to her dresser and dug through her humongous work purse. "You bet your sweet ass I did."

She pulled a folded piece of paper from her wallet. "I had him write and sign this before I agreed to go and had his personal assistant witness and date it to make it legally binding. Here," she handed it to her cousin. "Read it."

" I, Theodore Davis, network programming chef for EBS, agree to green light FAMILY DINNERS for Stacy Peters to develop and produce, and give her carte blanche for the hiring of a series director, star, and staff, after she acts as executive producer for the upcoming BEEF BATTLES contest for EBS, under the directorship of Dominic Stamp." Kandy set the paper down on her lap. "Wow. He really does want you on this project. Director *and* star choice is yours. That's unheard of."

"I know. His assistant was hyperventilating when she read that part." She rolled a pair of socks and stopped before throwing them into the suitcase when she spied the folded pile Kandy had made.

Drawing a huge breath, Stacy plopped down next to her cousin. "Tell me I'm not absolutely crazy to be doing this. Please?"

Kandy took the socks and tucked them into the suitcase, then tossed an arm around her cousin's shoulders and squeezed. "You're not crazy, Stace. I think I'd classify what you're doing as a huge step, career-wise."

"Kinda feels like professional suicide to me." She stared down at her empty hands.

With another squeeze, Kandy rubbed her free hand along Stacy's forearm. "You *have* been a primary producer before. It's not like you don't know what you're doing. Your track record is exceptional. Teddy knows that and is banking on you. Trust me, it won't be so bad."

"You're not the one who's going to be stuck on some God-forsaken prairie for two months with a director who eats television producers as an appetizer, Kandace Sophia."

Ever since Teddy Davis had called her into his office that morning, his cryptic summons telling her he had something that needed her immediate attention, Stacy's stomach had been rolling.

Just a week ago she'd sent him her proposal for a new reality food series she wanted to create and produce called *Family Dinners*, and had been waiting anxiously for his answer. She knew her concept was sound, had the potential to be a big hit for the network, and was a show that required relatively little in the way of funding. The budget she'd proposed was minor, something she knew the money-conscious programming chief would appreciate.

When Teddy's assistant had called requesting her presence, Stacy had been filled with equal parts joy and dread. To respond to a production idea in such a short time frame meant he was either thrilled with the concept or hated it. When she'd arrived at his office and been told what he actually wanted from her, Stacy had spent a long moment in panicked fear, and then a quick second on devising a plan that would benefit them both.

She hadn't grown up seeing her cousin manage a multi-million dollar cooking empire and not learned a thing or two about negotiation. When presented with her ultimatum—because that's what it had been—Teddy had acquiesced with surprising speed, something Stacy was just now considering.

"I know Dominick Stamp has a volatile reputation when it comes to his work," Kandy said, "but he really is a top notch technical director. You're going to learn an awful lot from him."

"If I survive." Stacy sighed.

Kandy laughed again. "You will. Guaranteed."

"How can you be so sure?"

"Because, Estella Elizabeth,"—Kandy grabbed her hand—"you're a natural survivor. Of all of us, you're the strongest of Sophie's grandkids."

Stacy's mouth flew open in shock.

"You know you are," Kandy said with a nod. *"No one* I know could have survived what you did and still grown into the amazing, smart, and wonderful woman you are. No one. Of us all, you're the most like Sophie."

Tears threatened. "I can't believe you think that. I've always thought you were the one who was the most like Grandma. In every way."

"I may have gotten the cooking gene," Kandy said, "but you got the backbone. Believe it. Just be your usual efficient, calm, and totally kick-ass self and all will be well in Montana. Now, let's get you packed. What time does your flight leave?"

"Five thirty. I've got a car coming at four," she added with a swipe at her eyes. "How you get up every day at that God-awful hour is beyond me."

"Years of practice."

An hour and three packed, over-sized, suitcases later, Kandy gave her cousin a hug and a kiss on the cheek. "Text me if you need to vent or be talked off a ledge," she said, with a grin. "Use our code word."

"Leech?"

With a laugh, Kandy nodded. "Anytime, okay? I'm always available for you."

"I know it, cuz," Stacy squeezed back. "Thanks for everything."

Alone in her apartment, Stacy dragged a hand through her hair. From her mental to-do list she ran through what she needed to still get done before she could crawl into bed so she'd be able to get up and out the door on time to make her flight.

After throwing out all the food in her refrigerator that stood to spoil for the next eight-plus weeks she'd be gone, she paid her rent on-line, notified the post office to hold her mail, and emailed her parents to tell them where she'd be for the foreseeable future.

She crawled into bed at eight-thirty with the two-inch thick binder Teddy had given her detailing all the information she needed to come up to speed on the show she was now in charge of producing.

Beef Battles was scheduled as a headliner for the upcoming midseason schedule and the network was betting on it winning its Wednesday night time slot. Ratings were the name of the game in television broadcasting and the EBS network had been slowly growing in popularity, ever since Kandy's show, *Cooking with Kandy*, had soared to the top of the Nielsen ratings and stayed there three consecutive years. When it ended, Stacy, who'd been Kandy's assistant throughout the run, had been approached by Teddy Davis to act as assistant producer for another of the network's reality shows. That program had been having internal troubles, but with

Stacy on board, it had turned around, and after one season had climbed in the ratings.

Knowing he had someone who could get along with any personality and who could remain calm during the most trying of times, Davis had given her another opportunity, this time to executive produce one of the network's most challenging programs, *Bake Off*. The hosts of the show were continually at personal and professional odds and the series was in danger of being cancelled due to overtime costs. Stacy came in, evaluated and identified the problems, and then turned the once combative co-hosts into on-air besties, pulling the show out of its dull ratings and into the top twenty.

It was during this time Stacy had come up with her own idea for a show and had researched and written her proposal. Now, with confirmation her idea would take off, she snuggled down under the covers and opened the binder.

Within two minutes she bolted upright in bed, fury heating her cheeks. *"That bastard!"*

She reached across her nightstand for her cell phone and was all set to call Teddy and back out of the job when her brain cooled down her emotions, forcing her to take a few deep, cleansing breaths and calm down. He hadn't told her that two producers had already quit before filming even began, citing a terrible working environment perpetuated by the director, or that Dominick Stamp's list of requests had already thrown the proposed budget to hell. And he'd failed to mention, or even hint at, the unusual living arrangements agreed to by the ranch's host in an effort to cut production costs.

Stacy fell back onto her pillows and closed her eyes. Pulling in air through her nose and gently blowing it out through her lips, her pulse slowed, and when her body relaxed again, she opened her eyes.

Grandma Sophie always said if you made a deal with the Devil, there'd be a heavy toll to pay. That statement had just proven true. If she wanted her own show she had to dance with the Devil—or in this case, Dominick Stamp in Lucifer's guise.

With another heavy sigh, Stacy reopened the binder and read it from beginning to end.

* * *

Eighteen hours and two planes later, Stacy exited the jet-way at Billings Logan International Airport tired and cranky. And if the email she'd received from Teddy's assistant was to be believed, she still had a two hour car ride to get to the ranch. Add in the time zone difference and Stacy could feel her internal clock boxing to be turned off.

A quick escalator ride down to baggage claim found her waiting for the carousel to spit out her luggage.

Stacy positioned herself as close to the metal carousel as she could and was just about to close her dry and tired eyes for a moment when she felt a tap on her shoulder. Turning, she found herself looking into an opened collared, sun-drenched neck covered by a deep copper colored, long sleeved shirt. She took a step back and lifted her chin.

"Miss Peters, ma'am?"

Stacy nodded as she stared up into the face of a man a few birthdays younger than her own twenty-nine. A broad and open smile lit the tanned face shaded under a white Stetson. Eyes so pale, Stacy blinked twice before she realized they were blue.

He stuck out his hand and said, "I'm Beau Dixon, Amos' son. I was sent to bring you back to the ranch."

Stacy took the proffered hand, and despite her sudden exhaustion, found enough energy to respond to his open and friendly smile with one of her own. "It's nice to meet you, Mr. Dixon."

"Just call me Beau, ma'am. 'Bout everyone does."

Nodding, she said, "And I'm Stacy. 'Ma'am' makes me feel like my grandmother."

His smile widened and he shook his head. "Well, we can't have a pretty little thing like you feeling like that, now, can we?"

The carousel alarm beeped and the metal rotors started their accordion movements, various luggage pieces suddenly rotating around them.

"I've got three bags," she told him.

With a nod he said, "You just point 'em out and I'll grab 'em."

"I was told it's a two hour drive from here to your ranch," Stacy said, while he lifted the first piece she indicated.

"Probably more like two and half, three, with this midday traffic. Once we get out of the city proper, though, it'll go fast. Don't you worry."

As soon as all three pieces of her luggage had been obtained, Beau carrying two of them as if they weighed no more than a piece of paper, he led her out of the building. Dry, hot air slapped her in the face as soon as they came through the revolving doors.

Get used to it, she told herself. This is what you're stuck with for the next two months.

A luxury town car waited at the curb, its hazard lights flashing.

"I didn't expect to see a car like this out here," she said while he stowed the baggage. Realizing a moment later how elitist that sounded, she added, "I mean, I just figured a truck would be the standard vehicle."

"I left the pickup at the ranch," Beau said, opening her door so she could slip in. He'd left the car running and the cool, refreshing air conditioning blasting through the dashboard vents was welcome. "Daddy thought this would be a more comfortable ride for you than in the cab of my truck."

He pulled them out into traffic and turned to grin at her. "Besides, he never lets me drive this beauty and I leaped at the chance when he offered."

Stacy grinned back. For several minutes he wove them through the busy traffic until they were onto the highway. "If you're tired you can just lay your head back and take a little snooze," he told her. "I expect with the time difference and the travelin' you're about bushed."

"In all honesty I am, but if I take a nap now," she said, "I'll never sleep through the night and tomorrow I'll be even worse. Why don't you tell me about your ranch? I've only been given the basics about it."

There was unmistakable pride in his deep voice when he launched into a speech about the cattle ranch. The cursory description Teddy's assistant had slipped into her binder had been adequate for her to get a picture of the business. But Beau was a wealth of knowledge about the intricacies involved in running it day-to-day.

"Now since we're almost into July," he told her after speaking almost non-stop for an hour, "most of our herd is out grazing, getting fat, and just waiting to either be sold or bred."

"Who makes that determination?" Stacy asked, her tired brain now spinning with all the facts and figures he spewed as if he were merely reciting the alphabet.

"My father and our veterinarian, Doc Burns." Beau tossed her a grin she was coming to think he was never without. "He's quite the character. Him and daddy have been friends since they were boys."

"That's sweet."

A sound remarkably like a foghorn blasted from him. "Don't know that anyone has ever had the notion to call Cal Burns sweet, but he sure is entertaining."

"My notes say you've got two older brothers and their wives, plus you and your father all living at the main house."

He nodded. "Hopefully pretty soon that number will increase by one."

"Oh?"

Something moved across his face while she watched him drive; something eager, expectant, slightly bashful.

"Well, you see, I've been planning—" He stopped and snuck a quick glance at her before turning his attention back to the empty highway.

"Yes?"

He took in a huge breath, pregnant with anticipation and then, after he expelled it, said, "There's this girl. Jessie. Jessica. She's...we've... well, she's my girl, see? We've been together since high school."

"Again, that's just sweet."

"Yeah, well, I'm gonna ask her to marry me."

"Oh! Congratulations."

"Thanks, but it's not a done deal yet. I need a ring. I need to ask her daddy, 'cause she's old fashioned that way, you know?"

"I do." Stacy smiled. Her heart sighed at the thought of being young and in love and having a shared future in front of you. Not that she considered herself old, but love wasn't something she'd ever felt for a man. Instead, she'd concentrated on moving in and out of every day, secure in the knowledge she'd made it through another twenty-four hours without the dark and miserable thoughts of her younger years breaking through and overtaking her once again.

It had been a long, hard fought internal battle against her many demons to get where she was today emotionally, spiritually, and physically and she'd come to terms with the fact a lasting, happily ever after wasn't in the cards for her.

Beau pulled the car off the highway.

"We should be at the main house in about fifteen minutes. All this land you see is Dixon land."

Stacy's view of the empty and never ending stretch of highway they'd just exited morphed into a length of road in front of them equally as vast, surrounded on both sides by fenced in fields of verdant, wind-blowing grass.

"We've got just shy of thirty thousand acres," he told her.

True to his word, not more than fifteen minutes later Stacy got her first peek at the Dixon Ranch, or as Beau called it, the main house.

In her mind she'd pictured the house as resembling the one from the 80's show *Dallas*. The Dixon house was nothing like that iconic structure.

Three stories high and filled from side to side with gabled windows, the house was composed of multicolored gray slab in a patchwork design, Ionic columns shooting up from the wraparound porch to the second story across the front of the building, and a set of double front doors made of solid, unstained oak.

Several American model trucks and cars littered the gravel road up to the house but Stacy's gaze zeroed in on three huge box vans parked off to one side with the initials EBS blazoned cross them. Satellite dishes covered most of the three vehicle's roofs. Several smaller box trucks surrounded them, all belonging to the network.

"The television trucks and crew arrived a week ago," Beau said.

"Did Mr. Stamp arrive with them?" she asked.

"No, Ma'am, uh, I mean, Stacy."

She was charmed when his cheeks reddened.

"Got here three days ago. He's been out with daddy, scouting locales for filming. They've been gone most of every day since."

When his lips pulled back into a dry grin, she asked, "What's funny about that?"

"Not funny, like you mean, Ma—Stacy. It's just Daddy's been as ornery as a hungry mountain cat. He likes to order people around, does Mr. Stamp. Daddy doesn't take kindly to following other people's commands."

Great. Now she not only had to try and control her dictatorial director, but she probably had to smooth the waters with their host as well.

The rumbling sound of a large vehicle coming up the drive had them both turning to the sound.

"Here they come now, in fact."

Stacy's gaze tracked the truck as it pulled in and parked. The driver's door pushed open and she got her first view of the ranch's owner, Amos Dixon. Put thirty years and fifty pounds on Beau and you had his father, right down to the Stetson on his head and the well lived-in jeans covering the yards of leg.

Dixon's eyes zeroed in on his son and then trailed to Stacy. A slow, steady and welcoming smile drifted across his mouth as he boldly stared at her. She was about to return it when the passenger door slammed, its occupant pushing around from the front of the truck.

His height mimicked the man next to him at about six-one. The similarities ended there. Where Amos Dixon was stockily built and barrel chested, his physique laying claim to the fact he labored hard for his living, Dominic Stamp was lithe and athletic, narrow hipped, but broad shouldered. Clad in jeans under a pure-white collared shirt, the last thing anyone would take him for was a rancher.

His eyes were hidden behind dark aviator sunglasses, his head hatless. Thick and wavy jet black hair tinged with white at the temples and hairline framed a face that could never be called soft. Angular planes cut into his high cheekbones, deep corrugations running down from the corners of his thick lips to his chin. Even though she couldn't see his eyes, she knew they were locked on her, just as she knew behind those sunglasses, heated antagonism was focused on her face.

Stacy had prepared what she was going to say when they finally met. Her little rehearsed speech died a horrible death before she was ever able to utter it as the director stomped toward her, his mile long legs eating up the dust and gravel beneath his feet, an angry scowl darkening his features. The hostility blowing from him sliced through her the closer he came.

Stacy took a deep mental *and* physical breath. She'd known his reputation before agreeing to take this job and had decided to do it anyway. Working with him was going to be difficult and the biggest professional challenge she'd ever set herself up for, but if there was one thing Stacy knew about it was she was determined to never quit. Anything. No matter what—or who—the challenge was.

With her mouth pulled into a determined line and her spine as straight and hard as a steel-forged rod, she moved toward the director, one hand extended.

Acknowledgments

Writing is a solitary endeavor. Thankfully, I have a huge support system who check on me frequently to make sure I exercise, eat, and have some form of human contact. That support system consists of people with skills—serious skills—who answer me when I have questions, and allow me to pick their brains when I need to learn new things.

So, for helping me learn about photography, thank you Jill Hart and Stephanie Krist. Just watching you two take pictures is like attending a master class in photography.

For several years, my husband and I, plus our daughter, were privileged to study karate with Sensei Rick Wilmott. For almost 10 years we got tossed to the floor more times than I'd like to remember when we sparred and grappled, and learned innumerable ways to defend ourselves against physical attacks. Many of the maneuvers we learned I incorporated into Gemma and Ky's story, so thank you, Sensei, for giving me that foundation of knowledge.

I want to acknowledge my husband, here. Two years ago he had the idea that it might be a fun thing for us to do as a couple to learn to shoot. City slickers though we were raised, we now live in a rural area where guns are not uncommon. He felt it would be wise—plus fun—for us to learn about gun safety and to take shooting lessons. When I envisioned Gemma, I truly saw her as a warrior, so since she could defend herself with her martial arts skills, it made sense she could shoot a gun as well. I would never have known the terminology to use, or what it actually felt like to hold a gun had my hubby not pushed for us to learn those skills. Taking those lessons helped me walk the walk and talk the talk of shooting.

Lastly, my continued thanks to my wonderful editor, Esi Sogah, and all the marvelous, smart, sassy, and book-market savvy professionals at Kensington/Lyrical. Your persistent encouragement and support has made me the writer I've always longed to be.

About the Author

Peggy Jaeger is a contemporary romance author who writes about strong women, the families who support them, and the men who can't live without them. Peggy holds a master's degree in Nursing Administration and first found publication with several articles she authored on Alzheimer's Disease during her time running an Alzheimer's in patient care unit during the 1990s. A lifelong and avid romance reader and writer, she is a member of RWA and is the Secretary of her local New Hampshire RWA Chapter. When she's not writing she can be found cooking. With over 100 cookbooks, dog eared and well loved, her passion for writing is only seconded by her desire to create the perfect meal for those she loves. Visit her at peggyjaeger.com.